**Books by Jonnie Jacobs**

Kali O'Brien Novels of Legal Suspense

SHADOW OF DOUBT
EVIDENCE OF GUILT
MOTION TO DISMISS
WITNESS FOR THE DEFENSE
COLD JUSTICE


The Kate Austen Mysteries

MURDER AMONG NEIGHBORS
MURDER AMONG FRIENDS
MURDER AMONG US
MURDER AMONG STRANGERS


Published by Kensington Publishing Corporation

# COLD JUSTICE

## JONNIE JACOBS

KENSINGTON BOOKS
http://www.kensingtonbooks.com

For Rod

KENSINGTON BOOKS are published by

Kensington Publishing Corp.
850 Third Avenue
New York, NY 10022

All Kensington titles, imprints and distributed lines are available at special quantity discounts for bulk purchases for sales promotion, premiums, fund-raising, educational or institutional use.

Special book excerpts or customized printings can also be created to fit specific needs. For details, write or phone the office of the Kensington Special Sales Manager: Kensington Publishing Corp., 850 Third Avenue, New York, NY 10022, Attn. Special Sales Department. Phone: 1-800-221-2647.

Kensington and the K logo Reg. U.S. Pat. & TM Off.

Library of Congress Card Catalogue Number: 2001095360
ISBN 1-57566-827-0

First Printing: June 2002
10 9 8 7 6 5 4 3 2 1

Printed in the United States of America

# PROLOGUE

A new year. A fresh start.

Although the holiday season was exciting, Anne Bailey preferred January. It was a month of possibilities. A perch from which to relish the wide expanse of one's future.

Not that any year in recent memory had lived up to its promise. Nonetheless, Anne remained an optimist. She had a bumper sticker on her new Lexus—*This is the first day of the rest of your life.* A collection of similarly sunny sentiments papered the front of her fridge, and a few had even made their way onto her desk at work.

Her friend Kali thought she went overboard on the positive stuff. Said it made more sense to brace oneself for the bumps and disappointments in life than to hold out hope they'd somehow vanish. That was one of the ways she and Kali were different. One of the many ways. But Anne knew that deep down, where it mattered, they thought alike.

Mindful of new beginnings, Anne set her purchases on the sales counter. Toothpaste, shampoo, and a home pregnancy test. She didn't really need the toothpaste or shampoo, but they somehow made the other purchase—the one she'd come for—seem less significant. Like it was no big deal. Like she was simply picking up everyday toiletries.

Anne wasn't sure whom she was trying to fool—herself or the pimply faced salesclerk. She'd apparently succeeded in the latter if not the former. The young man slid her purchases across the scanner and into a plastic bag without so much as raising his eyes. But Anne's heart raced as she handed over her money.

What would she do if the test was positive? She wouldn't have an abortion; she knew that. No matter what Jerry said. But would she stay married to him? The timing couldn't be worse.

Anne pushed the thought away, as if the very act of thinking about a baby might make it a reality. But the alternative was just as bleak. Her heart had already opened to the child she imagined growing inside her.

Plastic sack in hand, Anne walked through the dimly lit parking lot to her car. It was drizzling out, and dark. She almost wished she weren't meeting Kali for dinner. It would be a good night to curl up with a book. Except that Jerry would no doubt call. Or worse, show up at her doorstep drunk. And they'd fight. Again.

Then he'd try to persuade her to let him move back home.

*I need you, honey; you're the only woman in the world I care about. I swear on my mother's grave, it won't happen again.*

Sometimes she believed him. Other times she was certain the best course would be to file for divorce.

And now? Anne didn't want to think about that just yet.

As she approached her car, she saw that a panel truck had pulled in next to her, leaving only a narrow space between vehicles. In a parking spot designated for compacts, no less. And the lot wasn't even full. People could be so thoughtless.

Anne was reaching into her purse for her keys when she caught a blur of movement near the other side of the truck. An instinctive stab of fear sent her heart racing. Before she had time to react, she felt warm breath on her neck and a hand at her throat. Her last conscious thought was of the package she let fall to the ground.

She'd never know if she might have been a mother.

# CHAPTER 1

With an apology for her late arrival already on the tip of her tongue, Kali O'Brien stepped from the cold, wet January night into the warmth and bustle of Shooters. Her eyes scanned the crowded bar and the cluster of tables surrounding it.

No Anne.

Kali checked her watch. She'd only been delayed fifteen minutes. Surely Anne wouldn't have given up on her already. Especially after enticing her with the promise of "some interesting news." Kali let the mental reel of apology wind down. It would be a nice change to have Anne be the one proffering excuses.

She ordered a glass of white wine from the bar, then found an empty table near the door where she'd be sure to see Anne when she arrived. Kali pulled out a pen and the small notebook where she'd written a list of issues to be resolved if she and Anne were going to share an office, as they were talking about doing.

Anne Bailey was a friend from Kali's days in the DA's office. They'd both signed on right out of law school, then moved into other areas of practice in the years that followed. Now they were thinking of joining forces again, if the logistics and finances worked.

Joining forces, ironically, right when Dwayne Arnold Davis was once again headline news.

The Davis trial had been what brought Anne and Kali together initially. Fresh and eager, both of them. Burning the midnight oil for truth and justice. And the thrill of working with Owen Nelson, one of Alameda County's most accomplished prosecutors.

Now, with Owen making a bid for the governor's office, the grisly details of the Bayside Strangler murders and Davis's execution were somehow deemed freshly newsworthy.

Out of the corner of her eye, she saw a scruffy, large-bellied man approach her table. He'd been sitting at the bar with friends and giving her what she supposed were come-hither looks for the last ten minutes. As he slid into the seat opposite her, she caught a whiff of his stench—an unpleasant mixture of body odor, grease and beer.

"Buy you a drink?" Only it came out so slurred, it took her a minute to decipher. The man had obviously had too many himself already.

"I'm waiting for someone."

"You can still drink, can't you?" He laughed uproariously, banging the table with his hand. His fingernails were blackened with grime. "Hey, bartender. Give us a couple of beers."

Kali eyed him levelly. "Please leave."

"Please," he mimicked.

"Or I'll ask that you be thrown out."

"Feisty, huh? I like that in a woman." The man made no move to leave. Instead, he rocked back in his chair and again hollered to the bartender.

While Kali debated her best move, another man—clean cut and dressed in a sports jacket and tie—stepped in.

"Hi," he said to Kali, as if they were old friends. "Sorry to keep you waiting." To the man seated opposite her, he said, "Sorry, pal. Time to move on."

The drunk looked him over for a minute, then rose and lurched back to his place at the bar, where he and his companions had a good laugh.

"Thanks," Kali said, though she bristled slightly at the notion of rescue by male gallantry.

"No problem." Her knight had blue eyes and a friendly smile. Pleasantly attractive, though not someone you'd notice in a crowded room. "Guess I'd better stay for a bit," he added, "or your buddy there will come right back."

"I'm meeting someone," Kali said. There were different ways of hitting on a woman, and she wasn't in the mood for any of them.

The man smiled. "I figured as much. You don't look like the type to be hanging out in a bar alone. My name's Nathan Sloane."

"Kali," she said, omitting a last name.

Sloane sat down, folded his hands on the table.

Kali glanced at her watch again. It was half an hour after she and Anne had agreed to meet. Unusual for Anne to be late at all.

"I'm going to call my friend," Kali said. Rather than use her cell phone, she headed for the relative privacy of the pay phone near the restrooms. She called Anne's office and got nothing but the answering machine. Same result when she tried the house.

The tiny niggle of anxiety in Kali's chest tightened. Traffic accident? Another round with Jerry? Or maybe it was just the wet weather making it difficult to get across town.

When she returned to the table, she found that Sloane had procured a glass of wine for himself as well as a fresh glass for her, and a plate of potato skins. A part of her longed for the drunk, whom she wouldn't care about offending.

Well, she'd give it another fifteen minutes. Time enough for Anne to show, if she was going to. Time enough for half a glass of wine and polite conversation with Nathan Sloane. Dues paid.

"Did you reach your friend?" Sloane asked.

"She's on her way." Purposely vague.

He took a sip of wine, watching her over the rim of his glass. "Guess I must seem kind of pushy, huh? I elbowed aside the other guy who was bothering you, then moved in myself. It's just that I was watching from that table over there"—he waved in the direction of the back wall—"and it seemed like maybe I could help."

"I could probably have managed, but thanks."

"Now I've insulted you." Nathan had thick brown hair that kept falling forward over one eye. He brushed it back with his hand. "I'm sorry. I'm new to the Bay Area. Guess maybe I'm desperate for a friendly face. I mean, not that anyone would have to be desperate to spend time with you."

He looked embarrassed, and Kali sought to help him out. She owed him that much at least. "Where'd you move from?"

"Boston. I'm with Global Investment. Financial planning and management. How about you, you lived here long?"

"Since college." No point going into her life history. Some days she thought the three years in Silver Creek were best forgotten anyway.

Nathan regaled her with stories about apartment hunting in a strange city, his new boss, his many travels. He had a way of making even the mundane sound amusing, and in spite of her earlier misgivings, she was grateful for the company. But after twenty minutes, she began gathering her things to leave.

"You're not going, are you?"

"Afraid so. Thanks again."

"What about your friend?"

"She said not to wait more than fifteen minutes."

"I thought she was on her way."

A bit pushy, Kali thought. "She wasn't sure she'd be able to get away."

"No need to rush off. We've got a whole plate of food left."

"Sorry, I do need to go."

Nathan stood when she did. "Maybe I could call you some time."

"Probably not such a great idea. But I enjoyed talking with you."

His features pulled into a scowl. "Why not? You seeing someone?"

"Sort of." A total lie, but sometimes that was the easiest course.

"It doesn't have to be a date. I mean, we could just—"

"I don't think so." She smiled and extended her hand. "But thanks for the drink and the company."

She was almost to her car when she heard footsteps behind her. She turned to see Nathan not more than ten feet behind her. "You forgot your book," he said, and handed her the DayTimer she carried in her briefcase.

"How'd you get this?"

"It was on the floor by your chair. I noticed it after you'd left."

"Thanks." Kali took the book and shoved it back into her briefcase. It must have fallen out when she'd knocked the briefcase over on her way to phone Anne. She gave herself a silent reprimand. What a mess she'd be in if she lost the thing.

"Take care," Nathan said.

She could feel him watching while she got in the car and drove away.

# CHAPTER 2

Rainy nights were the worst, Abe thought. Worse even than bitter cold. Cold you could curl away from, layer on the coats and cardboard. But rain was wet and relentless. Doorways weren't much good against rain. Neither were trees or kiosks. BART stations worked, if you could stay clear of security, but they closed up at midnight. And just try getting into a shelter when the weather turned. You might as well hope to win the lottery.

Abe hadn't even bothered trying for a bed since he'd discovered the alley a couple of weeks ago. It smelled, on account of the dumpster at the entrance, but there was a private parking structure in back with a ventilation shaft that offered easy access. Abe thought of it as his private retreat.

The sky lit with a flash of lightning. Abe counted to nine before the thunder broke. He picked up his pace.

The left wheel on his cart wobbled, making it difficult to steer, and the plastic garbage bag that served as a raincoat hindered his movement, but he'd managed most of the distance already. Which was good, because it was getting late and Abe liked to be settled at night.

He passed a corner grocery. "Mom-and-Pops" they used to call them. Maybe they still did, though it was usually some foreigner behind the counter.

Abe fondled the bills in his pocket. He'd done well today. One thing rain was good for was people's guilt. They were freer with the handouts when it rained.

He pushed his cart up next to the door and peered inside. The aisles were narrow, the shelves crammed. Everything from onions to mousetraps. And sure enough, a dark-skinned foreigner was at the register.

And behind him were shelves lined with booze. Bottle after bottle of the stuff.

The sky again flashed with lightning. A night for the comforts of home, Abe thought. He counted his bills. Barely enough. But he'd eaten well at lunch. Some weary-looking mother with a screaming kid had gotten angry and tossed a whole ten-pack of chicken nuggets into the trash. Fries too. Abe didn't need dinner, really. Besides, the whisky would help him sleep.

He shuffled inside and bought a bottle. And was jubilant to discover he had enough money left over for a Hershey bar. It was going to be a good night. He tucked the bottle into his cart and picked up his pace.

As he neared the alley, he looked over his shoulder for a passing cop or some tender-hearted guy who felt he owed his dog a walk despite the weather. The path was clear. Abe ducked into the alley.

Working in the dark, he pried the grill from the vent, crawled through to the garage interior, then spread out his thin bedroll and opened the bottle of whisky. Home sweet home.

It was near daybreak when Abe awoke. The bottle beside him was empty, and his mouth was sour with the taste of having drunk too much. He groaned and tried to go back to sleep, but he knew he never would without taking a leak first.

Some guys, they'd just unzip and aim for the corner. What did they care? Not Abe, though. He had his standards.

He crawled out through the vent and took a couple of steps in the direction of the dumpster. He'd reached for the zipper of his fly when he saw what looked like someone slouched by the dumpster asleep.

He blinked, and peered again through the murky half-light of early dawn. There *was* someone there. A woman.

Abe thought of the garage as *his* place, and he wasn't happy about sharing it. On the other hand, no one deserved to sleep out in the rain like that. Especially not a woman.

He approached cautiously. He didn't want to scare her. But as he got closer, it became clear to him that she wasn't sleeping. She was dead.

# CHAPTER 3

Detective Lou Fortune reached his partner at home late Saturday afternoon. He could hear a female voice in the background, sultry and seductive. It didn't take a lot of imagination to figure out what his call had interrupted. He wondered if the voice belonged to the young dispatcher who'd been panting after Keating for the last few months or to one of his weekend pickups. Lou experienced a momentary pang of loneliness. Not that he wanted what Keating had; what he wanted was Jan.

"I don't suppose you're calling just to hear the sound of my voice," Keating said.

"You suppose right."

"Happens every time, you know."

"What happens?" Lou had been partnered with Bryce Keating for a little under six months now, and he still had trouble following the guy's logic.

"Every time we get called out on a weekend, I'm in the middle of something."

"As far as I can tell, Bryce, you're always in the middle of something." Lou was impatient to get to the crime scene before every bit of useful evidence was trampled by inexperienced investigators. It happened so often that he'd come to expect it. "I'll pick you up in fifteen. That give you enough time to disentangle yourself gracefully?"

"It's not like I have a choice."

"Right. Keep an eye out. I'll honk."

Lou pulled the unmarked sedan up to an alley near Oakland's City Center and parked behind the coroner's van.

"Looks like the gang's all here," Keating said.

"Looks like."

A uniformed officer Lou didn't recognize was keeping watch on an area cordoned off by yellow police tape. They showed him their badges, passed under the tape and made their way down the alley to a dumpster, which seemed to be the center of activity. Cops, police photographers, evidence technicians—Lou couldn't place half of them. It was getting so the rookies outnumbered everyone else.

"Jesus, " he said to the young uniformed cop standing at the entrance to the alleyway. "Think you have enough people tramping around? This is a crime scene, not a fucking photo shoot."

"Nobody's touched a thing," the cop said indignantly.

That wasn't true. Maybe nobody'd meant to touch things, but any activity at a crime scene altered the way it had been left. Lou wasn't in the mood to explain. "What have we got?" he asked.

"Female. Appears to be in her mid-thirties."

"Any ID?"

"None obvious. She looks like a hooker."

Keating turned up the collar of his leather jacket against the wind. "Like someone asking to be killed, you mean?"

The cop shook his head. "Don't go putting words in my mouth. If she was picking up guys, you might have a lead on her killer, is all."

"How'd she die?" Lou asked.

"Appears she was strangled."

"Who was it found her?"

"Old guy. Homeless. Sounds like he discovered her body this morning, but it took him till noon to report it."

"Why's that?"

"Says no one would listen to him. I guess they thought he was a rambling drunk. He's in a black-and-white out there on the street if you want to talk to him."

"Yeah. Make sure they hold him until we're finished here."

Lou moved closer, his eyes scanning the scene as he approached the woman's body.

She was in a sitting position, her back propped against the metal side of the dumpster. Her arms were folded neatly in her lap, but her legs were spread in what was clearly an unnatural position. She wore a sleeveless, black jersey tee, tight and cut low in a deep V at the neck. And one of those short stretch skirts that would barely cover her panties had she been wearing any. Now, it had ridden up, exposing the bare flesh of her thighs and buttocks, and a triangle of blond hair at her crotch. Impossible to tell if she'd been raped, though Lou saw no obvious abrasions or signs of bruising. No signs of semen either, but that might have been washed away by the rain during the night. In time, the coroner would be able to give them an answer.

Keating stepped in beside him. "Doesn't look like the face of a hooker, does it?"

"You can tell a hooker from her face?" But he knew what Keating meant. Life on the streets hardened women. This one looked like she belonged downtown with a briefcase. Or in her garden, watering roses while conversing with her cat. Her makeup was subdued and artfully applied, her hair a golden brown, lightly frosted. It framed her face with curls, even now when it was wet. Her nails were short, with clear polish. She had a fresh look about her, even in death. She reminded Lou of Jan when she was younger.

So what was with the clothes? These days it was hard to tell the whores from the models, but given the weather, he'd at least have expected something with sleeves.

Keating was sketching the scene in his notebook. "Looks like she was killed elsewhere and dumped here."

"Unfortunately for us." An outdoor crime scene was hard enough. It was harder still when it wasn't where the murder had actually occurred. There was less evidence, fewer clues to go on. "Only not really dumped," Lou added. "Whoever killed her took care to position the body."

"An added risk for our killer."

Lou nodded. The longer the guy stuck around, the greater his chances of being seen. Still, given the area, it was unlikely they'd find a witness.

"So why'd he take the time to pose her, you think?"

"Got me." But Lou knew it was a question they'd be coming back to in the course of the investigation. He donned a pair of latex gloves and examined the line of discoloration around her neck. Ligature marks. Clear but not deep.

"Looks like he used rope," Keating said, echoing Lou's own thought.

"Let's see if the coroner agrees." Lou rolled the body slightly to the side, checking for scratches or bruises. Nothing to indicate she'd fought her attacker. Nothing that made it appear she'd been dragged either. She wasn't a large woman, but it still took considerable strength to carry dead weight.

Lou eased himself to his feet. "Let's do a walk-through."

They walked the length of the alley, then back out to the street. There was precious little to go on in the way of helping them find her killer. "We'll see what the crime scene folks come up with in the way of trace evidence. On first impression, though, I don't see a lot here that's going to help us."

The old guy who found her wasn't much help, either. He talked in circles, and it took effort on Lou's part to get the story even halfway straight.

"What time this morning?" Lou asked.

"Don't got a watch."

"Approximately."

The guy looked at the sky, like he was going to tell time by the movement of the sun. "Hard to tell. Clouds and all."

"You see anyone else around?"

The old guy shook his head. Only he was so full of twitches it took Lou a minute to decipher the shake for what it was.

"Did you touch the crime scene in any way? Take anything, like her purse maybe?"

The twitches grew more pronounced. "I didn't take nothing of hers! Nothing! Why you gotta go accuse me like that?"

"Calm down. It wasn't an accusation."

"I got respect for people's property," the guy muttered.

Lou had pretty much despaired of getting anything useful from him. "How'd you happen to spot her?" he asked.

"Just passing through, checking for collectibles."

Dumpster diving, in other words. "And then?"

"Went looking for a cop, I did. Weren't a one to be seen."

Lou figured he'd gotten as much as he was going to. The man could have been lying, of course, and probably was about some of it. Most likely he'd been camped out rather than passing through. And his timing was off a little, so maybe he had been drunk, or hung over, and not gotten around to reporting it as soon as he should have. On the other hand, Lou could believe that he'd been dismissed by folks, too. Just the smell of him had been enough to keep Lou leaning against the open rear door of the black-and-white.

The uniformed officer approached. "Are you about finished here? The coroner wants to take her away."

"I think so. Let me check with my partner." Keating was on the cell phone, and Lou waited to catch his eye.

"It's the sergeant," Keating said. "There was a call not long ago. A woman who says her friend didn't show up for dinner last night and hasn't been home all day. Five-five, short hair, frosted blonde."

"What's the friend's name?"

"Anne Bailey. She's an attorney."

Lou remembered his first impression on seeing the body. *She looked like she belonged downtown with a briefcase.* He hated the thought that he'd been right.

"See if the caller is willing to give us an ID." He checked his watch. "Tell her to meet us at the morgue in an hour."

# CHAPTER 4

Kali pressed a knuckle to her mouth as she examined the face on the monitor. "It's her."

"You're sure about that?" It was the younger cop who spoke. Bryce Keating, as she recalled.

She nodded, not trusting her voice. *Breathe deeply,* she told herself. *Don't think about Anne right now.*

It didn't work. Grief slapped her in the face and brought tears to her eyes. Anne, with an open heart, an infectious smile, and a whimsical sense of humor. A woman who bubbled with enthusiasm for life. How could Anne be dead?

The older, heavyset cop by the name of Fortune offered Kali a tissue.

"What happened?" she asked finally. She wouldn't have been sitting here in a cramped room at the morgue with two homicide detectives if there hadn't been foul play of some sort. Beyond that, she hadn't a clue.

"We're not sure," Fortune replied. "It would be helpful if you could tell us about your friend and the dinner plans the two of you had for last night."

"How was she killed?" Kali asked. She wasn't going to tell them anything until she had a few answers of her own.

The cops exchanged glances. Neither of them was familiar to her, although she was acquainted with several homicide detectives from her criminal defense work. If they recognized her, they were keeping it to themselves.

"Look, I'm an attorney. I know you can't tell me the details, but I need to know what happened." She softened it with, "Please."

Fortune stuck his hands in his pocket. He was broadly built and carried extra weight around his middle. His ruddy face was set in a dour expression, but Kali thought she detected kindness in his eyes.

"It looks like she was strangled," he said. "But that's just a guess. We won't know for sure until after the autopsy."

"Strangled." Kali's hand went to her throat. She had trouble swallowing. "Where was Anne's body found?"

"In an alleyway near City Center."

"All the way down there? We were going to meet at a restaurant in Berkeley. Near where she lives." *Lived*, Kali amended silently.

"That's the kind of information we need. You feeling up to it?"

She wasn't. She could feel tears stinging her eyes, waves of sorrow building inside her. But she wanted Anne's killer found. "I don't know," she answered truthfully.

"How about we try?" Keating asked. He was about her own age, long-limbed but with broad shoulders and muscular arms. His nose jutted out between prominent cheekbones. Above, his eyes were gray and sharp. Not unfriendly, exactly, but there was none of the gentleness there she'd sensed with his partner.

"Okay." She took another breath and worked on shelving her grief for a later time.

"Would you like something to drink?"

Kali shook her head, then changed her mind. "Yes, a soda, if you don't mind." She usually qualified such requests with, "Diet, if you have it." But with the pall of death hanging over her, a hundred or so empty calories seemed nothing to quibble about.

Keating went to get their sodas while she and Fortune made small talk in the tiny, airless room. How many grief-stricken people had sat here over the years? And how many of the crimes remained unsolved?

When Keating returned with three Cokes, Fortune took out a notebook. "Tell us about your friend. Where she lived, what kind of work she did, husband or boyfriend . . . The more you can tell us, the better."

Kali took a deep breath and pushed away the mental image of Anne's face on the morgue monitor. "She was an attorney. We both worked at the DA's office right out of law school." It wasn't an important fact, but Kali didn't know where to start. She licked her lips and began again.

"Anne had her own practice, in Berkeley. She handled mostly family matters, trusts and estates, divorces, that sort of thing, although she had some business clients too."

"Married?"

Kali nodded. "She and her husband separated about two months ago, but they were trying to work things out."

She saw a flicker of something in the cops' eyes as Fortune wrote down Jerry's name and address. Kali knew he'd be a prime suspect, at least initially. She wondered what sort of alibi he had for the time of Anne's murder.

"Did you call him?"

"I tried last night when Anne didn't show up for dinner. There was no answer. Same thing this morning." At the time, Kali had half suspected that Jerry was simply ignoring her. He sometimes acted as if he were jealous of his wife's friends. Now, her stomach soured at the suggestion that he might have been involved in her death.

"Why'd they separate?"

Kali gripped her soda can and struggled to stay focused. "It was Anne's idea. I'm not sure why, really, except that she thought it might help." Kali knew there were problems in the marriage, but she didn't know the details. She could imagine Jerry might not be the easiest guy to be married to, but then, when you got right down to it, the same could be said about a lot of men. It was a thought Kali often used to reassure herself when she was feeling lonely.

"Any kids?" Fortune asked.

"No." Though she knew Anne wanted them and Jerry didn't.

"Other immediate family?"

"A brother. He lives in Palo Alto."

Keating drummed his fingers on the tabletop. "The two of them have a good relationship?"

"Reasonably good. I don't think they were close, but they got along."

"How about her parents?"

"Her mother died when Anne was in college. Her father remarried. He lives somewhere in Florida. Sorry, but I don't know any more than that."

"Was she dating other men?"

"Not that I was aware of. She wanted to make her marriage work."

Keating and Fortune took Kali through her last conversation with Anne, roughly thirty-six hours earlier. They'd spoken Friday morning, confirming their plans for that night and agreeing on a time. She'd gotten the impression that Anne would be coming straight from work, but she didn't know for sure. Yes, Anne would have been driving, and no, she wasn't the type to offer a ride to a stranger. Kali tried only to think about the questions and her answers, not the fact they were discussing a dear friend who'd been murdered.

"She do drugs?" This was Keating again.

"No. She wasn't even much of a drinker."

"She hang out with a bad crowd?"

"Not unless you include lawyers."

Neither cop cracked a smile.

Fortune rocked back in his chair. "What kind of dresser was your friend?"

The question caught Kali by surprise. "What do you mean?"

"Conservative? Flashy?"

"Not conservative, but definitely not flashy." Like so many women, Kali included, Anne had tried to find the right balance between looking professional and being stylish. "I guess I'd say she was a fashionable dresser. Suits and dresses for work, slacks and sweaters when she wasn't in jeans. Why?"

"Just trying to get a complete picture."

"She was nude when you found her?" Murder was hard enough to accept. Kali tried not to think about the horrors Anne might have endured before her death.

"Not nude," Fortune said, clearly trying to offer Kali some degree of comfort. "She was dressed. And on first impression, it doesn't look as though she was sexually assaulted, but we can't say for sure."

Kali was grateful for his efforts at kindness. "What do you think happened?"

It was Keating who replied, though not with any sort of answer. "At this point, anything we say is pure speculation."

They asked her a few more questions, then thanked her for coming down.

"You'll notify her husband?" Kali asked. She knew she'd call herself and offer solace, but she didn't want to be the one to tell him about Anne's death.

"Right away."

Talking had kept Kali focused, but the minute she stepped into the cavernous hallway, she felt tears again prick at her eyes. By time she made it outside, she was choking back sobs. Finally, in the relative privacy of her own car, she pressed her forehead against the steering wheel and let her grief flow.

Sunday morning Kali woke to gray skies but no rain. Loretta had padded into the bedroom at the first light of morning and nudged the bed with her muzzle. Kali could feel her waiting expectantly for any sign of human activity. Finally, Kali opened an eye, and the dog leapt to life with the throaty whimpers and soft barks of her morning greeting.

"Okay, girl. I'm getting up." Although she might not have without the springer spaniel's insistence. She'd slept fretfully during the night, experiencing a flood of sorrow anew every time she woke. Now that morning had arrived, all she wanted to do was bury herself again in sleep.

Kali showered, then fixed coffee and a bagel, and braced herself for the story of Anne's death that was sure to be front-page news.

It was, but only one column in width. There wasn't, apparently, a lot in the way of information to report.

The partially clad body of Anne Bailey, thirty-five, had been found Saturday afternoon in a narrow alley in downtown Oakland. She appeared to have been strangled. Anyone with information was asked to call the Oakland police department, homicide division. The final two paragraphs of the article were given over to a cursory summary of Anne's life, derived, Kali felt certain, from Anne's legal resume. Her work on the Dwayne Arnold Davis trial had not been overlooked. The article concluded by noting that her husband, Jerry, was in seclusion mourning the death of his wife.

She wondered how and when to offer her condolences, and found herself feeling grateful that it was too early in the morning to even think of calling.

Under normal circumstances, Kali would have taken a long and brisk walk through the hills near her home, or forced herself to work out at the gym. But this morning she felt as though her body were made of lead. She opted instead for a short walk with

Loretta—enough to let the dog sniff and squat—and then returned home, where she wandered aimlessly from room to room.

Until recently, Kali had had housemates—two elderly sisters who'd leased the house from her when she'd moved back to her childhood hometown, Silver Creek, and then had graciously sublet a portion of it back to her when she unexpectedly returned to the Bay Area. But Bea and Dotty had left last month for an extended stay with friends in Arizona. Instead of relishing the experience of having her home to herself again, Kali found herself face-to-face for the first time with the angst of being alone.

She knew it wasn't just the empty house. More to the point was an empty heart. Bad luck, bad timing, the wrong men—who could say why, but bottom line was, she had no one to share her life in the ways she cared about.

There were days on end, weeks even, when it didn't bother her. But today wasn't one of them. Anne's death had cast a gray shadow on her psyche and there was no shaking it.

Finally, because she *had* to do something, she tackled the stack of ironing that had been building for weeks. She was down to the last pair of khakis when the phone rang.

"Hi, Kali. It's Jerry Bailey."

She'd been uncomfortable, wondering whether or not to call him, and now he'd beat her to it. She felt a pang of guilt. "Jerry, I've been thinking about you. I'm so sorry about Anne."

"I still can't believe it. I'm in shock, I guess."

"If there's anything I can do . . ."

"Actually, there is." He hesitated, but only briefly. "I'm at the house, and . . . I could use some company, I guess. I was wondering if you wouldn't mind coming over."

"Of course not." Except that the idea of being in Anne's house now that she was dead saddened Kali beyond measure.

"The cops said you were supposed to have dinner with her Friday night."

"Right."

"I just want to talk to someone who, you know, maybe knew what was going on."

"I'm afraid I won't be able to add anything, but I'd be happy to come by. I can be there in about half an hour, if that works."

"Thanks. I appreciate this."

\* \* \*

Kali had made enough condolence visits to feel awkward about arriving empty-handed. On the other hand, bringing Jerry a casserole struck her as ludicrous. She opted for deli sandwiches and a bag of chips.

Jerry answered the door on the first ring. Strain showed on his face and his eyes were bloodshot. "Thanks for coming." He ushered her inside.

Anne's house, without Anne. It felt strangely quiet and stale. Kali caught sight of a lithograph Anne had purchased years ago with her first paycheck. She remembered Anne's excitement the day she'd returned from lunch having found "just the thing" for her apartment wall. Now, Anne's eyes would never gaze on the lovely snow-capped mountains again.

"You want some coffee or something?" Jerry asked.

The man was clearly feeling unsettled. His arms crossed at his chest, then dropped to his sides. He shuffled from foot to foot.

"Sure," Kali answered. Making coffee would give him something to focus on. "I brought sandwiches," she added. "I wasn't sure if you were up to thinking about food."

"Thanks. I'm not really. Hungry, that is."

They moved into the kitchen, and Jerry filled the coffeemaker with grounds, then flipped the switch.

He wasn't tall, maybe five-nine at most, but he was well proportioned and athletic looking without being particularly muscular. Dark eyes, curly black hair, and a mouth a bit too full for Kali's tastes. She'd never really warmed to Jerry, but then, she'd never talked to him more than in passing.

"I guess you know that Anne and I were separated," he said.

"She told me, but not much more than that."

"We were fighting a lot." He shrugged. "I'm not sure about what even, but we were. I know I'm difficult sometimes, but Anne could be too. She's so demanding . . ." He seemed on the verge of launching into a tirade about Anne's faults, then remembered that she was gone. "Anyway, we were working it out. The separation was temporary."

"Anne said the same thing."

The water in the machine gurgled, and Jerry stared at it as though it held answers to all that confused him. "When did you last see her?"

Kali thought it over. "Probably a week ago. We had lunch. But we talked on the phone other times. I talked to her Friday morning, in fact."

Jerry ignored the coffee and instead paced back and forth. Finally, he leaned against the counter and crossed his arms. "Who is he?"

"Who is who?"

"The guy she was seeing."

Kali shook her head. "She wasn't seeing anyone."

"Don't give me that bullshit."

The change in tone was so abrupt, it caught Kali by surprise. "I don't—"

"She must have talked about him. Women all talk. They can't keep anything secret. Anne especially."

"She never—"

"I want to know who he is, damn it!"

Jerry's eyes flashed with anger. Misdirected grief, Kali wondered, or something else? Whatever it was, it made her uncomfortable. "What makes you think she was seeing someone?"

"Our separation, her coolness toward me . . ." Jerry pressed his palm to his forehead. "There had to be someone else."

"Not necessarily. Maybe it was just that your marriage needed a little work." Listen to me, the woman who couldn't keep a relationship going for the life of her, giving advice.

But Jerry wasn't listening anyway. "And then, today . . ." He shoved a florist's box at Kali. "This was on the doorstep."

She opened it. A single long-stemmed yellow rose.

"Read the card," he said, his voice tight with emotion.

Kali lifted it from the box. It was a standard florist's card. White with a red heart in the corner. "Anne, you've made me so happy. I will love you forever." There was no signature.

Jerry's face was red. His eyes had narrowed. "Just give me the truth."

Kali slipped the card back into its envelope, careful to touch only the outer edge. There was no way she could tell him the truth, even if she was sure what it was.

But she knew she had to call Owen Nelson.

# CHAPTER 5

Owen Nelson popped another throat lozenge into his mouth and shuffled the papers in his lap. Ostensibly he was boning up on labor and immigration studies, but it was dry reading, and with the cold he was suffering through, staying focused took more effort than he could muster. Campaigning was hard work, made harder still by the fact that everyone wanted a piece of him. Owen was not a natural politician. In fact, he hated politics. But he wanted to be governor, and he couldn't get there without jumping through the necessary hoops.

Owen put the papers aside and watched Alex through the den window. His son was washing his old, dented truck the way he did everything—in an apathetic, half-baked fashion.

Twenty-three years old and the boy still acted like he was sixteen. Undisciplined, irresponsible, always looking for the easy way out. At twenty-three Owen had been putting himself through law school, building a life and a future. Alex had barely graduated from high school, and despite Owen's best efforts to help him find a niche for himself, seemed content to drift from one low-paying job to another. The boy had potential too, which made his indifference all the more difficult to accept.

Alex swiped the cloth carelessly over the driver's-side door, missing whole stripes of grime. Owen closed his eyes; he couldn't bear to watch. What was it Dr. Mooney had said—you have to pull back and let them live their own lives? Well, he'd tried and it hadn't helped. Besides, it was easy for Dr. Mooney to talk. Both his daughters were Yale graduates.

"Hey, Dad."

Owen sat up with a start. He'd drifted off without even realizing it.

"Sorry, I didn't know you were sleeping." Alex started to back away.

"That's okay. I didn't mean to. It's this damn cold I've got."

"Just wanted to say I'm taking off. Thanks for the use of the driveway."

"Anytime. You want to stay for dinner?"

"Not tonight."

"Selby's got fresh crab."

"Sorry, I can't."

"Big plans?"

Alex shrugged. "Just the usual."

Owen was never sure what the usual was. Alex lived alone, in a cramped and rundown apartment partially subsidized by Owen himself. If he had friends, Owen hadn't heard about them.

"Everything okay, son?"

"Yeah, fine."

There was a knock on the door, and Selby poked her head in. "You've got a phone call, Owen."

"Who is it?"

"Someone by the name of Kali O'Brien. She apologized for bothering you at home, but said it was important."

Owen pulled himself from the sofa. She probably wanted to make sure he'd heard about Anne Bailey's murder.

"Bye, Dad." Alex started to leave, pushing past Selby without a word.

"Son, you're forgetting something."

"It's okay, Owen." Selby had stepped into the room. She pulled her blond hair into a knot at her neck, a nervous habit that Owen found incredibly sexy. "Really."

"No, it's not okay," he insisted. "Alex, please. Let's do this right."

Alex was stopped halfway through the doorway. He looked at Owen, then at his stepmother. "Hi, Selby. Good to see you." His voice was overly loud, his tone fake. He gave her an untidy peck on the cheek, then left without another word.

Owen was fuming, but he wasn't about to get into a shouting match with his son in front of Selby. Damn it, though, the kid was going to start showing some respect or else.

He forced himself to calm down before picking up the phone. "Hello, Kali. This is a surprise."

"I'm sorry to bother you—"

"Not a problem. I was just looking over some very boring figures. This being a politician can get tedious."

There was a moment's pause. "Did you see this morning's paper?"

"About Anne you mean?" So he'd been right about the reason for the call. Both women had worked for him some years ago. He kept in touch with them, but only sporadically.

"Yes, about Anne. Do you know any more than is in the paper?"

"No. I'm sure I'll hear more tomorrow, but they don't call me on weekends unless there's some value added to having the DA himself involved."

There was a moment's pause, and then she said, "I need to see you, Owen."

It was an unexpected request. Not even a request really, more of an announcement. But Owen couldn't think of a way to gracefully decline. "I've got meetings scheduled all morning, but maybe I can find a few minutes later in the day. Why don't you call my secretary tomorrow and see if she can fit you in."

"I think it would be better if we talked today. In person."

"Today?" The cold was making him groggy.

"I can come over right now if you're free."

He hesitated, then finally relented. She'd lost a friend, after all, and Kali O'Brien wasn't one to go flying off the handle without reason. "Okay. You want to tell me what this is about?"

"When I get there."

# CHAPTER 6

Now that she'd reached Owen, Kali was beset with doubts. Was she reading too much into a simple yellow rose? And bothering Owen at home—was that really necessary? No, and yes. That's what she'd decided initially. And her instincts told her she was right still, but now, standing at the entrance of Owen's palatial home in Piedmont, she was aware of the butterflies in her stomach.

The door was opened by a woman with silky blond hair and high cheekbones. Selby Maxwell, Owen's new, and younger, wife. Kali recognized her immediately, although she appeared more petite in person than on the screen.

"Hi, I'm Kali O'Brien. Owen is expecting me."

Selby offered her hand. "Pleased to meet you. I'm Selby."

"I know, I'm a big fan of yours. I think I've seen all your movies."

"Not the latest one, I hope," she said with an easy laugh. "It was a disaster. Come in. Owen's in the den. He's feeling sorry for himself because he has a cold."

She lead Kali to a room at the back of the house, told Owen she was going out for a bit, then left the two of them alone.

Owen rose from the sofa. "Hey, Kali. It's good to see you again. It's been over a year, hasn't it?"

"At least." Kali offered her hand, but he ignored it, draping an arm around her shoulder instead. He gave her a friendly hug.

"It's good to see you, too," she said, and meant it, despite the circumstances. Owen was one of the few heavy-hitters who didn't let his ego eclipse his heart.

"I've followed your successes in the news," he said. "You've done well."

If doing well meant winning cases, she hadn't done too shabbily. But the rest of her life could use a little fine-tuning. "Look who's talking. *Mr. Governor.*"

Owen laughed. "There's a lot of ground to cover between here and there, not the least of which is the upcoming primary. Two more months, and if I manage to beat that idiot Tony Molina, then it's still a long haul until my face-off with Barton in November. A lot can go wrong along the way."

"You'll win, Owen. June and November both."

"I appreciate the vote of confidence." He stepped back and gestured to a chair. "Have a seat. Can I get you anything to drink?"

"Thanks, but I'm fine." She sank down into a soft leather armchair. Owen was looking good. He had to be at least fifty, but you couldn't tell it. He had a full head of hair, silvered at the temples, and a trim, athletic build. When she'd first met him, she'd found him imposing. Now those same qualities gave him statesmanlike stature. Not only would he make a good governor, he'd look the role.

"Congratulations on your marriage, by the way. I'm very happy for you."

"Thank you. I'm a lucky man. Though what a beautiful young woman like Selby sees in an old goat like me . . ."

"Stop it, Owen." He was launching into one of his humble, shuffle routines. Juries ate it up, but Kali knew him well enough to see it for what it was.

Owen popped a cough drop into his mouth. "Well, I am a lucky man. There's no denying that."

"How's Alex?" Kali asked, again stepping around the purpose of her visit.

"Still looking for his true calling, but otherwise he's doing well. Still in recovery, no relapses that I know of. And we're at least talking to one another these days."

Kali had always liked Alex. He'd been a skinny sixteen-year-old with an attitude when she first met him, but since she'd once been a sixteen-year-old with an attitude herself, she'd been more willing than his parents to take it in stride. Besides, she wasn't related to him.

It was Marilyn's death that seemed to really pit father against son. Owen had lost a wife; Alex, a mother. But instead of turning to one another for comfort, they'd been at each other's throats. Owen had found solace in work; Alex in drugs. Kali hadn't seen Alex since Owen had shipped him off to a school for troubled teens in Idaho.

"He's young yet," she said. "Give him time."

Owen made a face. "Not that young. He's wasting the best years of his life. You wanted to see me about something?"

She nodded. "About Anne."

"I thought that might be it. Her death was certainly a shock. She was a good lawyer. And a nice woman. It's terrible what happened to her."

"Awful."

"But as I told you on the phone, I don't know anything more than you do at this point."

"Actually, *I* may know more than *you*." Kali hesitated, then jumped in with both feet. "Her husband found a florist's box on the porch this morning, with a yellow rose inside."

"A rose?"

"A yellow rose. With a card that professed eternal love."

Owen's face blanched slightly, but he quickly recovered. "She and her husband were separated, weren't they?"

"That's not the point."

"Just because there was a yellow rose—"

"There was the card, too."

He nodded. "There usually is."

"But it doesn't fit. Anne wasn't seeing anyone. And it was a single rose, not a bouquet." She couldn't tell if Owen was playing devil's advocate, or if he honestly found nothing odd about the coincidence. "There's the trash bin aspect too," she added.

Owen rose and paced to the window, then back. "Dwayne Davis is dead, Kali. He couldn't possibly have killed Anne."

"But—"

"And he *was* the Bayside Strangler. We both know that, even if the jury wasn't convinced he was responsible for all the murders."

"But there were loose ends, you can't deny that."

Owen pressed a palm to his forehead and stared at her. "Don't tell me those bleeding-heart liberal supporters of his have gotten to you."

"Oh, come on, Owen. You know I'm no fan of Davis's."

"You've been working on the defense side for the past few years."

"That's irrelevant. What's important here is that Anne received a single yellow rose with a love note the morning after she was killed. Just like Davis's victims."

"Except for Wendy Gilchrist."

"Right." Wendy had received a flower but no note. Hers was also one of the murders for which Davis had not been convicted. "The police asked me about Anne's clothes," Kali added. "They wanted to know what kind of dresser she was. At the time, I thought her body had been found nude."

Owen's brown furrowed. "Did they say what she was wearing when they found her?"

"They wouldn't tell me. But they'd tell you."

A muscle in Owen's jaw twitched. And then one near his temple. "Jesus!" He pounded his fist against the wall, leaving a small chip in the plasterboard. "Just what I don't need. Especially now, with the primary heating up and Molina milking Davis's execution for every bit of press he can get."

"That's why I thought you should know right away. I figured you might want to poke around a bit and see what's really going on before they get wind of it." Although nothing was going to bring Anne back.

"You haven't spoken about this to anyone else, have you?"

"No, of course not." Kali couldn't help but feel offended, though she knew Owen was simply sorting things out in his mind.

"Thank you." He gave her a long look. "Really, I thank you. In the wrong hands, this could become a political disaster."

"Perhaps a legal one, as well."

Owen shook his head. "Davis was our man. I was certain of it then and I'm certain of it now. I'll find out what the cops have on Anne's murder, but if there's any connection at all with Davis, I guarantee you it's a copycat killing."

"The media will still love it," she pointed out.

Owen's expression was pained. "So will Molina."

# CHAPTER 7

Kali felt out of sorts for the remainder of the afternoon. She looked at the growing layer of dust and clutter around the house, and thought that tackling it might be a good use of her time. But when Margot called and suggested taking the dogs to Tilden Park for a walk, Kali leapt at the distraction.

Margot was a new neighbor, a flaming redhead a few years older than Kali, who wasn't, she'd confided one night over too much wine, technically yet a woman. She'd lived the first thirty-seven years of her life as Maurice and had an ex-wife who'd since discovered Margot to be a much easier companion than Maurice. Margot also had four spirited wolfhounds. Loretta was older and slower than Margot's dogs, but she didn't much seem to mind.

"Best take advantage of the dry weather while we can," Margot said when they'd unloaded the dogs from her van and headed out. "There's supposed to be another storm coming in tonight or tomorrow morning."

As usual, Kali scurried to keep up. Margot was several inches taller than Kali, with long, powerful legs. She was attractive in a highly "done" manner—a little too much makeup and layered hair with as much width and height as length—and surprisingly feminine in most respects, but Margot charged from point to point with an energy and focus that was decidedly male.

"Gosh, just look at that view," Margot said. "So spectacular it almost hurts."

They were hiking the Inspiration Point trail atop the Berkeley hills. Kali looked to the west, toward the broad panorama of San Francisco Bay. The recent rains had cleared the air, intensifying colors and shapes. It was almost as though she could reach out and touch the Golden Gate Bridge with her hand.

"It is amazing," Kali agreed. "Especially on days like this." The sun was low on the horizon, casting bands of purple and pink across the sky.

Kali slowed to drink in the beauty, but Margot pushed on ahead. Kali jogged to catch up. "How's the novel coming?" she asked. Margot was writing what she claimed was a "very high concept" thriller, though Kali had yet to wheedle out of her any hints as to subject matter.

"Slowly." Margot's answer was always the same. And then she'd change the topic, as she did now. She chattered on about a new Johnny Depp movie, then slid into a discourse about global warming. Margot was, among other things, an active environmentalist.

"You're awfully quiet today," she said, turning to Kali. "Feeling under the weather?"

"It's not that. It's . . ." Kali couldn't decide if she wanted to talk about Anne or not.

"Unpleasant, I can tell that much," Margot said gently.

"Did you see the piece in today's paper about the woman who was murdered?"

"The lawyer?"

Kali nodded. "I knew her. In fact, I was supposed to meet her for dinner the night she was killed."

"Oh, my God. I'm sorry. It never dawned on me she might be a friend of yours."

"We worked together at the DA's office just out of law school. We didn't see much of each other after leaving there, but recently we'd reconnected. We were even talking about sharing an office." And now Anne was gone. Kali experienced a fresh pang of sorrow.

Margot touched Kali's arm in a gesture of sympathy. "How terrible for you. It must be so upsetting."

Kali swallowed against the rising tide of emotion inside her. Anne's death was bad enough, and now there was the wrinkle of the yellow rose. Upsetting was only part of it.

"Did she practice criminal law?" Margot asked.

"Family law mostly. Divorces."

Margot grimaced. "A lot of nastiness in that line of work."

"Surprisingly, Anne loved it."

"Takes a special kind of person, I imagine. Even good divorces, like mine, are painful." Margot's face darkened momentarily at the memory. "The newspaper said something about the Bayside Strangler trial. Isn't that the guy who killed a bunch of women years ago?"

"Uh-huh. Anne and I both worked on that case. That's how we met."

"*You* worked on that case?" Margot untangled the set of leashes, which had become unmanageable as the four dogs pulled in different directions. Her hands were large, but her fingers were slender and delicate, capped with shiny nails of fire-engine red. And jewelry. Today it was a ruby ring and a wrist heavy with jangling bracelets.

"I was just a worker bee. Owen Nelson was the chief prosecutor."

"The same Owen Nelson who's now running for governor?" There was awe in Margot's voice.

"The very same. It was the Bayside Strangler case that really put him in the spotlight."

"But you were right there, in the middle of it. A part of history, so to speak."

Not the middle, thank God. The dead women and their families—they had been in the middle of it.

"There was a movie about it, wasn't there?" Margot asked.

"Not a very good one, in my opinion. And not totally accurate either. There was a book, too. By a respected journalist. The book is much better."

"The Bayside Strangler." Margot squinted in thought. "I wasn't living here then, but I remember reading about it. How many women did he kill?"

"Five, that we know of. But we only got convictions on two. Under the circumstances, even that was something of an accomplishment."

"What do you mean?"

"The DA at the time recommended dropping the charges for lack of evidence, but the judge in the case wouldn't do it."

"Wouldn't grant the prosecution's own motion to dismiss charges?"

"Mostly it was politics, I think. The DA was worried about losing, both in court and in public opinion. He didn't want to take the chance. But the judge thought the case needed to be heard." Kali did a quick two-step to avoid stepping on a large slug making his way across the path. "It ended up being dumped in Owen Nelson's lap, and he turned it into a personal victory. That was the case that cemented his reputation as a first-rate prosecutor."

"Who'd the killer turn out to be?"

"Dwayne Arnold Davis. He was executed last month, right before Christmas. You probably read about the protests and last-minute appeals."

"Sounds vaguely familiar. That stuff doesn't stick with me. I figure a guy like that deserves what he gets." She handed Kali the jumble of leashes. "Here, can you hold this for a minute while I take off my jacket. What was this Davis like, some Hannibal Lecter clone?"

"No. He was married with a young kid. Taught junior high."

Margot gave her an incredulous look. "You're kidding?"

"Mild mannered and well liked. It came as a real shock when the investigation focused on him. There's a whole cadre of people who still think he's innocent." Kali wasn't one of them, though there'd been moments when she'd had her doubts. She'd put them behind her with his conviction, but now with Anne's death and the seeming similarities, she was getting a queasy feeling in her gut.

"Were the victims people he knew?"

"Not really, but he did target them ahead of time. We were never sure how or why, but he'd single them out, then get to know them in some way. He'd collect information about them."

"Stalking?"

"Sort of. Only the women weren't aware of it. In retrospect, we learned that they'd had strange phone calls or missing mail . . . the sort of thing that happens to all of us and we don't think too much of at the time."

Margot gave a dramatic shiver. "Creepy."

The creepiest part about it, Kali thought, was how normal Davis had seemed. "He dressed their bodies in revealing clothing and left them near trash cans."

"Making a statement?"

"It certainly looked that way. Then he taunted the police with poems about their death."

"A depraved son of bitch, wasn't he?"

"Yes, he was." And the fact that he'd sat through the entire trial with a smirk on his face only strengthened those sentiments for Kali.

"So how come he was only convicted of two of the murders?"

"A lot of mistakes were made in the investigation, and Davis's attorney played on them in his defense."

"Like the O.J. trial."

Kali nodded. "There were no claims of flying DNA, but Davis *did* claim the police framed him by planting evidence. There were questions of valid search and seizure as well. And finally, the defense attorney was able to make credible hints about another suspect."

Race had also been an issue with Davis, although it came into play mostly outside the courtroom. Davis was black; the victims and the detectives who worked the case were white. There'd been heated debate about whether Davis would have been a suspect at all if he'd been white.

A bicyclist passed them going the other way. Margot bit her lower lip and walked in silence for a few moments. "It must have been scary knowing a killer was on the loose."

"It was." The killings had started during Kali's last year of law school. A young woman who worked as a nurse at Alta Bates Hospital. Kali remembered reading about her disappearance, the pleas of friends and colleagues who insisted she would never go off without telling someone. Then her car had been found by the estuary, and three days later, her body.

Suspicion focused on a man she'd been having an affair with, but there was no hard evidence, and eventually the investigation moved from the front pages. Two months later it was a young professor at UC Berkeley, Kali's own campus. Kali hadn't known her—she was a professor of chemistry—but with all the talk among students and staff, the murder of Joanna Paget had taken on an almost personal dimension. But the real swell of panic had come when the police announced there were possible ties between the two murders. You could feel the fear in the air. Women didn't go out at night unless they had to, and paired up for simple tasks like going to the store.

"It got so that you trusted no one," Kali said. "Not the mailman, or the plumber, or even the grocery clerk who offered to carry your bags. And because rumor had it that the killer posed as a policeman, you couldn't trust them, either."

"I'm certainly glad they got the son of a bitch," Margot said.

Kali nodded. But her skin tingled with dread all the same.

# CHAPTER 8

Hamburger juice dribbled down Lou's chin. He grabbed the wadded-up napkin next to his plate and mopped the mess before it could land on his shirt. Across the table from him, Keating speared a forkful of lettuce. Neatly. What kind of man chose salad over a burger? There were things about his partner Lou would never understand.

Bryce Keating wasn't someone Lou would have chosen to work with if he'd had his druthers. Nothing like Harry, his partner for nearly a dozen years. But Harry had retired to travel in his Winnebago, and Lou had been paired with Keating. "Think of it as mentoring," the captain had suggested. More like playground duty, Lou sometimes thought.

Although Keating wasn't exactly wet behind the ears.

He wasn't a bad partner, either. Lou could have done a whole lot worse. At least Keating was male, which was a big plus right there. Especially now that the department was making such an effort to reach out to women recruits. Lou wasn't sure he could have worked with a woman. And Keating was no slouch on the job. If anything, he went overboard in the other direction. But he was from a different generation. Different planet, maybe. And he'd clearly watched too many action thrillers during his formative years. Saw himself as a hero for the new millennium, a crusader in the urban jungle.

"What do you think of the husband?" Keating asked. He was hunched over his salad, both muscled forearms on the tabletop, as if Lou might be tempted to snatch a slice of cucumber from under his nose.

"Too easy."

"Too easy? Aren't you the guy whose mantra is 'don't overlook the obvious'?"

Lou grabbed a french fry and chewed it thoughtfully. True, the husband hadn't been as forthcoming as Lou would have liked. But the man had been reeling from the news of his wife's death. Under the circumstances, you couldn't fault him for being less than coherent.

"Why would he kill her?" Lou asked, though he knew as well as anyone that motives for murder were as elusive as dust.

"You're asking me *why?*"

"You studying to be a parrot, Bryce?"

Keating ignored the jibe. "They were estranged, don't forget. Right there that tells us they weren't the happy couple Jerry Bailey made them out to be. A domestic dispute gets out of hand, the husband loses his temper, and next thing he knows, he's crossed the line."

"Except it doesn't fit what we know of the crime. He'd have had to track her down. She was at work, going to meet a friend for dinner. Doesn't strike me as a setup for a heat-of-passion killing."

"Maybe his anger festered. Or he stopped by the office to see her and they got into it then."

"It's possible, I guess." Lou signaled the waitress for more coffee. "You get anything from the secretary?" he asked Keating. She'd come in to talk to them first thing this morning.

"Not really. She left the office Friday evening about six. Ms. Bailey was still there, working. There was nothing on her calendar except dinner with the friend. And nothing unusual in her day, according to the secretary. She says Ms. Bailey was a respected lawyer"—here Keating made a face that conveyed his general distaste for attorneys—"well liked by clients, blah-de-blah. Handled mostly divorces, trusts and estates."

"If she was any good, she probably wasn't so well liked by her clients' ex-spouses." The waitress filled Lou's cup and he gave her a nod of thanks, but she'd turned her back already.

"I thought about that, too. There was apparently one divorce that was particularly acrimonious." He pulled a notepad from his pocket. "Jeff and Judy Mason. She got the kids, the house, a hefty support check, and a restraining order. Sounds like all he got was the shaft."

Lou raised an eyebrow. "Could be that's what he deserved."

Keating shot him a look that Lou knew well. On this point, the line had been drawn in the sand from the day they'd started working together. Lou suspected it had something to do with Keating's own divorce, though he never talked about it.

"Anyway," Keating continued, "the secretary didn't elaborate. Client confidentiality issues seemed to dawn on her partway through our conversation." He speared the last tomato on his plate and pushed back from the table. "How'd the autopsy go?"

"Not my idea of a good time." In all his years on the force, autopsies were one thing Lou had never learned to handle easily. What he *had* learned, though, was that it was important to be there. A paper report, no matter how detailed, was never as complete. Answers and explanations were easier to get on the spot.

"Nothing that's going to help us find the guy," Lou said. "But there was one surprise. She was pregnant."

"Didn't look it."

"She was barely there, the doc says, but pregnant all the same."

Keating's face grew attentive. "Spells motive to me."

"Maybe."

"Give me an overview of the rest of it."

Lou circled his coffee mug with his hands. "She was strangled. Some kind of cotton rope, the doc thinks. About a quarter of an inch in diameter. Maybe clothesline, but rough, not that plastic-coated stuff." Her skin had been pale and unblemished, he remembered, making the purple band of bruising around her neck seem all the more abhorrent.

"Time of death?"

"Around ten p.m., give or take a couple of hours. With the rain and her body being dumped outside, it's hard to say."

Keating tapped his fingers on the tabletop. Fingers and feet, he had a habit of tapping them both. "Any signs of a struggle?"

"Nope. Looks like she was killed right off. No chafing on her hands or feet like she'd been tied up. No bruises or skin under her nails like she fought back."

"What about the abrasions on her legs?"

"Postmortem. Probably when he was positioning the body by the dumpster."

Keating stopped the finger dance. "Sexual assault?"

Lou shook his head. "And I checked with forensics. Not much

in the way of trace evidence. Some blue acrylic fibers is all. On her skirt. And lots of litter around the dumpster, of course, which was no doubt there long before our guy showed up."

"Doesn't look like this one is going to untangle easily."

"You're right about that." Lou hated cases like this, working from nothing. Trying to figure out who killed a woman everyone professed to love. He took another sip of coffee. "We got a call from the DA this afternoon."

"The big man himself?"

"Yep."

Keating's brow furrowed. "What did he want?"

"To know what we had on the Bailey murder. I guess the victim being a lawyer and all, he's especially interested."

Keating's phone chirped. He pulled it from his belt, carried on a brief, monosyllabic conversation, then disconnected. "They found her car," he said to Lou. "Near East Fourteenth. Stripped."

"Tough neighborhood."

"Maybe the lady had a drug habit." Keating must have read Lou's skepticism. "Happens more often than you'd think," he added.

Keating had worked Vice before moving into Homicide. It was a turf he knew well, and a connection that frequently paid off in his current assignment. But the Bailey woman's well-toned and athletic body made Lou think his partner was off base this time around.

"You going out there?" Lou asked.

"Why not? It may be that someone in the neighborhood has eyes." Keating scooted back his chair. "Besides, it's good to keep in touch with old friends."

Informants, he meant. People who had their fingers on the pulse of criminal activity in the city. That was one of Keating's strengths.

Lou headed in the opposite direction from Keating, toward Anne Bailey's office in downtown Berkeley. From the outside, the building was vintage sixties—a vertical cube of concrete and glass built with an eye toward cost rather than aesthetics. He entered the lobby and approached the security guard, a skinny young man who was busily flipping through a wrestling magazine. It wasn't a high-security building, and Lou knew the man's role was more information officer than guard, but his lackadaisical attitude irked Lou all the same.

Lou flashed his badge. The man didn't exactly shoot to attention, but he closed the magazine and looked directly at Lou. That didn't always happen these days. People were eager for a quick response from the police when they were the ones in trouble, but otherwise they were wary of authority.

"What can I do for you?" The man was missing a few teeth, giving him the appearance of a pasty jack-o'-lantern.

"Were you on duty Friday evening?" Lou asked.

"I work Mondays through Thursdays. Noon till seven."

"Pretty busy here in the evening?"

"People pour outta here from about five to six, then it gets pretty quiet."

"How late does someone remain on duty?"

"Regular shift till seven. Then we lock the doors. People who work here have keys, but they have to sign in. There's someone on duty till midnight when the building shuts up."

Lou took down the name of the man who'd worked the night of Anne Bailey's death. Maybe they'd be able to get a fix on what time she left, or if they were really lucky, a description of someone she'd left with.

Next, he headed to the garage where the husband said she regularly parked. This time Lou was lucky and happened on the same attendant who'd been working Friday evening. But there his luck ended. Monthly card holders exited through a separate gate. The man didn't recognize Anne Bailey's photo, and silver Lexuses, he said, were as common as fleas on a dog.

Anne's trail once she left her office remained a mystery.

Twilight had robbed the sky of color by the time Lou paid his daily visit to Jan's bedside. At the entrance to the nursing home, he braced himself, as he did every time, for the walk down the long corridor to her room. The home depressed him beyond measure. The stale, sweet smells of age and illness; the hollow, hushed sounds of life suspended; the vacant stares of patients he passed along the way. And this was one of the better homes he'd looked into.

Not that Jan was in any state to know. Brain dead in a surprisingly vital body. All those years of exercise and healthy eating, and this is what it bought her.

Lou pulled up his customary chair, ignoring the woman in the bed next to hers, who drooled and made ugly sucking sounds. It pained him that he couldn't afford a private room, much less in-home care. But he couldn't have managed even this without state help.

Brushing Jan's hair from her forehead, he leaned over and kissed her lightly on the cheek. "Hi, honey. How are you this evening?"

Jan's hair had been blond when they married, and with the help of her hairdresser, had remained blond until the auto accident. Now it was an uneven, yellowed gray. He'd asked the home to dye it for her, but they'd looked at him like he was nuts. Maybe he was. When you were comatose, what did the color of your hair matter? But he knew that it would matter to Jan.

Lou reached into the drawer of the bedside table for the latest Harry Potter book, which he'd been reading to her for the last couple of weeks.

In the beginning, the doctors had said that the sound of his voice, his touch, could make a difference. So he'd started holding her hand and reading to her. He'd tried the romances she used to like, but Lou hated them. And Tom Clancy, which he'd known wouldn't appeal to Jan, but which he liked. Lou had finally settled on rereading the classics. *The Great Gatsby, To Kill a Mockingbird,* and most recently, *Pride and Prejudice.* Harry Potter was something a bit different. Lou was surprised at how much he was enjoying the story.

He took Jan's hand in his and opened the book to the chapter where they'd left off. He'd long ago given up any hope that she heard his words, but it was easier to read than to sit in silence. Or to dwell on what he'd lost.

# CHAPTER 9

Owen glanced at the speedometer and saw that it was inching toward eighty. He eased his foot off the gas pedal even though he was far from the fastest car on the road. No point asking for trouble, which was what the media could make of even a simple speeding ticket.

"You're awfully quiet tonight," Selby said.

"Am I? Just thinking, I guess."

They were on their way home from a political gathering where Owen had given a well-received talk. Of course, he'd been preaching to the choir, but the spontaneous bursts of applause had pleased him nonetheless. The press had been there too. Owen hoped they'd picked up on the same swell of support from the crowd that he had.

Still, he had been relieved when it was finally time to leave. The ember of worry burning in his chest had made it difficult to concentrate on anything else.

"You usually do your thinking out loud," Selby said.

Owen laughed. "I'm trying to spare you."

"I like listening to your thoughts, even when they ramble. You know that."

He did. Selby was an attentive listener, and she was often able to offer a fresh perspective, especially regarding the so-called women's issues on which elections frequently turned. They complemented each other in that, as in so many ways. If only Owen could make Alex understand. His marriage to Selby in no way diminished his memory of Marilyn.

"You're ahead of Molina in the polls, honey. And gaining every day."

one trying to convince Owen of the similarities between Anne's murder and the Bayside Strangler. Why now, did she find herself resisting?

Owen rubbed his cheek. "The cops got one too. So did Jackson."

"Jack Jackson?"

Owen nodded. "I convinced him to sit on it for now, but I don't know how long he'll keep quiet."

"I'm surprised you were able to convince him even of that." Jackson was a decent man, but he was an aggressive journalist. He and Owen had collaborated on a book about the Davis trial, so maybe Owen had more sway with him than most people would.

"It wasn't easy," Owen said with a fleeting smile. "I promised him the inside track as long as he behaved himself."

Kali slid the paper back across the desk. A yellow rose and a poem. Neither was unique. It might still be coincidence. She *wanted* it to be coincidence. "Did you talk to the detectives?"

Owen nodded. "Anne was dressed provocatively, in clothes that weren't her own. Her body was posed and placed, as you yourself pointed out, near a trash receptacle."

Like the victims of the Bayside Strangler. "So now you're wondering if you've got a copycat on your hands or if we put away the wrong man." Even giving voice to the possibility made Kali feel ill.

"I'm reasonably sure Davis was the Bayside Strangler," Owen said.

"Only reasonably? A couple of days ago you said you were sure."

He hesitated. "Publicly, I'm absolutely certain. But you have to admit, I'd be a damn fool to categorically rule out the other possibility."

And Owen was no fool. His open mind was one of the things Kali had always admired about him.

Owen stood. He paced back and forth behind his desk. Worry pulled his expression taut, flattening his gaze. Kali could well imagine his distress. It was a prosecutor's nightmare, made worse by Davis's claims of innocence and the publicity surrounding the trial.

It was also the sort of thing that could crush a candidate for public office.

Owen turned to face her. "I'd like you to think about coming back to the DA's office."

This was so far removed from anything Kali had imagined that she was momentarily stunned. In fact, she wasn't sure she'd heard him right. "The DA's office?"

"On a temporary basis. To work on this case."

"Why me?" She felt light-headed. Flattered and dismayed at the same time.

"You know the history," Owen explained. "You were involved in the Davis case. You'll recognize what's different this time around and what's not. You're also familiar with the investigative screwups last time. I want to make sure we don't go through that again. When we catch whoever's doing this, I want an airtight conviction."

"You've got a staff."

"I'm short-handed right now." He rubbed his jaw. "My two senior deputy DAs both have big trials coming up. Another is set to go out on maternity leave."

Kali was still reeling with the shock of Owen's request. But she also found it tempting. "I've been a defense attorney for the last four years."

"All the better. People can't accuse me of orchestrating a cover-up." He stopped his pacing and stood behind his desk, his hands on the back of his chair. "This is going to hit the papers at some point. Better that we come across looking like knights than villains."

"Grab the bull by the horns, so to speak."

"Beats getting trampled." He leaned forward. "I hope it goes without saying that I'm also interested in getting at the truth."

She did know that, and it was the reason she found herself considering his offer. Owen wasn't without ego, but his integrity was part and parcel of who he was. "The other day you were certain there was no connection between Anne's murder and the Bayside Strangler."

"I'm still not convinced there is. But with the rose, the note, the way she was found—it might be chance, or it might be that we are dealing with a copycat. Either way, it's important that I take an aggressive role in this. I don't want anyone saying I'm trying to sweep dirt under the rug in order to save my ass."

She smiled. "But you wouldn't *mind* saving it."

"Of course not." He didn't actually smile, but his eyes softened. "That's not the most important thing, though. I certainly hope I'm not so much of a politician that I've lost sight of doing what's right."

That strong ethical stance, Kali thought, would be one of Owen's strongest selling points in the upcoming election. He was a straight arrow. A man who listened well but was not afraid to speak his mind.

"I trust you, Kali. That's important, too. There are cops out there who aren't happy with some of my judgment calls, people in my own office even. Many of them have come out strongly in support of Barton. I don't want to be in a position of second-guessing everyone's motives on this."

She weighed Owen's request in her mind. Her own legal practice was at a crossroads. After moving back to her hometown of Silver Creek, she'd returned to the Bay Area last year in order to fill in for Nina Barrett, a law school friend who was ill and no longer able to handle her small, independent practice. For a variety of reasons, Kali had stayed longer than she'd intended. But the time had come to make a move. That was why she and Anne had been talking about sharing an office.

"I don't know, Owen. Let me think about it, okay?"

"Fine, but not too long. I've got to assign someone soon."

For the rest of the day, Kali found it hard to concentrate. Sitting at her office desk, she could think of nothing but Owen's request and all the reasons it was a foolhardy thing for her to do. But she was also intrigued, and felt in some measure that she owed it to Anne. And, perhaps, to Owen.

By three that afternoon, she had bounced back and forth so often she felt dizzy. Was she too close to the murder given her friendship with Anne? Probably, but she also wanted to see Anne's killer caught and convicted. Being part of that would be a productive way to channel her grief.

And Owen had asked for her help. That, in itself, carried a lot of weight. It would be good to work for him again, but more important, she would be able to repay Owen for his faith in her years earlier.

"Hey, boss." Jared stuck his head through the open doorway. "You remember I told you I had to leave early today, right?"

"Right." Kali pushed her chair away from her desk. The office, Nina's office really, had a homey feel. Ficus in the corner by the bay window, watercolors on the walls, a sage green Tibetan rug on the floor. She'd known it was temporary from the start, but that didn't make the prospect of leaving any easier. "How are you coming on the Sullivan matter?" she asked.

"Settlement conference is scheduled for Thursday morning. I don't think we're going to make it to trial on this one." Jared sounded disappointed. At twenty-four and newly admitted to the bar, he was eager for the challenge of courtroom litigation.

The phone rang.

"I'll get it," Jared offered. He doubled as office receptionist. "For you," he said a minute later with the wide-eyed look of a star-struck groupie. "It's Owen Nelson."

"Hi." Kali made a *door-closed* gesture with her hand as Jared left.

"I don't mean to pressure you, Kali—" Owen said.

"But you'd like an answer." She couldn't blame him. This was the kind of potentially explosive situation he'd want to diffuse at the earliest possible stage.

"If you've got one."

Kali looked at the thick stack of files on her desk. She was winding down here anyway. Nina would be coming back in a couple of weeks and was already working on several matters from home. Jared would jump at the chance to pick up whatever slack there was. Besides, in her heart, she knew what she wanted to do.

"Yes," she told him.

"Yes, you have an answer or yes, you'll do it?"

"I'll do it."

"Thank you. I owe you." His relief was evident in his voice.

"I just hope you feel the same way when it's all over."

"There's going to be a meeting of the investigative team tomorrow afternoon at two. Think you can make it?"

"I'll be there."

Decision made, she managed to get in a couple of hours of work before thoughts about her new assignment intruded. She printed out the final rewrite of a will she'd drafted and was ready to call it a day when her office door swung open. The man who entered looked familiar, but she couldn't quite place him.

"Hi." He grinned at her like an old friend.

"Hello."

"Caught you by surprise, didn't I?"

"You certainly did," Kali acknowledged truthfully. Even his voice was familiar, but who was he? Another attorney? Someone she knew from Silver Creek? A neighbor? Then it dawned on her, just as he caught her confusion and introduced himself.

"Nathan Sloane," he reminded her. "From the restaurant the other night. You were waiting for a friend who never showed."

"Right. It took me a moment to place you." A part of her was pleased to run into him again, but what was he doing here in her office? As she recalled, she hadn't even given him a last name.

He leaned against the door jamb, his eyes registering amusement. They were bright blue and fringed with long, thick lashes. "I hope she had a good excuse for not showing."

Kali thought about brushing the question off with a flip response, but her sense of loss was too great. "She's dead. Murdered, in fact. That night."

The expression of humor on his face faded. "The woman in the news?"

Kali nodded.

"Jesus. I'm sorry."

Nathan sounded genuinely moved, and Kali liked him for that. But she was still puzzled by his sudden appearance at her office door. And acutely aware that most of the building's tenants had gone home for the day. "How did you find me?"

"Your organizer. You left it at the table, remember?"

And he had obviously taken a quick peek before chasing after her to return it. "Maybe a better question," she asked, "is, why? Are you needing legal advice?"

"I sure hope not. I was in the neighborhood is all, and thought I'd stop by to say hello."

She was mildly flattered.

"You made quite an impression on me," he added with the hint of a quirky smile.

She wasn't altogether sure that was a good thing. On the other hand, Nathan Sloane had a boyish charm it was hard not to warm to. She returned the smile. "Thanks for stopping by."

"I was hoping you'd have time for a drink later. Or coffee, if you'd prefer."

Kali had enjoyed the time they'd spent over wine Friday evening. But now that she'd agreed to work with Owen, she had a lot on her mind. She didn't want to waste a couple of hours making small talk.

"Sorry," she said, "I'm busy tonight." She softened it with a smile.

Nathan studied her a moment, then touched two fingers to his forehead in a goofy salute. "Yes, ma'am. I read you loud and clear. Can't fault a guy for trying, though." And he was gone as suddenly as he'd appeared.

Only later that evening, when she faced an empty house, an empty fridge and a bottle of wine with a crumbly cork, did Kali wonder if she'd been too hasty in dismissing Nathan Sloane. What was done was done, however. She had no way of reaching him even if she'd wanted to. And she didn't, really.

She crossed the street and borrowed three eggs and a high-tech corkscrew from Margot. She found some cheddar cheese that wasn't moldy or overly dried out, and managed to put together an edible omelette. Then she went to her closet and pulled out the large cardboard box in which she'd stored newspaper clippings and her own notes on the Bayside Strangler. She no longer kept news clips and articles, even on high-profile trials where she was the lead attorney, but the Strangler trial had been her first, and she'd amassed quite a collection.

The clippings far outnumbered her own notes, but they contained fewer details. As she read through them, refreshing her memory about the crime, she jotted key points on a yellow pad.

Five victims, ranging in age from seventeen to twenty-eight. All single. And all blondes, with straight, shoulder-length hair and slender, well-toned bodies. All of the women had been wearing revealing clothing when they were found, clothing that wasn't their own. In three cases, the victim had also been wearing a black leather dog collar around her neck.

All had been killed elsewhere, their bodies deposited and posed at the sites where they'd been found—near public trash bins. The ligature marks on the necks of all five women were sim-

ilar, as well. The coroner had established that they'd been strangled with a common type of rope, the kind you could buy in fifty-
foot segments at the hardware store. All but Wendy Gilchrist had
been raped.

Kali thought about Anne and felt the sourness rise from her
stomach into her throat. Was she really up to reading the details of
her friend's death? Kali stood and stretched. She walked across to
the wall of windows looking out over the bay. On a clear night the
lights sparkled like jewels on black velvet. Tonight, the fog had
rolled in from the coast and mist hung low in the air. The jewels
still shone, but with an eerie, almost surreal cast that made Kali
think of enchanted kingdoms and magic spells. It was a view she
never tired of.

Somewhere she had the number of the window washer Anne
had given her last fall. Clear View Windows if she recalled correctly. He was good, Anne had said, and not too expensive. Kali
would have to give him a call as soon as the rain stopped.

Anne again. Reminders everywhere.

Kali sat back down at the table where she'd spread her clippings. Anne didn't exactly fit the pattern of the Bayside Strangler
murders. She wasn't single, for one thing, although she and Jerry
had separated. She was slender and athletic, but her hair was
more brown than blond and it was cut short. She was a bit older
than the others too. Of course, by now, their killer would be older
too.

Except the person who'd killed the others was Dwayne Arnold
Davis, Kali reminded herself, and he was dead.

So who had killed Anne?

# CHAPTER 10

Arms crossed at his chest, Lou glared at the captain. Inside, he was fuming, but he tried hard to appear calm.

"What, exactly, does 'working closely with the DA's office' mean?" he asked. Cops worked with DAs on a regular basis, sometimes even at the start of a new case, like now, but this was the first time Lou had been directed to do so from above. It didn't sit well.

"The team approach, Lou. Two minds are better than one; three better than two." Burnell didn't sound any too happy about the arrangement himself.

"Why?"

Burnell shrugged. "Owen Nelson covering his ass, probably. Like I said, he thinks there may be similarities between the Bailey homicide and the Bayside Strangler murders awhile back."

"That still doesn't—"

"Dwayne Arnold Davis. Ring a bell? He was executed last month."

A person would have to be living in a cave not to have heard about it. Last-minute appeals, candlelight vigils, accusations of racial bias and sloppy police work. Lou would have remembered the case even without all that. It was the case he'd been yanked from when he was put on administrative leave following a shooting. That still rankled.

"Owen Nelson was the prosecuting attorney on that case," Burnell reminded him.

And now he was the district attorney, running for governor. The picture was clear enough. Not that it made Lou any more comfortable. He didn't think much of attorneys, and he thought even less of politicians. Lou had a job to do, and he didn't need some snotty-nosed assistant deputy DA second-guessing his every move.

"Nelson wants his office to be part of the investigation."

"He can do that?" Lou asked. Though obviously he could, since he had.

"The district attorney's office has superior jurisdiction. Owen Nelson could run his own investigation if he wanted to." Burnell leaned forward, the bald dome of his head shiny in the overhead light. "Nobody's taking the case away from you, Lou. Nelson simply wants his office involved from the get-go."

"Last DA who was part of a task force was a horse's ass."

Burnell gave him a look that said *my hands are tied*. "Try to be grateful for the help."

Lou humphed. The way he figured it, the captain was covering his own rear end, just like Nelson. Trouble was, Lou was the man on the front lines. The one who had to pay the price.

"And when you catch the guy," Burnell added, "you'll be able to hand the prosecutor a case that will stand up in court, and in the press."

That was it in a nutshell, Lou thought. Owen Nelson wasn't taking any chances with a repeat of what happened before. Nor was the captain. The only person on the hot seat this time would be the defendant.

"You get anything from the note?" Burnell asked.

"No prints, if that's what you mean. Nothing special about the paper either. It was done on a computer. I've got the lab running tests for saliva from where the envelope was sealed." Lou hoped the guy had been too stupid to use a sponge to moisten the flap.

"What about witnesses?"

"Still looking."

"I've pulled Maureen Oliver from patrol and assigned her to help you."

"Me and Keating, we do fine by ourselves." Lou was no longer able to keep the edge of irritation from his voice.

"I'm sure you'll do fine with Maureen's assistance, as well."

Great. Not only was he going to have a chaperon from the DA's office, he was going to have a rookie cop trotting at his heels. And both were *shes*.

The captain's phone rang. He picked it up, dismissing Lou with a nod.

Kali shifted in her chair, trying to find a comfortable position. There wasn't one, she decided. It was a hard, straight-back chair. In a dingy and windowless room. Standard police department conference room. There was nothing comfortable about any of it, including the faces staring at her from around the table.

There were four in all. Lou Fortune and Bryce Keating, the detectives she'd met earlier; Maureen Oliver, a uniformed cop several years younger than Kali; and a liaison from public relations, a black man who looked to be in his early fifties, whose unenviable duty it was to run interference with the press. He'd introduced himself simply as Emory.

They were looking in her direction, expectantly. She felt a moment's irritation. She hadn't called the damn meeting; Owen had. Pushed her off to do battle with little more than a metaphoric handshake.

"I know this must feel like a turf war," she began, "but let me assure you that's not what it's about. I'm here because I want the same thing you do—a successful resolution to this case."

Maureen Oliver acknowledged the remark with a minimalist nod. The others remained stone-faced.

"I was one of the district attorneys who worked on the Dwayne Arnold Davis trial," Kali continued. "As you know, he was convicted of the so-called Bayside Strangler murders. Two of them, at any rate. There seem to be similarities between those murders and that of Anne Bailey."

"There are also differences." This was Fortune, the older detective with a belly that strained against the buttons of his white cotton shirt. His tone was gruff.

Kali hoped it was as much out of habit as real pique. "I'm not trying to ram anything down your throats, detective. I have no agenda aside from doing what I can to see that we catch, and convict, a murderer."

She'd expected resistance to the notion that they might be dealing with a serial killer. She didn't blame them. And she'd like nothing better than to have them prove her wrong.

Emory spoke up. "Are you going to be the spokesperson for the DA's office on this?"

"For the moment, among ourselves. But the detectives are heading up the investigation. Any public disclosures should come from them." She looked to the two men. Fortune's expression softened some, but Keating continued to regard her with the same flat gaze he'd fixed on her when she walked in.

"Now, let's talk about where we are and where we're going," she said.

Fortune hunched forward, arms on his knees. "Where we are is nowhere. We found her car, abandoned and stripped, on a side street off East Fourteenth. No clue as to where she was grabbed."

"What about evidence *in* the car?"

"We've got a team going over it now. No obvious signs of a struggle. Nothing that jumps out at you like it shouldn't be there. My guess is, the killer never set foot in that car."

"How did it get to East Fourteenth, then?" Kali had her own ideas about that, but she wanted to hear what the detectives thought. Besides, if they were going to work together effectively, she had to convince them she wasn't out to step on their toes.

"Picked up by someone prowling for auto parts, most likely."

"You're thinking she met with her killer somewhere between leaving her office and getting to the parking lot?"

"Or between her car and the restaurant," Fortune added.

Kali felt a shiver. She hadn't thought about the fact that Anne might have been only a few hundred yards away from her when she met up with her killer.

"Then again," Fortune said, "maybe she stopped somewhere along the way. Home even."

From the wiggle of the detective's bushy brows when he mentioned stopping at home, Kali sensed that Jerry was high on their list of possible suspects. The spouse usually was, and the fact that he and Anne were separated couldn't help matters.

"No witnesses?" Kali asked. "No one who saw anything unusual?" It amazed her that with all the busybodies and watchful eyes out there, people could be accosted and killed without being seen, but it happened all the time.

Bryce Keating eyed her silently, his dark eyes unreadable. "People who see don't always talk," he said slowly. "Not without a little arm-twisting." She thought he winked at her. "Fig-uratively speaking."

Kali wondered if he was being sarcastic. It was hard to tell from his tone.

She'd already learned that Keating had a reputation as some-one who pushed the boundaries when it came to getting results. He also had an air about him—intense and self-contained. She didn't have a clue what he was really thinking.

"As soon as the press gets hold of the Bayside Strangler con-nection," Fortune said bleakly, "we'll have people coming out of the woodwork. Ninety-nine point nine percent of them, at a min-imum, won't know a thing. But we'll have to follow up on all the leads on the minuscule chance of finding someone who does."

Maureen Oliver ran a hand through the hair at her temples. It was cut short, almost like a man's, but her skin was so smooth and her features so delicate, there was nothing masculine about her. "How strong *is* the connection?" she asked. "I don't know all that much about the Bayside Strangler."

"Strong enough for concern," Kali said. "The poem from our killer follows the Bayside Strangler pattern. In all but the first of the murders, he sent a poem to the police referencing the victim by name and mentioning some personal bit of information about her."

"Owen Nelson and that reporter Jack Jackson got a copy of the poem as well, didn't they? But the Strangler sent his only to the police?"

"Right. But remember, Owen and Jackson weren't involved in the investigation of the Bayside Strangler. They came on only after Davis's arrest."

"What was personal about this last note?" Emory asked.

"It referred to the yellow rose of Texas. Anne was born and raised in Texas."

Emory whistled under his breath. "And Jackson really agreed to keep it quiet?"

"Apparently. For now." Despite Owen's assurances, Kali had half expected to see a front-page story in this morning's paper. Whatever hold he had over Jackson, this must have put it to the test.

"Then there's the yellow rose itself," Kali said, continuing to address Maureen's question. "The Bayside Strangler sent a single yellow rose and love note to his victims. Four of them anyway. In one instance, the note never turned up." She turned to the detectives. "You've talked to the florist whose name was on the box?"

"He didn't remember anyone buying a yellow rose," Fortune said. "And he had no record of a delivery to Anne Bailey's address."

"You think the killer delivered it himself?" Maureen asked.

"Could be," Kali said. "It wouldn't surprise me to discover he bought the rose at a different florist's, either, and substituted the box. That's what happened with the Bayside Strangler." She paused, pulling herself back to her original train of thought. "There are other similarities—the placement of her body by a trash bin, the clothes she was wearing—"

"You've had a chance to look at them?" Fortune asked.

"This morning." It hadn't been a task Kali relished. She'd told herself they were just clothes, but they weren't. They were the clothes Anne's killer had chosen for her. He'd stripped her to the skin, then dressed her in a skimpy, tight skirt and shell, no underwear. Kali had felt a swell of nausea when the evidence room clerk handed her the lightweight plastic bag.

"Did her husband take a look, as well?" Kali asked. "He'd know better than I would if they were hers."

"He didn't think so, but he couldn't be sure."

"Neither item was hers?"

"That's what he said."

Kali turned to Maureen to explain. "The Bayside Strangler dressed his victims in provocative clothing, but he always included one item that was their own."

"It's what I've been saying." Fortune tapped the tabletop emphatically with his index finger. "There are differences."

Assuming Jerry could be trusted to recognize Anne's clothing. Kali wasn't putting her money on it. There were men who noticed clothes, but from everything Anne had said, her husband wasn't one of them.

Still, the more differences there were, the better. And there'd been no dog collar either, Kali reminded herself. The Bayside Strangler had placed a dog collar around the neck of three of his victims. That was a critical detail because it hadn't come out at trial or in Jackson's book.

"He *wants* us to think he's the Bayside Strangler," Fortune said. "Doesn't mean he is."

"More likely it means he *isn't*, but he wants us to make the connection." Keating leaned back in his chair, stretching his arms in front of him. His shirt sleeves were rolled up to the elbows, revealing well-toned forearms and a diagonal scar partially hidden by the black band of his watch. "Her husband might have a reason to want her dead," he said.

"What? The divorce?"

"She was pregnant. Her brother says the husband wasn't interested in having kids."

Pregnant. So that was what Anne had meant by *some interesting news*. And why she'd told Kali she was in a quandary. Pregnant with a baby she'd always wanted right when she and her husband were deciding whether or not to split.

Kali didn't want Jerry to be their killer. To die at the hands of someone you'd loved seemed the ultimate betrayal. On the other hand, if Jerry *had* been the one who killed Anne, then Owen, and Kali, were off the hook about dealing with a serial killer. That would be welcome news.

"What does he say about the night she was killed?" Kali asked.

"That he spent the evening alone in his apartment."

Kali took a moment to think. Jerry would know about the Bayside Strangler case because Anne had worked on it. But he'd also have known to dress her in an article of clothing that was her own. Or would he? It had been a number of years since the trial. It might be something he'd overlooked. And he *had* been the one to make sure she knew about the yellow rose. Was he capable of killing Anne? Kali realized she had no idea.

"At this point," she said, "we don't know anything for sure. We're still feeling our way."

"You may be," Fortune grumbled. "We're working on a homicide. And as far as I'm concerned, we're wasting our time here. We about finished?"

She'd wanted to ask more about what they'd learned so far, but maybe that was better handled one-on-one. "For now."

Fortune pushed back his chair, scraping the floor loudly. Keating was still looking at her. Looking through her, maybe. His eyes were so dark, it was hard to tell. Whatever he was doing, it made her uncomfortable. She busied herself with some papers, and when she looked up again, he was gone.

The district attorney's offices were laid out along a narrow corridor. Kali had been assigned an empty office at the end, near the stairwell. She was busy trying to make it feel like her own when there was a knock at her open door.

"Got a minute?" Jack Jackson didn't wait for an answer before coming inside and sprawling onto an empty seat. Except for the addition of a beard, he hadn't changed much in the five years since she'd last seen him. Jackson was only a little taller than she was, maybe five-nine, and pleasantly rounded, like a medieval friar or one of Santa's elves.

"I dropped in to see Owen," Jackson said, "and he told me you were working here again. On Anne Bailey's murder."

"I hope he also told you that my lips are sealed."

Jackson laughed. "He didn't have to tell me." He was suddenly serious again. "Terrible, what happened to Anne. I ran into her just last fall, at the Rockridge BART station. She looked great, sounded very upbeat. As usual."

"Yeah, things were going well for her." If you didn't count a crumbling marriage.

Jackson tugged at one of his socks. "So how've you been? You look great too, by the way."

She smiled to acknowledge the compliment, even if it was something of an afterthought. "I've been good."

"I've seen your name in the paper. I tried to get assigned to the Harper case you tried last summer, but there was big stuff happening elsewhere. Man, that was something, the way it ended."

It had been something all right, but not the sort of something Kali liked to think about. She'd had nightmares for months afterward, and she still had moments when the tears seemed to come out of nowhere.

"Owen said you got the same note he and the cops did."

"Yeah. That's a new twist." Jackson seemed almost pleased. "Guess it's because of the book."

*Perfect Stranger.* Jackson and Owen's commercially successful account of the Bayside Strangler murders, the investigation and the ensuing trial. It had been enjoying a surge of renewed popularity because of Davis's recent execution.

"Did the note come to the office or your home?" Kali asked.

"Home. Why?"

"Just curious." Owen's had come to his home address as well. The Bayside Strangler had limited himself to sending notes to the cops, at work.

"Pretty intriguing stuff, huh?"

"Pretty awful, too." Kali thought Jackson seemed to be overlooking that part.

"You think maybe Davis had a partner?" he asked.

"I'm not talking to you about this, remember?"

"There was some talk at the time about his brother being involved. I interviewed the guy for the book." He paused, giving Kali a chance to respond. When she didn't, he said, "The guy really looked up to Dwayne."

"Jack, when we get ready to make a statement to the press, you'll be the first to know."

"I'd better be. And it's going to have to be soon. Like I told Owen, patience is not a virtue of mine." He tossed a business card onto her desk. "Home and cell numbers are on there too. Call me anytime. Day or night."

Kali knew Owen would have both numbers as well, but she filed the card carefully in her new, and largely empty, Rolodex.

# CHAPTER 11

Lou took a long gulp of his beer. It was ice cold and satisfied some elusive craving deep inside him. "How long's it going to be, you think, before word gets out?"

Keating was watching a basketball game on the television behind the bar. "Word on what?"

"Bayside Strangler, Part Two." It sounded like the title of a miniseries, which was what it just might become. "There'll be a frenzy of media attention. We'll have public hysteria. Public outrage too."

"Probably."

"The death penalty opponents will be up in arms. They'll milk it for all it's worth."

"I imagine so."

Lou gave his partner a sideways glance. They'd gotten together in the evening after work like this only about half a dozen times, and Lou remembered now why he'd promised himself every time would be the last. Keating was a lousy conversationalist.

Lou took another swallow of beer. "It's bad enough the victim being a lawyer and all. High profile from the start. Case like this, it's going to be a pain in the ass."

Keating nodded, his eyes still glued to the screen.

"I mean, everybody's a critic, right? And they're all watching, eager for results."

"Yeah."

"Serial killer cases are tough even without all that attention."

"The worst."

Lou was getting tired of carrying on a conversation with him-self. "That doesn't bother you?"

"Not much we can do about it." A banking commercial came on the screen, and Keating turned his attention to his partner. "Besides, we aren't dealing with a serial killer yet. We're not even sure there's a connection to the Bayside Strangler. Like the DA woman said, we're just feeling our way right now."

*The DA woman.* Trouble enough having any lawyer breathing down their necks, much less a woman.

"Must be hard, the victim being a friend of hers," Keating said.

"She better not let it get in the way of her doing her job." Lou hunched forward, eyeballing the amount of beer left in the bottle. "What did you think of her?"

"The assistant DA?"

"Right."

"She seems okay. At least she's easy to look at."

"Is that all you ever think about?"

"Not by a long shot." Keating punctuated the remark with a lewd laugh.

"See, you've proved my point. You oughta get yourself a hobby, Bryce. Something to think about besides your next lay."

"Gardening's not my thing."

"Doesn't have to be gardening, for God's sake." Nothing re-laxed Lou like puttering in his garden. He loved watching barren branches become sprays of lacy foliage, and tiny sprouts push their way through the soil into the sunlight. It was an interest he and Jan had shared since the early days of their marriage when they lived in the tiny duplex near the freeway. When Nikki came along, working in the garden became a family experience. Lou still smiled at the memory of his daughter's chubby fingers pat-ting the soil around newly planted seedlings. Now in her twen-ties, Nikki lived in Los Angeles and grew nothing but the mold in her refrigerator.

"Could be woodworking," Lou suggested, pushing the mem-ory of happier times from his mind, "or fishing." Two other pur-suits he enjoyed. "Anything, really."

Keating's beeper went off. He pulled it from his belt, checked the number, then reached into a pocket for his cell phone and re-turned the call.

"Yeah," he said by way of greeting. "Good. Where?" He returned the phone to his pocket and addressed Lou. "A friend from the old days. Says the two guys he mighta seen with Anne Bailey's car are in the neighborhood again. You want to take a ride with me?"

Lou would have preferred a second beer. But the sooner they got a handle on this case, the better. "Sure. Let's go."

Keating drove. He turned on the lights and raced at speeds Lou thought excessive. Which was why Lou usually jockeyed for the position behind the wheel.

They pulled up to a darkened street corner two blocks from where Anne Bailey's car had been found. A young Hispanic male dressed all in black approached the driver's side. Keating rolled down the window.

The kid muttered to him in Spanish. Keating responded in the same language. Lou didn't understand a word of it.

"Gracias," Keating said at last.

That, Lou understood.

Keating grinned at the kid. "Keep clean, Paco. You're doing good."

Paco said a few more words, delivered with a laugh. Then he disappeared into the night.

"What was that all about?" Lou didn't like being out of the loop.

"The pizza place," Keating said. "Assuming they're still there." He parked a block farther on, in front of a hole-in-the-wall pizza joint with windows so dirty it was impossible to see through them.

The minute they pushed through the door, four young men seated around a table at the back looked up and froze. Lou had seen it before. Street-savvy kids had a sixth sense. They could pick out a cop every time.

"Which one of you is Fadoul?" Keating asked.

No one spoke.

"All we want is information,"

The four shifted uneasily.

"If we don't get some cooperation," Keating said, leaning low over the table, "we may go looking for something besides information." He paused for effect. "And make no mistake, we'll find it."

In unison, three pairs of eyes turned to the boy with his back against the wall. He was about nineteen, slender, with cue-ball eyes and a pointy goatee. Keating grabbed his shoulder. "Okay, Fadoul, let's take a walk."

The boy pushed back his chair angrily, gave his companions the finger and a look that spoke louder than any words, then followed Keating outside. Lou brought up the rear, positioning himself a few yards away. Close enough that he was part of the conversation, but with a clear view toward the restaurant in case the others decided to join them. The streetlight overhead was burned out, and Lou strained to keep an eye on both Bryce and the doorway.

"I'm interested in the silver Lexus you stripped last week," Keating said.

"I don't know nothin' about no Lexus."

"Yes, you do, Fadoul. People saw you."

"People got me confused with someone else, then."

"Not so. But this is your lucky day, Fadoul, because we're not on car duty this week. All we want is answers."

"Told you, I don't know nothin'."

"Where'd you pick up the car?" Lou said.

"You got no proof of anything." The kid pulled a cigarette from his pocket and lit it.

Keating stepped closer. "You carrying? Looks to me like a gun under your jacket."

"What?" Genuine outrage. "No way, man, You think I'm stupid?"

So fast that it surprised even Lou, who knew what was coming, Keating knocked the cigarette from the kid's hand, twisted his arm behind him, and pinned him against the wall face first. Careful, Lou cautioned silently. He'd never seen Keating actually cross the line, but he came close more often than Lou liked.

"Yes, I think you're stupid," Keating barked. " All I'm asking for is a little information, but you've got to turn it into something big. Tell me what I want to know and I'm outta here. But you keep making me mad like you're doing, and I'm going to have to search you. Got that?"

The kid said something that got garbled by the pressure of the wall against his face.

Keating let up some of the pressure he'd applied. "What's that, Fadoul? You have to speak up."

"I don't know for sure, maybe I found a Lexus."

"Maybe?"

Lou saw Keating twist the kid's arm again. The kid grunted. "Geez, man, you're hurting me. Okay, so I took the stupid Lexus. It wasn't locked or nothing. Just sitting there, like it didn't belong to nobody."

"Where."

"Some parking lot."

"Which one?"

"How should I know?"

"This ain't brain science," Lou said, growing irritated with standing sentry. "Simple question. Where was the parking lot?"

"I dunno. It was, like, dark out."

Keating slammed the kid's shoulder against the wall.

"Okay, okay. Shattuck, the other side of University. Near that drugstore there."

The door to the pizza place opened, and two of Fadoul's friends emerged. Lou unbuttoned his jacket, putting his gun in easy reach. The boys pulled out cigarettes and lit them, eyeing Lou warily.

"When was this?" Keating said.

"Friday night. Late."

"How late?"

"More like Saturday morning, probably. 'Bout three. Place was mostly empty, which is how I seen the car."

"You're doing good, Fadoul. Now this next one's real important. Besides parts, what did you take from the car?"

"Nothin'."

"Come on, Fadoul. I said it was important."

"I'm telling you the truth! I looked, man, there was some papers and stuff, that's all. Nothin' interesting."

"No purse or wallet?"

"I swear on my mother's grave."

Lou was willing to bet the woman was as healthy as a horse. It was all part of the act.

"You think of anything else," Keating said, "you let us know, okay? Might keep me from remembering about that gun of yours."

"I ain't got no gun."

Keating still had the kid pinned against the wall. Lou stepped closer. The beer was taxing his kidneys and he was anxious to be gone. "Let's go, Bryce. We got what we came after."

"Put your hands on the wall," Keating told Fadoul, "and count to twenty before you even think about turning around." He glared at the two friends. "You too. No one moves until we're gone."

By the time they reached the pharmacy on Shattuck Avenue, Lou was ready to pop. For once, he was glad that Keating drove fast. Bryce asked to speak to the manager while Lou went off in search of a restroom. If he'd been thinking, he would have gone before leaving the bar, even though he hadn't felt the need. A curse of advancing years.

When Lou returned, he found Bryce showing Anne Bailey's picture to a small gathering of clerks. One of them, a coffee-skinned woman with a headful of tiny braids, was telling Keating she was fairly sure Anne Bailey had been in the store Friday evening.

"She's a regular customer," the woman said. "She likes almond M&Ms, same as me."

"Did you wait on her?"

"Not that evening. But I remember it was Friday 'cause I was thinking she probably had the weekend off and I had to work."

"Any idea of the time?"

The woman started to shake her head, then seemed to remember something. "I don't think it was late. That's why I thought of the work connection. Must have been around six or seven."

"Was she alone?" Lou asked. Now that he wasn't fixated on finding a toilet, he was able to think more clearly.

"I don't remember anyone else."

"What about a surveillance camera? Does the store have one?"

Although he'd addressed his question to the woman, it was Keating who answered. "Twenty-four-hour loop. I already checked."

If the tape had caught anything, it was gone now. Lou and Keating pressed the other employees, but no one had anything further to offer.

Outside, they made a sweep of the parking lot, not expecting to discover anything helpful. And they didn't.

"Let's have Maureen Oliver make up flyers," Keating said.

"Maybe we'll get lucky and find someone who remembers seeing Anne Bailey in the company of a stranger."

Maybe, but Lou wasn't going to hold his breath. Still, they had a pretty good idea where she was taken. And a pretty good idea what had happened. "Looks like she must have stopped here on her way to meet Kali," Lou said. "And her killer either caught her by surprise or enticed her into his car."

"Assuming he didn't get to her in her own car," Keating pointed out. "He could have returned it to the lot after killing her."

"Why return the car, though? Wouldn't he just leave it on a street somewhere?"

"Not if his own car was here."

Lou shoved his hands in his pockets and surveyed the parking lot. The lighting was uneven, and none of it very bright. On a dark, rainy night, it wouldn't be hard, he supposed, to slip into the shadows. Still, you'd think he would worry about being seen.

Unless, of course, the killer was someone Anne had known. What better cover than familiarity.

# CHAPTER 12

Jane Parkhurst studied the house from the outside. She couldn't imagine what it was about the place that had appealed to Mr. Smith. It did offer privacy, but at the price of a level yard and sunshine. Tucked in among the trees quite a distance from the main road, the building was nothing but a tar-and-gravel-roofed box, painted an ugly lime green, no less. And it was in a sad state of disrepair.

For whatever reason, the house had caught Mr. Smith's fancy. He'd driven by, he said, seen her name on the for-sale sign, come right home and called her to set up an appointment.

She punched in the code on the realtor's box and took out the key. Inside, the house wasn't much better, although with a few cosmetic changes and a fresh coat of paint, it could be made livable. It would take someone with a good imagination, though, to see the potential, especially now that it was vacant. Jane was determined to help Mr. Smith visualize the possibilities.

She pulled a saucepan from her tote, filled it with water and spices, and set it on the stove to simmer. She put an easy-listening tape in the portable boom box, adjusted the volume so that it wasn't too loud, then walked through the rooms opening the drapes and turning on lights.

Mr. Smith had been fairly tight-lipped about what he wanted in a house. Sometimes that was a sign that people weren't seriously looking to buy, but they were usually the ones trying to get a peek at the million-dollar homes, not some rundown bungalow from the fifties. Jane had made Mr. Smith a list of other properties he might be interested in seeing. And she'd tentatively arranged to show the best of those today if he had the time.

With the pot on the stove cooking away, the homey scent of cinnamon and cloves began to fill the rooms. It wasn't such a bad house, Jane thought. Just neglected. And the neighborhood was a good one.

She checked her watch. Mr. Smith was late. Probably caught in traffic if he was coming straight from work.

Jane passed the time by imagining the changes she'd make to spruce up the house and grounds. She'd probably start outside by cutting down some of the eucalyptus trees that were blocking the light. It would really open the place up. And she'd rip out the carpeting. The owners had said there was hardwood flooring underneath. She could imagine the floors stained a honey blonde. It would give the interior the warmth it currently lacked.

The doorbell rang. Jane pulled herself from her daydreaming and went to answer it. She was looking forward to meeting Mr. Smith in person. New clients were always an exciting prospect. You never knew what they would bring.

# CHAPTER 13

Because of the autopsy and investigation, Anne's funeral had been delayed until the second week following her death. The day was bitter cold and damp—a lousy day for burying a friend, Kali thought. Not that there was ever a good one.

The turnout at the church was large. Kali recognized Jerry, Anne's brother Paul, and a few faces from the legal community, but most were strangers to her. She saw Owen in the church as well, accompanied by Selby and Alex, and a couple of media types who she guessed were covering Owen's campaign. No doubt his presence at the funeral of a murder victim would make juicy news since it combined two of the public's perennial favorites—politics and gore.

She didn't have a chance to talk with him until after the burial. Which was probably just as well since during most of the service she'd found herself too choked to trust her voice. But as they headed from the grave site back toward the parking lot, Owen fell into step beside her. The press was blessedly absent.

"It was a nice service," Owen said.

"Except for the fact that it was Anne's." Kali didn't mean to sound snappish, but as she'd watched the coffin being lowered into the ground, the reality of Anne's death had hit her anew. *Nice* was a pale thing compared to life.

"Except for that," Owen agreed. They walked a few steps in silence. Kali's mind filled with images of Anne, and anguish at the terrible way she'd died.

"How's it working out with the detectives?" Owen asked after a moment.

"Could be worse." And in fact, it might yet get worse. But Kali felt she'd bridged their initial skepticism. "Do you know either of them?"

"By reputation. They're both well respected within the department."

Kali had heard the same thing from others. She'd also picked up a bit of gossip about Bryce Keating's "eye for the ladies," as her secretary, Gloria, put it. But she'd certainly not seen any evidence of that herself.

"You've done a good job keeping the details from the press," Owen said.

"That wasn't really my doing. You put the clamp on Jackson, and nobody else has picked up on it." She'd been surprised, in fact, how little coverage Anne's murder had generated. A couple of stories early on, then nothing. It saddened her to think the loss of precious life was so commonplace it was no longer newsworthy.

"Any progress finding her killer?"

"Nothing substantial. They think she was abducted from a parking lot in North Berkeley. That's where her car was before it was stolen by some punk kids. And one of the store clerks thinks she remembers seeing Anne the night of her murder. The cops have distributed flyers to shoppers there, hoping to find someone who might have seen what happened, but the response so far has been disappointing."

"Nothing more related to the Strangler murders?"

Kali shook her head and shoved her hands into her pockets. The tips of her fingers were numb with cold. "Her family and friends are offering a reward. Maybe that will elicit some response."

"I know. I contributed to it myself."

As had Kali. "Anne's husband has hired an attorney," she said after a moment.

Owen gave her a questioning look.

"Turns out Anne was pregnant. Jerry didn't want a family. And he has no clear alibi for the night of the murder."

"But the rose, the note—"

"I know. But the Strangler tie-in could be a clever cover." Keating was the one pushing this angle, and although Kali was far from convinced, she wasn't ruling it out either.

"Wouldn't that be something," Owen said.

From his tone, Kali could tell he didn't hold out much hope it would be that simple.

They came to Owen's car, where Selby and Alex were waiting for him. Selby nodded a greeting. She was clearly impatient to be gone.

Owen turned to his son. "Alex, do you remember Kali O'Brien?"

Kali extended a hand. Alex looked at her a moment, then responded with a reluctant handshake.

"Hi," he said.

Alex had grown taller since she'd last seen him; in fact, he was several inches taller than Owen. He'd bulked up, too. His shoulders were broad, his arms thickly muscled. Gone was the awkward adolescent who'd favored drugs over exercise.

"Kali and Anne Bailey worked for me at one time," Owen said.

"I remember," Alex said. "It was around the time Mom died."

There was something about the way he said it, Kali thought, that spoke louder than the words themselves.

But Owen seemed not to notice. "Keep me posted," he said to Kali.

"Will do." She leaned over to wave to Alex, who'd already climbed into the car. "Nice seeing you again."

His eyes met hers and he waved back. But he didn't crack a smile.

What did one do after a funeral? Kali recalled her mother's funeral twenty years earlier, when she'd gone home following the service, headed straight for her room and wrapped herself in her grief, waiting for her father to search her out and offer comfort. She couldn't imagine now why she'd ever thought he might. Her father had been a stone. A man whose feelings were so deeply buried, he'd forgotten what they were. Whether that was his true nature or an adaptive defense, she'd never know. But she was still paying the price for having had a father who scorned emotions.

What Kali ended up doing after Anne's funeral was what she often did when feeling unsettled—she took Loretta for a walk. Bundled against the sharp wind, she headed up the road past her house to a small park where the dog could run free under a canopy of eucalyptus. There she said her own, final farewell to Anne.

Twilight had settled in by the time they returned. Passing Margot's house, she was drawn by the warmth of lit windows and the smoky tang of a wood fire. She rang the bell.

"Hey, how'd you know?" Margot asked.

"How'd I know what?"

"That I was just going to call you." Margot's wolfhounds sniffed Loretta, whose excitement at finding canine friends made their task more difficult. "Come on in. You want something to drink?"

"Do you have any wine open?"

"I think so." Margot looked in the fridge and pulled out a bottle of chardonnay. "I can't say how old it is."

"It'll be fine."

Margot poured Kali a glass, then covered the bottom of her own tumbler with scotch.

Kali took a seat at one of the high stools in the kitchen. "Why were you going to call me?"

"I need advice."

"Legal advice?"

"Dating advice."

Kali burst out laughing, spilling her wine.

"You think my dating is funny?"

"Not at all. It's just that I'm the wrong person to ask."

"Oh, come on. You've had more experience at it than I have."

Kali leaned an elbow on the counter. "Experience maybe. But my track record isn't so hot."

"I've never done this before," Margot explained. "As a woman, I mean. Didn't do much of it in my former life either. I married my high school sweetheart."

"You have someone special in mind?"

"Not yet, but I'm working on it." Margot crossed her legs, revealing silken limbs. Who but someone new to being female would wear a skirt with pantyhose around the house?

"Think of it this way," Kali offered, "you're an expert on men. That's got to be a real advantage."

Margot made a face. "I'm not so sure."

Kali ended up staying for a second glass of wine and then a third over dinner. By the time she made it back to her own house, the disquiet she'd felt following Anne's funeral was considerably muted.

* * *

A shrill ringing woke her at quarter to six the next morning. She tried the alarm first, and when that did nothing, thought to reach for the phone.

"Hello." She looked out the window. The sky was still pitch black.

"Bryce Keating here."

Kali pulled herself to a sitting position and blinked to clear her mind as well as her vision.

"We've got another murder," he said.

"Another . . . " Her voice croaked. She swallowed. "Like before?"

He didn't offer an explanation. "How soon can you get here?"

"Where are you?"

"Lake Temescal. The parking lot at the north entrance."

Kali's mouth was cottony; her body cried out for a shower. "Half an hour?"

"That should be good. We need to wait for daylight before we can finish processing the scene anyway."

Forty-three minutes later, Kali showed her new district attorney ID to the uniformed officer at the entrance of the lot. He waved her through. Half a dozen police vehicles, including the coroner's van, were already parked there.

Temescal was an urban lake fed by runoff from the nearby hills and storm drains. In the summer, people swam in the lake—an undertaking Kali felt sure had to be fueled by desperation. In the late fall, the lake was often green with algae. Now, with the recent rains, she imagined it was muddy brown. It was still too dark to tell.

She found Keating in the far corner of the lot, where most of the activity seemed to be centered.

He looked at his watch. "Not bad considering you sounded like you were still asleep when I called."

Of course she'd been asleep. Most of the city was asleep even now. He didn't have to make it sound like she was a laggard. "I had to let the dog out," she explained, in case he was inclined to think she'd spent the intervening time primping.

"Of course." No inflection. Kali couldn't tell if he'd intended sarcasm or agreement.

Keating pointed in the direction of the lake. "The body's over there."

"Do we know who she is?" Kali turned up her jacket collar against the icy wind blowing in from the west. She wished she'd had time for a cup of coffee before leaving the house.

"Not a clue. White, late thirties I'd say, someone who took good care of herself."

"Strangled?"

He nodded.

"What makes you think it might be same killer?"

"Come see for yourself."

Floodlights from two cruisers were directed on an area near the outer edge of the asphalt, where a Port-A-Potty stood. "That's where he left her? In the outhouse?"

"Next to it." Keating handed her a pair of latex gloves.

Kali slid them onto her hands. She had seen plenty of crime scene photographs but she'd never visited a fresh scene, and she wasn't thrilled about the prospect of doing so now. Especially without the benefit of her morning cup of coffee.

Two evidence technicians were working the scene. One of them was down on his hands and knees with a flashlight. The other was conferring with a man in a jumpsuit that had CORONER printed on the back in block letters. Kali followed Keating to the body.

The woman lay on the ground, her upper torso propped against the side of the Port-A-Potty. One leg was bent at the knee, causing her skirt to ride up. Her hands were folded in her lap. Despite her attire, which to Kali's mind could be summed up as "provocative," her appearance was more elegant than sleazy. Chin-length hair of a rich chestnut brown, eye makeup that was subtly applied and expertly manicured nails. The only thing a little off was the bright red lipstick that had somehow stayed in place despite the horrors of her death.

A tremor of unease worked its way down Kali's spine. The similarities between this and the pictures she'd seen of Anne's body were unmistakable. And both bore an uncanny resemblance to the photos of the Bayside Strangler's victims. Except this woman was a brunette and not a blonde.

"Who found her?" Kali asked.

"An early-morning jogger. He doesn't live far from here. He headed straight home to call us after he found the body."

"Any missing-persons reports that fit?"

"Not yet. It looks like she hasn't been dead long, probably less than twenty-four hours. That's not much time when we're talking about a missing adult."

"No, I guess not." Kali tried to imagine how long it would take before someone noticed *she* was missing. A lot longer than twenty-four hours.

Keating bent down next to the body. The harsh light of the floods lent a surreal feeling to the scene.

"Look here," he said, "see the bruising around her neck. It's practically identical to the markings on Anne Bailey's neck. I'm not an expert on this, but I'm betting the coroner will tell us they were made from the same type of rope or cord."

Up close, the lifelessness of the woman's body was raw and real. Nothing like the quiet sleep Kali had seen in funeral homes, or even on the video screen at the morgue. This was a woman, not unlike herself, who'd been caught in an eddy of unexpected horror. Kali felt suddenly light-headed.

Keating looked up at her. "You okay?"

"I'm fine." She forced herself to kneel and follow Keating's discourse on ligature marks and angle of attack.

"Also similar posing of the body," he said, rising. "And the clothes. I'm guessing they aren't hers. Either it's a hell of a coincidence, or we're dealing with the same killer in both cases."

"So Anne's husband is off the hook?"

"Unless this is a ploy to throw us off."

"You don't really think that, do you? That he'd kill another woman just to divert attention from himself?"

Keating pushed his tongue across his inner cheek, a habit Kali had noticed he fell into when he was thinking. "I'm not saying he did, just that we shouldn't rule it out."

"If it wasn't him, though, we're dealing with a killer who's targeting women for God knows what reason." She hesitated. "Someone like the Bayside Strangler."

Keating nodded. The play of harsh artificial light and murky dawn cast his face in shadows, making it hard to read. "The very toughest type of killer to catch. I worked on a case like that in Los Angeles once."

"Did you get the guy?"

"No." It was almost a whisper. "Eventually the killing stopped but not before six women were brutally stabbed and dismembered."

"Dismembered." Her hand flew to her mouth.

"Your standard motives—greed, revenge, jealousy—those are the easy ones to solve. You get a psycho who's listening to voices in his head or wrestling with some kind of faceless internal rage, and there's no clear path from victim to killer. You're left with nothing to fall back on but dumb luck."

Which was how they'd caught Dwayne Allen Davis. A necklace belonging to one of the victims had shown up in his possession during a routine traffic check. Without that, who knew how many more women would have died.

Kali and Bryce Keating had moved to the perimeter of the cordoned-off area. "I need to finish things here," Keating said. "No point your sticking around. I'll let you know if anything turns up."

"You've got my cell phone number?"

Keating was already moving off in the direction of the crime scene van. He patted his jacket pocket. "You gave it to us the other day."

The sun had finally risen high enough behind the hills to offer daylight visibility. Crime scene personnel were moving with an increased sense of focus. As Kali headed back to her car, she noticed several news vans parked along the frontage road. A helicopter was approaching from the west. The second strangulation murder of a woman in a relatively short period of time—the media was sure to make the connection, even without comment from the police. How long would it take before someone brought up the name Dwayne Arnold Davis?

# CHAPTER 14

Kali had barely settled in at her desk with a latte from Peet's when the phone rang.

Jack Jackson wasted no time getting to the point of his call. "Is this one the same?"

"Is what—"

"Don't play games with me. You know what I'm talking about. The body that was discovered this morning near Temescal."

"There's been no ID yet."

"That's not what I asked." The journalist's voice resonated with impatience, and something else she couldn't quite put her finger on. "Does it fit the same pattern as the Bailey murder?"

Kali felt a flash of irritation at the ease with which he distanced himself from Anne's death. He'd known her, after all. "This is an open investigation, Jack. We're still at the early stage of figuring out what happened."

"So tell me what you do know."

"I'm not going to—"

"You seem to be forgetting that *I'm* sitting on a note. A note purporting to be from the Bayside Strangler."

"I'm well aware of that." Kali took the lid off the steaming cup and licked at the foam collected there. Easy, she told herself. The last thing she wanted was to piss him off.

"I've held back from making it public at Owen Nelson's request, but that can change at any moment."

Kali gripped the phone. "I don't like being blackmailed."

"And I don't like being kept in the dark." His voice softened. "Look, I understand your wanting to keep this quiet awhile. And I'm willing to play along, to a degree. But you've got to understand where I'm coming from. This is a hot story. I'm not going to turn my back on it completely."

She hesitated, and then relented. Partially. They'd issue a press release before the day was out in any case. It couldn't hurt to give him a tiny head start. "I don't really know how similar the two murders are. What I said about the investigation being in the early stages is true. But the woman *was* strangled."

"Did the body appear to be posed?"

"On first impression."

"What about her clothing?"

"What about it?"

"You know, skimpy, sexy clothing that wasn't her own. Like Anne was wearing."

"What makes you believe that's the way Anne was dressed?"

Jackson laughed. "You must think I'm awfully stupid. That was a hallmark of the Bayside Strangler murders. I asked Anne's husband about it. He described the outfit for me, said he didn't recognize it."

Jackson knew details about Anne's murder, yet he hadn't printed a word of it. Kali had to give him credit. It was more than most reporters would have done. "We don't want that information made public right now, but off the record, yes, it appears the latest victim was dressed in similar clothing. Whether it was hers or not, I haven't the foggiest idea. We don't know who she is."

"Who she was," Jackson corrected. "What else do you have on the victim?"

"Caucasian. Late thirties, early forties, I'd say. Her body was found by a jogger early this morning."

"Upper middle class?"

"I told you, we don't know—"

"But from appearances?"

"Yeah, probably."

"So now we wait for the yellow rose. And another note."

Kali thought he sounded almost eager.

Despite the chilly morning, the day turned out to be relatively mild. The sky was clear and the air calm. The sort of midwinter respite at which the Bay Area excelled. At noon Kali walked the perimeter of nearby Lake Merritt before stopping at a corner convenience store to pick up a carton of yogurt to eat at her desk. She'd just tucked the yogurt and plastic spoon into her bag and was fumbling with the change when she heard someone call her name.

She looked up into the face of Nathan Sloane.

"Geez," he said with deadpan humor, "we have to stop meeting like this."

She blinked. "What are you doing here?" It wasn't the most gracious greeting, but he'd caught her by surprise.

"I had a meeting with a client." Sloane paid the clerk for a can of Pepsi and a candy bar. "What about you? You didn't come all the way from Berkeley to buy yogurt, did you?"

"I'm doing some work down in this area of Oakland." She zipped her wallet shut and dropped it into her bag. "How'd you know I bought yogurt, anyway?"

"I saw you. Why, was it a secret?"

Not a secret. Not even so odd, now that she thought about it. He'd obviously seen her before she noticed him. She made a joke of it. "I'm a card-carrying member of Yogurt Addicts Anonymous."

"Can't stand the stuff myself." He made a shivery motion.

"It's better for you than soda and candy."

"You sound like my mother." They moved outside. He pulled on a pair of dark glasses against the sun's glare. He grinned at her. "I don't suppose three's a charm?"

"Three?"

"The first two times I asked you out, you were busy." He gave the last word a sardonic twist, making it clear he'd understood that *busy* covered a multitude of possibilities. "Do I dare try a third time?"

Maybe it was the unexpectedly fine weather, or the relief at having the morning behind her, or maybe it was simply Nathan's lopsided grin, but Kali surprised both of them by saying, "Sure, give it a try."

"How about one night this week? We can keep it simple."

"Okay."

"The Oakview Grille? Tomorrow night, seven?"

"I'll meet you there."

Nathan rocked up on his toes. "And to think I almost didn't ask."

Kali felt herself smile. Nathan just might turn out to be an interesting guy.

Later in the afternoon, Kali was studying the file of a case from her own practice when she sensed someone standing in her doorway. It wasn't a noise or change in light that caught her attention, but rather a field of energy so strong, it almost knocked the wind out of her.

"Do you know you squint when you read?" Bryce Keating asked.

She hadn't, but as soon as he said it she became aware of the tension around her eyes. She rubbed the center of her forehead with her palm.

He didn't move from the doorway but he studied her for a moment before continuing. "We have an tentative ID on the body we found this morning."

No longer just a body now; there was a name and history to go with it. Kali's stomach felt leaden. "Who was she?"

"Jane Parkhurst. A real estate agent whose car was found at a home she'd recently listed. Another agent was showing the place and noticed Parkhurst's car in the driveway. She didn't think much about it until the woman failed to show for an appointment at the office."

"Parkhurst meets the victim's description?"

He nodded. "I'm meeting the other agent at the morgue in ten minutes. Might be a good idea if you came along. Do you have time?"

Two trips to the morgue in as many weeks. Not a pattern Kali wanted to see continue. But that was the whole purpose, she reminded herself. To find whoever was doing this and put him away for good.

She hesitated, then nodded. "I can make the time." She struggled to find the shoes she'd kicked off after lunch.

They headed outside.

"Where's your partner?" Kali asked, getting into Keating's county-issue black sedan. He hadn't spoken a word since leaving her office.

"Home."

"Day off?" She was surprised the discovery of another body hadn't been enough to bring him in.

"A day off in the middle of a major homicide investigation?" He sounded incredulous, and a tad insulted. "That's not the way it works. Lou tripped on his porch stairs and threw his back out."

"Ouch."

"Yeah, it's pretty bad." Keating fell back into silence.

"Tell me," she said. "Is he as much of a grump as he comes across?"

Suddenly Keating laughed. It changed his whole appearance. His face lit up and his eyes grew bright. "You've noticed, huh?"

"Hard not to."

"Yeah, Lou can be a real pain in the ass sometimes. But he's a good man. A good cop too." He paused. "Not that we always see eye to eye."

Keating parked in front of the morgue and they went inside. An olive-complected woman in a beige wool pantsuit was waiting for them in the reception area.

"Mrs. Andros?" Keating asked.

She nodded, standing tentatively. She clutched her purse to her chest with both arms as though for support.

"Detective Keating. We spoke earlier. This is Ms. O'Brien from the district attorney's office. We appreciate your coming down on such short notice."

Déjà vu all over again, Kali thought. Only this time she wouldn't be the one having to make the identification. "Hello, Mrs. Andros. I know this must be a difficult experience for you."

"I'm hoping it's not Jane," she said shakily.

Keating led the way into the viewing room. "We're going to show you a picture on the video monitor," he explained. "You don't have to actually look at the body, just the picture. And you can take as long as you need."

Mrs. Andros sat where he directed her.

"You ready?"

She nodded.

Keating flipped on the monitor. A woman's face appeared. Even though Kali had seen the actual body that morning, she felt herself recoil at the image. Death bore its own, unmistakable imprint.

Mrs. Andros gasped and covered her face with her hands. "That's Jane," she said, her voice raw with emotion. "I'm sure of it."

Kali touched her arm. "I'm sorry. Believe me, I know how hard it is."

The woman was wiping away tears. "I was so hoping there'd been a mistake."

"What can you tell us about her?" Keating asked with a gentleness that caught Kali by surprise.

"This is terrible. Just terrible." Mrs. Andros continued to weep quietly.

Keating handed her a box of tissues.

"I don't know what to tell you. She was someone we all admired."

*Admired*, Kali noticed, not *liked*. But maybe it was just an inadvertent choice of words. "It would help if you could tell us a bit about her life. All we have so far is her name."

"We've worked in the same office for what . . . almost four years. She was very good at what she did. Organized. And ready to pitch in whenever anything needed doing."

"How about her personal life?" Kali asked.

Mrs. Andros took a couple of breaths and dabbed at her eyes with a tissue. "Jane is divorced. Has been since before I met her. Lately, she's been dating a doctor, but I don't know how serious it is."

"You know his name?"

"Keith, that's all I know. He's a radiologist."

"Did she live alone?" Keating asked.

"Yes. On Loma Vista. I'm not sure of the address, but it's on the left. Third house in. With a white picket fence."

"What about the house where you found her car?"

"It's vacant." She gave them the address. "The people who own it were transferred east last month. It's a definite rehab."

Keating wrote the house number in his notebook. "When did you notice the car?"

"This morning. I was showing the house to a client. I didn't even give it a second thought at the time. Usually, it's the agents who drive, but some clients, particularly men, they prefer to do the driving. I just figured Jane had met her client at the house and gone on to look at other properties in the client's car."

"How would we go about learning who her client was?" Kali asked.

Mrs. Andros dropped the wad of tissues into her purse.

Talking had seemed to quiet her. "If it was an appointment made through the office, there would be a record of it. But usually we make appointments ourselves. Did you check her appointment book?"

"We haven't seen it," Keating said.

"She always had it with her. When you find it, maybe you could let someone at the office have a look. We should probably notify her clients and let them know she won't be . . . keeping her appointments."

"I'll see what I can do." Keating looked at his watch. "When you were showing the house this morning, did anything strike you as out of place or unusual?"

Mrs. Andros thought a moment. "Not really. I knew Jane had been there because there was a pot of spice water on the stove."

Keating looked puzzled.

"It's a trick she uses. Makes the house smell homey. This place, though, it needs a whole lot more help than that."

Back in the car, Kali confronted her own black thoughts while Keating called for an evidence collection team to meet them at the house.

"Not much chance they'll find anything," he said to Kali, "but you never know."

Armed with the combination to the realtor's lock, they gained easy access to the house. It was small, only two bedrooms and a living/dining area, and terribly rundown. Mrs. Andros had been right, it was definitely a rchab, or more likely, a teardown. It was situated on a steep but decent piece of property offering almost complete seclusion. The neighborhood was mixed, but judging from the fresh look of several nearby homes, it was improving rather than declining.

The location was, however, an ideal place to commit a crime and not be noticed. No crime of opportunity here, Kali thought. The killer had clearly planned the whole thing in advance.

Keating examined the interior of the house without saying a word, and then checked outside. Kali followed, noting everything and finding nothing of significance. Keating must have fared no better because he finally stopped, sighed, and shook his head. "It's like he spirits them away. I sure didn't see any sign of a disturbance in there, did you?"

"No." Not that there was much to disturb. Realtors sometimes staged more upscale vacant homes, bringing in sofas and tables to make the place appeal to buyers. This house had been empty of everything but the stained carpeting.

"Let's take a look at the car," Keating said.

Jane Parkhurst's car, a jade-green Mercedes, was parked in front of the garage, unlocked.

"I doubt we'll get his prints from here," Keating said. "More likely he grabbed her in the house." Nonetheless, Keating used latex gloves to open the door and look inside. He whistled. "No prints, but I think we just found her appointment book."

Keating pulled a slim, leather-bound datebook from the car, flipped to Monday, and again whistled. "Here it is. Six o'clock in the evening at this address. Mr. Smith."

A name as meaningless as no name at all. "You think that's his real name?"

Keating shook his head. "No idea. Even if it is, doesn't help much. Let's see if anyone at her office can fill us in."

Jane Parkhurst worked out of an office located in the Montclair district of Oakland. Twelve desks in two rows, plus a reception area at the front. Kali could see a couple of glass-walled conference rooms off to one side. The desks were all empty when Kali and Keating arrived. Half a dozen people, including Mrs. Andros, were gathered at the back of the room. The women were teary; the men looked pale. Mrs. Andros had obviously spread the word of their associate's death.

They pressed Keating for details of the crime, and while there was little he could tell them, his compassion in dealing with their questions both surprised and impressed Kali. She had him pegged for the aloof, all-business approach.

None of Jane Parkhurst's co-workers was able to offer any concrete leads, although there was no shortage of suggestions as to who might have killed her—her boyfriend, a neighbor boy, a client who'd lost out on a house. The name Smith meant nothing to any of them.

While Keating interviewed office staff, Kali sat at Jane's desk and activated her computer. It wasn't hard to find a database of clients. There was only one Smith, first name Charles. There was also a phone number. Feeling more than a little pleased with herself, Kali copied it down and went to find Keating. She wasn't sure why she wanted to impress him, but she did.

A hint of a smile crossed his face as he took the number. "Good job."

Kali noticed again how a smile changed his features. Dark and brooding one minute, warm and gentle the next. And sexy.

Keating used his cell phone to place the call. Kali could feel her pulse racing in anticipation. Could it really be this easy?

# CHAPTER 15

Lou wasn't sure he'd heard right. "The garbage collection company? That's the number your Mr. Smith gave Jane Parkhurst?"

"The guy's playing with us," Keating said. "Probably falling all over himself laughing about it, too."

Lou was reclining in the only chair in the house where he could get anything close to comfortable. And it wasn't all that close. "You never know, he might actually work there."

"Not a chance." Keating hunched forward in his chair, arms on his knees, looking glum. "This creep's too smart for that."

"Sometimes it's the simple things that trip you up." Lou shifted slightly in his chair, and groaned. He couldn't even breathe without hurting.

"You ought to see a doctor," Keating said.

"Why? I know what he'd say."

"Which is?"

"Ice, heat and time." And some pithy remark about growing older. Coming from a doc who was barely old enough to shave, it really rankled.

"How about a chiropractor?" Keating suggested.

Lou glared. "Did I ask for your advice?"

"I want you back on the job. Hard though that is to believe."

Half the time, Lou thought, Keating acted like he resented having Lou for a partner. Or maybe it was having a partner at all that annoyed him. "You and me both," Lou said. "But having some quack crack my neck and dance on my back isn't going to make it happen any faster."

"Well, you look miserable."

"I *am* miserable, damn it." He'd been swallowing Advil by the handful, and it hadn't made a bit of difference.

Keating grinned. "Nothing injured about your ornery streak, I see. You ever think you might heal faster if you let go of some of the anger?"

"You ever remember you're a cop and not a goddamn shrink? Go grab us a beer from the fridge, why don't you. Best medicine in the world." Lou had been thinking about an icy beer all afternoon, but he'd been put off by the thought of raising himself from the chair and struggling into the kitchen. Last time he'd been in this much pain, Jan had been around to pamper him. He knew that was a lousy, selfish reason to miss her, but he was in a lousy, selfish mood right now.

Keating disappeared into the kitchen and returned with two bottles of Anchor Steam.

"Tell me more about the victim," Lou said.

"Forty-one, long-time divorced. No children. We haven't been able to contact her ex-husband. He lives somewhere in England. We did talk to the guy she's been dating. He called us after he got the word from one of her co-workers. Kali and I paid him a visit at his office."

"Kali?"

"The new DA."

"Jesus, just what I thought. She's going to be dogging us every step of the way."

"I asked her to come along."

"You asked . . ." Lou paused as recognition dawned. "Not this time, Bryce. Use your head. She may be a woman, but she's also a fucking DA. You want a good time, go call up one of those women who are always panting and pawing at your feet." Lou wasn't sure just what it was women saw in Keating, but the effect was almost universal. Like bees to honeysuckle.

"Lou, you got a dirty mind."

"What I got is experience watching you." Lou pulled the cold-pack from behind him and repositioned it.

"Isn't that a bag of frozen peas?" Keating asked, puzzled.

"Yeah, it's a trick Jan taught me. Molds to your body better than ice, and it doesn't drip." Only somehow Jan made it work better. Lou had already managed to split open one bag, sending partially thawed peas into every corner and crevice of his chair.

He hated to think what a mess he'd find when his back was mended enough so he could finally pull up the seat cushion.

"I'll have to remember that." Keating's tone was skeptical.

"You were saying, about the boyfriend . . ."

"Yeah, he's older. Maybe fifty-five."

"That's not so old." Though lately Lou was feeling every one of his own fifty-four years.

"I said older, not old." Keating leaned back in his chair, swung one leg over the arm. It made Lou's back hurt just watching.

"He's a doctor," Keating added. "Seemed genuinely broken up over her death."

"Some people are good actors."

"I don't think we're going to find our killer by looking at friends and family, Lou. Not this time. What we got here is someone who's operating on a whole different level from what motivates most crimes."

"You're assuming we've got the same killer here as in the Bailey murder." Lou was hoping that wasn't so. Serial killer cases got everybody's attention. The media, the politicians, the talk show hosts, they all wanted in on it. And they wanted a quick, airtight arrest.

Keating frowned and rubbed his temples. "I don't like the idea any better than you do."

"No yellow rose, though, and no note."

"Not yet. But we only discovered her this morning. And from the crime scene itself . . . I got to tell you, Lou, it looks the same. Too damn many similarities for it to be coincidence."

"Let me make sure I've got this straight." Talking about work helped take Lou's mind off the pain. Already he had gone a whole thirty seconds without thinking about his back. "Parkhurst met a client at a secluded house. Her car stayed there, she wound up dead."

Keating nodded. "A *new* client. Parkhurst apparently kept good records. If this Smith was someone she'd worked with before, she'd have had a record of it."

"But it's a fake name. Could be anyone. Even her boyfriend the doctor."

"Could be, but my gut tells me we're dealing with the same killer in both instances. That changes our focus, Lou. Motive, at least in the usual sense, goes out the window. If we want to catch this guy we've got to look at why he chose these particular women. They aren't crimes of opportunity, either. He had to have crossed paths with them at some point."

"All we have to do is figure out when and how." Lou snorted. Unless they got lucky, it would be like solving a Rubik's Cube. Too many cases like that went unsolved. "I got to head to the john. Don't go away."

Gritting his teeth against the torture of movement, Lou pushed himself from the chair. Immediately, he felt his back spasm.

"You need a hand, Lou?"

"I'm fine, I'm fine." The only thing worse than hurting was having others see you hurting. Goddamn invasion of privacy.

Lou hobbled across the room. It was a slow trip, but he managed to make it down the hallway and back. He half expected Keating to be gone by the time he returned.

"So where were we?" Lou asked, easing himself back onto his pack of peas. They were partially thawed now, and no longer ice cold.

"Talking about our killer."

"Or killers." Lou wasn't ready to concede their two victims had been murdered by the same man.

Keating either didn't pick up on Lou's distinction, or didn't want to. "You think maybe this guy really *is* the Bayside Strangler?" he asked.

"And not a copycat, you mean?"

Keating nodded. "You were around then, weren't you?"

"Yeah, but I wasn't involved with the case." Lou had wanted to be. Would have been too, if he hadn't been yanked from it by being placed on routine administrative leave following the shooting of a doped-up suspect in a domestic murder. Lou had been cleared of any wrongdoing, but he'd spent six months behind the desk dealing with bicycle theft when he should have been working the streets in homicide.

"Any chance Davis wasn't the one who killed those earlier women?"

Lou thought for a moment. "I don't know what to make of the defense allegations of planted evidence. You hate to think badly of your fellow cops, but we both know that rules sometimes get bent pretty far." He looked at Keating to gauge his reaction. Lou didn't know for sure, but he suspected that Keating was one of those who occasionally pushed the limits. "As for Davis, though, I suspect he was as guilty as they come."

Keating was quiet, his expression clouded as it often was when he was uncertain. "I wish I could be as sure, Lou."

# CHAPTER 16

Nobody said it was easy being the single mother of a seventeen-year-old son, but Debbie Hunt wasn't about to throw in the towel and give up. She knew women who did. Women who simply shrugged when their kids cut school, who turned a blind eye to drinking and drugs, and then rationalized their retreat by saying kids would be kids, and what could they do anyway that wouldn't alienate their children forever? But the truth was, they didn't have the energy it took to be a responsible parent.

There were times Debbie wanted to give in, too. Life would certainly be easier if she didn't always have to come across as the bad guy. But kids in their teens needed guidance and moral direction.

Bobby disagreed, of course. All he needed from a parent was a roof over his head, food on the table and use of the family car and television.

Debbie had hoped Bobby would be there to help her carry in the groceries when she got home from work that evening. But the house was empty. She could tell by the backpack tossed onto the table and the dirty dishes in the sink that he'd come home from school and then gone again. No note either, even though she'd asked him repeatedly to let her know where he was going.

She made herself a cup of tea, put away the groceries, and was starting dinner when she heard the phone ring. Not surprisingly, the handset wasn't where it should have been. She followed the sound, and her instincts, to Bobby's room. The caller had given up by the time she found the phone. It was on the floor, half hidden by an old T-shirt and a long, rectangular florist's box.

For a fleeting moment Debbie thought that maybe the flowers

were for her. Bobby could be very sweet when he wanted to be. But they were probably for Erin, the girl he'd been seeing for the last month. Her birthday? Or maybe the aftermath of a quarrel? Debbie wasn't above a little light snooping. She opened the box and admired the single yellow rose. How romantic, she thought. How classy. She'd done something right in raising Bobby after all.

A peek at the card, however, and her motherly glow evaporated.

> *"Dearest Jane,*
> *I can feel the warmth of your body still. I'm so happy to know you will be mine forever."*

The card felt like a stone in Debbie's hand. Who was Jane? And, more to the point, what had she and Bobby done? Whatever had happened, it didn't sound innocent. It certainly didn't sound like behavior she condoned. Her throat felt dry; her heart was pounding. A parental moment of the worst sort.

She heard the front door bang shut. Bobby was home.

"What are you doing in my room?" he screeched, standing in the doorway with both arms on the frame.

"I was looking for the phone."

He glared at the florist's box in her hand, his mouth slightly agape.

"Who is Jane?" Debbie asked. With no time to think about the best way to approach him, she'd blurted out the first thing that came to mind.

"What?" Bobby made it sound like an accusation.

"Bobby, I don't want to play games here."

"Then don't speak in riddles."

She held out the card and Bobby grabbed it from her hand.

He read it, then tossed it on the floor. "How the hell should I know who Jane is?"

"Don't lie to me, Bobby. You obviously bought her a—"

"Mom! The rose is for Erin. She had a bad fight with her father. I thought it might cheer her up."

"Why'd you write the card to Jane, then?" Never mind what the card implied. She wasn't up to dealing with that just yet.

"I didn't write it."

"The florist made a mistake? And where did you get the

money for this anyhow? You told me you were down to your last quarter."

Bobby sat down on his bed. "I didn't buy it. I found it on the porch of that lady's house, the one who was killed yesterday. She lived near Patrick."

Debbie had seen the story in the newspaper. A woman's body found near Lake Temescal. "You *stole* from her?"

"She's dead, Mom. She's not going to miss a stupid flower."

Debbie wasn't happy about any of it, but she couldn't help feeling relieved that she'd misunderstood the situation. Still, taking other people's property was stealing, no matter what the circumstances. "You take it back, right now," she told her son. "I'm going with you."

"The woman's dead, Mom. The flower will sit on her porch and rot."

"So be it. It's hers, not yours. Besides, I'm sure she has family and friends who might like to know about it. Come on, we're going there right now."

With Bobby directing her, Debbie drove to the house. She was herding Bobby up the walkway when the door opened and a young female cop stepped out.

Debbie nudged Bobby's shoulder. "Go on, tell her what you did." She hadn't expected to find a cop here, but she couldn't back down now. She only hoped she hadn't set Bobby up for bigger trouble than she'd intended.

But the cop wasn't much interested in Bobby's explanation. She took one look at the yellow rose and her face took on an intense and uncomfortable expression. She grabbed the box and thanked them hurriedly, brushing them aside as she headed for her patrol car.

So much for honesty and righting wrongs, Debbie thought.

# CHAPTER 17

Owen woke to the clamor of the alarm. It surprised him because he was sure he'd been awake all night. Tossing, turning, sweating and fighting the dread that pulsed through his veins.

He'd been working in his study when Kali called the previous night to tell him about the rose. He'd taken the news with outward calm, but he'd felt his heart hammering in his chest. No more deluding himself into thinking it was all a coincidence. Owen had to face facts. A killer was once again loose in the East Bay; a killer whose crimes, by design or happenstance, bore an uncanny similarity to those of the Bayside Strangler. For which Dwayne Allen Davis had been convicted. And executed.

The press was bound to latch on to it, build it into an even bigger story than it already was. People would love it. And Owen would be the center of controversy. This wasn't the sort of publicity he wanted.

Nor did he want to face the possibility that Davis had been innocent.

Owen felt ill thinking about it. In the bed next to him, Selby stirred, reached out to touch his shoulder, then returned to the stillness of deep sleep. Owen raised himself on one elbow and kissed her cheek. She was beautiful, even first thing in the morning without benefit of makeup or a hairbrush. Especially then, in fact. There was a softness about her, a vulnerability she worked hard to disguise once she was fully awake.

He'd been happier in the four months since they'd been married than he'd ever been. Some of it might have been the thrill of newfound love, but he couldn't recall feeling about Marilyn the way he did about Selby. Maybe that had been their problem all along. He had loved Marilyn, but he hadn't been *in love*. Even in the beginning. She had been a comfortable companion, a quiet, unassuming woman who made few demands on him. At the time, he'd thought that was enough. Now he realized what he'd been missing.

Owen showered, finishing off as he did every morning with a blast of cold spray. He made himself a cup of coffee and leafed through the newspaper. The Parkhurst murder had garnered only a single column on the inside of the second section, much of it a rehash of what had been covered, briefly, the day before. Now that they'd identified the victim, however, the story had expanded to include quotes from friends and co-workers. No mention was made of the similarities between this murder and the murder of Anne Bailey, or of the yellow rose. Owen breathed a little more deeply, but he knew the reprieve was only temporary.

He closed the paper and tried to likewise close his mind to anything but the full and busy day ahead of him. He simply couldn't afford to let his thoughts wander down the treacherous path of conjecture.

Owen gathered his briefcase and went back to the bedroom to kiss Selby good-bye.

She was awake now. "Will you be home for dinner?" she asked, propping herself up on an elbow.

"I'm giving a talk at the City Club, remember?"

"Right. I'd forgotten." She swung her legs over the side of the bed and eyed him mischievously. "Another rich meal. I'm glad I don't have to go with you tonight. Not only is campaigning hard work, it's hard on the waistline."

"Is there a hidden message there?"

She laughed. "Not unless you find one."

Owen sucked in his stomach and promised himself he'd skip dessert. "Little did you know what you were letting yourself in for when you married me."

"Oh, I knew." She stood and wrapped her arms around his neck. The nightie she wore was such a fine cotton that it was almost transparent.

Owen put a hand on the small of her back and pulled her toward him. "One of these days, we're going to get away, just the two of us. No deadlines, no ringing phones—"

"Sounds good to me." She kissed him, then headed off to the bathroom.

As Owen was getting into his car, he was surprised to see Alex pull up in front of the house. It was early for him, unless he'd never gone to bed in the first place. Which, from the looks of him, Owen thought highly likely.

"This is a surprise," Owen said as Alex lumbered toward him.

"I thought maybe we could go the cemetery together."

"Cemetery?" Owen's first thought was of the Parkhurst homicide.

"Mom's birthday, remember?"

He hadn't, and he could tell by look on Alex's face that Alex knew he hadn't.

"You don't even remember when her birthday is, do you?"

"Of course I know the date, it's just that I wasn't putting today's date together with—"

"You never even think about her anymore."

"Not true. I think about her every day."

Alex glowered. He was taller than Owen, and broad through the shoulders and arms. Too broad, Owen sometimes thought. He looked more like The Incredible Hulk than the sweet boy he'd once been. Marilyn had been stocky too, but she'd carried herself with a dancer's grace whereas Alex was awkward—and often sullen.

Owen mentally ran through his day. Not a spare half hour anywhere. "Why don't we go to the cemetery tomorrow. We can have lunch together first. Any place you'd like." Owen wasn't sure what his schedule for tomorrow looked like, but he'd find a way to make the time. His relationship with his son was paramount.

"You didn't pay any attention to her when she was alive, either," Alex said.

"What are you talking about? Of course I paid attention to her. It's not like we were newlyweds."

Alex shook his head. There was a look in his eye that reminded Owen that his son wasn't a kid anymore. "You never think about anyone but yourself."

An old lament. Owen wasn't in the mood. "I've got a busy day, Alex, and a lot on my mind right now. Can we have this talk later?"

"Yeah, I forgot. You're so important. *The* district attorney. The wannabe *governor* of California."

"I'd be busy whatever my job."

"You don't get it, do you?" Alex turned on his heel slammed the door to his van, and drove off with a screech of rubber on asphalt.

No, Owen didn't get it. He didn't get anything about Alex. The boy had been on Marilyn's case constantly during the last year she was alive. Angry, disrespectful, critical of everything she did. And he had barely mentioned her name in the years following her death. Until Selby came into picture. Then suddenly it was Owen's fault that Marilyn had died; Owen's fault that she'd come to rely on alcohol and tranquilizers to get through the day. Everything was Owen's fault. And now, he was at fault again for not putting his workday on hold at a moment's notice to visit his late wife's grave.

Where had the idea come from, anyway? Owen rarely went to the cemetery, but that didn't mean he wasn't thinking of Marilyn. As far as he knew, Alex hadn't been there for years himself.

Owen felt a knot of tension building at the base of his neck. He had enough things on his plate already. There was no room for an indignant son.

It was mid-afternoon, following a successful but intense power lunch with key contributors to his campaign, when Owen's secretary buzzed him.

"Selby's on the phone," she said. It was always Selby, never *your wife*. Claire had known Marilyn—they had, in fact, shared an interest in needlepoint. Owen had the sense that Claire looked upon Selby as an interloper.

He picked up the phone. "Hi, honey."

"I hate to bother you—"

"Anytime, you know that. There's no one I'd rather hear from."

She hesitated. "Owen, you got a letter today . . ."

He swallowed hard. He'd been half expecting it, trying hard to pretend he wasn't. But that didn't make it any easier.

"I wouldn't have opened it," Selby said, "except it was addressed to both of us."

"Your name was on the envelope?" Maybe it wasn't what he thought, after all.

"*Owen and Selby*, not even *Mr. and Mrs.*" She drew in a breath. "There was a poem inside. Typed on a full-sized sheet of paper."

Owen felt his stomach clench. His first response had been right, after all. But addressed to both of them? That was a new twist, and it made him queasy.

"Don't touch it any more than you have already." Not that it would make a difference. They'd never get prints. The guy was careful.

"I know, Owen. I already put it into a folder. Do you want me to read it to you?"

"Let me find a pen first. Okay, go ahead."

"It's four lines. 'Who knows/Where the rose/Goes/Next.'"

Not haiku, as Kali would point out. And different from the others in that there was nothing specific about the victim.

"That's the whole poem. But there's a photo, too. Grainy and kind of dark. Of a woman. It looks like it was taken through a window or something."

"You mean from outside the house looking in?"

"Exactly. It's creepy."

Owen offered a grunt of agreement.

"First the rose, and now this poem," Selby said after a moment. "It's like the murder of that woman who used to work for you, isn't it?"

"I'm afraid so."

"And the Strangler case from before."

Owen had mentioned the similarities only in passing, trying not reveal the full extent of his concern, but Selby had seen immediately how worried he was. "There are differences," he told her. "And I'm still convinced Davis was guilty."

"But I know how much it's been on your mind. You don't need this now."

"You're keeping the doors locked, right?"

"You don't think—"

"Just to be safe." He didn't want to scare her, but who knew where the killer would strike next? And Selby's name *had* been on the envelope.

\* \* \*

Kali's eyes fixed on the photo Keating had placed on her desk. He was talking to her about the note, but she couldn't take her eyes off the woman in the photograph. Jane Parkhurst. Kali might not have been able to recognize her from the original snapshot, but Keating had had the photo enlarged and computer enhanced to make it clearer.

Jane Parkhurst, dressed in a white terry bathrobe, was talking on the telephone. From the cabinets in the background, it looked like she might have been in the kitchen. How had the killer taken the picture? Had he called her himself? The idea of being baited was so intrusive, so sick, it made Kali shiver.

Keating tapped his fingers on her desk. "The guy's no poet," he said. "Even I can tell that."

Finally, she turned her attention to the note.

> *Who knows*
> *Where the rose*
> *Goes*
> *Next*

Kali's stomach felt as though it were weighted with lead. He was already planning his next kill. They no longer had a choice. They had to go public, to somehow alert women without causing a panic.

Once they did, the whole Bayside Strangler connection was bound to come into play. The very thing they'd been hoping to avoid.

"This is the first time he's actually hinted at more killing," she said at last.

Keating was standing over her at the edge of the desk. He now sat and leaned forward. "The guy's getting off on the gamesmanship of it."

Kali nodded.

"Were the earlier poems like that?" Keating asked.

"Earlier poems?"

"In the Bayside Strangler case."

"I'd have to go back and reread them . . . In fact, that's something I've been intending to do, but my recollection is that they were more subtle." She paused, trying to call up the words, but seven years was a long time, and the notes had faded in her memory. "The last one was different, as I recall. More amateurish. And it wasn't haiku as the others had been. Speculation was that maybe he was getting tired of the poems. Or that he was too busy to spend much time on it. Davis's father had a stroke only a few days after Wendy Gilchrist's death."

Keating rubbed the bridge of his nose. "How strong, really, was the case against Davis?"

"You're asking if the wrong man was convicted?"

"Isn't it possible?" Keating was studying her with such intensity, she could almost feel his eyes grazing her skin.

"I think Davis killed those women," Kali said quietly. "I thought so then, and nothing since then has made me change my mind. But the case against him wasn't as strong as we'd have liked."

"Because the cops screwed up."

"I didn't say that."

"But that's what happened, isn't it?" There was an edge to his voice that Kali had trouble interpreting.

"We had evidence the judge wouldn't allow the jury to hear—"

"And other evidence that *was* allowed in, only to be tainted by allegations that the police had planted it."

Kali nodded. "But in spite of that, Owen Nelson managed to get a conviction."

"And a real career boost." Keating gave her a sardonic smile.

"He did a good job."

"So I've heard." Keating's beeper sounded. He checked the number and reached across her desk. "Can I use your phone?"

The question was apparently rhetorical, since he'd already begun punching the keys. His side of the conversation was quick and clipped. He dropped the receiver back into the cradle and looked at her.

"The note was sent to a reporter as well."

"Jackson?"

Keating shook his head. "A local newscaster, channel four. He was home with a cold yesterday, so he didn't get the note until today."

"Maybe he won't know what to make of it."

"It came with a copy of Jackson's book. And he's apparently already spoken with Anne Bailey's husband. It will be all over the news by evening."

This was what they'd been afraid of. No one liked the idea of the media being in the driver's seat. "Did he get the photo, as well?" she asked.

"Not that I know of."

That was something in their favor, at least.

"We'll have to hold a press conference," Kali said. "In a couple of hours, if it's going to make the evening news. I'll get in touch with Emory and tell him to notify the key networks and papers." Her mind was racing. How much to make public, how best to package what they had. How not to fuel the fire of hysteria.

Or blow Owen's candidacy out of the water.

Keating regarded her through narrowed eyes. "This announcement coming from the DA's office?"

She shook her head. That wasn't her intention. Though she'd clearly taken the reins, it was more out of habit than design. "I think statements about the investigation would be better delivered by the detectives in charge."

Keating's expression softened, but just for a moment. "Let's get to it, then. We've got our work cut out."

At four that afternoon, Keating stood behind the podium in the press room facing a sea of minicams and microphones. Kali stood off to the side, wondering if the media attention would help or hinder them in the long run. It was, almost certainly, what the killer was after, and that alone made her uncomfortable.

Keating began by reading a prepared statement on the recent murders. He conveyed the pertinent information about each, noting there were similarities but not detailing them. He covered the single yellow rose, the accompanying note, and the poems to police and selected media contacts in the same informative but generalized manner. They were following up on several leads, he said, but they weren't yet ready to name a suspect.

He ended by urging women to be extra cautious until the killer was safely behind bars.

Although Keating never mentioned the Bayside Strangler, the reference came up almost immediately in the question-and-answer session following his formal statement. It was Jack Jackson who raised the issue, and though it would probably have been picked up by someone else anyway, Kali was annoyed at him for doing so.

"We are aware that certain elements fit the pattern of earlier murders," Keating said smoothly, "but there are differences too."

"Such as?" This was another reporter, a woman whose strawberry-blond hair was pinned on top of her head with the help of several dozen shiny barrettes.

"We can't get into that at this time."

Jackson picked up the ball again. "Does that mean you're not even looking for a connection between the two recent murders and those committed by the so-called Bayside Strangler?"

"We are exploring all possibilities."

"What are you not telling us?" asked a reporter from the back of the room.

Keating offered a thin smile. "As you all know, we withhold some information in every case so as not to compromise our investigation. But I've given you all of the key points. And we will keep you informed as new developments occur."

He was good, Kali thought, wondering why that observation surprised her. Maybe because *articulate* wasn't one of the words she'd heard associated with Keating's name. *Tough, cocky, loner, hardheaded* and occasionally something along the line of *stud muffin*, but nothing that had prepared her for the ease with which he was handling the role of public spokesperson. Then again, this wasn't the first time she'd found Bryce Keating to be a man of surprises.

A reporter near the front of the room spoke up. "Is it true the DA's office is taking an active role in the investigation?"

"We always work closely with the District Attorney's office. This is one of the instances where we have chosen to involve them sooner rather than later."

"Any particular reason?" Jackson asked, shouting to be heard above the others eager to ask their own questions.

"The task force approach has proven particularly useful when dealing with crimes of this nature." Keating looked at his watch. "We have time for one last question."

"What advice do you have for women living in the East Bay?"

"They need to be particularly vigilant in the weeks to come. They should keep an eye out for suspicious behavior and travel with a friend whenever possible." He read off the number of a hotline to call with information.

The room began to empty as soon as the press conference

ended. Through the open door, Kali could see reporters standing in the hallway, cell phones pressed to their ears. Meeting a deadline no longer meant beating your competition to the pay phone.

"Nice job," Kali told Keating.

"The proof will be in how it plays out in the news."

Jack Jackson grabbed Kali's arm as she moved toward the door. "You fucked with me." He spat the words at her with venom.

"What do you mean?"

"I thought we had a deal. I held back mentioning the first note, the one that came directly to me. In return, you were supposed to tell me before the story broke."

"It all happened so fast, Jack."

"How much time does it take to pick up the phone and call?"

Calling Jackson hadn't even crossed her mind that afternoon. It wasn't her deal with him anyway, it was Owen's. "It's not like I can read the killer's mind. How was I supposed to know he would send a note to some other reporter this time?"

"A phone call, Kali. That's all it would have taken."

"You still have more background—"

"Damn straight I do. And a story already sitting on my editor's desk. No thanks to you." He pushed past her and into the hallway.

"What was that all about?" Keating asked.

"Jack Jackson wrote a book on the Bayside Strangler. Collaborated with Owen Nelson, in fact. Jackson's the journalist who got the note following Anne Bailey's murder." Speaking Anne's name aloud, Kali felt the familiar ache in her gut. In some ways she welcomed it because it kept her focused on the victims as people rather than mere names and statistics.

"He wanted to scoop the story," Kali added.

"Then why did he raise the Bayside Strangler connection at the press conference?"

Kali had wondered the same thing. "Probably to get our reaction on record."

"He's in no position to complain," Keating said bitterly. "Now he can write another book. More fame, more fortune."

"He's not a bad guy, really."

Keating shot her a look of disdain. "Not a good guy either, I suspect."

# CHAPTER 18

Bryce Keating's step had a spring to it as he headed for the unmarked black sedan in the parking lot. The press conference
had gone well, he decided. It was impossible to know what slant
reporters would give the story, but he'd managed to avoid
putting his foot in his mouth or losing his temper, both of which
had been very real possibilities. And he'd fielded questions in a
manner that was fair but didn't give away too much. All in all, he
was pleased.

Kali had approved, as well. Why that should matter, he wasn't
sure, but her comment as they'd left the room together gratified
him. He'd caught her looking at him during the press conference,
tilting her head the way she often did when listening intently. But
he'd been unable to read her expression. That bothered him since
he considered himself a pro at reading people. Particularly
women.

He climbed into the car and punched Lou's number on his cell
phone. "Hey, Lou, how's the back?"

"Better, I think."

"You think?"

"Better, definitely. Not great, but . . ."

"Better."

"Yeah. I'm thinking I might head back to work. I mean, I can
be miserable on the job as well as at home, right?"

"Not really." The way Keating figured it, a disabled partner
was worse than none at all. And Lou was hardly a stoic. He
wouldn't complain outright, but he'd piss and moan about every
little thing. Besides, Keating had his own style, and it was different from Lou's.

"There's too much going on," Lou said. "Makes me itchy being on the sidelines. I want to be where the action is."

"There's damn little action."

"You getting enough help?"

"Yeah, Maureen Oliver has been doing a lot of the scut work. Doing it well, I might add. The captain has given the okay for adding another member to the task force if we need it."

"I'm going to come in tomorrow anyway." It sounded like a point of honor with him.

"Fine." Keating wasn't going to argue.

Lou hesitated a moment. " How'd the press conference go?"

"Where'd you hear about that?" It had only ended half an hour ago. Keating hadn't thought to check the radio yet.

"I've got my fingers on the pulse, Bryce. Good thing, too, since my own partner doesn't keep me informed."

"Your partner had a few other things on his mind this afternoon."

Lou mumbled something unintelligible.

"What's that?"

"Forget it. So, how'd the press conference go?"

"Good. Reporter by the name of Jackson, the guy who wrote the Bayside Strangler book, he lashed—"Keating caught himself about to mention Kali's name. The last thing he wanted was to give Lou more ammunition. "The guy got all hot and huffy because he didn't get a heads-up on this latest murder. The rest of the group behaved themselves admirably."

"I'll make sure to catch the evening news. Might even learn something." Lou paused. "Where you headed?"

"What do you mean?"

"You're on the street or in the car. I can tell from the background noise."

The guy might have a bad back, but there was nothing wrong with his hearing. "Thought I'd drop by Jane Parkhurst's home."

"The latest victim?"

"Right."

A beat of silence, then Lou said, "Why her home? Is there something going on I don't know about?"

Keating didn't want to discuss the photograph on a cell phone, where his words might be overheard. "I'd rather give you the details in person."

"Come get me and we'll head out to the house together. I've had about all the convalescing I can take."

Lou grimaced as he tried to extricate himself from the passenger seat of the sedan. His back hurt like hell. Maybe he'd made a mistake offering to come out.

"You want a hand?"

"I'm fine." He brushed aside Keating's offer of assistance and reached for the top of the door frame. A slow and painful process. Just as getting into the car had been. But he was damned if he was going to give Keating the satisfaction of helping him. Bad enough he had a back that gave him trouble, he didn't need a partner giving him trouble too.

Once he was standing, it was easier going. Lou joined Keating on the sidewalk.

"What do you think?" Keating asked, waving a copy of the photograph Owen Nelson received along with the poem from the killer.

"It's sick, is what I think."

"Yeah, I know that. But about the photo."

Lou pulled a pair of drugstore reading glasses from his pocket and examined the photo more closely. Very little of the house was visible. On the outside, just a little of the siding and part of a curtain. He could see an interior door in the background, just to the left of where the woman, Jane Parkhurst, was standing. The walls were papered in some sort of swirling pattern.

He glanced up at the actual house before him. It wasn't large. It wasn't even particularly well kept, which surprised him given that Parkhurst was in real estate. White stucco with a red tile roof, situated in a quiet residential area off College Avenue.

"Not a front-facing room," Lou said. "I couldn't say for sure that it's even the same house."

"Look here, though. The trim around the window and the pattern in the stucco. I bet it is."

Lou studied the photograph, and nodded.

"If the killer did snap the photo here," Keating said, "there's a chance someone in the neighborhood saw him."

There were areas of the city where people kept to themselves as if their life depended on it, which it often did. But most places, neighbors looked out for each other. Lou thought they were lucky this was the kind of neighborhood Jane Parkhurst had lived in.

While Lou stood at the bottom of the front steps, Keating rang the bell. It went unanswered, which was no surprise. The window shades were lowered, but Keating peered through a narrow slit of glass next to the door.

"What do you see?" Lou asked.

"Not a bloody thing. Let's try the back."

Keating took off down the narrow stone path that led to the rear yard. Lou hobbled after him. Back there, the windows were uncovered, and Keating pushed his way through the bushes near the house to look inside.

"Watch the pansies," Lou said. Pansies had been one of Jan's favorites.

"The what?" From the way he continued stomping through the flower bed, it was clear he didn't know a pansy from a doorknob. Or maybe he thought Lou was making a crack about gays.

"The flowers. No need to trample them." Although Jane Parkhurst wasn't going to care.

Apparently, neither did his partner. Keating retreated from one window and pushed his way toward another without so much as a downward glance.

"Bingo," he said at last.

"What is it?" Lou rested a hand on his lower back, pressing against the knot at the base of his spine. No matter how he shifted his weight, his back cried out for a different position.

Keating yanked the photo from Lou's grasp. "The picture was taken through that window." He pointed to the panel of glass he'd just come from. "Probably with some kind of telephoto lens. So our photographer would have been standing back a ways."

Lou examined the yard. It was small, deeper than it was wide, with enough bushes and small trees to hide a person who didn't want to be seen. There were single-story houses on both the left and the right, but the building behind had two stories. The perimeter of the yard was veiled by a canopy of branches and greenery.

Lou turned back to his partner. "I don't know . . . with all the shrubbery and stuff, it's not likely a neighbor would notice a stranger in the yard."

"Not likely, maybe, but not impossible either. You want to wait by the car while I ring a few doorbells?"

"Nah, moving's good for me." Just as long as he did it at his own pace.

They checked with the occupants of the houses on both sides. Lots of concern on the neighbors' part, but nothing at all helpful. The building to the rear turned out to be a small apartment house. The window most closely centered on Jane Parkhurst's yard opened onto a stairwell.

Lou held the picture at eye level and looked through the window.

"The angle's wrong," Keating said.

"So now you're Ansel Adams?"

"Adams photographed nature scenes."

"Look at all that greenery."

"He was known for composition and contrast, not angles. Besides, there's a screen on this window, and none in the picture."

"Well, it was a thought." Lou peered through the window again. He hadn't even seen the screen, and for all he could tell, the angle wasn't so far off. But nobody ever said he had an artistic bone in his body.

They were back at the curb in front of Jane Parkhurst's house when a heavyset woman in tight athletic leggings came out of the house across the street. Lou could never understand why a woman with fat thighs and a bulging stomach would wear leggings that left nothing to the imagination. In fact, it was a rare woman over twelve who could wear them at all.

"Are you with the police?" she asked.

Lou was dressed, as always, in a dark suit. Keating wore a sports jacket and slacks. How had she known? Lou couldn't see they looked any different than your average business types.

The woman smiled. "Don't ask me how, but it's written all over you. Anyway, my mother"—she gestured to her house—"she sent me out to get you."

Lou raised an eyebrow.

"It's about our neighbor who was murdered. I imagine that's why you're here."

\*   \*   \*

The mother, Mrs. Edna Greene, looked to be in her early seventies. There was a cane beside her chair, but she appeared otherwise fit. Her skin was remarkably smooth and her hair a bright emerald green.

*My God,* Lou thought, *did the poor woman have a disaster at the beauty shop?*

"She just did it last week," the daughter explained when she caught Lou staring.

"Because of her name?" Keating asked.

"To match my eyes," Mrs. Greene said, batting them in Lou's direction.

Lou figured she was as nutty as a fruitcake.

"You're investigating the murder of my neighbor." It was a statement, not a question.

"Do you know something that might help us?" Keating asked.

"There was a man, a couple of weeks ago. He was wearing one of those orange vests, like a workman. I saw him walking back and forth on the sidewalk in front of the house. Then I saw him again a couple of days ago."

Hardly suspicious behavior, Lou thought. "What makes you think he might be connected to the murder?"

"It's just a feeling I have."

The daughter rolled her eyes toward the ceiling. "Mother, they're not interested in your *feelings.*"

"Wasn't like he was *going* anywhere so much as fiddling around. Like he was casing the house, maybe."

Keating took out a pen. "Can you describe him?"

"About your height. And muscular. Not that you aren't." She did the eye-batting routine for Keating's benefit.

The description left the field pretty much wide open. "Anything else?" Lou asked.

"Not that I can remember." Mrs. Greene studied her hands. "My subconscious might know, though. Maybe if I was hypnotized . . ."

"Mom, please."

Lou had known she was a flake the minute he saw the green hair. This only confirmed it. "We only use hypnosis in rare situations."

"Couldn't this be one of them?"

"With all due respect, ma'am, there isn't much that ties this man you saw to the murder."

"Soon as I heard about her being killed, I thought of him," Mrs. Greene explained. "I'm sure he was up to something. If I was hypnotized, I might be able to come up with one of those, what do you call them, composed sketches."

"Composite," Lou said.

"Yes, that's it. My sister was hypnotized once at the county fair. Years ago. Quacked like a chicken, she did."

Lou groaned under his breath. Did Mrs. Greene really want to quack like a chicken?

"That's not how we do it anyway," Keating explained.

"Well, you change your mind, just let me know. I'm willing."

"Absolutely, ma'am. We'll be in touch."

The daughter shrugged as she showed them out. "What was I supposed to do? She said she'd gotten a glimpse of the killer."

Lou walked gingerly across the street to the car. "Not one of our more successful forays into detection," he said, easing himself into the passenger seat.

"At least we've determined that the woman in the photo is our victim and that her killer stalked her here at her own house." Keating started the engine. "I'm heading back downtown. Shall I drop you home first?"

Lou shook his head. "I'd rather get a head start catching up."

One look at this desk and Lou wished he'd put it off another day. It was worse than he'd predicted. The desk was piled high with paper. Messages, memos, folders he'd requested from records, solicitations from organizations he'd never heard of. A couple more days of being gone and he'd have had to dig his way through to find the telephone. He sat there awhile wondering where to begin. Finally, he shoved the whole mess to the side.

Next to him, Keating was sorting through his own, much smaller cluster of message slips. "They've finished the inventory of evidence from the Parkhurst murder," he told Lou. "Want to take a look?"

"Sure." It beat trying to sort his way through the paper jungle on his desk.

The crime scene lab was only one floor down, but no way

could Lou take the stairs with his back acting up the way it was. He headed for the elevator, and after a moment's hesitation, Keating followed.

The tech at the desk that afternoon was Joe Moran, a man who reminded Lou of a rabbit. He had big ears, big front teeth, and while he didn't actually hop, he seemed always to move in fits and starts.

Moran pulled the bin for the Parkhurst case.

"Jesus, what is all this crap?" Lou asked, poking through the collection of cigarette butts, loose change and buttons, pocket combs and gum wrappers.

"It was a public place," Moran explained. "Lots of debris. We got prints off the outhouse, though. And we had the septic guys hold the contents for processing."

Lou gagged. "Jesus, glad I'm not in line for that job." Sifting through shit had to rank as the least pleasant job imaginable.

"Someone's got to," Moran pointed out.

"This was at the scene?" Keating pointed to a tube of lipstick. "Any chance it matches what was on her lips?"

Moran's face grew flushed. "I don't know."

"Even if it does, so what?" Lou asked.

Keating tugged on an earlobe. "Kali thought Jane Parkhurst's lipstick looked fresh." He turned to Moran. "See if it matches. And check for prints."

Moran nodded. "The blue fibers on her clothing were like those found in the Bailey case," he said. "Something man-made, like nylon. Maybe from a car's interior. We're still working on that."

"What's with the lipstick?" Lou asked as they left the room.

"If you'd been abducted and feared for your life would you think about putting on lipstick?"

"I never think about it." Lou laughed at his own joke. "What are you thinking?"

"Maybe the killer applied the lipstick himself. He took pains to dress her, after all."

Lou grunted. "So our girl from the DA's office looks at a corpse and first thing she checks is the lipstick. Typical female."

"You know, Lou, you're really out of touch with the times."

There was probably some truth to that, but Lou wasn't about to lose sleep over it.

\* \* \*

Kali flipped on the television. She'd only have time to catch the beginning of the news before leaving to meet Nathan Sloane for dinner. If their news conference wasn't one of the lead stories, she'd have to tape it and watch when she returned.

Or forget about meeting Nathan. She had trouble remembering now why she'd agreed.

*Oh, come on, you know why you said yes. Nathan is an attractive guy and he's clearly interested in you. Why shouldn't you go out with him?*

*Because I'm not ready for another relationship. I don't even trust my own feelings anymore. And after what happened with Steven, I need time to heal.*

But living was what would help her heal, people said.

Too late to get out of it now, anyway. Besides, what was the harm in dinner? One date and that would be the end of it.

Loretta, who had been lying at Kali's feet, stood up, circled once, then plopped back down just as the news anchor led into coverage of the afternoon's press conference. Kali was tuned to channel four, the station that had received a copy of the poem, thinking they would probably have the most extensive coverage.

The news report began with a rehash of the murder and the station's own role, then switched to clips from the conference itself. Kali was impressed with Bryce Keating, just as she had been earlier. He was confident and in control, but managed at the same time to exhibit a genuineness not often seen in police personnel, particularly in public. The hotline phone number was prominently displayed on the right of the screen, and the reward for information leading to an arrest was mentioned at least twice. The phone would undoubtedly ring off the hook. Whether anything came of the calls was another matter.

And then came commentary from a reporter noting similarities between the two recent murders and those attributed to the Bayside Strangler. A quick clip from the Davis trial followed, along with a recording of his own words proclaiming his innocence.

The news anchor, a young woman with dark, doe eyes, looked directly into the camera. "Has the real Bayside Strangler been at large all these years, or has a copycat killer recently surfaced? That is the question police are asking themselves as they work

frantically to find an answer before yet another woman is murdered."

Kali switched channels in time to hear sound-bite interviews
with women on the street about their reaction to the recent murders and what they were doing to ensure their own safety. By the
time she checked her watch again, she realized she'd have to
hurry to make it to the restaurant in time.

Nathan Sloane was already seated when she arrived at the
Oakview Grille. He stood as she approached. "I thought maybe
you weren't going to show."

There was a thin but cool undercurrent to his tone that Kali
thought wasn't justified. She was barely ten minutes late, and that
was because a car fire had stalled traffic on Telegraph Avenue.

"Sorry I kept you waiting." She didn't bother with excuses.

He smiled and the ice melted. "Anyway, I'm glad you made
it."

He'd probably worried he'd been stood up, she realized. She
liked it that he felt a little vulnerable and wasn't one of those men
who thought they were God's gift to women. "A car fire caused a
major traffic jam," she explained.

As soon as she sat down, a waiter appeared with a chilled bottle of champagne. He poured a glass for each of them, then set the
bottle in an ice bucket next to the table. So much for the simple
meal Nathan had originally suggested.

"Cheers." Nathan raised his drink in a toast.

"Cheers." The champagne was cold and smooth. Almost immediately, Kali felt its effervescence hit her bloodstream.

The waiter returned with a platter of tapas. "I took the liberty
of ordering an appetizer for us," Nathan said.

Kali responded with a smile since the right words eluded her.
First the champagne and now this. He'd obviously arrived well
before the time they were set to meet. And gone a bit overboard in
trying to make a good impression. She was both flattered by the
attention, and a little uneasy with it.

Finally, she gave up analyzing the situation, sat back and
sipped her champagne. Nathan, too, appeared to relax.

"Tell me about yourself," he said. His eyes were a bright, almost iridescent blue, and he fixed them on her intently. This, too,
was both flattering and disconcerting.

"That could take forever," she said, keeping it light.

"I've got time."

Kali folded her hands around the stem of her champagne flute. "What would you like to know?"

He leaned forward slightly, leading with his chin. "Why not start at the beginning. Where did you grow up?"

"Silver Creek. A small town in the Sierra foothills." A town she'd returned to several years ago when her life in the Bay Area began crumbling. Now she was faced with deciding which place to make her permanent home. But she wanted to avoid that discussion tonight.

"Brothers and sisters?" Nathan asked.

"One of each. How about you?"

"Only child. My parents traveled a lot so I was raised mostly by a succession of housekeepers."

The waiter appeared, ready to take their orders.

"The duck is excellent," Nathan told Kali. "As is the pork tenderloin. You can't go wrong with either of them."

Giving in to the tiny voice of rebellion in her head, Kali ordered the grilled salmon instead.

Nathan laughed. "A woman who knows her own mind." He ordered duck for himself, then turned back to Kali. "Now, where were we?"

"In the early stages of the getting-to-know-you dance." She smiled, hinting at flirtation. "I thought you were new to the area. You seem to know a lot about the menu here."

"I like to eat well. And I'm a lousy cook." His brow creased slightly in concentration; then he seemed to remember the earlier thread of their conversation. "Family," he said. "That's where we were. You were lucky. I always wanted siblings. And parents like other people had."

Family was a subject Kali preferred to pass over. Whatever fond memories she'd had of her own upbringing had been permanently marred by her mother's suicide when Kali was sixteen. She steered the conversation in a different direction by asking Nathan about his work, and he obliged by telling her. By the time their food arrived, her head was swimming with talk of brokered deals, buyouts, and mergers. She wasn't sure she could have said exactly what it was he did, but she wasn't going to push the issue any further.

Over their meal, they covered movies, San Francisco attractions, lawyer jokes and problems with mass transit. There were moments when Kali found Nathan to be a bit presumptuous, but on the whole he was good company. She was enjoying herself with a member of the opposite sex, something she hadn't done in months.

"I caught your name on the news this afternoon," Nathan said. "Is it true you're working for the DA's office now?"

"On a temporary basis."

"They're shorthanded?"

"In a nutshell, yes, although it's actually a bit more complicated than that."

"Isn't it always." When she didn't offer to elaborate, he continued. "Must be exciting working on a murder investigation."

"Frustrating and depressing is more like it."

"Interesting what they're saying about Bayside Strangler case. Were you around then?"

"I was with the DA's office. Helped prosecute Dwayne Davis, in fact."

"Really?" He sounded impressed, which hadn't been her intention. Or had it? She'd caught herself playing up to him on several occasions.

By the time they'd finished dessert, Kali was in a mellow mood. She was glad she'd driven herself to the restaurant, and would drive herself home, or she might have been tempted to take the evening further.

# CHAPTER 19

Owen had never been a fan of power lunches. He preferred conducting business on the phone or around a conference table. Straight and direct. Since plunging into the world of politics, however, he'd been forced to adapt. More than adapt really, and he'd gotten quite good at it. Still, he wasn't looking forward to spending another noon hour (which usually turned into several hours) walking a tightrope of touchy issues over pasta in garlic sauce.

"The Davis question is bound to come up," warned Les Amstead, his key campaign strategist, as they walked through the city-owned garage toward Amstead's car.

"You talking about my stand on capital punishment?" Owen knew that wasn't what Les was referring to, but he wanted desperately to put the recent murders from his mind.

"That may end up being part of it, but what's going to be on the tip of everyone's tongue are the Bailey and Parkhurst murders. It was headline news in this morning's papers and the lead story on every radio news program I listened to."

"Wonderful."

"You read the piece in this morning's *Trib?*"

Owen had. It was a lengthy account of the Bayside Strangler killings and their similarities with the two recent murders. It sounded more like something he'd expect to find in the tabloids than the mainstream press, and he half suspected that Jack Jackson had authored it under a pseudonym. Jackson's own piece in the *Chronicle* bore striking parallels.

"There are times," Owen said, "I wish I'd never taken that case on."

"You might not be where you are today without it. Exposure is the name of the game here."

That was true. Owen spent as much time seeking out venues to be heard as he did planning what to say. Marketing was a big part of what separated winners from losers. He sometimes fantasized about chucking the whole thing for a quiet life in rural Idaho. Except that deep down he *did* want to be governor. Not for the power and ego gratification as his son and some of his critics claimed, but because he honestly believed he could do some good.

"I'll settle for wishing I'd not gotten involved with the book, then. Or the movie. People could remember the case without remembering me."

"I hate to break it to you, Owen, but the book and movie were what got you the exposure. The public doesn't give a rat's ass about your sound legal mind."

"Aren't you the voice of inspiration today."

"Just telling it like it is." Amstead pulled the car out of the garage and turned left. "Even without the Davis connection there'd be interest in the recent murders. So think about what sort of spin you want to put on them."

Spin. There it was again. The selling of Owen Nelson for governor. "Homicide is not a rare occurrence," he pointed out. "Most killings don't even make the news."

"Come on, Owen. You know this is different. We're talking professional, upper-class women. White women. The kind of victim that gets people's attention because it hits so close to home."

"I hope you never say that publicly."

"I'm not saying that's the way it *should* be, only that it's the way it is."

They'd reached the Sheraton, where Owen was meeting with would-be contributors. Amstead pulled up in front and waited for the valet parking attendant to take their car. "Besides," he said, turning to Owen, "murders like this capture the public's imagination in the way a simple drive-by, or even a shooting at the ATM, doesn't. With those, you get a brief news story and maybe a follow-up a few days later. Then interest peters out. This is different. We've got ritualistic murders where the killer has targeted his victims, then turned around and taunted law enforcement. It has Hollywood written all over it."

"I'm running for governor, Les. Not auditioning for a part in a movie."

"The two aren't as different as you might think." As they moved through the lobby, Amstead whispered, "Wait until word of the photo gets out. The wires will burn."

"I wish you wouldn't sound so gleeful."

"It's news, Owen. Like I keep telling you, exposure is good for the ratings."

"Unless I wind up looking like an ass."

Amstead grinned. "So make sure you don't."

A drone of voices, mostly male, greeted Owen as he approached the West Ballroom, where the luncheon was being held. He knew the buzz would quiet briefly when he entered, then pick up again as he worked the room, shaking hands and mixing generic greetings with popular sound bites. He could do this, Owen told himself. He was, in fact, good at it. But for a moment before he stepped through the double doors, he almost choked on the knowledge that two young women were dead and his fortunes were somehow tied to their murders.

When she was a little girl growing up in southern Kentucky, Diana Davis had fantasized about joining the circus. She wanted to fly from the highest trapeze, ride on the head of an elephant, crack the whip as the tiger stood atop his perch. She wanted to wear sequins and spangles, to wave to the cheering crowds and, most important, travel the world. Never in a million years would she have imagined herself as a waitress with a young son. But as she watched ten-year-old Teddy dribbling the ball down the court at the school gym, she couldn't imagine her life without him.

He was tall for his age and thin, like Dwayne, though not so dark-skinned. Teddy was bright, eager, kind and now, unfortunately, at an age when he was asking about his father. Really asking, and demanding answers. These weren't the "where's my daddy?" questions of childhood. Questions she could skirt with vague, ambiguous responses. Teddy wanted—deserved—to know whatever she was able to tell him.

But what did she know, really?

That she'd loved Dwayne once; that he'd stood by her when she discovered she was pregnant. That she'd been as shocked as everyone else when his name surfaced in connection the with Bayside Strangler murders.

She could recall, as fresh as if it were yesterday, how stunned she'd been when the police first questioned Dwayne. Impossible, she'd said then, like everyone else who knew him. Dwayne was a dedicated and popular teacher. But the police questioned him again, and again. And then, with the suddenness of a rattlesnake strike, they'd arrested him. She was certain there had to have been a mistake.

During the course of the trial, she experienced her first inkling of doubt. As she listened to the evidence, she realized with alarm that some of it fit. The diamond pendant Dwayne had given her for her birthday was exactly like the one Angela Morrelli had been seen wearing the evening she was killed. The Wednesday night of Christine Krichek's murder, Dwayne had called to make sure she and Teddy were truly at her sister's place. One by one the myriad of little lies she'd caught him in surfaced in her mind.

Once she started, there seemed to be no end to the things she remembered. She could recall the times he fell into dark moods, when he wouldn't speak to her for days on end; the angry outbursts when she knew she'd displeased him but didn't know how. *Controlling* was the word used by the therapist she'd seen early in their marriage. Dwayne was controlling and narcissistic. He saw the world only in terms of what it did, or didn't do, for him. And she'd felt a chill in her bones when she'd heard the psychiatrist testifying for the prosecution say the same thing about the killer.

She'd sat through the trial with her chin up the way the attorney, Al Gomez, told her to. Even without his prompting, she'd wept when the verdict came in. But she'd only visited Dwayne once in prison, and that was to tell him she was filing for divorce.

Still, she couldn't help wondering if some of it wasn't her own fault. Maybe if she hadn't gained so much weight when she was pregnant, or if she'd done a better job of keeping Teddy quiet in the evenings when Dwayne was home, maybe then he would have loved her, and that would have been enough.

Six years ago it had seemed like a good idea to pick up and start over in an area where no one recognized her. She'd piled Teddy in the car and driven south. They'd gotten as far as Fresno when the car broke down, so Fresno was where they'd stayed. It had turned out to be a good move. The city was growing like gangbusters. New faces weren't a novelty—even when they were the color of coffee rather than cream. And where you'd come from was less important than how you fit in. Diane had found good work waiting tables. Teddy had thrived in school. Fresno became home, and she put the past behind her.

In the beginning she'd even considered taking back her maiden name, but she'd ended up sticking with Davis because she wanted the same last name as her son. It was a common enough name that people never connected her with Dwayne. Even her fiancé, Colin, didn't know she'd once been married to a convicted killer. She knew she should tell him, but he and Teddy got along so great that she hated to take a chance on spoiling it. He'd have to feel differently about things if he knew that Teddy's father was the Bayside Strangler.

If Dwayne actually was.

That was what she always came back to. Had Dwayne killed those women?

And now there were two new murders. Did that mean that Dwayne had been innocent all along? Diana wouldn't even have known about the new murders if Al Gomez hadn't sent her the news clippings. He was always pressing her to speak out, to give interviews and make appearances, all, as far as she could tell, to further his own agenda. But so far he'd been good about respecting her privacy when she declined. With these new murders, however, she'd sensed a renewed energy on his part, and it made her nervous. She didn't want the life she'd left behind thrust in her face, or in that of her son.

The coach blew his whistle, and Diana turned her attention back to the game. A foul by the other team had put Teddy into free-throw position. He bounced the ball against the floor a couple of times, then took a deep, calming, breath. His long, skinny arms bent at his chest. Her own heart was beating as fast as his must have been. Teddy took the shot and dropped the ball smoothly into the center of the basket. And then again. He turned to look at her and grinned.

Diana beamed back. In her pocket, her fingers found the newspaper article Gomez had sent, and she felt a slender ray of hope that Teddy's daddy had not been a killer, after all.

*   *   *

Kali had intended to take the slice of chocolate cake home for dessert, but by two o'clock in the afternoon it was calling to her so loudly, she gave in. Bringing a cake on your birthday was an office tradition she remembered from her early days as a DA, and it apparently hadn't fallen out of favor. Gloria, the secretary she shared with another assistant DA, had turned fifty and was determined not to be morose about it. She'd bought a triple-layer chocolate mousse cake so rich looking that Kali was sure the fudge scent alone was filled with calories. She'd tried to politely decline, but Gloria had ignored her excuses and pressed a piece on her anyway.

Kali used the plastic fork Gloria had also pressed on her (just in case) and took a bite. Delicious. She would have liked a glass of ice-cold milk to go with it, but settled for coffee instead. At least that would help her stay awake.

She had spent the morning poring over interviews the detectives had conducted with friends and family of both victims. She'd tried to reconstruct the days preceding the murders, hoping to find a common thread. Nothing had jumped out at her as significant. Yet the killer had clearly been watching his victims and, in Jane Parkhurst's case, had been at least as close as her backyard. The notion of him hidden there in the bushes photographing her gave Kali the creeps. But creepier still was the thought that he could have appeared in his victims' lives, befriended them even, in just about any guise.

Like the Bayside Strangler.

All the time she'd been looking through the reports, images of Dwayne Davis had filtered through Kali's mind. She'd spent the hours since lunch looking over the Davis files and transcripts. Now, only several bites into her cake, she found herself engrossed in the testimony of Dr. Dunworthy, a psychologist who'd testified for the prosecution and had since made something of a name for himself as an expert on serial killers.

Owen had felt the jurors needed a framework for understanding how a seemingly respectable man such as Dwayne Davis could have committed multiple murders. Carl Dunworthy, a gnomelike man with a pointy goatee, had suited the purpose to a tee. With an academic background and an impressive list of publications, he presented a highly credible witness. He was also a showman who delighted in sharing with an audience.

Kali remembered wondering at the time what sort of person made his life's work the study of deviant minds and serial killers, and maybe that was what had colored her impression of him. It was nothing she could put her finger on, but the man struck her as a bit odd. A good witness, but not someone she took an instant liking to.

She took another bite of cake and then read further in the transcript.

Nelson: Can you tell the court, Dr. Dunworthy, how you came to be involved with this case initially?

Dr. Dunworthy: I first learned of the investigative task force by reading about it in the newspaper. It interested me and I immediately offered my services.

N: And what did you do by way of assistance?

D: Primarily, I helped them come up with a profile of the killer. Later, I also interviewed Mr. Davis.

N: What do you mean by "profile"?

D: Well, loosely, what we do is draw up a kind of psychological composite of the killer. As a start, we make a distinction between organized and disorganized killers.

N: I'm not sure I understand.

D: The crimes of disorganized killers tend to be opportunistic and impulsive. These killers pick their victims at random, use as a weapon whatever happens to be handy, take substantial risk of discovery, and rarely make any effort to hide or move the victim's body. The so-called organized killers, on the other hand, are more methodical. They plan their crimes in advance and target victims who fit some preconceived notion in their minds. Indeed, they usually take a great deal of satisfaction from the planning stages and the process of selecting the victim.

N: How do you make this determination about a killer?

D: From crime scene analysis and reconstruction of events surrounding the crime.

N: And what was your impression of the person responsible for the so-called Bayside Strangler murders?

(There was an objection here from the defense—it hadn't been established that all the crimes had been committed by the same individual—but the judge overruled it. As Owen had told Kali more than once, they'd been very lucky in their draw of Judge Harrington.)

D: These murders were clearly committed by a personality we call the organized killer. His victims were personalized. They were women he'd selected ahead of time and come to know on some level. He brought his own weapon to the crime scene and took it away after the commission of the crime. The planning for these crimes was quite elaborate as well—the clothing, the means of disposal, the rose sent to the victims. To say nothing of the taunting notes to the police.

N: What else can you tell us about the organized killer?

D: He often takes trophies—

N: Excuse me, Doctor. What do you mean by trophies?

D: Personal items belonging to his victims—earrings, a locket, that sort of thing. They allow him to recall the victim in his fantasies and often serve as an acknowledgment of his accomplishments. Much in the same way a hunter might admire the antlers of a deer he shot, the organized killer looks at the ring or necklace he's taken and relives the excitement of the crime. Sometimes trophies are given to the killer's girlfriend, wife or mother, and the killer finds added thrill in the fact that only he knows the origin of the object.

N: It's a game for them then?

D: In a sense, yes. These are people who've never outgrown the "me" stage that all children go through. They think only of their own needs and see themselves as the center of the universe.

N: What about the sexual aspects of these crimes?

D: It is an attribute of the organized personality that the sex act, if it occurs, is completed with a living victim. A disorganized killer often does not complete the sex act, or if he does, it is only after the victim is dead or has been rendered entirely inanimate. It's important to bear in mind, however, that we are not talking so much about lust as control, and the sex act as a means to this end.

N: What is it that motivates such killers, Doctor?

D: Nothing that is obvious in the sense we usually associate with crimes—greed, revenge, heat of passion. The kind of killer we're talking about is most often living out a private fantasy of some sort. That is why there is the similar signature in each crime.

N: Signature?

D: Most killers leave their own personal stamp at the scene. It is an unconscious pattern that includes the type of victim selected, the method used to control the victim, method of disposal, and so forth. Although certain details may change from crime to crime, the basic signature of the killer remains the same. Each new murder is not so much a new event as a different act in an ongoing drama.

N: Dr. Dunworthy, can you tell us how we would recognize this so-called organized killer were we to run across him? Would he appear crazed? Threatening?

D: Not at all. Such personalities are clever and inventive, and very skillful at presenting themselves to appear beyond suspicion. They are usually of above-average intelligence, reasonably good-looking, socially adept. Such a killer would look and act like any of us. You or me even.

Here, Kali paused in her reading and shivered. She remembered Dr. Dunworthy looking in her direction, fixing his small, dark eyes on her as if she were a bug under a microscope. She thought she saw the corners of his mouth twitch before he turned his attention back to Owen.

N: He would be well integrated into society, then?

D: Absolutely. You have only to look at the list of famous serial killers to see that. Ted Bundy and John Wayne Gracy, for example, were perceived as upstanding citizens. Intelligent, energetic and actively involved in the community. In fact, a hallmark of this type of killer is that he often follows the investigation closely and may become actively involved in it, as a volunteer or even a professional. I recall one case where the guy who handed out flyers on a missing child was also the killer, and another where the killer posed as a television cameraman.

Kali stood and stretched, as much to clear her mind as to relieve the kinks in her back and shoulders. Everything that Dunworthy had noted about the Bayside Strangler could be said of their current killer as well.

Did that mean the Bayside Strangler was still on the loose? No it did not, she argued silently. The evidence spoke just as clearly to the existence of a copycat. There was enough detail in Jackson's book, wasn't there, to serve as a blueprint?

And neither Anne nor Jane Parkhurst had been raped. That, too, spoke to the existence of a copycat. Kali wondered, though, if that was as significant a difference as it first appeared. The Strangler murders had taken place almost eight years ago, after all.

That brought her full circle. What if they weren't dealing with a copycat killer? It was the issue Kali had been skirting for days, like the shadow of a bad dream. It made her stomach knot and her skin feel tight.

Maybe it was just the chocolate and coffee, but Kali's mind was buzzing. Thoughts flew in, circled a bit, and either collided with other thoughts or were pushed aside by new ones. She couldn't hold onto any of them long enough to sort through the chaos.

Sitting again in her chair, she turned to the back pocket of her case binder from the Bayside Strangler trial. There, along with a few penciled annotations of her own, was a neatly typed list of contacts, telephone numbers and addresses. She slid her finger down the column to Dr. Dunworthy's name, then over to the entry for his number.

She punched in the seven digits and was connected to a woman with a lovely Irish accent, who'd never heard of Dr. Dunworthy. Kali hung up feeling discouraged. Then she remembered the proliferation of area codes since the Davis trial. Kali was in the East Bay and Dunworthy, as she recalled, had been from somewhere in Marin County. She tried again, this time including the area code. Dr. Dunworthy picked up on the second ring. He sounded harried, and it wasn't until she'd reminded him about the Davis trial and twice explained how the current murders might relate that he seemed to focus on what she was saying.

"I'm afraid I'm very busy," he said.

"Please, it's important. I'll only take an hour or so of your time."

"A copycat killer, huh?"

"That's one of the things we're trying to determine."

"But only two murders." Something about the tone conveyed disappointment, though Kali was sure he didn't intend it.

"Only two so far. We'd like to prevent a third."

Dr. Dunworthy sighed loudly into the phone. "I'm leaving town tomorrow to deliver a paper in Montreal. It's an important conference."

"I could be there in half an hour." Kali checked her watch. Half an hour wasn't really feasible, not with traffic what it was these days. But better to promise the moon than let him slip away.

A fact that wasn't lost on the psychologist. "My dear, I'm flattered that you're so eager, but you won't make it here from Oakland at this time of day in under an hour. Don't race just to get here. I'll be waiting."

"Thank you, Dr. Dunworthy. I appreciate this." She got directions, then, after a moment's reflection, called Keating and was patched through to his cell phone.

She explained briefly. "You interested in coming with me?"

"You bet." His answer caught her by surprise. In her experience, cops tended to lump psychologists with psychics and palm readers.

"I'm not far," Keating said. "I'll pick you up out front in about ten minutes." He paused. "Oh, and by the way, the lipstick is a match."

# CHAPTER 20

Dr. Dunworthy lived in the hills of Sausalito, up a long, narrow driveway. The house wasn't large, but it was exquisitely furnished—oriental carpets, sofas of buttery-soft leather, and chests of dark, highly polished mahogany. Where Kali's tables were cluttered with magazines and paperbacks, Dunworthy's displayed modernistic sculptures and large-format, full-color art books. It was clear there were no children living there, and Kali sensed there was no woman either.

Dunworthy looked pretty much as she'd remembered him. His goatee was a bit grayer, his waistline a bit larger, but he wore the same sort of soft-drape wool slacks and cashmere turtleneck, and he still smelled of stale cigarette smoke and coffee.

"I must admit," he said when they were settled in the high-ceilinged main room that functioned as both living and dining space, "that you've piqued my curiosity. Tell me more about these recent murders. I've seen the news, of course, but I want to know the details."

Kali let Keating lead off, then she filled in bits and pieces she thought Dunworthy might find significant in light of his work on the Davis trial. Dunworthy took notes as he listened, stopping them now and then to ask for clarification. When they'd finished, he sat silently for a moment, his gaze flat and unfocused.

"Most interesting," he said at last, tugging on his goatee. "Fascinating, in fact."

"So what do you think?" Keating asked. He was clearly impatient with the doctor's grandstanding.

"The two sets of murders—the original Bayside Strangler killings and the current ones—have strong similarities. Similarities beyond even the obvious. There are significant differences, however."

"Such as?" Keating prompted.

"Most notably, the two recent victims were not sexually assaulted. And they don't fit the mold of the earlier victims, who were not only younger, but all of a similar type."

"No dog collar with the recent victims either," Kali commented.

Dunworthy brushed her comment aside, literally batting the air with his hand. "That's really just window dressing, in my mind. What's important is that the Bayside Strangler murders had the earmarks of psychosexual fantasy. The killer enjoyed toying with his victims. As I recall, there was some evidence that he brought them to the brink of unconsciousness and then revived them long enough to again rape them. Even the body poses after death were erotic. And he took great care in dressing them. The two new murders feel quite different, even in light of the killer dressing his victims."

"How so?"

"I don't see anything to indicate the same sort of sexual fantasy. And from what you tell me, the killer's dressing of the bodies is more haphazard. The Strangler paid a great deal of attention to detail, not only in the choice of clothing itself but in making sure it was properly arranged."

Keating rubbed his jaw. "Our killer seems to have taken great care in posing his victims, though."

"Care, yes, but without the Strangler's focus on degradation."

Keating looked skeptical. "Both women had their skirts up around their waists. Looked demeaning to me."

"I'm not saying there wasn't an element of that, but from what you've told me, I think he also cared about them in some way. Hands folded in their laps, legs more together than apart. I don't pick up on the same sense of anger and contempt."

"It's been a long time," Kali reminded him. "If it was the same killer, wouldn't he have changed some?"

"Yes, in fact he would. Repeat, ritualistic killers are always evolving, tweaking and fine-tuning their art, if you will excuse the term, with each murder. But the underlying signature doesn't change."

Keating leaned forward in his chair. "What do you mean?"

"At the root of these types of killings are fantasies and hostilities nurtured in childhood."

"So we're looking for someone who's had a bad childhood?" There was just the hint of mockery in Keating's voice.

"Not necessarily. The instigating childhood trauma doesn't have to be odd or abusive. It could be something as simple as pressure to succeed in a parent's eyes." Dunworthy smiled at them. "Think of it as a pair of glasses through which the killer sees the world. He is acting out a drama that is uniquely his. Some of the peripheral touches may change, but the central plot and theme remain."

"You're saying that the two recent murders are part of a different drama?" Kali asked.

"That's certainly the way it appears to me."

Kali felt the knot in her stomach relax. Nothing said Dunworthy was right, of course, but she took comfort in his analysis nonetheless. Two sets of murders, two different killers. Davis, and now a copycat.

"We shouldn't entirely discount the superficial differences, either," Dunworthy continued. "No dog collar, as Kali noted earlier. And the poems are quite different. The photo is something new. As is this lipstick you mentioned." He turned to Keating. "You found a lipstick at the crime scene and it matched the color on the second victim's lips?"

"Right. But what got our attention was the fact that her lips were so freshly colored. Either she applied it right before she was killed, or her killer did it after death. I haven't had a chance to follow up and see if the same was true of the first murder."

Kali tried to recall the afternoon she'd identified Anne Bailey's body. Her eyes had settled on the video screen only long enough to know that it was Anne. Fresh makeup had been the least of her concerns. But looking back, Kali thought she remembered something off about Anne's appearance. At the time, she'd attributed the change to death.

Dunworthy stroked his goatee for a moment. When he spoke, it was as if he was thinking aloud. "Most likely what we have here is a copycat who has adapted the basic framework to fulfill his own fantasies."

"Why copy an earlier crime at all?" Keating asked.

"Good question. And that may be something that will help

you narrow the field some. There has to have been something about the Bayside Strangler case that struck a chord with your killer."

"It did get a lot of publicity," Kali pointed out.

"Yes, it did. But there have been other cases that have received as much, if not more, publicity." Again, the thoughtful pause. "I'd say the Strangler case was in some way personal to your killer. Not in a direct way necessarily, but in the sense that there was something about Davis himself your killer related to. Or perhaps the core fantasy of the murders touched a nerve with him. There must have been something that captivated the killer's interest and appealed to him on a very basic level."

Keating looked dubious. "Still doesn't explain why he'd copy someone else."

"The fact that it was someone else's program probably added to the enticement at first. It's like a kid who's fixated on an actor or rock star. He tries to copy his manner of speaking, dress and so forth. He chooses that particular movie star for a reason that's uniquely his, and he chooses to emulate someone else rather than develop his own style from scratch. What's interesting in the case before us is that the killer is already pushing the parameters, making the crime more his own."

"Adding his own touches, you mean?"

"Exactly. It's a copycat crime but it's his, too."

"What motivates someone like that?" Keating asked.

"Anger, a sense of powerlessness. My guess is that your killer feels alienated from those around him. He feels he's been mistreated, that life hasn't been fair to him. He's quick to blame others and loath to look inward and accept responsibility himself."

Keating gave a harsh laugh. "Sounds like half the population I deal with on a daily basis. That's not going to exactly help us find the guy."

"Where do we go from here?" Kali asked the doctor. "Any ideas?"

"Something about the Bayside Strangler murders made an impression on your killer. That's one avenue to explore. The other is to look at the victims. How does he find them? Why these particular women? You said they didn't look anything alike, but there's some reason he's targeted them and not others. The photo of the

Parkhurst woman makes it clear the crime wasn't a matter of simple opportunity."

Dunworthy checked his watch and stood abruptly. "Unless you have a last, pressing question, I'm afraid my time is about up."

"Thank you, Doctor," Kali said. "We appreciate your help, especially on such short notice."

He walked them to the door. "I'm sorry I'm not in a position to be more actively involved in the investigation. I do hope you'll keep me informed, however. It's quite fascinating how it's playing out."

When the door shut behind them, Keating muttered, "As if we'd *asked* him to be more involved."

"What did you think of him?" Kali asked.

"Aside from the overblown ego, you mean?"

She smiled. "Aside from that."

"Well, I don't know that it was particularly helpful, but it was interesting."

That was pretty much Kali's take on it as well, although she'd felt relief at hearing Dunworthy distinguish the recent crimes from those of the Bayside Strangler.

"Victim profiling is nothing new," Keating added. "As for the rest of it, bottom line is we're looking for a narcissistic copycat who was attracted to the Bayside Strangler murders. Doesn't offer much direction."

"At least it's a copycat."

"Maybe," Keating said. "Maybe not."

Lou knew next to nothing about women's clothing. Jan had always looked nice, he knew that much, but he'd never paid much attention to the details. In fact, he'd sometimes made the mistake of complimenting an outfit she'd dragged from the back of the closet in order to work in the garden or paint the porch. He was a fashion philistine and proud of it. So when Maureen Oliver had remarked that the dress Jane Parkhurst had been wearing when they found her body was a Carin original, he'd stared at her as if she'd spoken Sanskrit. But he'd gotten the gist of it quickly enough (she'd harped on it until he did), and now he was standing at the door of the exclusive Carin Gallery in Danville, dress in hand.

A buzzer sounded as Lou opened the door and the lone sales-clerk looked up. She was a slender woman in her early thirties with straight blond hair and bangs that hung half into her eyes. He approached, grateful to see that, except for the two of them, the place was empty. Didn't look like they carried much merchandise either. The store was small, half taken up with an overstuffed couch and chair. What few dresses there were hung singly on hangers about the perimeter.

Lou explained why he was there and showed the dress to the clerk.

She pulled back a bit, averting her eyes. "Someone was murdered in one of *our* dresses?"

"She may not have actually been murdered in it, but she was wearing it when we found her."

"How awful."

Lou wasn't sure if she was referring to the murder itself or the fact that the dress had been a part of it. "We're pretty sure the dress didn't belong to her."

"You think she stole it?"

"No, nothing like that."

"Borrowed it, then?"

Lou shook his head.

The young woman cocked her head and looked at him.

"We're trying to trace the person who purchased it." Lou knew he wasn't making sense, but he didn't want to get into the role of clothing in the murder. "If that's possible," he added, and he was pretty sure it wasn't.

The woman started to reach for the dress, then, seeming to remember that it had been part of a murder, shuddered. She pulled her arms back to her side. "Can you hold it up for me?" she asked.

Lou did so.

"That was a style we sold in early summer. What size is it?"

Lou had no idea. The saleswoman had to tell him where to look. "Size eight," Lou told her.

"Eight." The woman twisted her hair around her hand while she thought. Then she released her hold and let it fall loose. "Holly Spritzer," she said. "Or maybe Joan Robinson, but I think she took the six."

"You sold only one in each size?"

She gave him a trifling smile. "For any given style, there *is* only one Carin in each size."

He wasn't impressed, although he was fairly certain she expected him to be. "You wouldn't happen to have a phone number or address for either of the ladies, would you?"

"Of course." She went to the desk, hit a couple of keys on the computer, and wrote the information out for him on the back of a business card. "Holly was just in here yesterday. It's so weird that her dress would be part of a murder."

Lou heaved a sigh of relief when he exited the store. He should have let Keating handle it. He couldn't remember the last time he'd seen Keating look uncomfortable.

Lou picked up his cell phone to call Holly Spritzer, then realized he'd have trouble describing the dress, beyond the obvious. She might well own more than one black dress. So he drove to her place instead.

It was a lovely home near the Claremont Country Club. The woman who answered the door appeared to be in her late forties. She was fashionably dressed and had honey-blond, chin-length hair that probably cost her both time and money, but the image was marred by her scowl.

"No solicitors," she snapped. "Didn't you see the sign?"

Lou pulled out his badge. "I'm a detective with the Oakland Police Department."

She squinted at it and then at him. Her expression never softened. "What can I do for you?"

He held out the dress. "This look familiar to you?"

"It looks like the Carin I bought last summer." She examined the hem. "It *is* my dress. See, there's a grease stain that wouldn't come out." Her frown deepened. "What are you doing with it?"

Lou had questions of his own. "When did you last see the dress?"

She shrugged. "I donated it to one of those thrift shops. The Salvation Army, I believe. In the fall. Only wore it the one time. Some idiot sitting next to me slopped mayonnaise into my lap."

Lou groaned inwardly. This whole thing with the dress had been a long shot from the start. Now it looked impossible. How would they ever trace a dress through the Salvation Army? Still, he hadn't expected to get as far as he had, and it was an avenue that couldn't be ignored. You never knew what detail was going to break a case.

He hit all three of the Salvation Army stores in the East Bay and struck out, just as he expected. No one remembered the dress, and none of the stores kept track of inventory. But at least they knew their killer shopped at thrift stores. That was something.

It wasn't yet five, but Lou decided to call it a day. It was Saturday, after all. And his back was killing him. He wanted to go home, put ice on it and settle in with a beer.

He got to the nursing home earlier than usual and was surprised to find someone sitting in the chair by Jan's bed.

It took a moment before he recognized who it was. "Nikki. What are you doing here?"

"Hi, Daddy. It's nice to see you, too." The sarcasm was unmistakable, but for once she sounded more amused than angry.

"Why didn't you tell me you were coming?" Los Angeles wasn't exactly within "drop by" vicinity.

"I need to clear it with you before I can visit Mom?"

"That's not what I meant." Though Lou realized that on some level he probably did. Shouldn't a daughter forfeit some rights when she thumbed her nose at everything her parents had taught her?

"Anyway, I did try calling. You weren't home."

Lou stood with his hands at his side. He felt awkward, as he often did around Nikki. She'd been a pretty girl. A little pudgy maybe, but with her mother's soft eyes and the even white smile of an orthodontia graduate. Now, at twenty-five, she was rail thin. A brittle-looking bottle blonde with dark roots and enough body piercings to set off a metal detector. Lou noticed the flash of silver on her tongue, something he hadn't remembered from the last time they'd seen each other. He averted his eyes in disgust.

"You've got my work number," he said.

She shrugged. "I'm not sure I do anymore. How's Mom? Any change?"

"What's it look like?" His sore back and the surprise of running into Nikki made his tone shorter than he intended.

"Yeah, I guess it was a dumb question." Nikki looked over at Jan, and her chin quivered.

Lou felt a surge of affection for his daughter. "Why don't you come to the house for dinner? Or we can go out, if you'd prefer. That's probably a better idea given my skill in the kitchen."

"Sorry. Willy and I have tickets for Incubus tonight. That's why we're here."

*Willy.* The lazy, no-good, college dropout who had moved in with his daughter almost a year ago. Lou suspected Nikki was supporting him as well as sleeping with him. He couldn't decide which angered him more.

"Meet me for breakfast then," Lou suggested.

"Sorry, we're going back first thing tomorrow."

"You flew up from L.A. just for a concert?" Lou realized too late that it sounded like a reprimand. Mostly he was hurt she hadn't told him she was coming.

Her tone, in response, was cool. "Frequent flyer miles, Daddy. It didn't cost us a cent."

Lou pulled a chair from the hallway and sat at the foot of Jan's bed. Maybe he'd relate better if he wasn't towering over Nikki. He bit back his hurt and anger. "How are things going for you, honey?"

"Fine. Really good, in fact. I got a promotion. Production assistant."

"Great." He had no idea what a production assistant did. "Is it interesting work?"

"For now. How about you?"

"Yeah, things are, you know"—he shrugged—"about as good as can be expected."

"Bodies keep dropping, huh?"

"Afraid so."

They talked for a few minutes about Jan's health, then Nikki stood to leave. As she squeezed past him in the narrow space next to the hospital bed, she stopped to kiss him on the cheek. "Maybe you could come to L.A. and visit me," she said.

"Sure, as soon as I have some time."

She turned at the doorway and waved. "I'd really like it if you did."

When she was gone, Lou touched his cheek where she'd kissed him.

Bryce Keating rubbed his eyes. He was reading the words just fine, but they wouldn't stick. It was all a jumble of names and dates. Maureen Oliver had done a good job of collecting information about Bailey and Parkhurst. Everything from where they got their hair done to the stores they frequented. So far, he hadn't found a common thread.

The phone rang and Keating picked it up.

"Are you the one I should talk to about the reward?"

"What?" Keating had been only half listening.

"You know, that woman was killed. Got a handout here says there's a reward."

Keating was instantly alert. "For information leading to the arrest and conviction of her killer, yes. You know something?"

"I mighta seen someone in the parking lot that night."

"Might have or did?"

"I did see someone, absolutely. How much money we talking about?"

The initial surge of hope was quickly fading. "What's your name?"

"John Jones."

Yeah, sure. "Where can I reach you, Mr. Jones?"

"Uh . . ." The caller read out a number, stumbling once in the process. "It's kinda hard to catch me, though. I'm not here real often."

"Tell me what you saw."

"A car, man. And this dude kinda hanging around, like he was up to no good."

"Did you see him with a woman?"

"Yeah." The caller grew more animated. "He was kinda following her."

"And then?"

"That's all I seen."

"What kind of car?"

"Uh, old. Not real old, but not new either. And it was a van, not a car."

"Make? Model? Color?"

"Gray. Or maybe dirty white. It was night, you know."

"Big? Minivan? It would help if you could give us a few details."

The caller was quiet a moment, and Keating wondered if he was trying to remember or simply fabricating details out of thin air. "More like a panel truck, I guess. It had those two doors at the back instead of a hatch. And something hanging from the rearview mirror."

"How about the man," Keating asked. "Can you describe him?"

"Six feet, about. Maybe early twenties. Caucasian."

"What kind of build?"

"Average. Big through the chest and shoulders, though, like he was some mean punk."

"Any distinguishing marks or traits?"

"Like what?"

"I don't know, like maybe he walked with a limp. Or had a gold tooth."

The caller took his time thinking about it, but came up with nothing. "It was dark," he explained. "He mighta had those things and I just missed them."

Keating's head was beginning to hurt. "Okay, Mr. Jones. We appreciate your call. You think of anything else, let us know."

"What about my money?"

"We'll be in touch."

Keating filled out a form and tossed it into the special hotline basket, along with the other useless tips. Later, he'd enter the name and information into his own personal database. No doubt *someone* out there had seen their killer the night he grabbed Anne Bailey in the drugstore parking lot, maybe even Mr. Jones. But unless that person could give them something solid to go on, the tip wasn't going to prove particularly useful.

Keating went back to his notes, then gave up. Working weekends didn't bother him, especially when he was on a pressing case, but he hated spinning his wheels. They needed a break, and they needed it soon.

Before the killer stuck again.

Keating was feeling antsy. He wondered if there was any legitimate excuse to call Kali. He couldn't think of one.

Why hadn't he spoken up yesterday on the drive back from Dunworthy's? An offhand suggestion of coffee, or maybe dinner and a movie. Yesterday it would have been natural, but at the last minute on a Saturday evening . . . that wasn't the same thing at all.

Without thinking, Keating ran his thumb along the base of his left ring finger. Warm flesh instead of the once-familiar metal band. You'd think by now he'd no longer expect the ring, but somehow its absence always caught him by surprise.

He pushed back his chair, grabbed his jacket and headed for the Marquis. Maybe he'd get lucky. If he was desperate, there was always his little black book.

Inside, the air was thick with smoke and booze, this despite California law forbidding smoking in public places. Keating took a seat at the bar, ordered a beer, and checked out the action. For one brief moment he saw a woman across the room who might have been Kali, and his gut tightened. But when she turned, he saw they looked nothing alike.

He tried to work up some enthusiasm for approaching one of the two women sitting at the bar alone, but it seemed liked work, so he ordered another beer instead. He must be coming down with a cold or something.

Keating was lost in his own thoughts and didn't notice the young woman who slipped onto the stool next to him until she shoved a bowl of mixed nuts in his direction.

"Help yourself," she said, and smiled at him. Her complexion was rough, as though she'd had a bad case of acne as a child. It gave her a hardened look, but she wasn't unattractive.

"Thanks." He picked out a cashew and smiled back. It was an automatic response.

"My name's Linda."

"Nice to meet you, Linda." He was gradually falling into step. It was a dance he could do in his sleep.

"So what's your name?"

"Bryce."

"Like the canyon?"

"Yep. I've always been glad my parents went for that instead of Zion."

It took a moment, and then she laughed. Her lips were naturally thin, and he could see that she'd used lip pencil to paint them fuller. "I've seen you in here before," she said.

"You have?"

"Yeah, I come here with girlfriends pretty regular. They're all busy tonight."

"How come you're not?"

She made a face. "I got stood up."

"Can't imagine why a guy would pass on an evening with

you." The words tumbled out. Bryce felt like he was reading the lines in a bad play.

Linda gave him another smile. Her eyes were a mink brown, and very inviting. "What do you do for a living, Bryce?"

"I'm a cop." Most women were impressed, but not all. Tonight, Bryce didn't really care.

"For real?"

"Yeah."

"No, I don't believe you." She smiled flirtatiously. "Prove it to me."

What the hell? He showed her his badge.

"You got a gun, too?"

He opened his jacket to allow a glimpse of his shoulder holster.

"Guess I'm safe sitting here with you." She punctuated the words with just enough eye contact to make the double meaning clear.

"Absolutely safe," Bryce said. He was beginning to tire of the game already. Linda was a lot safer than she thought. "What's your line of work?" he asked.

"I'm a teacher. Third grade. Not very exciting, I know. Some of my friends are dot-commers. That's much sexier."

"But *you're* sexy," he said. It was the required line, and he delivered it without thinking.

"Am I?" She touched his knee and let her hand linger there. He could feel himself respond. But he wasn't interested.

He squeezed her hand and moved it back to her own lap. "You're very sexy, Linda, but you got me at a bad time."

"You still getting over someone?"

He shook his head. Kali's image flashed in his mind. "Just the opposite."

# CHAPTER 21

Kali got into work late Monday morning. She and Margot had gone to an arts fund-raiser Sunday evening—one of Margot's clients had offered free tickets—and they'd both had way too much champagne. Kali might not have pulled herself from bed at all if Loretta hadn't made such a pitiful plea for human activity.

Kali signed in, then stopped to confer with Gloria.

"Bryce Keating called," Gloria told her. "And someone named Hannah Slade. She said she needed to see you as soon as possible. I set an appointment for ten. Your calendar looked clear then." Gloria paused, then added with a touch of apology, "I expected you'd be in before now."

"Ten is fine." Although it gave Kali less than fifteen minutes to prepare for the visit. "Did Ms. Slade say why she wanted to see me?"

"Only that she'd read about the recent murders, seen your name in the paper, and needed to talk to you."

Kali's office had been closed up by the cleaning crew over the weekend. The blinds were drawn so that no outside light came in. She flipped on the switch and immediately headed for the window. When she turned back toward her desk, she muffled a yelp. Sitting there next to the blotter was an arrangement of yellow tulips in a clear glass vase.

She buzzed Gloria. "Where did the flowers come from?"

"Oh, I forgot to tell you. They were delivered Friday. After you'd gone. I put them in water so they wouldn't wilt. Is there anything left to them?"

The petals were, in fact, tight. Objectively, it was a lovely bouquet. "They're fine," Kali said, still feeling the shock of finding yellow flowers in her office. The box they'd arrived in was on her desk. She found the card and opened it with a shaking hand. *"Thanks for a great evening, Nathan."*

She relaxed, but only marginally.

It was a sweet gesture, she told herself. Romantic even. And they were tulips, not roses. But they were yellow, and that left her feeling queasy.

She moved the flowers to the narrow bookshelf behind her desk, where she wouldn't be constantly staring at them. She was crumpling up florist's tissue when Gloria ushered Hannah Slade into the office.

Kali held out a hand and introduced herself. "Can I get you some coffee or a soda?"

"No, thank you." Hannah Slade was barely out of her teens, with short black hair and heavy-frame glasses. Attractive in a no-nonsense sort of way. She took a seat where Kali indicated, perching on the edge of her chair as though she'd been summoned to Kali's office against her will.

"What can I do for you?" Kali asked.

Hannah appeared nervous. She rubbed her thumbs together. "About those two women who were murdered . . ."

"You know something that might help us?" Kali felt a surge of adrenaline.

"No, not really. It's just that I was hoping . . ." She stopped, took a breath and started over. "Slade is my married name. My family name is Gilchrist. Wendy was my sister."

Wendy Gilchrist, fifth and last of the Bayside Strangler's victims. One of the murders of which Dwayne Allen Davis had been acquitted.

Kali vaguely remembered seeing a younger sister at the trial, two of them in fact. Wendy's parents had appeared in court every day, but they'd kept the children away until the very end, when the jury returned. In the fevered pitch of tension that preceded the reading of the verdict, Kali had caught a glimpse of the family sitting in the gallery. But what she recalled most vividly was the anguished cry from Wendy's mother at the words "not guilty." Kali remembered thinking it a cruel twist of fate that Wendy's parents had tried to spare their children the grisly details of their sister's murder, and had given them instead a ringside seat to something equally painful.

"I'm sorry," Kali said. "I imagine these last years haven't been easy for you."

"Worse than you can imagine. My father died a year after the trial. Died of grief, my mother always says. It's true, I think. He pretty much lost interest in everything after that. My younger sister had a hard time too. She got into drugs, petty crime. She's more or less disappeared from our lives at this point."

The ripple effect of crime. There were always more victims than people realized. But Hannah didn't appear to be one of them. "How about you? Have you managed to make a life for yourself?"

"I saw a good therapist."

"I'm glad you were able to get help."

A thin smile. "Me too." She looked Kali in the eye. "The truth is, I hated Wendy. I was jealous of her because she always got the attention. She was prettier, smarter—"

"Older."

"I wanted to hurt her." Hannah's eyes grew glassy with tears. The girl with the good shrink disappeared, and in her place was a young woman weighted with guilt. "I did hurt her, too. Wendy only went out that night because I told her a lie. I said I had seen this guy she liked with another girl."

"Hannah—"

She held up a hand. "I said I had a good therapist, and I meant it. It will always be there, what I did to her, but I'm learning to live my life in spite of that. Which is sort of why I'm here."

Kali waited for Hannah to continue.

"News accounts of the recent murders keep referring to the Bayside Strangler. They say the murders are like the ones he committed."

"There are some similarities," Kali said carefully.

"Similarities?"

"Right. Little things that appear similar to what we found with the Bayside Strangler. The yellow rose, for instance. And the love note."

"But Wendy never got a note. Not that we knew about."

Kali nodded. "That's what makes this so hard. The earlier murders weren't identical, but there were key elements that tied them together. Some of those same elements have shown up in the recent deaths as well."

"So there's a chance that Dwayne Davis wasn't"—she swallowed and took a breath—"he wasn't the Bayside Strangler?"

So that was why Hannah Slade had come to see her. She wanted assurance that her sister's killer wasn't still out there.

Kali felt a wash of sympathy for the young woman. "At the time of the trial, I was convinced Davis was guilty, and nothing has made me change my mind. Owen Nelson feels the same way."

"Then why—"

"I suspect we're dealing with what we call a copycat killer."

Hannah's dark eyes narrowed in thought. "You mean someone who wants to make it look like Dwayne Davis is doing the killing?"

"More or less."

"But Davis is dead. How is framing him going to help the killer get away with it?"

"I don't think it's about escaping detection," Kali said.

"What's the purpose then?"

"It's complicated. And I don't claim to be an expert." Kali spread her hands on her desk. "But I'm guessing our current killer gets a feeling of power from copying the Bayside Strangler. Those murders made headlines for months. The trial was big news too. Then there was the book and the movie. I think he might simply like being part of the action, so to speak."

"He's doing it for the attention?"

"That's certainly part of it. He clearly *wants* us to see the connection with the Bayside Strangler case. And he's enjoying the gamesmanship of the chase."

Hannah shivered. "That's so disgusting. Thinking of killing as a game."

"I agree. But he isn't the first."

"These murders have stirred things up again for us. My mother, especially, is very upset. Not that we'd gotten over Wendy's death, especially since Davis wasn't actually convicted of her murder . . . but with his execution we felt some closure. Now it's, like, right there in our face again. My mother is reliving the whole nightmare, and I'm not doing so great either."

"I wish there were something I could do to make it easier on you."

Hannah took a breath. "Do you think you'll catch him?"

Kali's public persona would have responded with confidence, but Hannah Slade deserved an honest answer. "I don't know," she said. "And I don't know if we'll catch him in time."

"Before he kills someone else, you mean?"

Kali nodded.

During the course of their conversation, Hannah had slowly relaxed into the chair. Now she sat forward again. She brought her hand to her face, pressing her knuckles against her lips. "It's just so weird. Did you know the Bailey woman was murdered on the anniversary of Wendy's death?"

Kali sucked in her breath. At one time she'd known the date of Wendy's murder, and the four others, but not anymore. And despite their looking for parallels, neither Kali nor the detectives had thought to check the dates. How could they have missed something so obvious?

"Do you think he did that on purpose?" Hannah asked. "Part of the copycat thing?"

"It could be. I hadn't thought about the timing of the murders." She wondered if the date of Jane Parkhurst's death was equally significant.

Hannah stood. "Thank you for seeing me. It was my mother, really, who pushed me to talk to you, but I'm glad I did. We were worried there'd been a mistake. That Davis wasn't . . . That the real killer had come back."

Kali handed Hannah a business card. "Feel free to call me any time."

When Hannah had gone, Kali returned Bryce Keating's call from earlier that morning. He was out, so she left a message. Then she dug out the dates of the five Bayside Strangler murders. They'd occurred over an eight-month period, but none of them matched the date of the Parkhurst murder.

Kali poured herself a cup of coffee and sat at her desk mulling over the troublesome issue Hannah's visit had raised. What were the odds that two similar murders would occur on the same date simply by chance? Kali wasn't a statistician, but the odds had to be pretty slim. That meant their killer had made a conscious decision about when to start his murder spree.

Why choose the date of Wendy Gilchrist's murder, though, and not one of the others? Maybe because it was the last of the

Bayside Strangler killings. Picking up where the others left off, so to speak. Or maybe because her murder hadn't been pinned on Davis, at least not in court. And one thing Kali knew for sure about their killer was that he enjoyed taunting them.

It was possible, too, that the dates of the other four Strangler murders were important and she just didn't see how yet. Phases of the moon? Evening temperatures?

Or perhaps there was something about Wendy Gilchrist and/or her murder that appealed to their killer. Kali kept coming back to Dunworthy's theory that their killer felt some personal tie to the Strangler. What if the connection was to Wendy Gilchrist and not the Strangler?

She chewed on the possible significance of dates, noting days of the week and timing between murders in the margin of her notes. The days were random as far as she could tell. The timing was too. Five months between the first and second; two-and-a-half months between the second and third; only ten days between the third and the fourth; and then three weeks until Wendy Gilchrist's murder.

She remembered Dunworthy explaining that thrill killers often experienced an increasing and heightened urge to kill again. It was almost as though once they'd opened the door by acting on their fantasy, there was no holding back. They often tried, Dunworthy said, but the compulsion to kill became stronger with each "success."

And yet, Kali noted, the interval between the fourth and fifth murders was actually longer than between the third and fourth.

Unless you removed Wendy Gilchrist from the calculations. Kali sat forward, suddenly energized. Discounting Wendy's death, the interval between each murder was approximately half of the previous one. If she were to graph the acceleration, it wouldn't be a perfectly smooth slope, but the pattern was clear. Was that because Wendy's killer was someone other than Davis?

Kali's assurances to Hannah Slade seemed suddenly hollow. Perhaps she'd spoken too hastily.

Wendy Gilchrist's murder had always been problematic. At seventeen, she was younger than the other victims, although she hadn't looked it. There'd been no note sent with the rose, and no dog collar around her neck. But there'd been no dog collar with the first victim, Joanna Paget, either. They'd theorized it was a touch Davis added after the first murder, and then, for some reason, overlooked with Wendy Gilchrist.

But the rest of it fit. She'd been strangled, though it appeared her killer had used something softer than rope. Her body had been found near an overflowing trash can in a secluded area of the UC Berkeley campus. And like the other victims, she'd been dressed provocatively.

Unlike the other victims, however, Wendy Gilchrist had not been raped. Neither had Anne or Jane Parkhurst. What's more, none of the three had been posed in the same degrading fashion as the first four Strangler victims. Dunworthy had said that was important, as she recalled.

A knot formed in Kali's stomach as a new thought took hold. Was it possible the Bayside Strangler had been not one individual, but two? Two separate killers who by plan or happenstance followed a similar pattern in their attacks?

The sound of her own pulse echoed in her ears. She needed to talk to Owen.

When Kali reached Owen's office, she caught him about to leave for a meeting with his campaign staff.

"I was hoping to talk with you," she said.

He glanced at his Rolex. "I've got a few minutes still. What's up?"

"Wendy Gilchrist."

"The Bayside Strangler's last victim?" He'd placed the name immediately. "What about her?"

"Her sister came to see me this morning. She was troubled by news reports playing up the similarities between those murders and the recent ones."

The fan of wrinkles at the outer corners of Owen's eyes grew more pronounced. "We are all troubled by the similarities."

"She pointed out that Anne's murder occurred on the same date her sister's did, eight years ago. I'm thinking the timing has to be somehow significant."

"We know the killer wants us to make the connection with the Bayside Strangler murders." Owen's tone was deliberately cautious.

"But what if the jury was right in acquitting Davis of Wendy Gilchrist's murder? What if there was a second killer operating at the same time, and he's resurfaced?"

"Eight years later?"

She knew it wasn't a scenario Owen was eager to embrace. On the other hand, he'd hired her because he wanted an investigation that was above politics. "If you look at the dates of the Strangler murders," she said, "it's clear the interval between killings is less with each one, except for the last—Wendy Gilchrist's."

"Killers aren't robots, Kali. You have to look at general trends and not get too caught up in minor deviations."

"Also, the murders we're dealing with now are more like Wendy Gilchrist's than the others."

"How so?"

"No dog collar, for one. And the poem sent to the police after her death wasn't haiku as I recall."

Owen raked a hand over his cheek. "No offense, Kali, but you put too much store in this poetry business. Nobody but you even recognized the poems were haiku."

"She wasn't raped either."

"No, but she had her period, right? Wasn't that how we dealt with that discrepancy?"

Kali nodded. Owen's calm made her reconsider. Had she been too quick to see meaning where there wasn't any? "You think I'm off the mark, then?"

"Jesus, a second killer." Owen raked a hand through the silver hair at his temples. "There was talk about that at the time of the trial."

And the prosecution had effectively countered it.

"I guess it can't hurt to quietly explore the possibility," Owen said, after a moment. His voice was low and throaty. "Maybe look at some names the cops had before they zeroed in on Davis. I hope you'll be careful though"—he paused and cleared his throat—"extremely careful not to make it appear we're now looking at someone other than Davis as the Bayside Strangler."

Even though they both knew in their hearts it might be a possibility, no matter how slight. Owen's expression was set, and ever so slightly guarded. Not one Kali had seen him wear before.

What would Owen do if faced with credible evidence that Davis wasn't the right man? What would *she* do?

And what would happen with the election? Owen was, to Kali's mind, the best candidate by far for governor. Her support of his candidacy went beyond loyalty to a friend and mentor. Owen had the integrity and foresight California so badly needed. Qualities so lacking in his opponents that it was frightening. Owen had to win the primary.

In theory, Owen's role in putting Davis away shouldn't be an issue, but Kali knew how it would play out in the press and in people's minds if it turned out Davis was innocent.

"I'll be careful," she said.

"I know you will. That's why I asked you to do the job you're doing." He picked up his briefcase and pushed back his chair. "Sorry, but I need to get going."

Kali walked with him to the elevator. "How's the campaigning?"

He grimaced. "Being governor, should I be so lucky, will be a piece of cake compared to running for office." And then he laughed. "But neither is as hard as being a father."

"Alex giving you trouble again?"

"Not trouble really, but I certainly can't do anything right."

She smiled. "My only experience in that regard is as a kid, but I gather tension between parents and kids is a fairly universal phenomenon."

Owen's expression registered skepticism. "I think Alex takes it into new territory."

Kali returned to her office just as the phone on her direct line was ringing. It was Bryce Keating.

"We traced the dress Jane Parkhurst was wearing," he told her. "It's some exclusive designer type, only one made in each size. The woman who bought it got a stain on the dress and gave it to the Salvation Army." Keating's voice carried a hint of disdain. "So we know where our killer shops, though we haven't been able to take it any further."

"There can't be many designer dresses sold at Salvation Army stores."

"No, but the salesclerks don't pay a lot of attention to people's purchases, either."

Nor, Kali imagined, would they recognize a designer dress if they saw one. She certainly hadn't.

"We've asked them to keep an eye out in the future," Keating said. "For all the good it will do."

"In Davis's case we managed to find several purchases he'd made through catalogues like Victoria's Secret. They matched some of the clothing found on the victims. But that was all after the fact, in preparation for trial." Kali paused, her conversation with Owen still fresh in her mind. "Are the case files from the Bayside Strangler investigation still around?"

"I don't know. They must be, but no place readily accessible."

"The lead detective on the case, Sam Eastman. I know he's retired now. I don't suppose you know how to reach him?"

"As a matter of fact, I do. He moved up to the Truckee area. Why?"

"No reason, really. Just thinking about the parallels, then and now." She wrote *Truckee* on a message slip. It was a long drive, probably easier to call. "I had a visit today from the sister of Wendy Gilchrist, the last Strangler victim."

"Any particular reason?"

"She wanted reassurance, I think, that her sister's killer wasn't still out there."

"Understandable."

"She raised an interesting point, though. Anne's murder took place on the anniversary of Wendy Gilchrist's death." When Keating didn't respond, she added, "In some ways our recent murders are more like Wendy Gilchrist's than the other four Strangler victims'."

"How's that?"

Kali went through the same explanation she'd given Owen. "I'm not sure what it all means, though. Maybe it was the Gilchrist murder that struck a chord with our killer, not the Strangler himself. Or even . . ." Kali paused, then pushed ahead. "There was some speculation during the Davis trial that the Strangler murders were the work of two different killers."

"That's why you were asking about Eastman."

The man was quick.

There was a moment's silence during which it sounded as though Keating was getting ready to say something more; then, abruptly, he ended the conversation with a "Got to run, talk to you later," and was gone.

In the late afternoon, Kali finally reached Sam Eastman. The first time she'd called, no one answered. The second time, his wife said he was asleep. On the third call, however, Sam Eastman answered the phone himself. Kali remembered him from the trial, a burly man with deep-set eyes and weathered skin. The sort of cop who could intimidate a suspect just by looking at him. She was surprised that he remembered her, as well.

"Sure, there were two of you gals as I recall."

Kali found his terminology amusing, though she knew women who would have called him on it in an instant.

"And a young black man. I always suspected Owen had him on board to counter the defense's race argument."

Corey Redmond, who'd married money and traded the practice of law for a seat on the boards of several family-owned companies. Last she'd heard, he had twin daughters and his own jet.

"The other woman on the team was murdered recently," Kali said.

"Really? Sorry to hear that. What happened?"

She gave him an overview of the murders.

"I heard something about that on the news."

"It's actually why I'm calling."

"A Bayside Strangler copycat, huh?"

"It looks that way. Unless maybe he was working in tandem with Davis all along."

"Nah, Davis would have turned him over to us if that were the case. Maybe even saved his neck in the deal."

Kali hesitated. "Assuming he knew who the other killer was."

"You saying you think Davis was good for only some of the crimes?"

"What I think is that we need to consider every possibility. Were there other suspects you looked at before arresting Davis?"

"Absolutely. We only latched onto Davis because of a lucky break."

The necklace they'd found in the car when they stopped him for suspicion of driving under the influence.

"I remember we questioned a number of people, even explored the possibility that Davis hadn't acted alone. But in the end, we were sure Davis was the right man. Still," he continued, "it's not a bad idea, looking at the other suspects. I remember one case we had years ago where one of our suspects in an earlier murder turned around three years later and killed a woman he did gardening for. It's always bothered me that maybe we planted the seed in his mind by questioning him as a murder suspect."

That was a permutation Kali hadn't considered. It presented an interesting possibility, especially in light of what Dunworthy had said about the killer having ties to the Strangler case. There was nothing like being a potential suspect to make the crimes seem personal.

"Do you remember the names of other suspects you looked at in the Bayside Strangler case?"

"This will be a test of the old gray cells." Eastman laughed. "Let me think a minute. One was a sex offender, which is how we first picked him up. Robert O'Dell, I believe was the name. We looked at him quite seriously. There were also two brothers. Silva was the last name. First names went together, Larry and Barry, if my memory serves. There were others along the way, but those were the serious contenders. All that was before we stumbled onto Davis, of course. Once we had him, all bets were off."

Kali jotted down the names. "How about members of the public who showed particular interest in the investigation? Maybe a volunteer or a concerned citizen?"

"The whole damned county showed interest. If people weren't calling us with advice, they were calling with questions. It was probably the most chaotic investigation I ever worked on."

"I take it, then, that none stood out?"

"Afraid not. Say, Owen Nelson's really gone places, hasn't he? Wouldn't that be something if he were the next governor of California. You think he stands a chance?"

"A good chance." If the Bayside Strangler case didn't come back to haunt him.

"Got remarried, I hear. Not too long ago."

"Last September."

"Well, good for him. It was a terrible thing his wife dying while the trial was going on. I mean, terrible that she died at all, but I admire the dedication he showed in finishing the trial."

Owen hadn't really had a choice about seeing the trial through to the end, though his focus and determination under such trying circumstances amazed Kali, too. But that was how some people, particularly men, handled pain. They ignored it. There were times Kali envied them that.

# CHAPTER 22

Lou Fortune spread the sketch artist's composites across his desk. Three drawings, and none of them looked like the same guy. Lou was willing to bet none of them looked much like the killer, either. He had suspected all along that, as a witness, Mrs. Greene would fall short when pushed for details. Her window was too far from Jane Parkhurst's house to give her a good look at the man even if her eyesight and memory were to be trusted. Still, her sighting of a "suspicious male" was noteworthy in a case where they had damn little else to go on.

He'd used their best sketch artist, a man who knew how to probe a witness's memory for forgotten details. Lou had instructed him to take his time. The three separate sketches spoke to the care he'd taken. Unfortunately, they also spoke to the muddle of Mrs. Greene's observational skills.

He studied the drawings again. White male, that was something useful anyway. When Lou looked closely, he could see all three had similar faces—wide and full. And all of the sketches depicted a fringe of hair at the nape of the neck poking out from under the baseball cap. Their suspect, if that's what he was, wore his hair on the long side. Beyond the obvious, however, the drawings differed widely. In one, the eyes were narrow and closely set; in another they were round with heavy lids. One had a pointy chin while the other two depicted a much squarer jaw. No way they were going to find the man on the basis of these drawings.

Lou had checked with both the utilities district and Pacific Gas & Electric. Neither had reported any workmen in the neighborhood during the time Mrs. Greene had spotted the man she found suspicious. That still left everything from tree trimming to road work, however, or even a FedEx driver who happened to be wearing an orange vest. Plenty of opportunity for legitimate activity.

But it could also have been someone up to no good, just as Mrs. Greene thought. It couldn't hurt to show the sketches around the neighborhood, Lou decided.

He turned to Keating. "Hey, Bryce. What d'ya think the odds are that Mrs. Greene actually got a look at our killer?"

Keating was writing intently and didn't bother to look up. "Doesn't matter the odds. Even if she did, it's not going to help us find the guy."

How could a man abduct and murder two women, and not be seen? It was like he was invisible or something. Which brought Lou back to the orange vest. People didn't notice workmen, and didn't think anything of them when they did notice. Not actually invisible, but pretty damned close.

Lou gathered the sketches. "I think I'll see if these ring a bell with any of the other neighbors. You want to come along?"

"You go on. I want to talk to a couple of the early Bayside Strangler suspects."

Lou stood slowly, pressing a hand against his lower spine where the muscles were still tight, and ran Keating's words through his mind a second time. "Didn't know we were looking at them," he said after a moment.

Keating shrugged. "Kali's got a theory that our murders have a lot in common with the last Strangler murder, which was different than the others. It's also one Davis dodged."

Kali again. Lou noticed how Keating rolled his voice around the name. He'd only been partnered with the man six months, but that was long enough to recognize the signs. Keating was looking to put another mark on his scorecard. Lou sometimes suspected Keating's womanizing was more show than substance. He wore his reputation like a badge of honor, and cultivated it at every opportunity. Maybe he actually liked the image, but Lou noticed it was also a way for Keating to keep himself emotionally distant.

"You're thinking the last victim might be the work of our killer?"

"It's a theory."

A fairly farfetched one, Lou thought. "Keep me posted."

"Will do."

Lou turned to leave. "And take it slow, will you? She's a fucking DA, remember?"

Keating tapped his pen against his palm, a glint of amusement in his eye. "You've got a dirty mind, Lou."

"Yeah? Well, I know where I got it."

The phone rang and Keating looked at Lou. "You in or out?"

"Depends on who it is." For a brief second, he thought it might even be Nikki, although he hadn't the foggiest notion where he'd gotten that idea.

Keating picked up and immediately made a face. "Listen, Jackson," he said after a moment, "we're running an investigation here, not writing a gossip column. When we've got an announcement to make, you'll hear about it."

Lou slid out the door before Keating found some excuse to pass the call off on him.

It was late afternoon, almost time for her scheduled coffee break, when Mitsu Yamamoto noticed a man picking through the rack of women's lingerie. It wasn't unheard of to see men buying women's clothing. She saw more of that here at the Salvation Army store than she had when she worked at Penney's in the mall. She probably wouldn't have thought twice about it if a memo hadn't gone around asking employees to keep an eye out for just this very thing.

Mitsu was at the cash register, waiting on a toothless woman buying a bathrobe and slippers, but she kept her eye on the man in lingerie. He didn't look particularly sinister or dangerous, just a little odd with his thin, fox-like face and prominent Adam's apple. Most likely he was buying a gift for his wife or girlfriend. Or even himself. Since moving to the Bay Area, Mitsu had run across her share of cross-dressers.

She didn't know why the police wanted to be notified about a man buying women's clothing, and she wasn't sure how she felt about getting involved. This was America, after all, where people had a right to privacy. Maybe it didn't apply to shopping, but she didn't see why not.

On the other hand, the police wouldn't be involved if it wasn't important. A big shoplifting ring maybe. Or something to do with drugs. She'd read that a lot of crimes were drug related.

Mitsu wasn't supposed to leave her post at the register, especially with a line of customers waiting to be rung up, so what could she do, anyway? Still, something about the man kept drawing her eyes back.

She could see that he had chosen a black slip and bra, and had now moved on to the rack of blouses and tops. He must have felt her watching because he turned suddenly and looked straight at her. His eyes were beady and dark, like an animal's. Mitsu shivered. She looked around for one of the other clerks, but they were all occupied and oblivious to the sighting of a man the police might be looking for.

Finally, she caught the eye of Thomas, who was carrying a customer's bookshelf to the front of the store. When he'd set it by the door, he followed the woman to the register and handed Mitsu the sales tag.

"Call the police," she whispered.

"Huh?"

"The police. Didn't you see the memo?"

He looked around. "What memo?"

It was useless. She was probably the only person in the store who'd taken the time to read the thing.

The woman with the bookshelf drummed her fingers on the countertop with impatience. She looked like the type who expected royal service wherever she went. "Is something the matter?" she asked, none too kindly.

Mitsu shook her head and rang up the purchase. Thomas scratched his chin. "Who'd you want me to call?"

"Never mind."

The man from lingerie kept glancing her way every few minutes, which made Mitsu nervous.

There *was* something strange about him, she decided. It was his manner as much as his appearance. Besides, the police wouldn't have gone to all this trouble if it wasn't an important case. What if she let this guy get away and later found out he committed some horrible crime? She wouldn't be able to live with herself.

Mitsu looked back toward the spot where she'd last seen the man. He was gone. She felt a flutter in her stomach.

Then, out of the corner of her eye she caught a flash of him leaving the store. His jacket bulged on one side where he'd no doubt stuffed the articles of clothing he'd been carrying.

"Stop! Thief!" She pointed toward the door. Mitsu thought she'd yelled loudly, but only a few people turned to look at her, and no one made a move to assist. Before she had time to think about it, she tossed the bookshelf woman's purchase receipt across the counter and shouted at Joyce to cover the register. Then she raced out the door in pursuit.

The man walked rapidly, and when he saw that she was following him, he picked up his pace to a trot. He crossed against the light, narrowly escaping collision with a fast-moving truck, and ducked around the corner. Mitsu reached the corner herself, just in time to see him pull away in a dirty white Econoline van with a dented fender. The car sped down the block before she could read the whole license plate but she caught the beginning and committed it to memory.

Kali had never been partial to color-coded organizational schemes. She'd had friends in college who used variously hued index cards when they researched papers, and she knew lawyers who plotted their trial strategy with colored ink, but Kali generally found the fewer the distractions, the clearer her thoughts. She'd been staring at her notes all morning, however, looking for patterns and connections she'd missed, and growing increasingly desperate. Finally, she picked up a red pen and began scribbling.

Why choose the anniversary of Wendy Gilchrist's murder? First possibility was that Wendy's killer was responsible for the two recent murders, as well. And the eight-year moratorium? The most likely explanation was prison. Perhaps he'd been picked up on an unrelated charge and only just released. Kali was anxious to hear what Keating had learned about the names she'd gotten from Eastman.

The second possibility was that there was something about the Gilchrist murder that was meaningful to their killer.

If only she had some clue what that was.

Kali pressed her palms to her temples and sighed. There were so many possibilities—a likeness in Wendy to someone their killer knew, a television account that touched a raw nerve with him. Or maybe his mother's name was Wendy. Hadn't Dunworthy said that serial killers were often acting out the unresolved conflicts of their childhood? Unless she was inside the head of the killer, she had no way of knowing why Wendy's murder was significant to him.

She glanced at the clock and was gratified to see that it was time to meet Keating. As she grabbed her coat and purse, the vase of tulips caught her eye. She made a mental note to get rid of them when she returned. Nathan would never know.

When she got outside, Bryce Keating was parked at the curb, waiting for her. Kali climbed into the black Ford sedan, noting that it smelled faintly of sweat and aftershave. It wasn't the unappealing combination she would have imagined.

"We got lucky," Keating said, pulling into traffic. "Two of them are still local."

"Were you able to get a look at the old files?"

"Like I said, they're in storage."

"But surely—"

"The cases are closed, remember?" He paused. "We got a conviction, in fact."

*And an execution.* He didn't remind her of that.

"If it seems important, we can always pursue it later," Keating said.

A polite way of letting her know he'd agreed to follow up on O'Dell and the Silva brothers only to humor her?

"I did run the names through the system," he added. "Nothing came up."

"Meaning they've been straight?"

"Or lucky."

Kali braced herself with a hand on the dashboard as Keating took the corner without slowing down.

"Are you afraid he's about to leave the country or something?"

Keating's face registered confusion. "Who?"

"Whichever one of them we're headed out to visit first."

"O'Dell's first up," he said.

"You drive like we're in a hurry," she explained, since he seemed intent on not understanding.

She'd been pleased that he'd followed up on her idea of looking at suspects from the Bayside Strangler case, and likewise pleased that he'd thought to ask her along. Now that she was in the car with him, however, holding tight, as though she was riding a runaway roller coaster, she was less enamored of the idea.

Keating grinned. "You and Lou could form a chorus."

"This is your standard driving mode?"

"Sometimes I'm not so slow and careful."

Great, Kali thought. Keating fancied himself a comedian as well as a race-car driver. Why had she ever thought him cute? "I'd like to get there in one piece, if you don't mind."

"I'd like to get you there that way too." He gave her a sideways glance, and what she thought was a wink.

Okay, so he *was* cute. He wouldn't be the first cute asshole she'd run across. Kali gripped the door handle and said a silent prayer for safe delivery.

For the remainder of the trip, they talked about shopping at secondhand stores (something Kali had actually done, which seemed to amuse Keating no end), and the odds of Anne Bailey being murdered on the same date as Wendy Gilchrist. Keating didn't find it as strange as Kali did, though he did concede that in light of everything, it might be important.

O'Dell's house was a weathered pink stucco bungalow in the flatlands of East Oakland. The door was answered by a bird-like woman in a housecoat, who seemed not at all surprised to find the police on her doorstep.

"We're looking for Robert O'Dell," Keating explained.

"You'll have to speak up, I can't hear so well."

"Robert O'Dell," he repeated.

"Senior or junior?"

Keating shot Kali a look. "Junior," she said. Senior was no doubt the woman's husband, and too old to be the man they wanted.

"I figured as much." Her tone was weary. Kali could tell she was a woman who'd been down this path many times before.

"Are you his mother?" Kali asked.

"I raised him. He's my late husband's boy."

"That would be O'Dell senior?"

The woman nodded. "He passed away almost a year ago, but there's still bill collectors show up looking for him."

"You know where we might find your stepson?" Keating asked.

"What's that you said?" She cupped a hand around her ear.

"O'Dell junior," Keating repeated. "Where can we find him?"

She pulled back, her face pinched with suspicion. "Is this some kind of trick?"

"A trick, ma'am?"

"He hasn't escaped, has he?"

Kali frowned. "He's in prison?" So much for Keating's running the names through the system. She wondered if he'd even tried.

"Sent away last August. Got caught with a twelve-year-old girl." Her voice registered disgust. "Wasn't the way he was raised, I promise you that."

"August," Keating mumbled, sounding confused. "Where was he arrested?"

"Outside of Tucson. He was visiting my brother's family." She looked them in the eye. "So what's this about?"

"Sorry to bother you," Keating said. "Our information isn't as up-to-date as it should be."

As they headed back to the car, Keating muttered under his breath. "Tucson. No wonder there was no record of his arrest in California."

At least Keating had taken her theory seriously enough to run the names.

With Barry Silva, they were luckier. Not only was he not in jail, he was at home—a rundown apartment building near the Coliseum. He opened the door only a crack.

Silva was a slender man who looked to be in his late thirties. He had a pointy nose and wild, frizzy hair that made Kali think of the stereotypical mad scientist.

"Whatever you got, I ain't interested," he said.

Keating identified himself and slipped a foot inside the door. "We'd like to talk to you."

Silva's eyes flashed. "I got nothing to say."

"You don't really want to go that route, do you? Make us haul you downtown and all?"

"You got no reason to take me in. No reason to be here at all. You guys messed with my life once, you ain't going to do it again."

"Messed with your life?" Kali asked.

"That Bayside Strangler thing. Soon as I heard 'bout those new murders, I knew you all'd be showing up here wanting to talk to me."

"We're just covering all the bases," Keating explained.

"I ain't got nothing to do with any of it."

Keating nodded. "You know how it is, though. We have to

check off all the boxes. Might be better if we had this conversation inside. More private and all."

"We ain't having a conversation," Silva said.

Kali had to hand it to the man. He could hold his own.

"So what are you doing these days, Barry? You working?"

"Yeah, I'm working. Night manager at the Mobil station on Ninty-eighth Avenue. Go ahead and check if you don't believe me. I got me an alibi for the night of them murders, too."

A little too quick with the denials, Kali thought. "How do you happen to know what nights those were?"

He shot her a hostile look. "Was in the news, lady. You're wasting your time thinking it mighta been me."

"What about your brother Larry?" Keating asked.

"Larry's dead. Crashed up his motorcycle about six years ago." Silva laughed. "Got hisself an alibi, too."

Keating's pager went off just then. He looked down to check the number. "Let us know if you plan on leaving town," he told Silva.

"Yeah, right." In a tone that said, *Screw you, buddy.*

In the car, Keating pulled out his cell phone. Kali could tell from the eagerness in his voice that it wasn't a routine call. When he disconnected, he turned to explain. "A Salvation Army sales-clerk saw a man looking through women's clothing. He took off without paying, and she followed him. Got a description of the car and a partial plate."

"Do you have his name?"

"Not yet, but we will."

It was only then that Kali realized she'd been holding her breath, afraid that the call had been signaling the discovery of another murder.

# CHAPTER 23

Kali's house wasn't large or elegant, but it offered one real luxury: a west-facing wall of windows with an ever-changing panorama of the San Francisco Bay. It was a view that never failed to soothe her. As she wound her way through the darkness up the narrow road toward home, she was already looking forward to a glass of wine and the calming effect of shimmering lights against the evening's blackness.

She was feeling oddly discouraged after the interviews with Silva and O'Dell's stepmother. From a strictly logical perspective, it was foolish to have expected anything to come of the leads. If either man had been a serious contender in the Strangler case, the police would have followed up at the time. Or so she liked to think.

At least Keating hadn't scoffed at her idea of looking at suspects in the Strangler case.

Keating. Bryce. His name brought a tingle to her skin.

Her thoughts stayed with Keating as she shifted into second for the hairpin turn near the top of the road. There was no denying the chemistry between them. Kali found him increasingly attractive, yet her head told her she was being ridiculous. He was nothing like the kind of man who interested her. Beer and ball games if she had to guess. A big-screen TV, maybe a car in parts in the garage. And a brashness that practically knocked you over. Not her type at all.

Besides, experience had taught her it was a mistake to mix business and social pleasure.

Kali turned left onto her own street. As the headlights swept the roadway, she saw a light-colored van pull away from the shoulder in front of her house. A visitor? The vehicle didn't look familiar. She waited for a moment to see if the driver would turn around now that she was home. The van slowed for a moment about five houses down, then took off again with a squeal of tires. Clearly not anyone looking for her.

Funny, though, that it had been parked directly in front of her house. The road was narrow and winding, and there were better places to stop if you were going to one of the other houses in the neighborhood.

Loretta greeted Kali with her usual canine enthusiasm. She barked and danced at Kali's feet, sliding on the polished wood flooring like a four-legged break dancer.

"I know I'm late," Kali said. "Couldn't be helped."

Loretta rubbed against Kali's legs. Instant forgiveness.

Kali poured food into Loretta's bowl and added a bit of canned soup out of guilt. She poured the rest of the soup into a pot for herself, though it was a decidedly unappetizing prospect for dinner. Not that she had a lot of choice. She couldn't remember when she'd last been to the grocery.

She was sorting through the day's mail when a niggling memory dislodged itself from the back of her mind and smacked her between the eyes. The motion sensor light next to the driveway had been on when she rounded the corner to her street. It could mean nothing. That happened sometimes when a bird flew across its path, or a spider happened into the infrared beam.

But combined with the strange van, it spooked her.

The phone rang, and she jumped.

"Good, you're home," Margot said. "I'm hungry for sushi. Want to join me?"

Relief flooded through her, though she wasn't quite sure why. Had she been expecting a call from the killer? She pushed the thought aside and glanced at the unappealing pan of soup on the stove. "I'd love to."

"I'll pick you up in about ten minutes?"

"Fine." Kali hesitated, then asked, "Margot, did you see anyone here just a bit ago?"

"At your place?"

"Right. Outside. There was a van parked in front when I came home. It left just as I pulled up."

"I didn't see anyone, but I wasn't looking either. You were expecting someone?"

"No. That's why it's odd."

"Maybe a do-gooder collecting for world peace. See you in a bit. I'll toot when I'm out front."

Though Miyako was crowded, they were eating late enough that there wasn't the usual long wait for a table. They were seated right away and ordered without looking at the menu.

"I'm glad you called," Kali said. "I'm overdue for a trip to the grocery."

"It's your karma, darling. I've never seen anything in your fridge but the basics."

"That's not true. I buy all sorts of stuff, then I never get around to using it and have to toss it."

"Maybe you should take a cooking class."

"I know how to cook," Kali protested. It was just that the effort involved was usually more than she wanted to put forth. That was a downside of living alone. One of many.

Margot picked up her chopsticks and held them aloft in slender fingers capped with nails of deep sienna. As usual, a collection of bracelets jangled at her wrist. "It wasn't meant as an insult. Besides, if you cooked more you wouldn't be as eager to join me in dining out."

"How did your date work out, by the way?"

"Randy? All he did was talk about himself and make lewd comments that I suppose he thought were romantic."

"Not atypical," Kali said dryly.

Margot rolled her eyes. "Men," she said with a glint of amusement.

Kali laughed too, then turned serious. "Can I ask you a personal question?"

"Sure."

"How did you decide to become a woman?"

"Wasn't a matter of deciding, Kali. It's who I am. Somehow I got stuck in the wrong body is all." Margot paused, chopsticks held midair. "Not that SRS is an easy decision."

"SRS?"

"Sexual reassignment surgery. I've been a woman now in

every other way for close to three years. Longer than most doctors require. But I haven't taken that final step."

"It's a big one." Kali tried for noncommital. She was more than willing to accept Margot as a friend, and wanted to know her better, but now that she'd raised the gender issue, she found she wasn't entirely comfortable with the intimate details.

"The initial stages were actually the hardest," Margot continued. "New ways of relating, having people treat me differently. And the hormones—" She laughed. "Don't ever underestimate the power of hormones."

"I can see that would be hard." Kali tried to imagine presenting herself as a man. She had trouble enough changing hairstyles. She couldn't fathom what it would be like to change genders.

"But also very exciting and liberating," Margot added, then thankfully moved the conversation in a new direction—Nordstrom's shoe sale.

After their meal, they browsed a neighboring bookstore, each swearing her to-be-read pile was too high to accommodate more books, and then buying a couple anyway. Kali was pleased to see that she and Margot shared an appreciation for many of the same authors. When Margot dropped her off in front of the house, Kali half expected to see the driveway light illuminated again, but it didn't switch on until she triggered it herself.

She went through the greeting routine again with the dog, and took her for a quick evening walk. She didn't think to check her messages until much later that night as she was getting into bed.

Nathan had called.

"Sorry I keep missing you. You're not avoiding me, are you?" He punctuated the remark with a self-conscious laugh. "Hope you liked the flowers. A token thanks for a nice evening. I really had a good time."

Kali played the message a second time. Straightforward and simple. Why, then, did it leave her with an unsettled feeling? Must be something to do with the damned flowers. She should have acknowledged them, however. It was the polite thing to do. She promised herself she'd call Nathan in the morning.

Alex Nelson held the hand-rolled joint between his thumb and forefinger and took a deep drag. He held his breath as long as he could, looking away from Ben to keep from laughing. He had no idea why Ben was cracking him up tonight, but every time their eyes met, Alex was overcome with spasms of laughter.

Finally, he exhaled, glanced at Ben, and succumbed to a fit of giggles. "This is good stuff, man."

"Yeah." Ben reached for the joint. "Got it from my dad's cookie jar."

"Your dad smokes dope?"

"Not very often, but he goes only for the best. Like in everything else, top of the line." Ben put his feet on the coffee table. "Guess your old man wouldn't be caught dead with the stuff."

"You guess right." Alex giggled at the thought. "Thinks of himself as Mr. Morality."

"Wouldn't it be a hoot if he actually won this election? You'd be the *governor's son*."

"Spare me. I don't think his ego can take getting any bigger than it already is."

"He's really that bad?"

Alex nodded. Ben's dad might be a pretentious ass, but at least he treated Ben like a person. Alex sometimes felt like he was invisible where his own father was concerned.

"Now that he's got Selby," Alex added, "he's so smug it makes me want to puke."

"Must be weird having a famous father and a famous mother."

"Stepmother."

"Whatever." Ben took another toke and held his breath while talking. "I saw that movie *Stranger Next Door*, the one that's supposedly based on the Bayside Strangler case. Harrison Ford played your dad, right?"

Alex grunted. "Right. On top of everything else, now he thinks he looks like Ford."

"Who cares? They're both old."

Old and phony. "The cops might have gotten the wrong man, you know." Alex took another hit and fell into a fit of coughing. "Shit, that hurt."

"You mean the dude they executed wasn't the real killer?"

"Haven't you heard about the two women who were murdered recently?"

Ben frowned. "They think it's *him?*"

"Might be. My dad's about ready to shit a cow. There goes the election, up in smoke." Alex snickered. "Or down the toilet." He stood up. "Man, I've got the munchies."

"There's some bread in the kitchen. Some cheese too, but it's kind of moldy."

"I got the munchies for ice cream. Let's go to Fenton's."

"At three in the morning?"

Alex checked his watch. Ben was right. "Okay, so we'll go to Safeway instead."

"How are you going to do that? You're stoned out of your mind."

"It's not that far. I can drive."

"Oh, sure. I bet you can't even *walk* a straight line."

Ben was such an old lady. He was always finding reasons they couldn't, or shouldn't, do things. Half the time Alex didn't know why he bothered to hang out with Ben. "I'm fine," he said. "Look." He stood on one leg and touched the tip of his nose with his finger.

"You're supposed to shut your eyes, too," Ben said.

Alex tried it with his eyes closed and listed to the left. Well, he wasn't going to *drive* with his eyes closed so what did it matter? "Picture this," he told Ben. "Jamoca fudge ice cream, chocolate sauce, marshmallows, nuts . . ."

"Okay, all right." Ben fumbled with tying his shoes, and gave up. "You sure we should do this?"

"Yeah, I'm sure."

Two blocks from Ben's house Alex entered an intersection and narrowly avoided hitting the car coming from his right.

Ben grabbed the dash. "Watch it."

"I am."

"Why didn't you stop at the corner? I told you we shouldn't have come out."

"The stupid sign was hidden behind a bush."

A block later, Alex saw red flashing lights in his rearview mirror.

"Shit," he said.

Ben turned around to look. "Damn. Guess we won't get our ice cream."

"Let me handle this." Alex pulled to the side of the road and eased out of the car, steadying himself by holding on to the door.

The cold air on his face brought a moment of clarity. It had been stupid to drive when he'd been smoking. He didn't need this kind of trouble.

"Let me see your license," the cop said.

Alex handed it over, contrite and deferential. "Geez, officer, I'm sorry. It was so dark out, I didn't see the stop sign until it was too late."

"Stop sign?"

Alex backtracked. "Hey, maybe there wasn't one after all. It would explain why I didn't stop." He laughed lightly, the way he'd heard his father do at parties.

"You were driving with your lights off," the cop said.

"Oh."

"You been drinking?"

"No, sir. Not a drop."

The cop eyed him suspiciously. "This your vehicle?"

"Yes, sir. But it's registered in my dad's name. Owen Nelson." Alex waited to see if the name had the desired effect.

"Nelson? The candidate for governor?" The cop seemed impressed. He looked at the license and back at Alex. "He's a good guy, your dad. He's going to get my vote."

Alex tried for humble. "Sorry about the headlights, sir. My friend and I were just going out for milk and cereal. Guess with all the street lighting we didn't even notice."

"I'll tell you what," the cop said after a moment. "I'm going to let you go with a warning. But remember to turn those lights on."

"Absolutely."

"What about the ice cream?" Ben asked as Alex turned the car back in the direction they'd come.

"Forget it."

"Oh, man. You got me craving ice cream and chocolate sauce. You can't hang me out to dry now. Can't we just—"

Alex snapped, "I said, forget it."

"No need to get mad about it. You were cool. Real cool."

And damned lucky.

# CHAPTER 24

Lou was having a bad morning. He'd nicked himself shaving, hit his shin against the dresser and spilled coffee on his pants. Now the captain was reading them the riot act for not making better progress with the case.

"We've got public opinion to consider," Burnell said, running his hand over the shining dome of his head. "Not to mention public safety."

Lou leaned back in his chair, trying not to say something he'd regret. "We're anxious to solve this too."

Keating nodded agreement. Lou could tell from his partner's posture that the captain's remarks didn't sit well with Keating either.

"Yeah, yeah, but *I'm* the one with city officials breathing down my neck. You have any idea what that's like?"

"Not pleasant, I imagine." Of course, that was why Burnell's salary was what it was, which was a whole lot more than Lou's.

"Not pleasant doesn't begin to cover it. Everyone's nervous as hell waiting for this guy to strike again."

"That's what he wants," Keating said.

"Well, he's certainly getting it." The captain drummed the desktop with his fingers. "You think there's any chance we're dealing with the actual Bayside Strangler and not a copycat?"

"It's possible. But there's nothing about the crimes the killer couldn't have gotten from news accounts or Jackson's book. And neither woman had a dog collar around her neck, which is one bit of information that *wasn't* in the book. So I'd say the odds favor a copycat."

"Besides," Lou explained, "our guy is adding some twists of

own. The lipstick, for example. And the photograph, in Jane Parkhurst's case."

Burnell pressed his palms together, elbows resting on his desk. "Owen Nelson must be sweating bullets. He's taken a stand in favor of the death penalty. He can't be happy about talk that the wrong man was executed."

"The press is certainly having a field day with it," Lou agreed.

"So where are we? Any luck with that witness in Parkhurst's neighborhood?"

"The artist did three different composites," Lou told him. "I showed them around to other neighbors. Didn't ring a bell with any of them."

"How about simply seeing a stranger around her property? We know the killer was there at least once to snap that picture of her."

Lou nodded. "Seems she had lots of work people around the place—gardeners, a housecleaning service, a recent roof repair—so it wasn't unusual to see strangers wandering about. The neighbors more or less stopped noticing."

"And the call that came in from the Salvation Army clerk—anything come of that?"

Keating rubbed his chin. "We're still waiting to hear back about the partial plate the witness got. Lou and I both talked to her. She didn't recognize the man from the composite sketches, but she gave us a fairly detailed description."

"You want us to try for another composite from her?" Lou asked.

"Let's wait and see what comes up on the plate. Most likely what we've got is a man buying a gift for his girlfriend."

"Stealing." Besides, Lou had trouble imagining a woman who wouldn't take offense at receiving used clothing as a gift.

"You need more people on this?" Burnell was stingy as hell when it came to pulling people off other cases, and he'd already given them the go-ahead for patrol backup. Lou took the offer as a measure of the pressure the captain was under.

Lou and Keating spoke at once. "We're fine."

"You need anything, just ask." Burnell's tone signaled the end of the conversation.

When Lou got back to his desk, there was a message that Diana Davis was waiting in the lobby. He buzzed Martha at the front desk. "Who's Diana Davis?"

"Former wife of Dwayne Davis." She didn't have to elaborate.

Lou sighed. The day's bad luck was continuing. He wished Keating hadn't just stepped out. This wasn't going to be an easy meeting. "Send her up."

Diana Davis stood hesitantly at the doorway, gripping her pocketbook against her chest. She was an attractive woman, on the plump side, with warm brown skin and a head full of those tiny braids that seemed to be so fashionable.

Lou held out a hand and introduced himself. Her own grip was so weak, it was barely there.

"Can I get you some coffee?" Lou asked, showing her to a chair.

"Thank you, but no." She sat primly on the edge. "I'm wondering about these two women who were murdered . . ." She paused to clear her throat. "There's been quite a bit in the news."

"Yes, there has." He'd expected outrage; her tentativeness caught him off guard. "What about them?" he asked, though he thought he knew where she was going.

"I'm interested in . . . well, in whether or not you think it's the same person who . . . who was responsible for the Bayside Strangler murders."

"And by inference, whether your husband was innocent."

She gave a very slight nod, as though she were afraid to acknowledge the thought with anything more. "There's been so much speculation, people saying the Bayside Strangler has returned and all. There was even a cover story in one of those supermarket tabloids. Right there at the checkout counter."

Lou scoffed. "The only interest any of them have is selling papers."

"But there was all that controversy about the evidence against Dwayne, too. . . ."

"Controversy trumped up by his attorney."

Lou didn't think he'd sounded especially harsh, but he must have because Diana Davis cringed.

"Please," she said. "I didn't come here to argue. I only meant that I've never really been sure . . ." She took a breath, looked him in the eye for the first time. "I have a ten-year-old son, detective. Do you have any idea how hard it is for a boy to learn he's the son of a murderer?"

Lou hadn't thought about that before, and he still wasn't sure what she expected from him. A ray of hope? Closure and certainty? He couldn't give her any of it, though it surprised him to discover he wanted to. The woman looked close to tears.

"Your husband was convicted in a fair trial, Mrs. Davis, and that conviction was upheld on appeal. There is nothing about the current murders that makes me think the verdict was unjust."

"But on the news they said the victims got a yellow rose, and they were dressed . . . you know, like before. Mr. Gomez even says—"

"Gomez?"

"Dwayne's attorney during the trial. He says it shows Dwayne didn't murder those other women."

"What it shows is that Gomez is still playing advocate." And playing on the hopes and fears of a vulnerable woman for the purpose of furthering his own agenda. The guy disgusted Lou. "Most likely what we've got here is a copycat."

"Most likely?"

She had him, though she seemed to take no pleasure in it. "I'm not God, Mrs. Davis. Only God and fools are ever certain about anything."

Another minimal nod. "Not knowing makes it so hard."

Lou felt stirrings of sympathy, but it struck him that she was in a no-win situation. Either Davis had been innocent and unjustly executed, or he'd been guilty of multiple murders. Neither alternative seemed appealing. He wondered which of them offered Diana Davis the most peace.

"How is your son doing?" he asked finally.

"Good." She paused. "I haven't told him about Dwayne. He asks about his dad and I say he's dead. I used to tell him that even before Dwayne was executed. But he's getting to the age where he wants to know more . . . you know how kids are."

"Yeah." His thoughts jumped reflexively to Nikki. She'd peppered him with questions from the time she was old enough to speak. And for every answer, she'd return with a new question. Now, she never asked his opinion about anything. "I wish I could help you, Mrs. Davis."

A wan smile. "Yeah, me too."

"Why don't you leave a way for us to get in touch with you in case something comes up."

She took the pad of paper he gave her and wrote down a phone number. He recognized the area code as belonging to the Central Valley.

Diana Davis had barely left his office when Maureen poked her head through the open doorway. "I've got some names for you on that plate you wanted run. Of light-colored Econoline vans in the greater Bay Area, there were sixteen matches. If the clerk was wrong about the make, then the number is much higher."

Sixteen. They could handle that easily. And the sales clerk had seemed fairly confident about the identification once she'd looked at photos of different vehicles.

"I cross-checked the registration against the driver's license information, as well."

Lou took the list Maureen handed him. "I appreciate the quick response."

"I want the killer off the streets yesterday. This guy gives me the creeps."

Lou's first cut was to eliminate, at least initially, vans registered to women and old people. That brought it down to thirteen. And since the guy they were after was shopping in Oakland, Lou started with cars registered to drivers living in Alameda County. That narrowed the list to three. One of those, Kurt Lancaster, had a record for burglary. He'd been out of prison for three years, but since the other two names came up clean, Lou decided to start with Lancaster.

Keating came through the door.

"Don't take your coat off," Lou told him. "We're headed out."

"Where to?"

Lou read off the address. "We got some names on the plate that Salvation Army clerk gave us. Three good fits, one of them an ex-con. Name's Kurt Lancaster."

"Kurt, as in rhymes with Burt?" Keating shook his head. "The things parents do to their kids."

"Probably thought it was cute. How'd you make out, by the way?"

"Zippo. Whoever our killer is, he isn't bragging to his friends."

"Maybe he has a higher class of friends than your band of informants."

Keating laughed. "Wouldn't be hard."

\*   \*   \*

Lancaster lived in an apartment near the Emeryville border, just east of San Pablo Avenue. Rundown building, burglar bars, weeds, and chainlink fencing. It wasn't the sort of neighborhood anyone aspired to live in.

Lou found a parking space half a block away.

"Hey, will you look at that?" Keating said as they walked toward the apartment building.

A white Econoline van—dented. Lou couldn't believe their luck. "We must be living right," he said. "It's not often we score right out the gate."

They knocked on the door, waited, then knocked again. Finally Lou heard movement inside. The man who opened the door had a prominent Adam's apple, just like the salesclerk had described, and a nervous tic in his shoulders. It was looking more and more like they'd found the right guy.

Lou took the lead. "Mr. Lancaster?"

"Yes."

"Oakland Police. Mind if we come in?"

Lancaster closed the door an inch or two. "What is it you want?"

"We want to talk to you."

"I haven't done anything wrong."

"Might be better if we had this conversation inside," Keating said. He moved forward, pushing Lancaster aside. Lou wasn't comfortable with that sort of in-your-face approach, but Keating was tough enough to pull it off.

"I been reporting to my parole officer regular. I'm in the clear. You go check the record if you don't believe me."

"That's not why we're here," Lou said. He followed Keating inside. The apartment was small and dimly lit. It smelled of stale cigarette smoke. Lou almost wished they'd stayed on the doorstep. "Where do you work these days?" he asked.

"B and B Janitorial. I work nights is how come I'm home now. Office buildings mostly."

"How long have you worked for them?" Lou looked around the apartment. The furniture had seen better days, but the place was as neat as a pin. The kind of neat that made Lou uncomfortable because it didn't seem natural.

"Three years," Lancaster said. "Ever since I got out of prison. I'm crew supervisor now."

"Nice to see a man turn his life around." Keating's tone was only slightly sarcastic.

"What I did before was stupid. I didn't have my head screwed on straight. But I did my time, and now I want to forget it."

Lou studied the man. He fit the salesclerk's description to a T, but except for the longish hair, he looked nothing like anything Mrs. Greene had given them. That didn't mean shit, though. "Mr. Lancaster, were you shopping at the Salvation Army store in Oakland yesterday?"

His expression was suddenly alert. "What of it?"

"Were you?"

"It's a free country."

"Clerk there thinks you took something without paying."

"Uh-uh. You can't prove that."

"Shopping for yourself, were you?" Keating asked.

Lancaster was growing agitated. "What difference does it make?"

"You wear ladies' undies, Lancaster?" Keating wandered across the room and into what appeared to be a bedroom. He stopped short and whistled under his breath. "Hey, Lou. Come look at this."

Lancaster was at Keating's side in an instant. "You can't go in there," he said indignantly. "That's my studio. You have no right."

Lou peered between the two of them into a room full of life-sized dolls. Mannequins, cloth forms, plastic dummies. All female. "Jesus."

One of the cloth dolls appeared to be under construction; the rest were posed around the room in chairs, on the bed, seated on the floor as though at a dormitory slumber party. Some were elaborately dressed, down to shoes and a pocketbook, while others were clad in nighties or underwear. It was an odd and unsettling sight.

"Stay out of there," Lancaster sputtered. His right eye twitched uncontrollably.

Keating ignored Lancaster's protests and moved into the room.

"Don't touch them. They're mine." Lancaster's voice was high and thin, and held a glint of rage.

Lou readied himself to reach for his gun. Keating had a way of pushing a situation to the point where it sometimes turned ugly.

Keating found the light switch and flipped it on. "What *is* this stuff?"

"It's a hobby of mine," Lancaster explained with the air of righteous indignation.

"Playing with dolls?"

"It's not *playing.*"

"What is it then?" Keating snickered. "You don't have sex with them, do you?" He poked at the doll under construction, lifted the skirt of another, no doubt looking for anatomical details.

Lancaster went berserk. He grabbed the doll and hugged her to his chest. "Don't touch her. Get your hands away."

"Well, do you?"

"You're disgusting. You've got no right to be here. Either one of you. I've done nothing wrong." He looked close to tears and more than a little crazed.

Lou caught his partner's eye. "Come on, Bryce. We got what we came for."

"Not quite." He grabbed a flimsy black something from a pile of clothing on the dresser. "This look to you like what the clerk said was missing?"

Hell, it was a negligee, or maybe a slip. Lou couldn't tell. And the clerk wasn't certain what the man had taken, if, indeed, he'd taken anything. "Yeah," Lou agreed. "Looks like it to me."

"I didn't steal it," Lancaster protested. "It was a gift."

Keating smirked. "Sure it was. Don't go anywhere, Lancaster. We'll be in touch."

Outside, Keating asked, "What do you think, Lou?"

"The guy's a fruitcake. With extra nuts. Those dolls of his gave me the willies."

"They were strange, all right." Keating started the engine and pulled away from the curb.

"He's a perverted son of a bitch, you ask me." Lou had never worked Vice the way Keating had. Maybe you got used to the kinky stuff, but thank God he'd never had to find out.

"Could be it's art."

Lou glanced sideways to see if Keating was serious.

"They weren't sex toys, Lou."

"Well, they weren't art either. And those stacks of women's clothing . . . I say we arrest him right now."

"For what? Playing with dolls?"

"Think about it, Bryce. He gets off on dressing those dolls, just like the killer does with his victims." That was what made the dolls so creepy. Well, they were creepy no matter how you looked at it, but the overlap with the murders was what really did it for Lou.

"Some guys dress *themselves* in women's clothing. None of it's illegal."

"It ought to be." Lou had taken Nikki to the city once when she was younger, arriving on BART in the middle of the Gay Pride parade. Whole brigades of men dressed as brides, nuns and hookers. Bare-chested women on motorcycles. He'd just about had a heart attack.

"If anything," Keating said after a moment's reflection, "this gives Lancaster a legitimate reason to be buying women's clothing."

"Legitimate. Hah."

"Try his parole officer, why don't you?"

Lou pulled out his cell phone and called. He wound his way through the system for a couple of minutes before finally managing to reach Lancaster's PO, a man named Gaines.

"Sure, I know Kurt Lancaster," Gaines said. He had a soft voice, a faint Texas drawl. "Name like that, how could I forget. He in trouble?"

"We're looking at him in connection with a crime we're working."

"Burglary?"

"Homicide."

Gaines drew in a breath. "Homicide? You sure you've got the right guy?"

"No, we're not sure, that's why I'm calling." Seemed obvious to Lou.

"I gotta tell you, this is a surprise. The parole business, it's mostly a revolving door. But Lancaster isn't like that. Jail time was a wake-up call for him. He's been straight as an arrow since the day he got out."

"Meaning what, exactly?" As far as Lou was concerned, the guy was anything but straight.

"Meaning he's kept his nose clean. Reports in when he's supposed to, holds down a steady job. Never any hint of trouble. His employer gives him high marks."

"What about his personal life? You know anything about that?"

"I know he had a girlfriend for a while. Seemed like it might be serious, but it never worked out. It didn't send him back over the line, though. Not as far as I heard anyway."

A romance gone south. Did that explain Lancaster's interest in dressing up dolls? It certainly dovetailed with anger against women. "The girlfriend, you know anything more about that?"

"Just that Lancaster took it hard. I think he'd kind of pinned his hopes for a new life on her, and when it fell apart, he felt he'd failed."

"When was this?"

"Couple of years ago. I'd have to check my records if you want anything closer than that."

"I'll let you know if I do. Thanks for the help." He ended the call and turned to Keating. "Bleeding-heart liberal," Lou muttered. "He's like every PO I ever met. Thinks ex-cons walk the road of salvation."

"What did he say?" Keating asked.

"Lancaster seems to be passing parole with highest honors."

"You sound skeptical."

Lou grunted. "I am." No man who filled his apartment with life-sized dolls was completely normal. Maybe Lancaster could fool a soft touch like Gaines, but Lou saw things more clearly.

# CHAPTER 25

Kali squinted against the glare of early morning sun and crossed the street without waiting for the walk sign. Eight-thirty and already the block was closed to traffic in anticipation of the noontime rally. A pair of Port-A-Pottys sat on the corner nearest the freeway. Closer in, the sponsors were setting out orange cones and stringing wire for the sound system. Energy filled the air, accompanied by a flurry of activity.

The event had initially been billed as a protest of capital punishment, with the late Dwayne Davis as poster boy, but Kali had word that it had grown to encompass a demonstration against police corruption and a show of support for Tony Molina, Owen's arch rival in the upcoming primary. This being the Bay Area, she wouldn't have been surprised to find exotic dancers, animal rights' crusaders and the extraterrestrial support league staking out a piece of the action as well. Especially given the nice weather.

She wove her way through the crowd-control barricades and took the elevator up to her office. The yellow tulips were still on the credenza behind her desk. She hadn't gotten around to tossing them, after all. With the open petals and arching stems, they looked like something out of an Impressionist painting.

They were just flowers, she decided. Lovely flowers at that. Tulips were among Kali's favorites. She could understand why she'd reacted so negatively at first, but at the same time, she chided herself for doing so.

Kali dug around in her desk drawer until she found the note that had accompanied the arrangement. In retrospect she was flattered that Nathan had cared enough to send them. And a little ashamed of herself for ignoring him.

Kali checked her watch. Eight forty-five. If Nathan wasn't yet at work, he'd find her message when he arrived. A message was often easier than conversation anyway.

He'd told her he worked for Global Investment, but hadn't said which office. Kali tried the Oakland office first, and when she had no luck there, she dialed San Francisco. When that got her nowhere, she pulled out the yellow pages and tried offices in Walnut Creek and Pleasanton before asking if there was a company-wide directory.

"I'm looking for an employee named Nathan Sloane," she told the woman. "I don't know which branch office he's in, however."

"Let me check." The woman put her on hold, and Kali sat through a recorded sales pitch for the company, as well as two renditions of "Your call is important to us; please stay on the line."

Finally the woman again picked up. "I don't find a record of anyone by that name."

Kali was sure he'd said Global Investment. "He's new there," she explained. "Would there be a different list he might show up on?"

"We're computerized," the woman said. "Unless he was hired this morning, he'd be in the master directory."

Maybe she'd misunderstood the name of the company. "Thanks. I appreciate your looking for me." Kali tried directory assistance next, looking for a home number. There were numerous Sloanes, but no *Nathan* and no *N*. An unlisted number? She might have pursued the matter further if Owen hadn't dropped in just then.

"Did you see what's going on out front?" he asked.

"Setting up for the rally?"

He nodded, and sank into the chair opposite hers. "I don't know what in the hell they think they're doing."

"Angling for some major media coverage, from the looks of it."

"It's bad enough there's a killer terrorizing the city, but to dredge up Davis and the Bayside Strangler murders..." He pressed his fingertips together and shook his head. "It serves no purpose except stirring people up for the sake of controversy."

"I don't know that it's just for the sake of controversy, Owen. But it *is* too bad they had to drag politics into it."

"This is exactly the sort of thing I wanted to avoid." His voice rose in anger. "I thought if we took an aggressive position on these murders, we might take the wind out of their sails."

"We're talking about a single demonstration," Kali reminded him. "By next week, no one will remember what it was even about."

"Wrong. Molina's people will make sure they do." He gave an irritated sigh. "These murders couldn't have come at a worse time."

"Especially for the two victims."

Owen winced. "Okay, so I'm tripping on my own ego. It's just that it's so unfair. They're making me the scapegoat." He rubbed his palms on his pants legs, took a breath and sat back. "I sound like Alex, don't I? Thinking only of myself, moaning that things aren't going my way. And my response to him has always been 'get over it; no one said life was fair.'"

Kali smiled. Owen was as ambitious as any politician, but what set him apart and endeared him to his supporters was this ability to step back and see himself objectively. "It's not over until it's over. Once there's an arrest, this will all be history."

"I sure hope so." He didn't sound convinced.

When Owen left, Kali finally got down to work. She made a few calls and confirmed that Robert O'Dell was still behind bars in Arizona. Of the identified suspects in the Bayside Strangler murders, that left only Barry Silva as a possible perpetrator of the recent crimes. Kali hit the computer to see what she could dig up on him. Not as much as she'd hoped, despite the search techniques she'd learned in a continuing education class for lawyers. And nothing that helped her determine if Silva warranted further attention.

It would be helpful if she could find a common thread in Anne Bailey's and Jane Parkhurst's lives. Each of them had somehow crossed paths with the killer. And not just at the moment of their deaths. The killer had known Anne was from Texas; he'd taken a photo of Jane Parkhurst at her own home. He'd chosen them, individually and specifically, as his victims.

When she'd worked in the DA's office before, Kali had tried a case involving a string of home burglaries. The defendant had cased the houses, and the victims, when he delivered newly purchased mattresses and bed sets. Once the police had determined

192 / *Jonnie Jacobs*

what the victims had in common, zeroing in on the culprit had been easy. Kali recalled reading about other, similar cases. The trick was finding where the victims' lives intersected.

Which brought her back to Barry Silva. He worked at a gas station. Just the sort of place where two otherwise separate lives might overlap. Had Jane Parkhurst purchased gas at Silva's station? Had Anne? Kali had no trouble envisioning effervescent Anne chatting, in passing, about her childhood in Texas.

The Mobil station where Silva worked wasn't convenient to either woman's house, but that meant nothing, Kali reminded herself. While most people had a preferred station or two, everyone occasionally bought gas at other locations as well.

Kali picked up the phone, called Anne's husband at work and was told he was no longer employed there. She started to try the house, then had a better idea. The noise from outside, amplified by loudspeakers, made her antsy anyway.

As she left the building, she stayed to the fringe of the gathering crowd. Several of the demonstrators carried placards bearing photos of Anne Bailey and Jane Parkhurst with the caption *Bayside Strangler strikes from the grave*. It annoyed Kali to see tragedy exploited. The photo of Anne was particularly hard for her to take. The sense of loss was like a sharp stab to her belly.

Did the protesters honestly believe Davis was innocent? And if the rally was really a demonstration against capital punishment, why bring Anne and Jane Parkhurst into it? The whole thing reeked of political manipulation.

Toward the back of the assembly, she passed a bearded man hawking Jack Jackson's book. That she found even more disturbing. The event had taken on a circus-like quality. She got into her car feeling prickly and agitated.

Kali pulled up to the curb in front of the house that had been Anne and Jerry's just as Jerry and another man emerged through the entry door carrying a dresser. She had spoken to Jerry only once since that morning three weeks ago when he'd shown her the yellow rose, and she felt a twinge of guilt now that she hadn't called more often to see how he was doing.

Jerry and the other man were loading the dresser into the back of a pickup truck already crammed with furniture when Kali approached. Jerry's expression registered surprise. "What are you doing here?" he asked.

She put the question aside. "How have you been?"

Jerry's laugh was harsh. "I've been better. I see from the TV you're working with the cops now."

"More accurately with the district attorney."

"They thought I killed her." Not surprisingly, he sounded angry.

"Friends and family are always suspect."

"No, not always."

The other man muttered something about rope and went back into the house. Jerry pushed the dresser flush against the side of the truck. "I guess I'm off the hook in light of the second murder. At least no one's accused me since it happened." He paused and wiped his forehead, suddenly suspicious. "That's not why you're here, is it?"

"No." She stepped out of his way as he shifted an upholstered chair farther to the back of the truck bed. "Are you moving?"

"Just getting rid of some stuff. There are too many reminders of Anne in the house."

Kali would have thought that might be a comfort, but apparently not.

"Tell me what's going on," he said, his tone softening. "I get nothing from the cops."

"They're working on it. They seem fairly certain that Anne and the second woman were killed by the same person." A thought floated across her mind. "Anne didn't know Jane Parkhurst, did she?"

"The cops asked the same thing. I never heard the name before."

"Parkhurst was a real estate agent. Could Anne have been working with a real estate firm?"

"We were already living apart. Why would she want another place?"

"Just asking." Anne had never mentioned to Kali that she was house hunting either. "Did Anne have a regular gas station?" Kali asked.

Jerry frowned. "What is this, twenty questions?"

"I'm looking for ways she might have crossed paths with the killer."

"You've got a suspect who works at a gas station?"

"No suspects, just idle speculation."

He'd finished rearranging the bed of the pickup, and now began tucking the blue crew-neck tee into his jeans. "I don't know where she usually bought gas, probably some place near here or the office. I could check through the credit card statements if you'd like."

"That would be helpful. Keep an eye out for a Mobil station in the vicinity of Ninety-eighth Avenue."

"Okay. It was usually Shell or Chevron, though, I'm pretty sure about that." He laughed. "And it had to be one of those auto-pay stations. It drove her nuts to wait in line to deal with a real person."

Kali understood. She felt the same herself.

Jerry jumped down from the truck bed. "I'll give you a call when I've had a chance to sort through the receipts."

"Thanks." She hesitated. "I called your number at work. They said you'd left the company."

"Yeah. I finally had it with that place. I'm thinking I'll take six or eight months, maybe do some skiing, some traveling, and then look for a job that suits me better."

Kali remembered it was Anne's life insurance policy that provided Jerry his newfound freedom. She had a fleeting thought that the detectives had been too hasty in dismissing him as a suspect. "Sounds like things are working out well for you," she said, not accusingly but with a certain reserve that couldn't be easily ignored.

"Nothing is going to bring Anne back," he said, looking at her levelly. "And nothing is going to stop me from missing her. But since I can now afford to quit a job I've hated for years, I don't see why I shouldn't. Do you?"

"No, I guess not." But she left with the uneasy knowledge that Jerry had wasted no time in turning Anne's murder to his advantage.

Back in her car, Kali tried to think how she could learn if Jane Parkhurst had frequented Silva's Mobil station. Again, credit card statements would help. She made a mental note to contact Jane's parents, then decided getting a court order would be quicker. In the meantime, she'd take a look at Jane Parkhurst's house and neighborhood.

\* \* \*

Kali had no sooner rung Jane Parkhurst's doorbell, on the off chance a friend or relative was at the house, when she caught sight of a woman with colorful green hair tottering across the street. Mrs. Greene, no doubt. Kali had assumed the detectives were exaggerating when they talked about the green hue of her hair, but if anything, they'd failed to do it justice. It was a color you might find on a Berkeley teenager, and even then you'd do a double-take. On a woman who looked by all other attributes to be in her early seventies, it was a real jolt.

"Are you a reporter?" Mrs. Greene asked, hobbling up the walkway with the use of a cane.

"I'm with the DA's office."

"Ah, then you might be able to help me. I haven't seen my sketches in the newspaper."

"Your sketches?"

"The ones by that police artist fellow. I saw a suspicious man around Jane's house, you know."

Kali nodded.

"Don't they usually do that?"

"Do what?"

"Run them in the paper. So if anyone out there recognizes the man—"

"They do that sometimes," Kali explained. "But not always." And only when there was an accurate eyewitness observation of a person reasonably considered to be the perpetrator of the crime.

Mrs. Greene studied Kali for a moment. "I was just making some tea," she said finally. "Would you like some?"

It was information Kali really wanted, and she'd take it where she could get it. "I'd love a cup of tea," she said.

Mrs. Greene ushered Kali into a kitchen so dated it might now be called stylishly retro. The countertops were tile—teal and black, the stove an old Wedgewood. The table where Kali sat was of chrome-trimmed yellow Formica of the sort she remembered fondly from her grandmother's house as a child.

"Did you know Jane Parkhurst well?" Kali asked, watching Mrs. Greene pour boiling water into a china teapot emblazoned with pink roses.

"We were neighborly. I'd pick up her mail for her when she

went on vacation, borrow eggs or sugar if I ran out. But we weren't close friends."

Not the sort of relationship that invited confidences, but people sometimes said things in passing that later proved important. "You don't happen to know the kind of gas she favored, do you?"

"Probably the expensive stuff. She drove an expensive car." Mrs. Greene handed Kali a cup and saucer. Desert rose, her grandmother's pattern. "Sugar?"

Kali shook her head. "I'm fine. I meant the brand of gas. Shell? Mobil?"

"I haven't the foggiest idea."

Not surprising. Kali herself couldn't have answered the question about her closest friends. "Do you know if she was out in the vicinity of Ninty-eighth Avenue recently?"

"Being in real estate, she got around quite a bit I imagine. But Ninty-eighth Avenue is kind of far out. That wasn't really her area. Why? Is it about her murder?"

"I'm just trying to retrace her steps," Kali said. Silva was a long shot anyway. It wasn't likely either of the victims had been at his station, much less both of them.

"Something like this," Mrs. Greene said, "it really shakes you up. Jane was a nice woman and she led a quiet life. You don't expect someone like that to get murdered. It goes to show, you just never know."

"You never do," Kali agreed, looking for a way to politely extricate herself from what she could see might become a long afternoon.

Mrs. Greene rubbed at a spot on the table with the sleeve of her sweater. "There used to be an older woman lived next door to us when I was growing up. Real grandmotherly and sweet. She'd invite us kids over for cookies and ice cream and homemade fudge. Turned out she'd butchered her husband some years earlier and kept him in the freezer. He was there all that time."

"My God, right there in the house? What a shock that must have been."

"More for my poor mother than us kids. We just wanted to know if her husband was in the same freezer where she kept the ice cream."

"Was he?"

She laughed. "I doubt it, but I don't know for sure. My parents were all very hush-hush about the whole thing." Mrs. Greene picked up the teapot. "More tea?"

"I think I'd better be going. This was lovely, though, thank you." Setting her cup on the counter, Kali caught sight of a business card. Clear View Windows. A name she recognized. "Have you used this company?" she asked.

"Not yet. I want to wait for the rainy season to pass before I call."

"That's funny, I'm doing the same thing. A friend of mine recommended them highly." A friend who was now dead. Kali felt a lump forming in her throat as it did whenever she mentioned Anne's name.

"Jane used them too," Mrs. Greene said. "That's where I got their card."

Kali's pulse skipped a beat. There it was. The connection they'd been looking for. A current of excitement made her skin tingle. A window washer would have ample opportunity to find out about the occupants, either from papers left lying about or by talking with the women themselves. It fit so perfectly, it almost took Kali's breath away.

"Don't call yet, Mrs. Greene. I've just remembered someone who had a bad experience with them."

# CHAPTER 26

Kali tried calling Bryce Keating from her cell phone the moment she left Mrs. Greene's. When she didn't reach him, she returned to the office, where a sidewalk littered with discarded placards and fast-food wrappers was all that remained of the rally. She was relieved the approach to the building was clear; her mind was already unsettled enough.

Now she sat at her desk, palms pressed to her forehead, willing herself to recall exactly what Anne had told her about Clear View Windows.

Kali could recall the occasion of the conversation vividly. They'd been in Anne's office. An autumn day in full, vivid color, just before Thanksgiving. The sun angling through the window had warmed Kali's back and cast a golden glow on the room. Kali had commented on the clean windows, and that was when Anne had given her the name of her window washer. "He does my windows at home, too," Anne had explained. "He's cheap, fast and thorough." And Kali, who'd just that morning noted the layer of grime that dulled the large wall of windows in her living and dining rooms, wrote the name and number of the window washing service on a scrap of paper and tucked it into her purse, fully intending to call that evening. She hadn't, although she'd filed the paper away where she could find it later.

If she *had* called, might she have met the same fate as Anne? Kali felt nausea roll over her and took a deep breath to steady herself. Then she reached for the phone and punched in the number. An answering machine picked up. Male voice. Fuzzy and hard to decipher. She rang the number again. An individual's name rather than a company, but Anne had said the man worked alone.

Next, she checked with the county to see if Clear View Windows was registered with the county. It wasn't. Not that failure to register the name necessarily held significance. People doing business under a name different than their own were supposed to register, but small service businesses like housecleaning or gardening sometimes overlooked that step.

Kali took another deep breath and tried again to step back in time. What else had Anne said? Kali was sure there was more, but it hadn't seemed important at the moment. Something about the man's wiry build and intrepid maneuvering of heights, as she recalled. But nothing to indicate that he appeared in any way threatening.

Kali was still working the memory when Lou Fortune and Bryce Keating showed up at her office door.

"We got your message," Bryce said. He crossed in front of Kali's desk and leaned against the wall near where she was sitting. A faint whiff of spicy aftershave followed. Kali couldn't name the scent, but she'd come to associate it with Bryce Keating and the pleasant sensation she felt in his company.

Lou grimaced as he sat in the straight-back chair closest to the door. She could tell from the way he lowered himself to the seat that his back still bothered him. "How'd you find out about this window connection?" The question sounded almost accusatory.

"I saw a business card in Mrs. Greene's kitchen," Kali explained. "She told me Jane Parkhurst had used the cleaning service and given her the name. It was familiar because Anne had recommended the service to me."

"You've used them too?" This was Bryce. He looked directly at her, and she felt her skin grow warm.

"No, I never got around to calling. It strikes me as an interesting coincidence that both Anne and Jane had their windows done by the same company. It's just the sort of connection that ties them to the same killer."

Lou picked up the card from Kali's desk and tapped it against his knee. "What do we know about this outfit?"

Kali told him what she could remember of her conversation with Anne. "I checked fictitious business names. There's no Clear View registered."

Bryce looked at his partner. "Let's give the number a try."

"I already did," Kali said. "It's a recording. Very fuzzy. I tried it twice to make sure I was dialing right. It sounded like a home answering machine. The voice was male, but that's all I can say for sure."

"Was Clear View identified by name?"

Kali shook her head. "As I said, the tone was garbled, but it sounded like the guy said his name was Burt Lancaster."

There was a moment of deafening silence during which Bryce and Lou exchanged meaningful looks. Their reaction wasn't what Kali expected, and it made her uncomfortable.

"Like the actor—you know, Elmer Gantry. At least, that's what it sounded like. That's why I tried a second time. I thought I'd misdialed."

"Could it have been Kurt instead of Burt?" Bryce asked.

"Kurt Lancaster? Sure. It could have been a lot of things."

"Son of a bitch." It was said with a sense of amazement.

"I knew it." Lou slapped his knee. "I told you the guy was a pervert."

"You know him?" Kali hadn't followed the whole nonverbal exchange, but she was pretty sure she'd understood the gist of it.

"Just met him," Bryce said. "He's the guy who was buying women's clothing in the secondhand store."

"Kinky too," Lou added. "He had these dolls—he made some of them, in fact. Life-sized. And lots of different outfits. He dresses them, kind of the way girls play with their Barbies."

"He works for a janitorial service." Bryce seemed to be thinking out loud. "It fits. Works evenings for the company, moonlights during the day doing windows on his own."

Lou rose to his feet. "Let's bring him in."

Kali was torn. Her heart pounded with excitement at the prospect of catching the killer, but her role here was to make sure it was done right. "It's going to be tough convincing a judge that we have enough evidence to hold him."

"Fuck that," Bryce said. "By the time we're finished with him, we'll have the evidence."

"That's not—"

"You want us to leave him out there on the streets where he can kill again?" His tone was sharp.

"Of course not." Was Bryce being purposely argumentative?

"We're going to need solid evidence, though, if we want the charges to stick."

"We'll get it," Bryce said with a smugness that made her wonder momentarily why she found him attractive.

"Solid, reliable evidence," she added, recalling the fiasco surrounding Dwayne Allen Davis.

"Thanks for the vote of confidence."

"I'm just thinking ahead to—"

"We don't need your permission anyway." This was Lou weighing in.

"But it will come to me soon enough. How am I going to charge him without sufficient evidence?"

Bryce shot her a silent look and the detectives left.

Kali didn't get a glimpse of Lancaster until later that evening when Lou and Bryce brought him downtown for questioning. They stuck him in an interrogation room and left him there for nearly an hour while they trumped up excuses for keeping themselves busy.

"Probably best if we question him alone," Lou informed Kali as they conferred over Styrofoam cups of bitter black coffee. Not hostile, but not asking, either.

"There's a two-way mirror against the back wall," Bryce said. "That way you'll be able to tell if we screw up." He gave special emphasis to the last two words.

Kali had no problem not being part of the initial questioning. That was pretty much standard practice. She *was* bothered, however, by the barbed undertone in Bryce's delivery. And when she tried to clear the air, he brushed her efforts aside.

"We've all got a job to do." He looked at her a moment and then left.

Lou showed Kali the door to the viewing room. She took her coffee and settled in front of the mirror where she could watch without being seen.

She was struck right off the bat by how wiry and delicate Lancaster was. He wasn't much taller than she was and probably weighed only a few pounds more. The type of man who'd have been teased a lot growing up, even without the unfortunate name.

Could Lancaster have overpowered women who were athletic and fit? Yes, she told herself. All he had to do was catch them unawares. A hand around their throats in just the right place and they wouldn't have stood a chance.

Lancaster was fidgety and seemed upset, but Kali would have been, too, in his position. Finally, Bryce entered the interrogation room carrying a can of soda and a candy bar. He handed them to Lancaster. "Sorry to keep you waiting. Paperwork and phone calls. Too much happening all at the same time."

Lancaster took the soda but ignored the candy bar. "What's this about anyway? I don't bother nobody."

Bryce sat down and folded his arms across his middle. Casual conversation mode. "Those dolls, the way you have them set around the apartment like they lived there, it's pretty neat. I've never seen anything like it before."

Lancaster rubbed a palm against his thigh. "It's something I do."

"And the ones you make yourself are really something. Must take a lot of patience."

"It does." The response was couched in wariness.

"Where'd you learn?"

"Taught myself mostly."

"You ever sell them?"

Lancaster reacted with agitation. His Adam's apple bobbed and his skin looked pasty. "No. That would be . . . it wouldn't be right."

Bryce nodded with understanding. "They're . . . special. Like your friends or something."

"Yes, that's it. Most people don't understand. They think it's a hobby, like . . . like photography."

Kali was intrigued. Not only by his doll making, but also the reference to photography. The killer had sent them a photo of Jane Parkhurst, after all.

"My partner should be here any minute," Bryce said, stifling a yawn. "I gotta warn you, he's a tough old bastard and he's in shitty mood. I'll try to keep him reined in for you." The door opened. "Ah, there he is now."

Lou entered the room. Even through the glass Kali could feel the change in atmosphere, and she knew that it was intentional. The old good-cop, bad-cop routine.

Lou pulled out a chair as if to straddle it, then apparently remembered his back. He leaned over the table instead. "Anne

Bailey. Jane Parkhurst. Those names mean anything to you, Lancaster?"

He thought for a moment, licked his lips nervously, then nodded. "I know them. I've done work for them."

"*Knew* them, dipshit. They're dead. Both of them."

Lancaster started to twitch. Head, shoulders, legs. Like a marionette with tangled strings. "What are you saying?"

"Dead, as in murdered. But you know they're dead, don't you?" Lou leaned farther over the table until he was almost nose to nose with Lancaster. "You know it better than anyone."

"Whad'ya mean *murdered?*" Lancaster looked from Lou to Bryce.

Kali could see his Adam's apple bobbing frantically.

Bryce pulled himself from his slouch. "Hey, Lou, read him his rights. Mr. Lancaster here deserves some respect."

"What are you talking about? You think *I* killed them?" Lancaster's voice rose to a fevered pitch. "That's what this is about?"

"Did you?" Bryce's voice was so soft that Kali had trouble making out the words.

Lancaster's hands shook. His body rocked in his chair.

Lou pulled a card out of his pocket and read off the standard Miranda warning. Lancaster barely listened.

"You . . . you think I k . . . kil . . . killed them?" he asked again.

"Yeah," Lou said, "that's what we think."

"You . . . you're wrong. I . . . I . . ." He turned to Bryce. "Wh-wh-why would I do something like that?"

"You tell us," Bryce said calmly.

Lancaster's twitching grew more pronounced. As did his stuttering. "I-I-I di-di-didn't. You-you-you don't understand."

"We understand plenty," Lou bellowed. "You play with those stupid dolls of yours, dressing them, undressing them, dressing them again. Then you wanted something a bit more, isn't that right? So you went after real women. Dressed them up just the way you do your dolls."

"No!"

"Why'd you do it, Kurt?" Bryce's voice was gentle, entreating.

"I di-didn't."

"If you tell us why," Bryce said reasonably, "maybe we can

help. Maybe you didn't really mean for them to die. Maybe they even liked having you dress them."

There was no response, only more twitching.

"Yeah, I bet that's it," Lou said. "It's not really his fault."

Where Bryce's tone was gentle, Lou's was thick with disdain. Kali knew they'd taken on the roles deliberately, and knew that both were manipulative, but even so she found herself drawn in by Bryce's empathy.

"Some little voice in your head tell you to do it?" Lou snickered.

"Only the voices of the angels," Lancaster said.

"Angels, is it? They talk to you?"

"Sometimes."

"Fallen angels, more like it. You know about fallen angels, don't you?"

"I didn't kill anyone!"

Lou's face wore a look of disbelief. "Where were you last Tuesday?"

Lancaster looked at Bryce. "Shouldn't I have a lawyer?"

Kali reacted immediately. *We want this clean*, she reminded them silently. The last thing they needed was a confession that would get tossed out at trial.

Bryce rubbed his jaw as if having a lawyer present had never crossed his mind. "Sure, if that's what you want." In a manner that said, "What would be the point in that?"

It was remarkable how much could be conveyed by tone and nuance. Kali hoped he'd keep it at that.

"But maybe you could help us out a little first," Bryce added. "See, all we want is to know where you were Tuesday. If there's someone who can vouch for you, then you couldn't have done it, right? You'd be in the clear."

"I was at work," Lancaster said without hesitation. "Six at night till two in the morning."

"Can you prove it?"

"I-I don't know. Somebody must have seen me."

"Give us some names."

Even from where she sat, Kali could see the panic in Lancaster's eyes. "I . . . I don't remember exactly."

"You work in teams?"

"We've been short-staffed. I've been working alone." The explaining seemed to have calmed Lancaster. His jerky twitches and stammering were less pronounced. "I can give you some names, though. You ask. Somebody musta seen me."

"Where were you working?" Bryce asked.

"Downtown. On Harrison."

Lou pulled his chair up close to Lancaster and finally sat down. "Nothing says you couldn't have left work for a while, done the deed, the kidnapping part anyway, then gone back to the job."

"Why do you think I—"

Lou tossed a coil of rope onto the table. "We found this in the back of your van, Lancaster."

Neither detective had mentioned the rope to Kali. She hoped they'd obtained it legally, though the search requirements for parolees were a lot looser than for the general public.

"I try to keep some there," Lancaster explained.

"The women were strangled with rope like this," Lou said.

"I-I k-keep it for emergencies. Comes in handy, lots of times."

"Like for tying up women."

"N-no, n-no, I—"

Lou put a hand on Lancaster's chest. "Listen, genius. My partner asked you where you were Tuesday. You're the one who immediately jumped to evening. Which, by the way, coincides perfectly with the timing of Parkhurst's abduction. Only way you'd have known that was if you were there."

"No, I'm sure you said evening." Lancaster's eyes darted between the two detectives.

"How many others did you do?"

"Others?"

"Besides Anne Bailey and Jane Parkhurst." Lou poked him again with each name.

Bryce made a gesture restraining Lou. He addressed his comments to Lancaster. "We hear about it from your lips first, that's good, you know what I mean? We find out after the fact . . ." Bryce shook his head. "They'll charge it as a capital offense for sure."

He was walking a fine line, Kali thought. Nothing he said was untrue, but the slant was definitely misleading.

"So it's definitely better to tell us, Kurt. How many others?"

"None," Lancaster protested. "No one else!"

Kali's heart was pounding. Was that a confession?

"Just Bailey and Parkhurst?" Bryce asked.

"No, not them either! You're trying to trick me."

"We're trying to help you," Bryce said calmly. "Only way we can do that is to understand what really happened."

"Don't I have a right to a lawyer? You said I could call one."

"You ready to confess? Sure, we'll go find you a lawyer. Maybe even work out a plea. You might be able to get it down to life."

Easy, Kali thought. Deny him his right to counsel and you'll lose anything he tells you.

Lancaster was breathing quickly, as if he'd just run up a flight of stairs. "I don't want to confess. I just want a lawyer."

Lou snapped at him. "You dumb shits are all the same. Know what happens once you call a lawyer? He warns you not to cooperate. Zip your lip, he says. Don't give them anything. So you sit in a cement cell for months on end, sometimes even for years, while he's out earning himself a nice income messing with your life. He has lunch at Skates by the Bay, goes home to his pretty little wife. What does he care how long you stay rotting in the system?"

"It's up to you," Bryce said. "I know if it was me and I was innocent, I'd want to clear my name as quickly as possible."

"I want a lawyer!" Lancaster seemed near tears.

"I've had it." Lou stood and shoved the chair roughly. He headed for the door. "Let his sorry ass rot."

Bryce whispered something to Lancaster that Kali couldn't hear, then he, too, left the room. Lancaster folded his head in his arms and sobbed like a child.

Kali stood and stretched, suddenly aware of the knot in her shoulders. She felt flooded with relief. For a while there she'd been afraid the detectives would push it too far.

# CHAPTER 27

Kali popped the lid from her afternoon latte and dropped it into the trash next to Lou Fortune's desk. She'd gotten to bed late last night and slept poorly. She was counting on caffeine to get her through the day.

"Guys who've been in the system before," Lou said with disgust. "They know not to say boo without an attorney present."

"It's their right," Kali reminded him. She shared his frustration, however. After Lancaster's request for an attorney the previous evening, the detectives had been unable to question him further. Lancaster was scheduled to meet with a public defender today, but Kali knew his counsel would be to say nothing. Now she faced the prospect of filing charges in a case where she had more questions than answers. It didn't help that Owen wanted an arrest so badly, he'd practically salivated when she told him about Lancaster.

Bryce pushed his chair back from his desk and stretched. "Anyone who watches TV knows they have the right to an attorney."

"Most don't insist on it, though," Lou said.

"What about the search of his apartment?" Kali asked. "Did anything turn up?"

"Nothing obvious, but the full report isn't in yet."

"Camera?"

"Yep. With a telephoto lens. No pictures of Parkhurst though."

"And his van?"

"Blue interior," Bryce said. "Similar fibers to those found on both victims."

"Similar to what's found in thousands of vehicle interiors, too," Kali pointed out.

Bryce rolled his shoulders, stretching further. *"White van, two rear doors* also fits with what that witness in the Bailey murder reported seeing."

"Nothing dangling from the mirror, though."

Lou shot her a contentious look. "So he took it down."

"What about the rope?" Kali asked.

"Size and material fits. But it's standard rope, available at any hardware store. I talked with his employer this morning. Lancaster called in sick on the night Anne Bailey was murdered. He was supposedly working the night of Jane Parkhurst's death, but there's no way to verify what hours he was actually in the building."

"Did you talk to other members of the crew?" Kali asked.

"Of course we talked to them." Lou's tone was disdainful.

"What I meant was, what did they say?"

"Might have seen him, might not," Bryce replied. "The evenings all blur together. No one could remember the night in question with any certainty, much less what time they remembered seeing Lancaster."

"But a couple of them admitted it's conceivable Lancaster could have left the job site early, or left and come back. We asked them that, too," Lou added pointedly.

"Sorry, I wasn't being critical."

Lou looked at her for a moment, started to say something, then changed his mind.

Kali didn't want to be sidetracked by a petty turf war. "I wish we had something that clearly tied him to at least one of the murders," she said.

Hard, physical evidence wasn't absolutely necessary, but it put the prosecution in a much stronger position. And given the politics involved, if there was ever a time they needed a strong case, this was it.

Lou pulled a pack of spearmint gum from his pocket and offered it around before taking a stick himself. "Don't forget those dolls of his. They're downright spooky."

Kali agreed. She'd gone by Lancaster's apartment that morning when the cops were executing their search. It wasn't just the dolls, although they were bizarre enough in themselves, it was also the way Lancaster had them positioned around the house, like his own private harem. But eccentric, or even kinky, she reminded herself, wasn't against the law.

"Has Mrs. Greene seen his photo?" Kali asked.

"Yeah," Lou said. "Doesn't recognize him. She's sure he's not the same man she saw 'snooping' around the Parkhurst house." He rolled the gum wrapper into a ball and tossed it into the trash. "Nothing says the stranger in an orange vest she claims to have seen is the man we're looking for, either."

"True." But so far they had precious little on Lancaster. "Do we know where Lancaster was eight years ago when Wendy Gilchrist was killed?"

"Prison." Bryce slid a page across the desk toward her. "That's a summary of his record."

Kali's eyes scanned the printout. A couple of small-time drug arrests and the one that sent him away, burglary of a residence. "No mention of violence," she noted.

"It's a summary rap sheet," Lou said. "Not a full-blown biography. He coulda killed his mother for all we know, and not been caught."

"It doesn't put us on very solid footing," Kali said.

"What about the shoplifting charge?"

"His word against the clerk's."

"Still, we oughta be able to hold him a couple of days," Lou said. "He's on parole, don't forget. That makes shoplifting a felony."

They could hold him forty-eight hours, regardless. It was what they did after that worried Kali.

She rose. "I guess that's it for now. Keep me informed if there are new developments."

Bryce stood also. "You headed back to your office? I'll walk with you." He held the door for her. "Good catch you made, recognizing that Lancaster had done work for both victims."

"It was pure chance."

He raised an eyebrow. "You're quick to deflect credit."

"Just telling it the way it is."

His dark eyes held hers for a moment, and the corners of his mouth smiled. "So what do you do when you're not unveiling killers?"

"Defend them." It was the sort of seat-of-the-pants response she tossed off among close friends. She regretted it instantly. "That's not entirely true," she amended. "Criminal defense work is only part of what I do, and so far I've been lucky enough to represent only innocent clients."

"But you couldn't have known for sure that they were innocent when you agreed to represent them."

"No." In several instances, in fact, she'd had serious doubts. And it troubled her. She knew the arguments in favor of defense representation as well as the next person, but when it came to personal feelings, theory didn't hold much weight. And the last person with whom she wanted to explore the issue was a cop.

"It's interesting the way you have a foot in both camps," Bryce said, walking slightly askew to address her face on. "I'd like to hear more about it sometime. But what I was really asking is, what do you do for fun?"

"Fun?" Her mind was still on weightier matters.

"You do believe in fun, don't you?"

"Yes, of course." Didn't she?

Just then Lou poked his head into the hallway and called out. "Hey, Bryce, you've got a call."

He turned to Kali. "Save that thought. I'd like to continue this discussion. Maybe over coffee some morning?"

"Okay."

"Or drinks some evening?"

She smiled. "Even better."

Bryce gave a small salute and headed back toward the homicide room, leaving Kali warm with the recognition that she'd just been hit on.

Owen popped a braised mushroom cap into his mouth and washed it down with a gulp of Pellegrino. As fund-raisers went, this wasn't a bad event. Less formal than most, and since Owen was familiar with many of the names on the guest list, it felt more personal as well. Not quite as comfortable as an evening with friends, but definitely an improvement over the glad-handing and forced repartee of the last fund-raising dinner he'd attended.

The Hobarths, formidable political wheeler-dealers as well as long-time acquaintances, had offered to host the evening at their luxurious Pacific Heights home. Though the food and service were catered, Beth Hobarth's practiced hand was evident in everything from the valet parking at the curb to the party decor, which featured the California state flag with Owen's picture superimposed.

They'd told him to expect a crowd of about fifty, which Owen thought might be overly optimistic in light of the thousand-dollar-a-head cost of attending, but looking around the room, he now decided their estimate had actually been on the conservative side. The guests were all wealthy and influential people who would potentially make much larger contributions once they'd met Owen in person and heard firsthand his vision for the state's future. It was this underlying element of salesmanship that kept Owen from fully enjoying the evening. It was also the reason he was holding a glass of designer water instead of wine or even, God forbid, a nice scotch.

At least now they had an arrest in these murders. He was no longer fielding so many questions about an ongoing crime spree and uncanny parallels to the Davis case. That was a pleasant change from the last few weeks when Owen had felt squarely situated on the hot seat.

Not that Lancaster wasn't a topic of conversation, too. Though the print media had little in the way of hard facts, they'd put the story of his arrest on the front page, filling two whole columns.

Like everyone else Owen had talked with this evening, the couple across from him were interested in knowing more.

"Why did he do it?" the husband asked.

Owen remembered the man was involved in some biotech start-up, but he couldn't for the life of him remember the fellow's name. It was one of Owen's pet peeves that name tags were considered tacky at exclusive events such as this. In fact, he sometimes thought life would be easier if people had name tags permanently affixed to their lapels.

"Why? I'm afraid I have no answer for that. We may never know."

"You must be relieved to have gotten him so quickly."

"Yes," Owen agreed. "Very relieved. It was a top-priority investigation, but we were also lucky." He added the last because it was true, and also because he felt that a touch of humility made a good impression.

"Why did he copy the Bayside Strangler?" the woman asked.

Owen shook his head. "We don't have the full story yet. We

aren't even sure whether it was just coincidence or if he copied intentionally."

"The similarities are a bit close to be simple coincidence, don't you think?" The husband took a smoked-salmon roll from the silver platter of a passing waiter.

Owen had been eyeing the salmon all evening, but he was always on the wrong side of the gathered group. He tried to catch the waiter's eye, but the young man had already moved on. One would think a perk of being the honored guest might be that the servers would make sure he wasn't overlooked.

"Harvey is right," the wife said. "It *is* odd. The yellow rose, the poems, the way he dressed them."

Harvey Blakewell. Owen remembered the name now. He tried to imprint the name in his memory, but Owen knew it was a lost cause. His biggest political failing was his inability to remember names.

"He must have wanted you to think the Bayside Strangler was still around," Mrs. Blakewell added.

"You sure he isn't the Bayside Strangler?" Her husband's tone was joking, but Owen heard a thread of doubt in the question.

"Yes," Owen said with a confidence he hoped was warranted. "We're sure. Frankly, I think we're dealing with a copycat, but it's quite plausible too that whoever committed the recent murders was operating entirely from his own imagination."

Mr. Blakewell scoffed. "What are the odds of that?"

"Not as long as you might think," Owen responded. "There are certain patterns we see time and again with serial killers. For instance, their murders often involve ritual, especially dressing, posing or putting makeup on the body. There are also numerous cases of killers stalking their victims and then reveling in their accomplishments via notes or poems. Even flowers are a recurring theme."

"But a single yellow rose . . ." Mr. Blakewell was not ready to give up.

"Maybe," said his wife, "this Lancaster fellow was an admirer of the Bayside Strangler. Many years ago when the Zodiac killer was preying on women of this area, my neighbor's nephew collected . . ."

Owen was tiring of playing spin doctor. He'd barely had time to digest the arrest himself, and since he'd missed Kali's latest call, he was short on details. "Our man wouldn't be the first copycat killer, for sure. And there was a book about the case, so the specifics—"

"Right," Harvey Blakewell said. "I remember reading it. You made a name for yourself with that case. Got yourself elected district attorney, and you've been a damn good one too, I might add."

Back on comfortable ground. Owen breathed a sigh of relief. "I appreciate the kind words, but I hope my appeal as candidate for governor goes beyond the realm of crime."

"Absolutely. Your stands on accountability in education and the economy—"

Another man, the senior partner at a boutique intellectual-property law firm, joined them just then, picking up on the conversation. "But crime is a big concern in the state right now. There are strong feelings about the death penalty, especially with the DNA testing in death-row cases. And with the three-strikes law, well, I think most people didn't understand how it worked. They're all for getting tough on crime, but they want to be fair about it too."

"That's my motto," Owen said with a self-effacing grin. "Tough but fair."

"You going for the death penalty on this one?"

No need to ask *which* one. "We haven't decided yet."

"Who's representing him? One of the big guns?"

"Public defender's office," Owen said.

"That ought to make it an easy win for the prosecution."

Civil lawyers liked to win. That was the name of the game for them. Lawyers in the district attorney's office liked to win, too, of course, but they were charged with going after the truth, not simply winning at all costs. Owen was always a little uneasy when the two sides were unevenly matched, especially when the stakes were so high.

"Well, I'm glad you've moved so quickly and we can now put the Davis matter behind us once and for all. This one could have brought you down, Owen. Or at the least, done major damage. A group of us were talking just the other day. We all had the same reaction when the story broke, and we were a bit leery about throwing our support behind you."

"And now?" Owen hoped he didn't sound desperate. Or resentful. With all the important issues facing California in the years ahead, it annoyed him that so many people got hung up on a single, narrow issue.

The man gave him a hearty slap on the back. "I think you'll find the money coming in a bit more easily."

Another man elbowed his way next to Owen, introduced himself, and started in on the subject again. Owen scanned the room for Selby and felt a moment of unease when he didn't see her. Then he spotted a streak of red. Ah, there she was, in her form-fitting, one-shouldered scarlet gown, charming a group of admirers. She was his best campaign asset, he sometimes thought. He'd get votes not because people wanted to see Owen as governor, but because they wanted Selby as the state's first lady.

Owen caught Selby's eye and gave her their secret signal, a tug on his left earlobe. She was at his side in little over a minute.

"Owen, darling," she cooed. "I wonder if I might have word with you." She turned and flashed the large man next to Owen her most winning smile. "I'm so sorry to interrupt, but wives have that prerogative."

The men chortled with good humor, their eyes riveted on Selby. She slipped her arm through Owen's and they walked to a quiet corner on the far side of the room.

"You having a rough time of it?" she asked.

"Just tired of talking about murder."

"And one trial in particular, I bet. I've had my ear bent on that subject, as well."

Owen looked around the crowded room. "Not one person has asked me about the workfare program I outlined last week during my talk at the World Trade Club. Not one person."

"That's nuts-and-bolts stuff, Owen. Important but hardly as engrossing as murder."

"Nuts and bolts is what running the state is about, damn it." He caught Selby's look, which was sympathetic but also slightly amused. It was the look she wore when she thought he was taking himself far too seriously. A not infrequent occurrence.

Owen sighed. "I wish I knew more about this guy Lancaster."

"And you don't because . . . ?" Selby tilted her head to the side the way she often did when she was coaxing him out of a grumpy mood.

Because he'd been campaigning when he should have been

working. "I missed Kali's call and haven't been able to reach her since. Besides, it's early in the process. Between now and the trial, there will be quite a lot unveiled."

Selby squeezed his hand. "What matters, Owen, is that Lancaster's arrest makes you look good."

"But it's not—"

Beth Hobarth swooped in on them in full hostess mode. "Owen, what are you doing off in a corner? No hiding allowed." She wagged her finger at him. "Come on, I'll introduce you."

Owen handed his glass to the bartender for more Pellegrino and lime, gave Selby a beseeching look, and let Beth lead him across the room where he was immediately surrounded by a group of potential supporters. Half an hour later, he caught sight of Jack Jackson in the crowd and made his way over to him.

"You coughed up a thousand dollars for this?" Owen asked.

Jackson laughed. "Of course not. I'm here in an official capacity. In fact, there are a couple of us sympathetic press types sprinkled among the masses."

"Do I detect the hand of Les Amstead?"

"Indeed you do, and a very nimble-fingered hand it is. He's doing a good job overseeing your campaign, Owen. He knows how to market you."

"He's a good man to have on board." Owen sometimes thought Amstead seemed more determined to win than Owen himself.

"So what can you tell me about Lancaster?" Jackson asked.

"You need to talk to Kali O'Brien. I've been keeping my distance with respect to the day-to-day developments on the case."

Jackson sipped his wine. "I couldn't reach her. And the cops won't give me the time of day. They issued a very brief press release yesterday morning, and there's been nothing since."

"I'm sure there will be more after Lancaster is charged."

Jackson eyed him. "So your office is going ahead and prosecuting?"

"Of course. Why?"

"Just curious. Not all arrests lead to prosecutions."

"My office has been working closely with homicide on this from the beginning." Owen had about had it with this subject.

"I don't suppose you know whether he washed windows for any of the Bayside Strangler victims?"

Owen was momentarily stunned. "What's the matter, Jack? You didn't express any doubts about Davis in the book." Not entirely true, Owen conceded silently, since Jackson had included enough controversy to propel the book onto the bestseller lists.

"I'm not expressing doubt now, either," Jackson said. "Just asking what strikes me as a rather interesting, and obvious, question."

"Two different killers, Jack. Remember that. Davis was the Bayside Strangler, and he wasn't around to commit the new murders."

Just then another man approached and Owen was off again, shaking hands and trying his best to impress. Out of the corner of his eye, he caught Jackson watching. He wasn't thinking of parlaying these latest murders into another book, was he? Owen tried to work his way back to ask Jackson that question directly, but the wave of people greeting him pushed him to the far side of the room. At least there, the conversation focused on education.

By the time they left for the evening, Owen was hoarse. And badly in need of a glass of scotch.

Selby fixed one for each of them as soon as they got home, and they took the drinks to their bedroom. Selby slipped out of her dress and hung it in the closet, then came up behind Owen and gave him a hug. "I love you," she said, her chin pressed against his back.

"That's good, because I love you." Her very presence made him feel whole and grounded. He was lucky to have met her. Luckier still that she'd shown any interest in an aging bureaucrat when she'd been surrounded by Hollywood charm.

"I think you won over a lot of people tonight," she said.

"It was an audience predisposed to be won."

"Yes, but there's a difference between perfunctory approval and genuine admiration." She was leaning against the dresser now, gazing at him with her soft blue eyes. "You have a winning way with people, Owen."

"We'll see how much of that translates into public endorsements and monetary support."

Selby sighed. "It's sad that's what politics comes down to." She turned to look at her own reflection in the mirror, pulling her hair back from her face with her hands. "You know, I hadn't realized until tonight that I knew that real estate agent who was killed. Jane Parkhurst."

"Knew her? How?"

"Maybe *knew* isn't really the right word. I'd met her. Remember when we were thinking of selling the house?"

Owen nodded. Last year, following their engagement. Moving had been Selby's idea. She wasn't keen on the idea of living in "another woman's house," as she'd put it. But once she'd started looking at what else was available, she'd more or less given up on the idea. Instead, she'd redecorated.

Owen undid his tie. "You were working with someone by the name of Carol, I thought."

"Right, Carol Johnson. But she had a couple of her fellow agents look at this house to give us an estimate of how much we might get for it, remember?"

Vaguely. Owen had left the matter pretty much in Selby's hands.

"I'm sure Jane Parkhurst was one of the women Carol asked."

"And?"

Selby let her hair fall loose again. "And nothing. It just dawned on me tonight that I'd met her, that's all."

It was an instance of what Owen thought of as woman's logic. Random thoughts that came out of nowhere and somehow took on significance. He kissed her forehead. "I've had enough murder talk for one night. Can we put it behind us now and go to bed?"

"And?" she said playfully, echoing his own question a moment earlier.

He gathered her into his arms. "Definitely not *nothing*."

# CHAPTER 28

Kali woke during the night with a start, her heart pounding and her bedclothes in a tangle.

She'd heard a noise. A faint, unfamiliar scratching.

Or had she?

She'd been dreaming, she realized now as she came more fully awake, though she couldn't recall anything about the dream but a rush of fear. Had she imagined the noise?

Kali pushed back the covers and listened. Nothing. Loretta was sleeping, undisturbed, on the floor at the foot of her bed. Granted, she was no watchdog, but she was usually quick to react to anything out of the ordinary.

Just as Kali began to relax, she heard it again. A fleeting sound from somewhere outside.

Again, Kali listened intently. Her muscles were taut and her body stilled. She held her breath, wanting nothing to get in the way of her ability to hear.

There it was once more, an uneven scraping near the kitchen. She eased herself out of bed, grabbed the cordless phone from the table, and moved quietly into the hallway.

Despite the cold, she went barefoot rather than risk the shuffle of slippers on wood. The noise was coming from outside, she reminded herself; she didn't have to worry about an intruder hearing her. Still, she preferred the cover of stealth.

She crept down the hallway, through the living room to the kitchen. The house appeared undisturbed, the doors and windows locked. She checked the lower level, as well, and found nothing amiss. Finally, she returned to the kitchen and flipped on the outside light. A movement caught her eye and her heart stopped until she determined that what she'd seen was only a paper bag flapping in the wind. It was caught on the leg of one of her deck chairs that had itself been blown close the house. As she listened now, she heard the sound for what it was, merely the rustling of paper against wood.

Kali felt her body relax and she breathed deeply for the first time since waking. She had really let her imagination get the best of her this time, and that didn't happen often. It must have been the dream, she decided. Kali tried, and again failed, to recall what it had been about. But the aura of fear that had been so central to the dream still clung to her. It took her over an hour to get back to sleep.

Rain arrived with the first light of day. A forceful, pounding rain that made Kali happy to be warm and dry and comfortable in her own bed. Twenty minutes after the alarm had gone off, she was still huddled under the comforter. Finally, she forced herself to get up, but even then she moved more slowly than usual. Rainy days did not bring out the best in her.

Kali fixed coffee, and to fortify herself against the wet weather, allowed herself an English muffin with jam. She lingered over the paper, where Lancaster's arrest was front-page news, and then coaxed Loretta outside for her morning constitutional. Instead of hunting for a spot to squat, the dog made a beeline for the paper bag that had wakened Kali the night before.

"No, you don't," Kali said, dashing barefoot into the rain to grab the bag before Loretta tore it to shreds. "Do your business and come back inside."

It was a Safeway grocery bag with two Dove candy wrappers and the remnants of a tuna sandwich inside. No wonder Loretta had been attracted to it. Kali wadded the thing up and tossed it into the garbage.

She was rinsing her hands when curiosity got the better of her. Retrieving the bag, she checked the cash register tape. The purchases had been made the day before at eight-thirty in the evening at a store nowhere near her neighborhood. The candy and the sandwich were part of a larger order that included gum, film, beer, hair gel and cigarettes. So how had the bag ended up outside her door? She remembered the wind from the night before. No doubt the bag had blown from a neighbor's yard.

Kali again tossed it into the garbage. She let Loretta back into the house but only after wiping her muddy paws with an old towel. Finally convinced that the rain wasn't going to let up anytime soon, Kali headed for her car.

"I don't suppose we've lucked into a confession?" Owen asked when she was seated across from him in his imposing office later that morning. As he folded his hands, his gold stud cufflinks clanked against the polished surface of his desk.

"Far from it. He says he didn't do it."

"No surprise there, I guess." Owen leaned back. "We'll have to build a case the hard way, piece by piece."

Kali shifted in her chair. Owen was apparently leaning toward forging ahead. "The evidence against him isn't as solid as we'd like," she said.

"Enough for the prelim, though?" His tone made it a question, but it was clear he thought the answer was obvious.

"I'm not even sure about charging him."

"What?" Owen looked annoyed. "How can we not charge him? We need to put an end to this."

"But what if he's not the right one?"

Owen hesitated. He looked at her, then away. "What do you mean?"

The office was cold. Kali rubbed her hands together. "He's squirrelly, Owen, but I'm not convinced he's our killer."

"You're an expert on serial killers now?"

Kali couldn't tell if the words were meant to sting, but they did. "You always told us that as prosecutors, we were warriors for truth. That we shouldn't proceed with a case unless we genuinely believed justice was on our side." In theory, that was the tenet for prosecutors everywhere, but in too many instances, politics and personal grandeur came first. Owen, though, was a man of principle. Or he had been at one time.

"Come on, Kali. Don't go soft on me."

"Soft? All I—"

Owen snapped at her. "Maybe you've spent too many years as a defense attorney."

"And maybe you've devoted so much energy to running for governor, you've lost sight of the fact that you're still the district attorney."

The silence that followed was palpable. Kali felt the bite of her own words as much as she did Owen's.

She started to apologize, but Owen cut her off. "No, I'm the one who was out of line. You're doing what you should be doing. What I asked you to do in the beginning." He dropped his head into his hands and kneaded his forehead with his fingers. "You're right. We can't charge him until we're sure we've got a case against him."

"With luck, we'll have the evidence soon." Maybe not soon enough, but she was relieved she didn't have to battle Owen over it.

"I just want this mess done with," he said, sounding something like a petulant child. "The primary is less than two months away."

"I know, the timing is bad." Worse, even, for the victims. But she knew Owen well enough to feel certain he hadn't lost sight of that.

He raised his head. "This morning's *Chronicle* ran the results of their latest poll, conducted yesterday after word of the arrest was out. My popularity increased by seven points." He gave her a skewed grin. "It was one of those quick and dirty surveys so the results are probably meaningless, but it was still a nice feeling."

"If the voters had half a brain, you'd be so far ahead this case wouldn't matter."

He smiled. "Thanks. But unfortunately, it matters a lot. Even with the seven-point gain, I haven't reclaimed the edge I had before this all started."

It wasn't just the murders, Kali realized, but the play they'd received in the press. She was sure that Tony Molina had done what he could to keep the interest alive.

Owen sat back in his chair and ran a hand through his full head of silver hair. "So, tell me what doesn't sit right with you about Lancaster."

That was hard to explain because it was more a feeling than anything concrete. She looked out window. The rain had not let up. "He's not strong, for one thing."

"It doesn't take strength to strangle someone," Owen responded. "Just know-how."

"But he had to accost his victims, move them at some point, pose the bodies."

"Know-how, again."

"He can't spell worth a darn," Kali said. "And I doubt he's much of a poet."

Owen gave a short laugh. "Our killer isn't much of a poet either."

"You know what I mean. If Lancaster was going to write a taunting note, I bet it wouldn't be in the form of a poem. Besides, he doesn't even own a computer."

"There are dozens of places where the public can access computers."

Was he simply playing devil's advocate, or was Owen actually trying to talk her into something? Political ambition colored the thinking of even the most honest men.

"Lancaster had connections to both victims," Owen pointed out. "That in itself raises a red flag. The fibers from his van were similar to those found on both Anne's and Jane's clothing, and the rope in his trunk was consistent with that used in the murders."

"None of that is conclusive."

Owen pressed on as though she hadn't spoken. "His van matched the description given by a possible witness to one of the murders, and he *did* call in sick the night Anne Bailey was killed."

"There's no hard evidence, though. It's all circumstantial."

"That's often the case, as you well know."

But this felt different somehow. "It's the total picture, Owen. Our killer wants us to think he's the Bayside Strangler. He's clever and manipulative. A gamesman, in fact. Lancaster is just some dopey guy with a kinky interest in dolls."

Owen scratched his cheek. "I don't see that those two portraits are so far off. He's certainly playing games with those dolls of his."

"But why the Bayside Strangler? He claims never to have heard of the earlier murders or Dwayne Allen Davis."

"You don't honestly believe every word he says, do you? Especially now that he's got an attorney at his side."

"Of course not." Lancaster's attorney, a veteran public defender, had no doubt coached him well.

"I understand the point you're trying to make," Owen said reasonably. He leaned forward, resting his forearms on his desk. "But I think you should ask yourself if you're being overly cautious. Sure, prosecutors are supposed to believe in their cases, but that doesn't mean there's never the slightest doubt. We'd never prosecute anyone if that was the standard."

*Was* she being too careful? That was part of the reason she'd decided years ago that she wasn't cut out to be a prosecutor. There was always a niggling of doubt in her mind.

Lancaster had the means and the opportunity to commit the crimes. As for motive, who could fathom what went on in the mind of a serial killer? All Kali knew was that his dressing of the dolls was eerily similar to what had happened to their victims.

"I don't want to press charges if we can't make a case, Kali. But neither do I want to let this case hang in limbo if we don't have to." Owen pushed back his chair and stood. "In any event, I'd like to issue a press release. So far there's been very little official comment from either this office or the police, and I think it's time to put our own spin on events. Nothing detailed or specific, but if we don't come forward with *something*, all the public will have is media speculation. Can you have a draft ready by this afternoon?"

"Sure."

"Get it to me by two o'clock if you can."

Kali returned to her desk by way of the coffee machine. If it weren't for the wet weather, she'd have gone out for a cup of the good stuff, but even the prospect of a full-bodied latte couldn't tempt her from the relative comfort of a dry office building. She took her cup back to her desk and had just begun working on the press release when her phone rang. She picked it up on the first ring.

"Hi, it's Nathan. Hope I'm not interrupting anything important."

"On a day like this, I welcome interruptions."

"One of those times you'd rather be anywhere but work?"

"Sort of. Speaking of which, I tried calling you. To thank you for the flowers. I couldn't find anyone at Global Investment who recognized your name. What office are you in?"

An embarrassed laugh. "No office anymore. I had a run-in with my boss and quit."

"Quit? Just like that?"

"I've been thinking about doing something different anyway."

"What?"

"Oh, I'm exploring a couple of options. Let me give you my cell phone number. It's probably the best way to reach me."

She jotted down the number he rattled off.

"Glad you liked the flowers. I considered roses, but then thought they might be too much for a thank-you."

Kali felt a prickle of anxiety. "Why roses?"

"Aren't they woman's best friend?" He laughed. "Or maybe that's diamonds. Anyway, I enjoyed spending the evening with you. I'd like to do it again. Soon." He paused, maybe waiting for her to jump in. When she didn't, he asked, "How about dinner tomorrow night?"

Kali had wanted to thank him for the flowers because it seemed the polite thing to do. But she wasn't at all certain she wanted to see him again. And this talk of roses cast a bit of a pall over whatever warm feelings she might have had for him. "I'm afraid I'm busy tomorrow evening."

"You free tonight by any chance?"

"Sorry." This, at least, was a legitimate excuse. She had plans with Margot.

"Guess I shouldn't wait until the last minute."

"I'm sorry, I—"

"So pick a date. My evenings are open."

Now he'd put her on the spot. She hedged. "My calendar is at home. I'll check and get back to you."

"You're a popular woman." His voice had become cooler.

She tried to keep it light. "Not really, but this is kind of a busy period for me. A big case at work, a couple of other commitments . . ."

"Hey, it's okay. You aren't the only fish in the sea, you know." Cool had turned to ice. He hung up abruptly.

What a jerk. She was glad now that she'd been busy.

When the phone rang again a few minutes later, she thought it might be Nathan calling back with an apology. But instead it was someone who identified himself as John Jones.

"When do I get my money?" he asked.

"Money?"

"Yeah, for the reward. You got the guy, right?"

She mentally arranged the pieces. "Are you talking about the reward money offered in connection with the two recent murders?"

"Yeah. The twenty grand."

"How'd you get my name?"

"It was in the paper. No one was answering at the other number."

"What other number?"

"One I called the first time."

Slowly, she was beginning to understand the sequence of events. He'd called the tip line originally and was now calling back to arrange for payment. Kali found a pencil and wrote "John Jones" on a sheet of yellow paper.

"What makes you think the money should be yours?" she asked.

"I called up and told them what I seen."

"Which was?"

"A man in that RiteAid parking lot. Same night that woman got kidnapped and killed."

*That woman*, Kali realized with a start, was Anne Bailey. "You saw who took her?"

"I saw a man. Built like he worked out, you know?"

"But you didn't see him with the woman?"

"No, never saw no woman. But I saw one of those flyers with information about the reward. Store had them in the window."

"What makes you think the man you saw had anything to do with her murder?"

"Looked like a punk."

If they arrested everyone who looked like a punk, the jails would be overflowing. "Give me your number. I'll see what I can find out. But the reward is good only if the information leads to a conviction." And his description didn't even sound much like Lancaster.

She called the detectives. Bryce answered. His brusque tone softened the minute she said her name, a reaction that Kali found pleased her.

She explained about John Jones's call.

"Yeah, he's the guy who saw a white van in the parking lot."

"What else did he see?"

"Let me check the log," Keating said. He put her on hold for a moment. Then came back. "I took the initial call myself. Maureen Oliver followed up on it. Jones is apparently missing a few brain cells. Said he saw some guy standing next to his vehicle smoking. Never went into the store, just parked and smoked."

"And what made him think this guy had anything to do with Anne's murder?"

"The reward most likely. We get tips like this all the time."

"Then his description of the van doesn't do us much good with Lancaster, does it?"

"We've got other stuff on Lancaster."

Too bad the caller hadn't seen a slender, wiry man, Kali thought. But that gave her an idea. "Can you look through the list of tips and see if any of them might implicate Lancaster?"

"Will do. Meanwhile we're running Lancaster's prints against every bit of evidence we've got."

All they needed was one solid piece of direct evidence. It might not be enough to ensure a conviction, but it would make Kali feel much better about pressing ahead with the case.

# CHAPTER 29

Bryce Keating opened the database on his laptop and scrolled through the list of people who'd called with tips about the murders. He wasn't optimistic about coming up with anything Kali would find useful, but you never knew. He'd been a cop long enough to know that seemingly inconsequential details were sometimes pivotal in breaking a case. He had to assume the same was true in prosecuting one.

Then, too, he wasn't about to pass up having an excuse to call her.

Not that he generally needed an excuse to call a woman. He was, in fact, quite adept at such things. But Kali was different. Bryce hadn't figured out yet just how or why, but she was.

He was clearly attracted to her, but he felt an unusual wariness as well. It wasn't that he wanted to admire her from afar (the very idea was depressing as hell), but every time he thought about making a move, he hesitated.

She wasn't the kind of woman he usually went after. Maybe that was the problem. Kali was more of a challenge. At least Bryce hoped that was all it was. After the divorce, he'd promised himself no woman was ever going to get under his skin again. He worked hard at making sure that didn't happen, and he didn't like to think he'd found a weak spot.

Bryce sorted the list of names using several different criteria, and pulled out five for further consideration. Rereading the notes on each of them, he whittled it down to three. He loved the way computers eased the storage and retrieval of information. Lou wouldn't get within five feet of a computer. He relied on his notebook and pen, and a drawer full of file folders he never looked at.

The first homicide they'd worked on together, Lou had accumulated so many bits of paper that you couldn't see the top of his desk. Bryce had everything he needed on a three-inch floppy.

He printed out the summary of information and went to see Kali.

She was bent over her desk, pen in hand. Her other hand fiddled with a wave of curly auburn hair that fell over her eyes. She hadn't heard him approach, and he watched her silently for a moment before knocking.

"Don't pin your hopes on these tips," he told her, handing over the printout.

She looked up and smiled. "Wow, that was fast."

"The benefits of modern technology." Bryce leaned against the door jamb. "The first name there, Mills, is a man who had a conversation with a stranger in a bar. The stranger apparently talked about having sex with a corpse. Mills thought the guy was pulling his leg, but when he read about the murders, he called us. The stranger's description could fit Lancaster.

"The second name is a woman who saw a man and woman struggling the evening of the Parkhurst murder. She said there was a lot of name calling and the man hit the woman, but in the end, the woman got into the man's car and they drove off. Again, the man might fit Lancaster's description. The third is probably your best shot. A florist who recalls a man buying a single rose. Maureen Oliver talked to her in person and got only the vaguest description—white male, indeterminate age. But maybe if she saw a picture of Lancaster it might jump-start her memory."

Kali rubbed the bridge of her nose. "It would be terrific if she recognized him."

"And if she doesn't?"

Kali hesitated. "Let's cross that bridge when we come to it."

She was silent for a moment. Bryce watched her. He liked the way her green eyes darkened when she was lost in thought. She had nice eyes. You could tell a lot about a person by her eyes.

"You're not seeing anyone, are you?" he asked. The words were out before they'd even formed in his mind. He didn't have the foggiest idea where they'd come from. She'd already said she would meet him for a drink sometime.

She gave him an odd look, then shrugged. "I was for a while, but I stopped a couple of months ago. Why?"

"I wouldn't want to step on any toes."

She made a small noise, something between a hiccup and a laugh. Whatever it was, it stuck in her throat. She took a couple of swigs of coffee to wash it down. Her cheeks grew pink. Bryce could have sworn she was embarrassed, although it might just have been her cough.

Finally she looked at him and managed a smile. "You wouldn't be."

God, how could she have been so dense? Kali pounded her forehead with her palm. Her mind had been someplace else altogether. One of those weird mind leaps borne of associated memory. When Bryce had asked if she was seeing anyone, she'd thought he was talking about a shrink. At the encouragement of just about everyone she knew, and some she didn't, like the police chaplain, last fall she'd gone to see Dr. Sadler, who insisted on endlessly rehashing what had happened with Steven. It reminded her of the movie, *Groundhog Day*. She figured when she finally got it right, he'd pronounce her cured. But in the end she'd simply quit going. She still had the nightmares sometimes, but her sessions with Sadler hadn't done anything to relieve the terrible memories.

Bryce, however, had apparently been asking about her social life. Kali felt an involuntary smile on her lips. She couldn't imagine that she and Bryce Keating would have many interests in common, but in terms of pure chemistry, she had a feeling it didn't get much better.

The idea was so appealing that she had to force her mind back to the job at hand. She finished drafting a press release, ran it by Owen and gave it to Gloria to fax to the major media outlets. Then she took Lancaster's photo and set out to track down the three names Bryce Keating had given her.

She tried the florist first. A middle-aged Asian woman who wanted very much to please, but was sadly unable to identify Lancaster as the man who'd purchased a rose.

"It might be him," she said. "But maybe not, too. We get so many customers, they all seem the same after a while. Flowers I remember. A beautiful bouquet of iris and baby's breath for the gentleman yesterday afternoon, or Peruvian lilies for a lady with

234 / Jonnie Jacobs

the little black dog. But people . . ." She looked at Kali sadly. "I'm sorry I cannot be of more help."

Kali thanked her and left. At least the woman hadn't ruled Lancaster out.

She tried Mills next. He was a man in his fifties. Distinguished, even in blue jeans and a corduroy shirt. He'd taken early retirement, he told her. Best thing he'd ever done. The way he bent her ear, though, Kali had a feeling his days weren't as full as he let on. He spent time studying the photograph before saying definitively that Lancaster was not the man he'd had the conversation with in the bar.

Likewise, the woman who'd seen a couple fighting was reasonably sure the man wasn't Lancaster.

By the time Kali had finished, she was exhausted and grumpy. Bryce had told her not to pin her hopes on any of these people, but that hadn't stopped her from secretly believing one of them would provide the corroboration she needed. If Lancaster was their killer, there had to be ways to tie him to the crimes.

Back at her desk, Kali tried calling Dr. Dunworthy, fully expecting to get an answering machine. Instead, the man himself picked up.

"Sorry to bother you again. If you're in the middle of something, I can call back."

"Not at all. I read there was a suspect in custody. I'm quite interested to hear how he fits the characteristics we discussed." Dunworthy's voice resonated with anticipation.

"I'm not sure he does," Kali said. "Not fully, anyway."

"Tell me about him."

"We're still filling in the pieces. What we know now is that he's thirty-six, never married, works as a janitor, with his own window-washing service on the side. His boss says he's a good worker, keeps to himself but in a friendly way. Neighbors say the same thing. He helps an elderly couple in his building when they need little things done around the apartment."

"What about family?"

"He's got a mother in Colorado. No brothers or sisters, and the father hasn't been in the picture for years."

"That part's not so far off," Dunworthy volunteered. "An only child from a single-parent home—there's potential there for issues of rage and control."

An overly simplistic assessment, she thought. But she made note of the point all the same. Fleshed out, it might provide context if the case went to trial. "But here's the interesting part," she said. "He makes and collects life-sized dolls."

"You say he makes them?"

"Some of them. They're constructed of cloth like the old Raggedy Ann dolls. A few had porcelain faces. But he also had mannequins and at least one that was actually a sex toy, though he dressed her conservatively. He has them set up all over the apartment. Like roommates or something. He has a complete wardrobe of clothes for them."

"Most interesting." Dunworthy sounded almost as though he were talking to himself. Kali could picture him stroking his goatee, his small, dark eyes narrowed in thought.

"They're like grown-up Barbies. I think he probably dresses them, moves them around, talks to them. The way kids do when they're playing with dolls or action figures." Kali was always fascinated watching her friends' children weave stories as they played. Their make-believe world was every bit as real as the physical one.

"You said before that the killer could be acting out his own personal fantasy with the murders," she continued. "Would he act it out both with the dolls and in real life?"

There was a scratchy sound, like the phone was being transferred from one ear to another, or walked between rooms. "I can't say I've encountered this before, either in my own experience or in the literature, but I wouldn't rule it out." Dunworthy was breathing heavily into the phone. Kali could imagine his excitement at discovering some new wrinkle in serial killer behavior. A major paper and the lecture circuit beckoned.

"I would have to speak to this man to know with any certainty," Dunworthy continued. "Perhaps the games with dolls no longer satisfied him, and his fantasy required the real thing. Fantasies do have a way of escalating. In fact, I'd very much like to interview him."

Dunworthy was an expert, Kali reminded herself. A man who'd written and lectured widely on the very sort of thing they were now discussing. So why should his clinical interest in Lancaster bother her? But she wasn't eager to have him questioning Lancaster for his own interests.

"I don't think that would be appropriate at this point," she told him.

"Perhaps as the trial approaches."

Kali mumbled something noncommittal. "Another thing, Doctor. When we last spoke you'd pointed out that our killer, as opposed to the Bayside Strangler who was meticulous in dressing his victims . . . that our killer has been more haphazard."

"Right." He dragged the word out, no doubt wondering if he'd been too hasty in his pronouncement. "Based on what you told me, it sounded like there was a difference in the way the two killers treated the victims. But what you're saying now is that this man you've arrested dresses his dolls with great care?"

"In a nutshell, yes." She waited to see if he would elaborate on his theory.

"Well, again," he said slowly, "without studying the evidence in more detail, I'm not in a position to speak with conviction, but I do understand your point. Nonetheless, one would assume that dressing a real body is much different than dressing an inanimate doll. There is also the discovery factor. The killer was no doubt under some pressure to get the bodies dressed and disposed of before someone saw him."

"I thought of that, but isn't there a core—uh, signature is what you called it, I think. A personal stamp, so to speak, that is unique for each killer?"

"Yes, yes. But that is with regard to actual killings. What we're talking about here is something different. These dolls, however bizarre they may strike you, aren't real living women."

"So you couldn't say one way or the other if he fit the pattern of our killer?"

"No. Certainly not without interviewing him directly."

Had she really expected Dunworthy to give her a definitive answer? Would she have believed him if he had? Still, she was disappointed. Maybe all she was looking for was an easy answer. "One last question, if you don't mind. The first of our victims was killed on the anniversary of the murder of one of the original victims, Wendy Gilchrist. Any idea why the killer might do that?"

Dunworthy's laugh sounded almost gleeful. "My dear, that seems quite obvious. This type of killer is enamored of ritual and the game aspects of murder. It's clear he likes taunting the police."

Kali picked up a paperclip and toyed with it. "Why that particular victim of the Bayside Strangler, though, and not some other?"

He seemed to think about it for a moment. "Well, he had to choose one, didn't he? There's also the possibility the date has some significance for him aside from the two deaths. We all make connections in our mind, often in ways that defy logic."

Kali remembered the tangled path of mental associations that had led her to think Bryce Keating was asking if she was getting professional help when he'd really been inquiring about her social calendar.

"I remember one case," Dunworthy continued, "where a man murdered three women, three years apart. All on August sixth. It was only after he was in prison and the subject of intense study by a colleague of mine, that it was determined August sixth was the day his mother had punished him as a child by making him play in the front yard in a dress. That happened when he was eight years old, and the first murder didn't take place until eighteen years later."

"He remembered the date?" Kali couldn't remember dates that were only a week past.

"The subconscious is a powerful thing, my dear."

As Kali was bending the paperclip with her fingers, it twisted and poked her thumb, drawing blood. She grabbed a tissue and tried to ignore the fact that it smarted. "Taken to its logical conclusion, your example implies that our current killer was responsible for Wendy Gilchrist's death as well." Except that Lancaster had been in jail at the time.

"I was simply making a point about the personal significance of certain dates." He paused. "But it's an interesting idea you raise. Wasn't the Gilchrist woman the one who most deviated from the pattern?"

"Right." Kali hesitated, reluctant to open the proverbial can of worms. But she'd come this far, she might as well finish the thought. "In fact, her murder is similar in many ways to the recent ones."

"Ahh, that raises some fascinating questions, doesn't it?" Again, Dunworthy's tone resonated with what Kali could only think of as delight.

"Do you think it possible that our killer wasn't so much fascinated with the Bayside Strangler as with the murder of Wendy Gilchrist?"

"Certainly, but I bet there's not as much distinction as you think."

"What do you mean?"

"It's like having a favorite actor. You like most everything he does, but there may be one movie in particular that's your favorite. Your killer could be fascinated with the Bayside Strangler and still exhibit preference for the Gilchrist murder." Dunworthy's delivery was growing clipped, as though he were in a hurry. "I'd be happy to discuss this with you in detail. But another time, I'm afraid. I have a commitment at the moment, and I really must go."

She thanked him for his time and hung up, not sure that she'd gleaned anything helpful from the conversation. Certainly nothing that relieved the gnawing uneasiness she felt.

Heading home, Kali promised herself she wouldn't think about the case for the remainder of the night. A good movie and Margot's company would keep her occupied.

She would have been true to her word if the previews of coming attractions hadn't included clips from a film about a wrongly accused man on death row.

"I guess that one's a little too close to home," Margot whispered.

Kali nodded. That brief reminder was all it took. Doubts about Lancaster churned at the back of her mind throughout the entire feature. It was a romantic comedy of the sort that would usually have absorbed her, but though she laughed occasionally, she never fully relaxed.

Afterward, Kali and Margot stopped for pizza and got to talking to the two men at the next table. It amused Kali to watch Margot flirt with them. Both men were overweight and had spent the early part of the their dinner talking about an old Mustang one of them was rebuilding. Kali suspected Margot wasn't so much interested in the men themselves as in flexing her feminine skills. At least she'd stopped short of handing out her phone number or last name, for which Kali was grateful.

Finally Kali pleaded exhaustion and dragged Margot away.

"You're giving the fair sex a bad name," Kali chided when they got into the car.

"I was just having fun."

"You're like a teenager."

Margot laughed. "That's not so far off. I'm still experimenting with my new identity. You've had all those years I missed."

"Heartache and angst. Be glad you missed them."

"You think I didn't have heartache and angst? Imagine how you'd feel if you'd spent your youth imprisoned in a man's body."

This was a conversation they'd had before. And while Kali understood in theory, she had trouble imagining herself as anyone but who she was.

Margot turned on the radio and began humming along with a rendition of "Yesterday." Kali, grateful not to be the one driving, closed her eyes and let the movement of the car gently rock her.

Margot stopped humming. "Had those guys even asked for their check by the time we left?"

"I don't know. Why?"

"I could swear we're being followed."

Kali opened her eyes and started to turn.

"Don't do that," Margot yelped. "They'll know that we know. Besides, you can't see anything but lights."

"Then how do you know it's them?"

"I don't. But someone has been on our tail since we left the restaurant. You think maybe I should drive around a bit before heading home?"

"Definitely. And lock the doors."

Margot hit the master lock. Abruptly, she turned left onto a side street. They were only one block from the bright lights and traffic of Shattuck Avenue, but the neighborhood was residential and quiet this time of night.

"What are you doing?" Kali felt fear rise in her chest. "We should stay where there are people."

"Sorry, I didn't realize how dark it was down here."

"Well, it is."

"I know, I know." Margot's voice reflected some of the same fear. "I just wanted to see if they were really following us."

"Are they?"

"Afraid so."

Margot slowed for a speed bump and Kali held her breath, half afraid the car behind them would take the opportunity to knock into them. "You're going to circle the block and get back to Shattuck, right?"

"As fast as I can." Margot pushed the speed between bumps. "I've learned my lesson. I'm through flirting with strange men."

"It might not be them, you know."

"Who else would it be?"

"Two women have been murdered recently, remember?"

Margot started to laugh, then stopped and turned to Kali. "You're serious, aren't you?"

"Like you said, I've lived more years as a woman than you have. It never hurts to be careful."

"I thought they arrested someone."

"They did," Kali said. "Why don't you head up Ashby. We'll go to the Claremont where there's a parking attendant and a doorman."

They'd gone only about a quarter of a mile farther, when Margot heaved a sigh of relief. "I think they turned off."

Just to be safe, Margot and Kali took an indirect way home. Margot was silent, leaving Kali to ponder her instinctive remark about murder. For a moment, she had completely forgotten that Kurt Lancaster was in jail.

# CHAPTER 30

Lou had not slept well. Too much MSG in the kung pao shrimp, or maybe too many beers to wash it all down. In any case, he'd tossed and turned, and rolled out of bed Sunday morning more tired than when he'd gotten in it the night before. The weather was gray and cold, which didn't help matters. The day loomed before him like a vast stretch of empty desert. He wanted only to get through it.

Not so long ago, weekends had been special. Even when he was on call, Saturdays and Sundays held a certain magic for him. No waking to the shriek of the alarm clock, a leisurely breakfast of Jan's blueberry pancakes instead of a hurried cup of coffee, the promise of an afternoon football game on the television. Jan and Nikki filling the house with energy, rounding out the hollow corners of his soul. He'd taken it all for granted. Didn't even realize what he'd had until he no longer had it.

So what if he hadn't needed to set an alarm this morning. It didn't matter, he'd been awake since five o'clock. And now, as he faced an empty refrigerator, he saw little appeal in a leisurely breakfast of stale Cheerios.

He ought to get himself a dog, he decided. Something to break the monotony of these long, solitary days. Nikki had begged for a dog when she was younger. Lou couldn't remember now why he and Jan hadn't agreed to it. Something about work and responsibility and the preservation of Lou's garden, most likely. It seemed the height of irony to get a dog now to fill the quiet Nikki left behind.

Having a dog wouldn't help with his breakfast dilemma, either. Lou closed the refrigerator door. What he wanted was eggs and bacon and hash browns. A real breakfast. And he wasn't going to get it by standing around feeling sorry for himself.

Fifteen minutes later, he was seated at Denny's trying to decide whether he wanted toast on the side, or English muffin. He went for the toast, gave the waitress his order, and unfurled the morning paper. Starting with the comics, as he always did, he was well into his scrambled eggs by the time he turned to the in-depth report on Kurt Lancaster and the latest murders. The article bore Jack Jackson's byline, which didn't surprise Lou. Having hit the big time with his book, Jackson seemed to be milking the recent murders for more publicity.

Lou read with interest, finding his own name mentioned in several places, and, he was pleased to note, in a favorable light. While Jackson rehashed parallels between the Bayside Strangler and the two current murders, he didn't fan the fire of doubt about Davis's guilt. Lou gave him credit for that. But neither did the article suggest certainty that Lancaster was the killer. Had Jackson talked to Kali O'Brien and picked up on her doubts? Or was he simply being the cautious journalist? Either way, Lou couldn't help but feel irked. They had an arrest in the case; that was what the papers should have been focusing on.

Lou chewed on a strip of bacon. He wondered if Diana Davis had heard about the arrest, and whether it would settle anything in her mind. The story might not have been covered outside of the Bay Area. He made a mental note to dig out her address and send her a clipping.

When his beeper went off, he glanced at the number, fully expecting it to be Keating. Instead it was a number he didn't recognize. He returned the call and was greeted by a female voice.

"Hi, Lou. It's Maureen Oliver. I hope I'm not interrupting something."

"What would you be interrupting?"

She laughed, sounding self-conscious. "I don't know. You weren't at home. I tried that number first."

"I was having breakfast."

"Oh." She sounded unsure. Maybe she'd taken his response as a reproach.

"Just finished. Is there a problem?"

"No problem. I'm calling with good news. At least I think it's good. I'm over here at Kurt Lancaster's apartment. I found something interesting."

"What is it?" Lou asked. If Maureen was going to make it in police work, she was going to have to learn to get to the point.

"One of his dolls," she said. "A mannequin, actually, had a purse draped over her shoulder. Jane Parkhurst's library card was stuck in an inside pocket."

Kali spent Sunday afternoon at the gym, then drove home to shower. She'd forced herself through a rigorous workout. Rigorous by her standards at any rate, and she was feeling pleasantly exhausted. She greeted Loretta, then checked her answering machine while the dog sat at her feet getting her ears scratched. Three calls. Her friend Nina, a hangup, and a long message from Nathan, who apologized for being short with her. He hoped they could get together soon. Kali was glad she hadn't been there to take the call. She'd decided the best way to handle Nathan was to ignore him.

She poured herself a glass of water and drank thirstily. The aroma of the chocolate cookies she'd baked earlier lingered in the air. Something so she wouldn't go empty-handed to Nina's that evening for dinner. She'd eaten two before heading off to the gym, and she was determined to avoid further temptation.

She took a shower and was toweling her hair dry when the doorbell rang. Peeking through the window, she saw a familiar car in the driveway, a black sedan with not-so-discreet patrol lights on the sides. Her first thought was of trouble.

Her hand was shaking as she opened the door.

"Oops," Bryce said, with an eye toward her wet head. "Looks like I should have called first."

Kali cinched her bathrobe tighter across her middle. Her heart did a little flip-flop at the sight of him. Still, she'd rather have been fully dressed with at least minimal makeup. "What's the matter?" she asked.

"Nothing. In fact, I'm the bearer of good news." His eyes crinkled at the corners. "There's new evidence linking Lancaster to one of the victims."

"Who?" She wasn't sure if she wanted it to be Anne or not. Being part of the investigation meant walking an emotional tightrope.

"Jane Parkhurst."

Relief. That was what she felt. So much for keeping her professional distance. As much as she wanted, and needed, details, she was never able to forget that Anne had been a friend.

Bryce leaned forward, peering into the interior. "Can I come in?"

She ran a hand through her wet hair. What was she going to do, tell him to come back in twenty minutes when she was presentable? She'd have liked to. Instead, she opened the door and stepped back. As they entered the open hallway, Kali was aware of the clutter of newspapers and books strewn everywhere. Weekends did that to her housekeeping.

But Bryce's gaze was on the panorama framed by the wall of windows. He whistled. "Nice view you've got." He moved closer. It was a typical reaction from first-time visitors.

"It's the reason I bought the house," Kali said. And even now she never tired of looking at it. Every day was different. Every hour. The sky, the bay, the lights and shapes of the city. Sometimes so crisp and clear she felt as if she could reach out and touch the towers of the Golden Gate. Other days, like today, muted by gray light, like an Impressionist painting.

"I can see why."

"So what's the evidence you've found?"

"Jane Parkhurst's library card was in a purse in Lancaster's apartment. Maureen Oliver found it."

Kali raised her eyebrows. "Nothing else, just the card?"

"Right. Lou's over there now. The way they figure it is, Lancaster took her purse, dumped the contents, and didn't realize the library card was stuck in an interior zipper compartment."

Kali felt a swell of relief. They'd gotten their man, after all.

The smallest slipup by an offender could be a godsend for police and prosecutors, and it looked as though luck had been with them this round.

"It will be even better if we can identify the purse as hers," Kali said.

Bryce nodded. "We're dusting it for prints. And Maureen suggested asking some of her friends if they recognize it. If Lancaster kept the purse, he may have kept other items as well, so they're going over everything again with a fine-tooth comb."

They were still standing. Kali waited for Bryce to add to what he'd told her about Lancaster, and when he didn't, she thought he would depart. Instead, he picked up a book from the sofa table.

"*Avoiding Mr. Wrong.*"

Kali felt herself blush. "It was a gift from a friend."

"She thinks you need help?"

"I don't know what she thinks. It was just a joke."

Bryce looked amused. "I wonder if there's an *Avoiding Ms. Wrong.*"

"Are you asking out of personal interest?" He'd put her on the spot. It was only fair to turn the tables.

He laughed. "Too late for me. I was married to her." He placed the book back on the table and sniffed the air. "Smells good in here. Like chocolate."

"Cookies. I baked some earlier. For a friend."

"Same friend?"

"Different."

He gave her a look. "Lucky friend." About as subtle as her teenage nephew.

"Would you like one?"

"If you have enough." He grinned.

"Coffee?"

"I prefer milk if you have it."

Cookies and milk. Kali suppressed a chuckle. Bryce Keating was full of surprises, but that wasn't a bad thing. In his jeans and tattered sweater, he didn't even look the part of hard-ass cop.

She showed him to the kitchen, poured two glasses of milk, and set a plate of cookies on the table.

"These are good." He finished his first and reached for a second. "Guess Owen Nelson can rest a little easier now."

"Because of the new evidence against Lancaster?"

Bryce nodded. "You admire the man, don't you?"

"Yes," Kali said. "I do. You don't?"

"I have nothing against the guy personally. But there are a lot of cops in the department who feel he doesn't understand the pressures of the job. Being a cop isn't like being a lawyer, where you've got time to deliberate and plan. Front-line crime fighting is tough and dirty."

"I don't think Owen's unaware of that fact."

Bryce scowled. "He's been pretty quick to speak out against cops who don't follow his plan."

"His *plan*, Bryce? You mean the law."

"The letter of the law."

"There's a difference?"

"Subtle but important. I'm not talking about flagrant misconduct by cops. That kind of behavior ought to be exposed and stopped. But when you're dealing with scum who by all rights should have been in prison years ago, too much precision can be counterproductive."

It was a familiar lament among cops. They were expected to put their lives on the line, but when it came to rights, suspects won out over cops every time. Kali didn't totally agree with the view, but she had sympathy. "You'd prefer Tony Molina?"

Bryce made a face. "I don't think there's a cop alive who'd vote for him."

"You're in Greg Barton's camp, then?"

"Not with any enthusiasm. Trouble is, he can't see past the end of his own nose."

"Or the latest contribution from a special-interest group."

Keating grinned at her. His eyes were dark and soft, and fixed on hers in a way that made Kali's skin tingle.

"At least we have that in common," he said.

Kali wasn't sure how to respond. It was clear that he'd tilted the conversation in a more personal direction. But he was being coy about it. "At least that," she said finally.

He leaned back in his chair, sucked on his cheek as though thinking, then stood. "Guess I'd better let you get dressed."

Kali gave a half a moment's thought to flinging off the robe and saying to hell with it. She had a feeling Bryce was thinking the same thing.

A vague smile played across his lips. Then he took a step toward the door. "Thanks for the cookies."

"Thanks for the good news about the library card."

The moment had passed.

Kali walked with him to the door, then down the front path where she could retrieve the throwaway circular in her driveway. That was when she saw the recycle bin, upturned, under the window at the side of the house. And next to it, a crumpled Dove dark-chocolate wrapper. The same sort of wrapper she'd found in the grocery bag on the deck two days earlier. She stopped dead in her tracks.

"Something the matter?" Keating asked.

"Sorry, just thinking."

"Not pleasant thoughts apparently."

"Nothing important." Maybe it had blown loose from the bag before she picked it up. "Thanks for coming all this way to deliver the news in person. You didn't have to do that."

There, again, was that look that made her skin tingle. "I know I didn't," he said. "But I wanted to."

"He's a bastard." Ruby blinked back tears. "All those months of putting my life on hold for him, arranging my schedule to please him, and he decides he's not going to leave his wife after all."

"I don't mean to rub it in," Carla said, "but I did warn you that messing with a married man was trouble." She was glad they were sitting in one of the booths at the back of the bar where it was quieter. What Ruby needed was simply to talk and cry a little.

Ruby licked the salt from her margarita glass and took a large swallow, then another. "You told me many times in fact. I should have listened to you." She took a trembly breath. "But I love him. What am I going to do?"

That Ruby should have had more sense didn't stop Carla from feeling sorry for her. Ruby deserved better than she had. She was sweet and trusting, and probably a little too eager to please, which was how she so often found herself shortchanged.

The two women had been friends since third grade, when they'd discovered they had the same birthday and the same last name. They used to pretend they were twins, though with Ruby's rich, Mediterranean coloring and Carla's obvious Nordic heritage, they looked nothing alike. By the time they roomed together in college, they'd traded the twins fantasy for that of being psychically joined, which, to the extent Carla believed in such stuff, was pretty close to the truth. When Ruby broke her leg skiing last winter, Carla had had such a sudden, shooting pain in her own leg that she'd needed to pull over to the side of the road. And when Carla went into premature labor with Becky in the middle of the night four years ago, Ruby had dreamt that precise thing.

Now Carla reached across the table and touched her friend's

arm. "I know it seems like the end of the world," she said softly, "but you will get past it, Rube. And I predict you'll find someone much better."

"You just don't like him."

"I don't like what he did to you. He never treated you with the respect you deserve, and he never cherished you the way someone who really loved you would."

Ruby drained the last of her margarita. "In the beginning it was really good. His wife was traveling a lot then. He took me places. And I don't mean just out to dinner. I went to functions with him. I even met Owen Nelson. The man who's running for governor."

Carla laughed. "I know who Owen Nelson is, Rube. Just because I spend days up to my elbows in Play-Doh and *Sesame Street* doesn't mean my brain is completely fried." Though there were times that wasn't too far from the mark.

"I didn't mean that." Ruby signaled the waitress for another drink. "It was a fancy party, lots of big names. He introduced me as his cousin." She giggled. "Good thing no one saw us in the coat closet."

"What's Owen Nelson like?" This was a far safer course than rehashing a failed affair.

"Charismatic," Ruby replied. "And genuinely nice. This was before he was running for governor, so I wasn't paying a lot of attention to the political stuff. But I liked him. Still do from what I've read."

"Was he married to the actress then?"

"I don't think so. He was at the party alone." The waitress brought Ruby a fresh drink, and she took a big swallow before continuing. "I'm half tempted to tell his wife."

"I thought she was dead."

"Not Nelson's wife, silly. I'm talking about the asshole."

"I wouldn't advise it," Carla said dryly.

"Don't you think she deserves to know what a piece of shit she's married to?"

"There's a certain logic to that, I guess. But you're doing it to get even, not because you care about her."

"I could tell the whole world, in fact. Serve him right." Ruby stood and tottered unsteadily on her feet. "I'm going to the little girl's room. Don't go away."

She bumped against the table next to them when she returned, then slid heavily into her own chair, glassy-eyed. Ruby was more than tipsy, Carla thought. She was bombed. "You've had enough, Rube. It's time to go. And I'm driving you home."

"I can manage."

"No, you can't. In fact, why don't you spend night with me?"

"And your perfect family? No, thanks. That would be rubbing salt in my wounds."

"Larry's far from perfect." The kids probably were too, but Carla had more trouble being objective where they were concerned.

"He's good in bed, though. You told me that." Ruby's voice was becoming loud. God, she was totally sloshed.

"Let's go," Carla said. "I'll drive you back in the morning for your car."

"You go on, I'm not ready."

Carla reached for Ruby's purse and extracted her car keys. "You coming with me or you want to call a cab?"

"Party pooper." Ruby stood and staggered. She slung her purse over her shoulder. "But you're taking me home, not to your place."

"I don't know that you're in any shape—"

"Who appointed you chief of the tribe?"

"I'm trying to help."

"I need to be alone." Ruby gave her a pleading look. "Please?"

Carla hesitated. "Okay," she said finally, "I'll take you home, but you should go right to bed."

They rode in silence through the nighttime drizzle. Ruby's house was dark when they arrived.

"Didn't you leave a light on?" Carla asked.

"I wasn't thinking, I guess. Too busy crying."

"Shall I walk you to the door?"

"Good grief, Carla. You're turning into a mother hen. No point your getting wet too." Ruby was fumbling for the door handle. She sounded angry.

"I'm worried, is all."

"I'm not going to slit my wrists over him, if that's what's you think."

"It's just that you don't always take care of yourself, Ruby. Wasting all those years with a no-good—"

"See, I knew it. You never did like him."

It wasn't an argument she was going to win. "What time do you have to be at work tomorrow? I'll drive you to your car. Any time after seven."

"I'll take a cab."

"No, really, I'd like—"

"Get off my back, will you?" Ruby's mood had turned foul. Carla handed over Ruby's key chain. "Sleep well, honey."

She watched Ruby weave up the path to the front door. She waited until the inside light went on, then drove home.

Larry was already asleep. Carla tiptoed in and kissed her sleeping children, then brushed her teeth and crawled into bed next to her husband, who may not have been perfect, but was a darned nice guy. She sometimes envied Ruby her freedom, but she wouldn't have traded places for all the money in the world.

Two hours later she awoke from a sound sleep, drenched in sweat. Her heart was racing. She must have been dreaming, she told herself, though she couldn't recall what the dream was about. She sat up in bed, feeling light-headed. The panic gripped her as much now as that moment she'd first awakened.

Then it came to her—she'd heard Ruby calling her name. Most definitely a dream. Still, Carla got out of bed and peered outside. The rain was coming down heavily now and wind whipped through the trees. Maybe that was all she'd heard.

No, it was Ruby's voice. Carla felt sure of it.

Knowing she was being foolish, she went downstairs and phoned. Didn't friends have the right to overreact sometimes, because they cared?

The machine picked up.

"Ruby are you there? It's me, Carla."

No answer.

Maybe she was still angry with Carla. Or sleeping so soundly she hadn't heard the phone. Carla remembered how Ruby passed out and snored when she drank too much.

Carla would have to needle her about it when Ruby was in a better humor.

# CHAPTER 31

It rained heavily during the night, a pounding storm that woke Kali with its energy. By morning, however, she was heartened to find only a light sprinkle falling. Though the paper promised afternoon clearing and dry weather for the remainder of the week, she wasn't going to count on it. Kali found the *Chronicle*'s forecasts were wrong as often as they were right. She'd been told, by someone who claimed to have heard it from a reliable source, that the entire weather page was written and produced in a windowless cubicle in the middle of Nebraska. No doubt by the same people who penned messages for fortune cookies.

Clouds of misty gray hung over the bay, obscuring her view of San Francisco but imbuing the horizon with an almost ethereal, dreamlike quality. She sipped her coffee and contemplated the day ahead of her.

With the discovery of Jane Parkhurst's library card, Kali was filled with a renewed confidence about proceeding with the case against Lancaster. She felt as though a heavy burden had been lifted from her shoulders.

She'd been afraid the DA's office would come under fire if they didn't prosecute, but stood little chance of prevailing in court if they did. What people didn't understand was that identification of a suspect was only one step in the criminal justice process. The prosecutor still had to find the evidence sufficient to charge him, and the jury had to find it sufficient to convict. Only then was justice served.

She took the last swallow of coffee and put her cup into the dishwasher. Too bad she had a dentist appointment that morning. Not only would she rather be just about any place on earth than the dentist's chair, but she was also eager to talk to the detectives and find out if they'd turned up anything more that might tie Lancaster to the crimes. The stronger the evidence against him, the more likely it was he would enter a guilty plea. Especially if she could convince Owen to offer a deal that spared Lancaster's life.

Then they could put the whole awful mess behind them.

When she arrived at work later that morning, one side of her face still numb from her visit to the dentist, Kali saw Gloria gesturing to catch her attention. On the phone she was saying, "Wait a sec, here she is right now."

Kali gave her a questioning look. Gloria knew better than to put her on the spot like that unless it was important.

"It's Detective Keating," Gloria explained, covering the receiver with her hand. "Do you want to take it in your office?"

"Tell him I'll be right with him." Kali felt a tingle of anticipation at the call, and not just because he might have news about the search of Lancaster's apartment. She'd spent most of yesterday afternoon mentally choreographing different conclusions to Bryce's visit—conclusions which almost always ended up in the bedroom—and wondering if he were doing the same.

She picked up phone without taking off her coat.

"We've got something here you should see," he said without preamble.

The tingle became lead. It was a business call. "Are you at Lancaster's apartment?"

"No. A house in the Dimond district." He gave her the address. Flat and cool, as if they were strangers.

"You're asking me to come there?"

"Yeah, I think you'll want to see this."

Kali wasn't sure what to make of the cryptic responses. "You going to tell me what this is about?"

"Might be better if you saw for yourself."

She felt a flicker of annoyance. She had a busy morning and was already behind, although she conceded that wasn't actually Bryce's fault. It wasn't his fault she'd been hoping for something different from the call, either. Still, why couldn't he tell her what they'd found and let her decide for herself how important it was?

"Okay," she agreed reluctantly, "I'll head over there now."

Bryce thought it required her attention, and that ought to be reason enough. Kali scooted her briefcase under her desk and retraced her steps, explaining to Gloria that she was going out again.

The address he'd given her was at the end of a cul-de-sac. The house was single story with a wide front porch and what looked to be wisteria twisting its way along the roofline. A white picket fence spanned the front of the property, set off by pansies and sweet alyssum. The house, like the others on the street, was small and showed signs of age, but it was clear the owner was trying to emulate the English country cottages that graced the covers of so many home magazines.

The scene was far from idyllic, however. Kali's stomach knotted at the sight of yellow crime scene tape securing the perimeter of the yard and the small crowd of neighbors gathered on the far side of the street. But there was no ambulance or coroner's van parked anywhere nearby. And only a single police car other than the detectives'.

Kali ducked under the tape and approached the uniformed officer standing by the door. Bryce saw her and waved her inside, where an overturned floor lamp and shattered pottery pot put the hairs of her arm on edge.

"There's a body?" Her mouth was so dry she had trouble forming the words.

"Not yet," Bryce said.

Her gaze fell on Lou Fortune, sitting across the room, cell phone pressed to his ear. "Not yet?"

"Follow me." Bryce led the way down a hall to the second of two bedrooms.

Here, too, the English country look prevailed. A rustic pine-frame bed, with a coverlet of white cotton eyelet and a profusion of matching pillows. The dresser was antique pine and the two chairs under the window were made of an old-fashioned, tight-weave wicker. The appeal of the room was marred, however, by the array of items carefully laid out on the bed. A slinky red beaded dress and, below it, garter belt, stockings, and backless heels. To the side were a pair of panties and a bra.

On the pillow at the head of the bed was a yellow rose tied in a ribbon.

It took a minute for Kali to absorb what she was seeing.

Clothing laid out as though adorning a body. She swallowed against the unpleasant taste that filled her mouth.

"There was a poem, too," Bryce said.

"Poem, and not a note?" In the past, the poem had come later, delivered to the media.

He nodded and handed her a piece of paper in a plastic sleeve.

> *Macy's weekend crush*
> *An armload of bathing suits*
> *Pink bikini wins.*

"Not exactly haiku," Kali said after reading it a second time. "But close."

"That's what I thought. The syllables are right, even if the spirit isn't."

Kali was impressed. "Who is she?"

"Woman by the name of Ruby Wings. Twenty-nine, single, works in medical records at Kaiser. Her neighbor saw the front door of the house open this morning and thought maybe it hadn't been latched properly, so she came over to check. When she got here, she heard a muffled sound like a dog whimpering, saw the overturned lamp and was concerned enough to call the police. The uniforms took one look and called us."

"You've looked through the rest of the house?"

"Through it, under it, around it. The dog was in the bathroom. His muzzle was taped shut, but he seems otherwise unharmed."

"But no sign of Ruby Wings?"

Bryce shook his head. "Her car's gone, so maybe she wasn't even here when this happened. Maybe she's visiting her mother or something."

Kali thought that unlikely, and by the tone of his voice, so did Bryce. But a thread of hope, however fragile, was better than nothing.

"Somebody's having fun playing with us," Bryce said after a moment.

And it couldn't be Lancaster. He was in jail.

Kali's chest was so tight, she could hardly breathe.

\*   \*   \*

Lou had a bad feeling about this whole thing. In some ways it was worse than an actual crime scene. There at least you knew what you were dealing with.

He stepped around the broken ceramic vase and made his way down the hall. Kali had arrived while he was on the phone. Now she stood in Ruby Wings's bedroom looking glum.

"Ruby Wings hasn't shown up for work today," Lou said. "Hasn't called in, either."

"And it isn't like her at all," Keating added, looking for confirmation.

"Right. And Maureen Oliver found her purse in the hall closet."

"Look like anything's missing?" Keating asked.

"Wallet's there. Cell phone. All the basic stuff."

Kali drew in a breath. "Anything yet on the car?" she asked.

"No accidents," Lou replied. "That's all we've got so far."

"I don't suppose the neighbors saw or heard anything unusual?"

Did she think they had superhuman powers? They'd only arrived at the scene fifteen minutes before her. "Not that we've uncovered so far," Lou snapped, "but we're just getting started." He couldn't help sounding defensive.

"Woman next door saw her Sunday midday," Keating added. "She was going into the house with a bag of groceries. A couple of the lights were on when the uniforms got here, so my guess is whatever happened, happened last night."

A voice called to them from the other end of the hallway. "Detectives, you'd best come take a look. One of the garage windows was forced."

Lou led, while Keating and Kali followed. They made their way outside, where a cement walkway abutted the attached garage. Lou noticed the campanula under the window had been trampled.

"See this?" The uniformed officer working the shift was young and earnest. He gestured to the window frame. "Tool marks. From here, it would be easy entry into the house unless she locked the interior door. Most people don't."

"Dust for prints," Keating said. "And check the surrounding area both inside and out."

"Are we looking for anything in particular?"

"Just the usual—footprints, fibers, cigarette butts, you name it."

Lou grunted. "The perpetual optimist."

"You got a better idea?"

"I'm not criticizing, Bryce, just tossing in a dose of reality." Truth was, Lou was becoming the perpetual pessimist. He didn't like that about himself, but seemed unable to change it.

Keating turned to Kali. "No point your sticking around while we process the scene, I just wanted you to see this firsthand."

"You think it's the same as the others?"

"Certainly looks that way."

Kali shifted her gaze from Keating to Lou and back to Keating again. "Guess this leaves us up a creek as far as Lancaster's concerned?"

Lou shoved his hands in his pockets. Keating looked away. Neither of them answered her.

"But what about the library card?" she asked. It was the same tone Nikki sometimes used when she thought Lou was being unfair. Not whiny really, but full of protest. "He had Jane Parkhurst's purse and library card, remember?"

"I know." Lou hated it when cases went this way. Which they did all too often.

"Maybe he's in on it, but not alone," Keating said. "Or maybe this is a setup by some friend of Lancaster's to make us think we've got the wrong guy."

"We want to keep this quiet," Lou said. "No press conference, no nods to the media. Maybe we'll figure it out before word gets around."

"But we've still got Lancaster to deal with." She rocked forward on the balls of her feet.

"Can't you hold him on the shoplifting charge? Or a parole violation?"

She turned to Keating in a flash of anger. "You wanted Lancaster off the street. Public safety, you said. Looks to me like putting him behind bars got us nothing but egg on our face."

"You think *I'm* happy about this?"

"Hey, we're on the same side here," Lou reminded them.

Kali sighed. "I'll see if I can run damage control in the DA's office." She turned and headed for her car.

Lou watched Keating, whose eyes were following Kali's re-treating form. "She still on your list?"

Keating didn't bother to look at him. "It's none of your damn business, Lou."

"Sorry, it's just that you'd said . . ." Lou held up a hand in surrender. Keating was right, it wasn't any of his business, but this was the first time Lou had seen Keating bristle about it. "Forget I asked." Truth was, Lou didn't really care, as long as Keating didn't let his personal life interfere with their work.

Keating glanced back at the house. "It's gotta be the same guy."

"I think so too."

"But it's a big shift from what he's done before."

"Setting up the scene of the abduction?"

Keating nodded, his hand clenched into a fist. "This is about more than simply killing women; our guy is enjoying jerking us around."

"And getting cocky about it, too."

"That's what I mean about the shift. It's almost like the victims are peripheral."

"To what?"

"The game." Keating bit his lower lip. "This is the type of killer who likes to associate himself in some way with the investigation. It's almost a textbook case."

"Or hang around the fringe." Lou knew it wasn't an uncommon phenomenon, but he'd personally come across it only once. He'd been in homicide a couple of years, already partnered with Harry. There'd been a rash of attacks on elderly women, including four murders. They'd finally pinned them on the ambulance driver who showed up at each of the crime scenes.

Lou eyed the dwindling crowd of onlookers. "We'd better check through the lookey-loo names. Maureen says she got contact information for most of them."

"Good. I suspect what our guy gets off on isn't so much a need to control his victims, as a *screw-you* challenge to power and authority. He'd like nothing better than watching us stumble."

Keating was thinking out loud. Lou played along. "I agree. The focus doesn't seem to be sexual."

"There's all the peripheral stuff like the poems and photographs. And now we've got a *scene* without a crime or a body.

It's a game for him, Lou. And *that's* the real turn-on as far as he's concerned."

This wasn't the first time they'd had this conversation, and for the most part Lou agreed. But recently he'd begun to wonder if they were missing something obvious.

"There's another possibility," he said. "Maybe it's not a text-book serial killer."

"What do you mean?"

"Think about who stands to benefit most from these murders."

"Benefit? In what way?"

"Could be that someone's trying to put a cork in Nelson's chances for the election."

Keating looked skeptical. "You really think Tony Molina would stoop to murder?"

"Not the big man himself, but some of his supporters." It wasn't a theory Lou necessarily believed, but he thought it warranted looking at. "Al Gomez, that lawyer who defended Davis, he's been trying to stir up trouble ever since Nelson announced his candidacy. I heard a radio interview with him not long ago. He and Molina grew up in the same neighborhood."

"But murder? I don't know. You must have been smoking some bad stuff, Lou."

"Only thing I smoke is cigars."

"They're the worst."

Lou chuckled. "You know, for a mean bastard, you have unbelievably sissified tastes."

"Refined tastes, Lou. There's a big difference." Keating checked his watch. "You put out an APB on the car?"

Lou nodded. "I have a bad feeling about this, Bryce. Whether we find the car first or the body, it's not going to be pretty."

"Lancaster seemed so perfect for the crimes, too." Keating sounded pissed, and Lou didn't blame him. He felt the same way himself.

"I'm going to talk to what's left of the flock over there," Lou said.

When Keating went back into the house, Lou moseyed across the street. Four women, a sprinkling of children, and two men. One looked to be in his seventies, the other considerably younger.

"Has something happened to Ruby?" one of the women asked. "The cop who was over here earlier said they were investigating a break-in, but Joanna Singleton, she lives there—" the woman pointed to the house behind them—"she was the one who called the police in the first place. She said she tried calling Ruby at work and was told she never showed up today."

"Any of you seen her this morning?" Lou asked, sidestepping the woman's question.

None of them had.

Three of the women lived in the neighborhood; the fourth was the visiting daughter of the older gentleman. The remaining man said he'd been taking a walk when he saw the crowd gathered and stopped to see what had happened. His driver's license showed that he lived about a mile to the east. He taught guitar out of his home, he said, mostly to school-aged kids, which was why he was free in the mornings.

"You walk this way often?" Lou asked him.

"Almost every day."

"You ever see anything unusual going on?"

"Can't say that I did. Sorry."

Lou probed further with the neighbors, learning nothing aside from the fact that Ruby Wings was well liked, then headed back to join Keating.

At the curb, he stopped to analyze how visible the intruder would have been from the side of the garage. Practically hidden. But he'd have had to park somewhere, and presumably get back into his car with Ruby. Unless he'd taken hers.

So maybe he'd approached the house on foot, Lou thought. Fat lot of good it did, though, if no one had seen him. As Lou headed back up the walkway, his eye caught something red and shiny on the dirt under the daylilies. He stopped and retrieved two foil candy wrappers. Dove dark chocolate.

Ruby's? Neighborhood kids? Most likely. But Lou had been trained by some of the best cops in the business. He carefully dropped the wrappers into one of the baggies he always carried in his jacket pocket.

Kali shook hands with Lancaster's attorney, a veteran public defender named Eric Pogue. Short and pudgy, with heavy jowls and an immutably grim expression, Pogue reminded her of a bulldog. She offered a smile as she introduced herself; he didn't.

"I'm going to advise my client not to answer any questions,"

Pogue said, bristling with righteousness. He had large lips, and an unpleasant habit of spraying saliva when he talked.

Kali stepped back. "I want to go over his statement to the police," she explained. "Make sure he feels it's a fair representation of the facts." And more importantly, get a feel for how Lancaster was connected, or not connected, to the murders.

Pogue scoffed. "Fair? He says he didn't do it; that's what you should be listening to."

There were two ways to approach a client's defense—work with the prosecution or dig your heels in and cry foul at every turn. She could see that Pogue had cast his fates in the latter camp. That made it much harder.

"Believe it or not, Mr. Pogue, I am only trying to get at the truth."

"And I've got a bridge I could sell you."

They entered the small interview room near the holding cells. Kurt Lancaster was already seated at the table. A guard stood behind him.

"We'll take it from here," Pogue said.

The guard looked at Kali, who nodded. "I'll be just outside if you need me," he said.

Pogue pulled out a chair and sat kitty-corner from his client. Keeping his distance, Kali noted, and his grim countenance. He didn't look directly at Lancaster, or address him personally. It was a job for him, Kali thought. And the attraction was in the rhetoric, not the people.

Kali sat closer to Lancaster, on purpose, and pulled out his file. "I'm the assistant district attorney assigned to this case," she explained. "I've read the statement you gave to the detectives, and I want to be sure it's accurate."

Lancaster nodded. He was, as she'd noted before, an odd-looking man, with deep-set eyes and a pointy chin, but up close there was also something vulnerable about him. Like the homely kid in elementary school who was the butt of every practical joke.

"You've done work for both Anne Bailey and Jane Parkhurst, is that correct?"

"I work for lots of people. I have my own window-washing business, part time."

"But Ms. Bailey and Ms. Parkhurst were among your regular clients?"

Pogue leaned forward. "You don't have to answer that."

"He's already admitted it," Kali pointed out with impatience. "And we've got corroborating third-party evidence to that effect."

"I did work for them," Lancaster said. "Ms. Parkhurst for several years."

"Can you tell me what you were doing the evening of January fourth."

Pogue interrupted, again spraying spittle. "I'm advising my client—"

"I already told the cops, I was sick. Achy, you know? And a fever."

"You were home alone and didn't talk to anyone at all?"

"Don't answer," Pogue said.

Kali waited a moment. This time Lancaster listened to the advice of his attorney and remained silent. She pressed on. "What about the evening of January thirteenth?"

"I was at work."

"Yet we've found no one who can vouch for the fact that you were there after signing in."

"I told—"

"Don't try to explain," Pogue said.

"But I want—"

"There will be time for that later."

Kali tried a direct appeal. "Mr. Lancaster, despite what you may think, we're not interested in charging an innocent man. If you can help us understand how we're misinterpreting the evidence, it would be in your best interest to do so."

Lancaster looked to Pogue and then back to Kali, but he said nothing.

"We know from your ATM records," Kali continued, "that you were in the area of Jane Parkhurst's house twice in the few weeks before she was killed. That's nowhere near your own home."

He shrugged. "I work all over the area."

"Your neighbors and co-workers say you're a good man." Kali kept her eyes on Lancaster, willing Pogue to keep from interrupting. "I'm thinking you might not be the one who was really behind these murders. Maybe you and a friend were in this together. Maybe it was all his idea. If you give us the other name, we're not going to be looking so hard at you."

"There wasn't anyone else."

"Shut up," Pogue said. "She's trying to trick you."

"I didn't do nothing wrong." Lancaster's eyes were dark and pleading. "I didn't touch those women."

"The police have searched your house, Mr. Lancaster. They found Jane Parkhurst's purse and library card there among your things."

Pogue pushed back his chair. "This interview has gone far enough." He turned to his client. "We'll deal with all this in court, Kurt. Not here."

Lancaster ignored him, giving Kali a pleading look. "I can explain about the purse. Mrs. Parkhurst gave it to me."

"She gave you her purse?"

He nodded vigorously. "It was on the front steps. A bunch of stuff she was giving away. I asked her, I didn't just take it. I got a blue sweater and a blouse, too."

Kali felt as though there was a lead weight in her stomach. They had no case against Lancaster. No case at all.

"Would you be willing to take a lie detector test?" she asked.

"Forget it," Pogue barked. "They are totally unreliable."

Also inadmissable in court. But the results might make Kali feel better about letting Lancaster go.

"I'll do it," Lancaster said.

# CHAPTER 32

"Hey, Dad," Alex called from the kitchen, "you want another beer?"

Owen wasn't much of a beer drinker. The one can he'd already downed had about pushed his limit, but in the interest of father-son bonding, he acquiesced. "That would be great, Alex. Thanks."

It wasn't often they were together like this, just the two of them kicking back in easy camaraderie. Selby was out for the evening with her college roommate, who was in town for a conference, and while Owen was disappointed that she'd left on one of the rare evenings he was free, he'd seized the opportunity to invite Alex to have dinner with him. He could never predict Alex's mood, and Owen had braced himself for some smart-ass response like "Why would I want dinner with you?" He'd been pleasantly surprised when Alex not only agreed but seemed appreciative. Perhaps there was hope yet for mending their relationship.

They'd decided that eating in was better than going out, although Owen suspected his new large-screen television had something to do with Alex's opinion on the matter. Now, fortified with enchiladas and chips they'd picked up at their favorite Mexican place, they were settled on the leather sofa in the den watching the basketball game. Alex had been in surprisingly good spirits all evening. Owen had even gotten out of him the name of a girl he was dating. Not *dating*, Owen corrected himself as Alex had corrected him earlier, *seeing*. Apparently *dating* wasn't something young people did anymore.

Alex returned from the kitchen with two cans of beer and a

bag of cookies. "Did I miss anything?" He handed Owen a beer, then plopped down at the far end of the couch.

"Four commercials, all of which were advertising sex and only incidentally whatever product was alluded to at the end."

Alex laughed. "You're a prude, Dad."

"Hardly."

"A dinosaur then?"

Owen was willing to give him that. He smiled. "Probably." Then he leaned back and privately basked in the glow of sharing an evening with his son.

They concentrated on the game with only an occasional "hold on to the ball, stupid," or "watch that shoving," to punctuate the silence. By halftime, Owen was feeling pleased with the way the evening had turned out.

"You ever think about college?" he asked.

Alex gave him a funny look. "I barely made it through high school."

"That's only because you never really tried. You're a bright boy, Alex. You could do anything you put your mind to."

"Brain surgeon?" The words were thickly sarcastic.

Owen wanted to send a positive message. "If that's what you wanted, yes. I'm willing to pay your tuition, help with living expenses. It's an opportunity—"

"For you to look like a hero."

The words smarted. Owen brushed them aside. "An opportunity to make something of yourself."

"College doesn't interest me," Alex said flatly.

Owen could feel his blood pressure rising. He bit back the urge to lecture.

"I'm starting to get interested in film," Alex said after a while.

"Film?"

"Like, making movies."

"Great." Another pipe dream, Owen thought. Like so many of Alex's interests. "Only it's not very practical."

"What do you mean?"

"Do you have any idea how hard it is to break in? How slim the chances of success are?" As soon as the words were out, Owen realized he'd gone about it all wrong.

Alex shot him a pointed look. "You saying I wouldn't be any good?"

"No, that's not what I'm saying." Though Owen was sure that Alex had no idea of the work and perseverance involved. He'd make some fly-by-night stab at it and expect immediate success.

"What I meant," Owen said with deliberate patience, "was there's a lot of luck involved."

Alex slid down on the couch, swinging one leg over the arm. "Doesn't matter. It's just something that's crossed my mind." Ignoring the marble coaster, he set the beer can directly on the walnut coffee table.

"Not on wood, Alex. You know better than that."

"What's the matter, Selby got you pussy-whipped?"

Anger flashed in Owen's gut, but he exercised restraint. He'd gotten that much from those counseling sessions. "I don't like that kind of language," he said evenly.

"Especially not about precious Selby, right?"

"Come on, son, don't spoil a good evening."

"Don't *son* me. It sounds so phony, like we have some sort of relationship."

"We don't?" Keep it light, Owen reminded himself.

Alex folded his arms over his chest. "This was my house before it was hers."

What did the house have to do with it? Alex had been living on his own for over two years. "Alex, I want nothing more than for us to get along, but you've got to do your part."

"My part?" Alex's voice spiraled in the course of two words. His tone was laced with anger. "What about your part?"

"That's what—"

"You were never here for us. Ever. You still aren't, except when it serves your own purpose."

Owen was stung as much by Alex's hostility as by the words. Part of him wanted to lash out, argue the point, but he bought time to calm himself. "Us?" he asked.

"Mom and me. You were always too busy. Always trying to make yourself look important."

"That's not true."

"You were so caught up in your own importance, you barely noticed she died."

Owen set down his beer can, on the coaster. "What are you—"

"You kept right on with that stupid trial like nothing had happened."

"I had a duty, Alex. We were in the middle of a very important and very high-profile trial. I couldn't just walk away."

The expression on Alex's face was dark and twisted with anger. Though he said nothing, Owen knew what he was thinking—that Owen had a duty to his family as well. That had come through loud and clear during the counseling sessions. What Alex didn't understand was that life rarely presented itself in simple either/or format. Far more common were the trade-offs and tensions of conflicting obligations. Those were things adults understood.

Alex continued to look at him. "It's your fault she's dead, you know." The very quietness of his son's voice was as disturbing to Owen as the earlier anger.

"Alex, please."

"It is. If you'd cared about her, it never would have happened. She wouldn't have been so depressed. She wouldn't have been taking all those pills. . . . You might even have noticed she needed help."

"She was getting help," Owen snapped.

"Sure. More pills."

The official cause of death was accidental overdose, and Owen fervently believed that was what had happened. Did that mean he was totally blameless? No. In fact, he'd often questioned his own role in failing to make Marilyn happy. It wasn't true that he hadn't loved her, however. He had. Maybe not in the way she'd wanted, but he'd done his best.

"Alex, your mom had been troubled—"

"From the time I was born. I know that."

"Even before that." The last thing Alex needed was to feel himself responsible for her unhappiness. "Your mother had always—" The phone rang and Owen started to rise.

"Let the machine pick it up," Alex said. "We're having a *conversation*." The last comment was snide.

"It might be important," Owen explained on his way to the phone. "I won't be long." He answered and was greeted by Jack Jackson.

"Hey, Owen, sorry to bother you at home."

"What's up, Jack?"

"Just wondering what went on today out at the house on Willow."

Owen caught Alex's eye and held up a finger, indicating he'd just be a minute. Then he turned back to the phone. "I haven't the foggiest idea what you're talking about, Jack."

"There were a couple of police cars parked in front all morning."

"So? This is a city. Police cars end up in front of all too many houses. I hear about only a fraction of them, and then usually after the fact."

"Here's what's interesting," Jackson said. "Detectives Fortune and Keating were there, too. Aren't they working exclusively on the recent murders?"

Owen felt uneasiness snake down his spine. He tried not to let it show. "Jack, I'm the district attorney, not the chief of police. Why don't you ask them what they were doing there?"

"I tried. They told me to get lost."

"That surprises you?" Owen was anxious to end the call and reach someone who could tell him what was going on.

"If it was a simple burglary, wouldn't they just say so?"

"Depends."

"Why would they be called out on a burglary anyway?"

Owen heard a car door slam. He looked out the window. "I've got to go, Jack. Sorry." He hung up abruptly and got to the door just as Alex pulled away from the curb.

Lou shoved his hands into his pockets to warm them. The day was overcast and very cold. He noticed that the small puddle of water in the gutter was still frozen.

Parked at the curb was the red Mustang registered to Ruby Wings.

"You called for the tow truck?" Lou asked.

Keating nodded. "Should be here any minute."

Lou didn't think they'd find a body. He put a lot of trust in his nose, and his nose told him the trunk would be empty. He suspected the interior would be clean too. But they wouldn't know for sure until the car was towed, the trunk opened, and the evidence team had finished working its magic.

A patrol officer had discovered the car earlier this morning parked in a metered, two-hour zone near Jack London Square. There were three tickets on the windshield, all issued yesterday.

"Wouldn't you think," Lou muttered, "that by the third one

the meter maid might get the idea that something more than a long lunch was involved?"

"You'd think so." Keating wasn't in a talkative mood. In fact, he'd been grumpy all morning.

"I see a number of different scenarios here," Lou said after a moment. It wasn't so much that he was aching for conversation as trying to make sense of the evidence they had. "One, someone else drove her car here for whatever reason, maybe to throw us off. Two, she drove it here herself. She could have gotten into trouble here and the stuff at the house was just frosting on the cake."

"Or three," Keating added, "none of the above."

"Either she drove it here or she didn't."

Keating shook his head. "She could have lent it to a friend. It could have been stolen. She could have driven it here, locked herself out, and taken a cab home. The possibilities are almost limitless."

"Smart-ass." Keating was right, of course, and that irritated Lou. "Why don't you try a few of the local establishments. See if anyone remembers seeing her. I'll wait for the tow truck."

"Do you still have that photo of her?"

"In the car."

Keating retrieved the photo and disappeared into a restaurant across the street. Lou saw him emerge and then enter another building farther down the block. The department tow truck arrived, and the driver went to work hitching the car.

"Is there a body in there?" the driver asked.

"I don't know."

"Gives me the heebie-jeebies thinking I'm towing a body. Happened once." He looked through the window. "Inside looks clean. I've towed some gruesome stuff."

"I can imagine."

Keating returned about five minutes later with a smile on his face. "It's our lucky day, Lou. A bartender with a good memory and an orderly stash of charge slips. Not only was she here Sunday evening, I have the name of the woman she was with. A Carla O'Neill. I already called it in and got the address. Want to head over there now?"

Lou checked with the driver to make sure he had everything he needed from them. The car would be towed and the evidence team would go over it with a fine-tooth comb. Lou wanted to be there when they opened it, but the wheels of procedure ground slowly. He knew if he followed the driver there now, he'd end up cooling his heels on the other end for an hour or so.

"Yeah, let's go."

Carla O'Neill lived in an older, two-story stucco house in the Crocker Highlands area of Oakland. Like the other houses on the street, hers was well maintained and neatly landscaped. This was the kind of neighborhood Jan had always wanted. But every raise Lou got, the cost of housing went higher too. Now it didn't matter. If it weren't for his garden, Lou would sell the house and move into an apartment. He didn't need more than a bed and a table, and even the latter he could do without.

Lou rang the bell. He could hear a television cartoon show playing inside.

A raven-haired woman opened the door. She looked at them and instantly her face fell.

"Carla O'Neill?"

She nodded. "You're with the police, aren't you?"

Another one, Lou thought. How could they tell?

She didn't wait for an answer. "Is it about Ruby?"

"What makes you ask that?" The suspicion in Keating's voice was only thinly veiled.

"Oh, dear. I knew it." Carla pressed her knuckles to her mouth, her eyes wide with worry. "Is she hurt?"

"Missing." Lou pressed the earlier question. "What made you think something had happened to her?"

"I've had this awful feeling. It's hard to explain, but it's almost like we can read each other's minds sometimes. And . . ." Her voice trailed off. She looked at Keating and then Lou. "What do you mean, 'missing'?"

"Mind if we come in?"

She stepped back and directed them toward the dining room with a sweep of her arm. "The kids are watching TV in the living room."

Lou could see two little heads peering over the cushions of the sofa. He waved at them and they dove for cover, giggling.

Carla sat at one end of the oak-plank table; Keating and Lou sat on either side of her.

"You were with Ruby Wings Sunday evening?" Keating asked.

Carla seemed momentarily stunned. "Wow, you're good. How did you figure that out?"

"The bartender had the credit card receipts."

"Ah."

Keating asked, "Which of you left first?"

"We left together. Ruby had a bit too much to drink, and I insisted on driving her home."

That explained the car. "What time did you leave?" Lou asked.

"About nine."

"Anyone follow you?"

"No."

"Anything else unusual?"

Carla O'Neill shook her head. "No, I . . . Wait a minute, I remember the porch light was off. Ruby noticed it too. She said something about forgetting to turn it on, but she sounded kind of perplexed by it. And then the strangest thing happened. I woke up about midnight in a panic. Bolt awake out of a sound sleep with a horrible sense that Ruby was in trouble."

Keating shot Lou a glance. "What made you think that?"

"Like I said, we have this kind of . . . I don't know what to call it. It's almost like ESP or something. I kept telling myself I'd had a bad dream, was all, but then I couldn't sleep, so I called her. The machine picked up."

"What about later? Did you try calling again?"

"The next morning. I'd offered to drive her back to pick up her car, but then I overslept, and since she hadn't called me . . . Anyway, she didn't answer. I figured she'd taken a cab or bummed a ride from someone else and was already on her way to work."

"You were worried enough about her to call in the middle of the night, but you didn't follow up?" Lou asked. For all her talk about being able to read Ruby's mind, Carla O'Neill seemed to have adopted a fairly passive posture in all this.

"By morning it didn't seem so odd. And we'd had kind of a . . ." She bit her bottom lip. "A difference of opinion that night. I told myself she was just keeping her distance."

"What did you argue about?" Lou asked. To heck with this *difference of opinion* crap.

Carla seemed to weigh her words before answering. "Girl

stuff," she said after a moment. "How did you find out she was missing?"

"The neighbor noticed an open door and signs of a struggle. Called us. It was clear something wasn't right. She never showed up for work yesterday, either."

"So no one has seen or heard from her since I dropped her off?" There was a rising tide of alarm in Carla's voice.

"Seems that way."

"What wasn't right about the house?" she asked.

"There were clothes laid out on her bed," Keating explained.

Carla's expression was puzzled. "Like she was packing for a trip?"

"Like she'd laid out a complete outfit, shoes and all. The dress was red, tiny straps, deep slits up both sides."

"Sequins across the bodice? It's one she bought for a special dinner last year. You think she was getting ready to go out?"

"Do you think so?"

Carla scraped some wax from the tabletop with her thumbnail. "Not Sunday night, for sure."

"There was also a poem on the bed," Lou added. He recited it for her. "Does it make any sense to you?"

Carla O'Neill's face had gone white. "That part about the bikini. Ruby was shopping for a bathing suit on Saturday. I was with her. One of the ones she tried on was a pink bikini."

# CHAPTER 33

Kali picked up the phone and punched Owen's extension. She dreaded making the call, but delaying would only make matters worse. Kurt Lancaster had passed the lie detector test with flying colors. And now, with Ruby Wings's disappearance, it made no sense to continue the case against him.

From a legal perspective, there was no problem dropping the charges. It happened routinely when new evidence was brought to bear on a case, or when prosecutors realized the case was too weak to try. But in this instance, the political repercussions were going to be a nightmare. Not only was the actual killer still on the loose, prowling for his next victim, they'd arrested an innocent man. *Again*, would be the inference. Lancaster's release was sure to be headline news and talk-show fodder, all of it fueling the debate about Davis.

Kali let the phone ring three times. She was ready to hang up before it could roll over to Owen's secretary when she sensed someone standing in her open doorway. She looked up to see Owen himself.

"I was just calling you," she said.

"And here I am." He entered and shut the door behind him. His brow was furrowed and Kali noticed, for the first time, dark circles under his eyes. He stood behind one of the chairs facing her, gripping its back with his hands. "Is it as bad as I think?"

"It's not good. What have you heard?"

"Only that we might have another murder on our hands. Jackson called me, said he'd seen Keating and Fortune at a house out in the Dimond district. As far as I know, they're only working one case."

Kali picked up her pen and ran a thumb along the side of it. "The good news is that it's not a murder. Yet."

"And the bad news?"

"It looks like the work of our killer." She told him about Ruby Wings's disappearance, the clothes laid on her bed along with a yellow rose and a typed poem. "It was sort of haiku," she added.

A nerve in Owen's jaw twitched. "Lancaster's still in jail?"

"Right. There's no way he was anywhere near Ruby Wings's house. What's more, he's got a reasonable explanation for having Jane Parkhurst's library card and purse in his possession. And he passed a lie detector test."

Owen made a sound, as though he'd had the air knocked out of him. He came around and sat down in the chair, pressed his fingers against his temples. "The media is going to jump on this," he groaned. "And you can be sure my name is going to show up in neon."

"People can hardly blame you for the murders, Owen."

He rubbed his forehead. "You know how these things take on a life of their own. Logic has nothing to do with it. Look at what's happened in the press already."

Some of the coverage had leaned toward sensationalism. Fed, no doubt, by Tony Molina in his increasingly frenetic appeal for support. But Kali credited most voters with enough common sense not to be swayed. "How can people think badly of you for declining to prosecute an innocent man?" she asked.

"Lancaster's not the real issue. It's what the recent murders imply about the Bayside Strangler case that has people riled up. Until we can tie up these new cases, doubts about Davis's guilt are going to continue to shadow me."

Owen got up, paced to the tiny window behind Kali's desk, then back to the chair. "What do we have so far with this disappearance? Any leads on what might have happened?"

Kali shook her head. "The feeling is that someone broke into her house and took her from there. They found tool marks on one of the windows. A couple of the inside lights were on, so speculation is that it happened at night."

"Breaking into a home is a first for him, isn't it?"

"So is laying out her clothes."

"And neither was a pattern the Bayside Strangler followed."

Owen seemed to be struggling to find a ray of hope in the differences.

"Right. Our killer is copying the old murders, but he's layering on his own signature as well. Little by little. The lipstick in Jane Parkhurst's murder was a new touch, as was the photograph."

"Reminds me of those goddamn bacteria that mutate every time scientists get a fix on them."

"It *is* a little like that." Only in our case, Kali thought, we never even got a fix on the killer.

"I hope to God he's only copying the earlier murders," Owen said irritably.

"Are you having doubts about Davis?"

"I try not to go there, Kali, even in my own mind. But sometimes I wonder, what if it's the Strangler himself who's evolving? Or maybe, as you yourself suggested, there were two killers all along."

"Why wait all these years to start up again?"

"Who knows. Maybe Davis's execution rekindled something in him." Owen pressed a palm to his forehead. "You got any aspirin? My head is killing me."

Kali rummaged around in her purse for the plastic pill case she carried and handed it to him. "I agree that none of this is terrific news, but since there's nothing you can do about it right now, it's probably best to try not to let it get to you."

"It's my political future, Kali. Kind of hard not to let it get to me." Owen didn't exactly snap at her, but it was close. "The primary's only weeks away, remember."

"You're right." It was easy to give advice. And hard to put worry on a back burner.

"I appreciate that you're trying to be encouraging," he said after a moment. "I'm in a foul mood, that's all." He shook out two aspirin and held them in his hand.

"Understandable. I would be, too, with all that pressure."

"It's not just this stuff with the murders." Owen paused, studying the pills in his hand. "Things aren't going so well with Alex, either."

"I'm sorry to hear that."

"He says I never think about anyone but myself. You think that's true?"

A loaded question, and one Kali didn't feel competent to answer. But there was something about Owen's tone, genuine dismay tinged with a plea for guidance. She didn't feel right about brushing him off either. "You're a good man, and your heart's in the right place," she said after a moment. "I know you care about him a great deal, but I imagine Alex is sensitive to unintended slights."

"In other words, I *do* put myself first."

"You wouldn't be where you are today if you didn't. But when it comes to family, there are different expectations. I imagine Alex wants a father he feels connected to, not one who simply goes through the motions."

Owen's gaze was flat. Kali realized suddenly that she'd gone too far.

She'd recognized so much of her own teenage angst in Alex when she'd first met him. He'd been sixteen then, sullen and resentful. But his eyes had spoken of hurt, not anger. Over the course of the trial, she'd seen him frequently, especially at the "working bar-b-cues" Owen regularly hosted. She and Alex became ping-pong buddies, and when Marilyn died, she'd talked to him about her own experience losing a mother. In truth, though, she hardly knew Alex now.

"I'm sorry," Kali offered. "I shouldn't have said that."

"No, no, I asked you. It's the same thing Marilyn used to say. Same thing the family counselor said, too. I thought I was getting better."

"I'm sure you are."

He smiled and stood. "Apparently I've still got a ways to go."

"You'll get there."

"I was thinking I might ask Alex if he wanted to take a trip this spring after the primary is over and before the main campaign gears up for real. Just the two of us. Maybe down into Mexico. Alex always talked about us doing that when he was younger."

"Sounds like a good plan."

Owen's expression relaxed. "I hope Alex thinks so too."

The minute Owen was out the door, Kali's phone rang. "Detective Keating called," Gloria said. "He asked you to call him as soon as you were free. He said he's at his desk."

Kali returned the call and Bryce picked up on the first ring. "We found Ruby Wings's car," he said without preamble.

"Where?"

"Near Jack London Square. She apparently met a friend there Sunday evening for drinks. Had a few too many so the friend drove her home. That's the last anyone saw of her."

Kali shivered, picturing what must have followed. But she also felt a glimmer of hope. They had a lead. "Who's the friend?"

"A woman. Lou and I talked to her. She claims she had some sort of ESP experience the night Ruby Wings disappeared, but otherwise she seems fairly together. She told us Ruby tried on a pink bikini at Macy's the day before."

"The reference in the poem?"

"Right. Either Ruby Wings mentioned it to her killer or he was there in the store, watching her."

"He was watching Jane Parkhurst, too." A killer who stalked his victims. It made Kali's skin crawl. "When was she at the store?"

"Saturday afternoon, sometime between one and four."

"You'll want to talk to whoever was working there that day."

There was a beat of silence; then Bryce laughed. "You think I wouldn't have come up with that on my own?"

Kali could feel the blood rise to her cheeks. She was doing a good job of putting her foot in her mouth today. "Sorry, I didn't mean to tell you how to do your job."

He didn't sounded offended. "Hey, it's like the old saying— two sets of eyes are better than one. And when it comes to shopping for women's bathing suits, you've got a leg up on me. A rather nice leg, I imagine."

She was glad he couldn't see her blush.

"I just talked with Bevin Moore, the head criminalist on the case," Bryce said. "We should be getting the evidence reports from Ruby Wings's house any minute now. If you have time, why don't you come by and take a look?"

"Will do."

Kali completed the draft of a press release explaining why the DA's office wasn't going to be pressing charges against Kurt Lancaster, printed out copies to run by the detectives and Owen, then headed out. She got as far as the lobby, where she caught sight of Nathan Sloane just as she exited the elevator. He was standing by the revolving door, one hand in his pocket.

Damn. She hadn't returned his last phone call because she'd

decided she wanted nothing more to do with him. She started to retreat back into the elevator. He saw her and waved. Double damn.

"What you doing here?" she asked when he approached. She tried for a neutral tone, but didn't quite pull it off.

"Hoping to run into you, actually." He gave her a quirky little smile. "You haven't been returning my calls."

"I've been busy."

"I wanted to apologize. I shouldn't have been so short with you on the phone."

Kali was still adjusting to the shock of finding him waiting for her. "No, you shouldn't have been," she said after a moment.

"I guess I was hurt that you seemed so uninterested." When she didn't say anything, he continued. "I thought we had a good time the night we met for dinner. I know I did. I was hoping to convince you to do it again." He rocked back on his heels and gave her a lopsided smile.

Now that he was standing in front of her, Nathan seemed like a nice-enough guy. Maybe a little goofy but in an appealing sort of way. And he was obviously interested in her. That, in itself, intrigued her. But when she was away from him, the image she carried in her mind left her feeling a little uneasy.

Best not to get involved. How did she explain without coming across like a snob?

"I did have a good time," she told him. "But I don't really see the relationship going anywhere."

"How do you know if you don't give it a chance?"

"I'm not really in a place to—"

"Besides, why does it have to go somewhere? Can't people just have fun?"

"Of course." She didn't know why she'd made the remark in the first place. It seemed whiny.

"How about after work tonight? We could go out for a drink."

She grimaced. "Sorry, I'm busy."

"Tomorrow?"

"Sorry again." Couldn't the guy take a hint?

"Three's a charm, right? Are you free Thursday?"

She tried putting him off. "I'm not sure how the week will play out in terms of work. Let me call you later, okay?"

"You won't forget?"

Kali shook her head. This way, at least, she'd have time to figure out how to tell him she didn't want to see him. "But I need your number. All I have is your cell phone."

"It's the best way to reach me."

Kali hated calling people on their cell phone. You never knew where they were or what you were interrupting. "Don't you have a home phone?"

"I'm never there." He grinned at her and started for the exit. "I hope you can make it on Thursday."

Kali made her way to the homicide room. Lou and Bryce were seated at their desks. Between them, in a plastic visitor's chair, was a woman about Kali's own age. She had a heart-shaped face, lightly freckled, and short feathery hair that was frosted at the crown. Kali's first impression was of a pixie.

Bryce looked up as Kali entered. The sight of him caused her stomach to do a little flip-flop whereas the sight of Nathan never did.

"Perfect timing," he said, meeting her eyes with a smile. "Have you met Bevin? She's one of our best evidence technicians." He made the introductions, then pulled up a second chair.

Bevin shook Kali's hand. "Pleased to meet you. I was just telling the detectives, we didn't find much."

"Did you come up with *anything?*" Lou asked.

"A number of prints. Of course we don't know if any of them belong to our guy. But here's something—a print on one of the shoes on the bed matches another found in the bathroom."

"Couldn't it be Ruby's?" Kali asked.

"Unlikely, since there were just those two. We don't have hers for comparison, but there were a lot of the same ones all over the house. We're guessing those are hers."

Lou rubbed his cheek. "Does it match any of the ones pulled from the Port-A-Potty in the Parkhurst case?"

"Afraid not. We also found a metal Levi's button in the garage." Bevin looked at Kali. "Could be Ruby's, of course, but all the jeans in her closet were from the Gap."

"Could have come from a friend's jeans," Bryce added. "In any case, Levi's are hardly a specialty item."

"I told you, Bryce, there wasn't much." The twinkle in Bevin's eye spoke of a familiarity that caused Kali a flicker of jealousy. She noted it and tucked it away to analyze at a later date.

"There was also a trace of cigarette ash in the toilet bowl," Bevin said. "Again, could have come from anyone, but friends don't usually hang out in the bathroom to smoke."

"There was a cigarette found at the Parkhurst crime scene," Kali noted.

"What about the poem?" Lou asked. "Anything there?"

"No prints. Nothing unusual about the paper. It's standard twenty-pound, white printer paper. But the font is Goudy Old Style. Not one of the more common ones. Were the other poems the same?"

"They looked the same. We never actually focused on the font."

Kali looked up to see Maureen Oliver approaching.

"Sorry to interrupt." Maureen addressed the two detectives. "A call just came in from the southern division. I think we've found your missing woman."

# CHAPTER 34

Kali drove her own car, following the detectives by probably a good twenty minutes. She'd had to retrieve the car from the lot, and had then taken her time on the road. In her heart, she'd known the call would come sooner or later, but she'd tried holding on to the hope that Ruby Wings was alive. Even now, a part of her was willing to believe the body that had turned up was unrelated to the case.

She exited the freeway and headed east across the railroad tracks, both literally and figuratively. She entered an area of housing projects, boarded-up buildings and broken windows. Undoubtedly a lot of broken dreams, as well.

Kali spotted the cluster of official vehicles on a side street near an empty field. A clear signal to anyone passing by that something was amiss. Some of the local residents were, in fact, peeking out from behind curtained windows, but there wasn't the usual gathering of curious onlookers. People in neighborhoods like this were wary of police, whatever the reason for their visit, and they weren't about to get any closer than they had to.

Kali parked outside the cordoned-off area and walked into the cold wind the half block to where a uniformed cop was standing sentry. He was one of the few cops she recognized, and he apparently recognized her, as well.

"You're becoming a regular at our little festivities," he said with a touch of gallows humor.

She smiled. "Can't stay away from a party."

"The action is down there." He pointed to the far end of an open lot.

She crossed the rutted field and passed through a large tear in the adjacent chain-link fence. It was wide enough to drive a tank through, and so old the metal had begun to rust. A hole like that defeated the purpose of having a fence in the first place. But in this area of the city, maintenance was not a high priority.

On the other side of the fence was an open cement culvert, probably ten feet across at the top, filled with slimy green water. The surface was pockmarked with algae and every kind of debris imaginable. Rags, tires, a shopping cart, even a baby carriage.

"Watch your step," Bryce called. He and Lou were huddled with one of the evidence technicians.

Kali looked down. The narrow ledge that ran along the culvert was uneven and badly cracked. She didn't want to trip. The thought of slipping into that cesspool of a culvert gave her the willies.

"Was she in the water?" Kali asked when she caught up to the detectives. She felt more sure than before that she didn't want to view the body.

Bryce shook his head. "Against the fence. Propped up with her hands folded in her lap like she was at the beach watching the sun set."

Kali picked up on the sarcasm in his tone, but there was something else too. A brittleness maybe. She couldn't put her finger on it.

"Is it Ruby Wings?" Kali glanced at the center of activity about twenty yards ahead. She saw Bevin talking to another criminalist who was sweeping the area and carefully depositing his pickings into a collection of paper bags.

"We don't have a positive ID yet," Lou said, "but it looks to be her."

"Same MO as before?"

"Pretty much."

A uniformed cop called to them from the other side of the fence. "The boys who found her are getting antsy," he said. "What do I tell them?"

"Guess we'd better talk to them," Lou said.

Bryce kicked at a broken piece of cement. "You and Kali go ahead. I want to check a few things with Bevin."

Lou turned to Kali. She could tell he wasn't happy with the arrangement. Neither was she.

"Let's go," he said with a sigh. "They're in the cruiser at the corner."

She followed Lou back across the field. It was a community sports field, she realized, only with so many potholes and boggy spots that anyone moving at more than a careful clip was bound to end up with a sprained ankle.

Lou opened the back door to the cruiser and invited the two boys inside to step out. They were in their early teens, dark complected, probably Hispanic. Skinny and awkward, with baggy pants and baseball hats turned backward. The taller boy had tattoos on his neck and hand. The other boy sported what he no doubt envisioned as a beard but was really a scraggly collection of chin hairs. They were street kids, and not the Berkeley, regular-allowance-from-mom-and-dad variety.

"What are your names?" Lou asked.

The boy with tattoos answered. "I'm Mando. He's Gus."

"We appreciate the call," Lou told them. "Tell us how you found her."

The boys were jittery. "We already told someone."

"And now you're going to tell us."

"We gotta get home, man." It was Gus who spoke this time.

"You live around here?"

Mando gave Lou a look of disgust. "Course we do. Who else you think come here?"

Kali reached for her phone and offered it to Gus. "You want to call your mom and tell her you'll be late?"

He gave her a sullen look. "I don't got a mom, and his"—he pointed to his companion—"she ain't home."

"So what's the rush?" Lou asked.

"We got shit to do, man, that's what."

More likely, Kali thought, they were simply eager to be done with all the questions. And the police. Little had they suspected what they were letting themselves in for when they'd reported finding a body.

Mando sighed. "What you want to know?"

"Start from the beginning, why don't you."

"We was fishing the river—"

"You fish in that?" Kali couldn't help herself.

A thin smile pulled at Mando's mouth. "Not for fish. For, you know, stuff."

Cheaper than a flea market, Kali supposed, but she cringed at the thought of children, even toughened kids like these, playing in such a place.

"We seen her, didn't think much about it. Some drugged-out whore sleeping it off, you know. Wouldn't be the first. Then we get closer, and we're like, hey, this ain't right."

"Did you take anything?" Lou asked. "Touch her?"

Gus jerked his head in contempt. "What you think we are, man? She fat and ugly."

From the picture Kali had seen, Ruby had been an attractive woman. Then it dawned on her that Ruby's body was probably horribly swollen and disfigured from being a day or more dead.

"We called the cops right away," Mando said.

"And they make us sit here, wait forever."

"We appreciate your help," Kali offered.

"What time did you first see the woman?" Lou asked.

"Couple of hours now."

Lou checked his watch. "You don't have school today?"

Mando shrugged. Gus looked like a bull facing down a red cape. "We cut out a little early."

"Do you come here often?" Kali asked.

"Every day just about."

"Yesterday?"

"Yeah."

Lou blew on his hands. "You think you'd have seen her if she was here then?"

"Guess so."

"Did you ever seen anyone around who looked like he didn't belong?" Kali asked.

"Whad'ya mean?"

She knew exactly what she meant, but not how to put it into words. "Someone you wouldn't expect to find nosing around a culvert," she said at last.

The boys thought for a moment. "Some lady and a man," Mando said.

"When was this?" Lou's voice was edged with eagerness.

Kali shared his excitement. It might be the break they'd been hoping for.

"Last summer. I heard 'em talking. She with some agency was going to clean the place up, but ain't ever happened."

"How about more recently?" Lou's tone made it sound like a reprimand.

"No one who don't b-e-e-long," Gus said snidely, looking at Kali. "Only people we ever seen round here are the kind like you'd *expect* to find nosing in a culvert."

Kali felt the pinch of guilt. Insulting them was the very thing she'd tried to avoid.

"Watch your tone," Lou said brusquely. He called to the uniformed cop to make sure their names and addresses were on record. Then he turned back to the boys. "Think about it. Ask around. If it turns out you remember seeing someone, give us a call. You tell us something helpful, there might be some money in it for you."

"How much?" Gus asked.

"Depends." When the boys were gone, Lou muttered, "Tomorrow's leaders. Doesn't fill me with optimism."

"They *did* call the cops," Kali pointed out. "That's more than lots of people would have done."

"You sound like my daughter."

He probably hadn't intended it as a compliment, but there was no missing the affection in his voice. Kali liked him better for that. She was beginning to understand, too, that he wasn't the tough, gruff cop she'd pegged him for.

"You think they know more and just weren't talking?" she asked.

Lou shook his head. "I doubt it. But someone in the neighborhood might know more, and those kids will have better luck getting the word out than we would."

They trudged back across the field. Kali could see that the coroner had arrived and was examining the body. News vans gathered, and overhead a helicopter was circling.

Kali raised her voice to be heard over the thump-thump of the chopper. "You know what I just realized," she said. "Our killer didn't put the body next to a garbage can or dumpster this time."

"He didn't have to. The whole place is a dump."

Lou was right. And it struck Kali suddenly that the killer was upping the ante each time. The Bayside Strangler had used garbage cans. With the new murders they'd had a dumpster, an outhouse, and now this noxious cesspool of a culvert. Part of his game?

Bryce moved to join them. "What did you find out?"

"The kids found her and called the cops," Lou said. "They didn't touch anything and didn't see anything. They don't think she wasn't here yesterday. We're going to get really far with that." He nodded toward the coroner. "What did Malkin say?"

"You know Malkin, he doesn't say diddly until he's good and ready." Bryce turned to Kali. "Come look at the body. There's something I think you should see."

Kali hesitated. She thought of the swollen flesh the boys had described. "I'm not sure—"

But he was already heading off down the narrow edge of the culvert. Reluctantly, she followed. Earl Malkin was near the fence, bent over examining a human shape on the ground. Kali braced herself.

"The DA here wants to have a look," Bryce said.

"Actually, I really—"

"Sure, I'm finished anyway," Malkin said.

He stepped to the side, leaving a clear line of vision to Ruby Wings's body. Kali didn't even notice the swollen flesh and distorted features. Instead, she focused on what Ruby was wearing—a pink bikini and some sort of necklace.

"Is that the pink bathing . . ." And then it struck her. She felt her chest catch. It wasn't a necklace around Ruby Wings's neck.

It was a dog collar.

Lou shifted uncomfortably in his chair.

The captain drummed his fingers and didn't say a word. Then he stood, shut the door and returned to his desk. Lou glanced at Keating, silent and brooding in the next chair. They'd come straight from the crime scene to deliver the news to Burnell in person, which was how they'd both agreed it had to be handled, but Lou had done most of the talking and now he felt the heat of the captain's scrutiny.

"A dog collar," Burnell said.

"Yes, sir."

"Same as with the Bayside Strangler victims."

It wasn't a question but Lou nodded anyway.

"Same type?"

"Plain black leather. Kali says she thinks it's similar to the ones used before, but we don't have the details yet."

"You know what this means, don't you?" As usual, the captain didn't wait for an answer. "It means the killer has information that's available to only a limited number of people."

Members of law enforcement—and the Bayside Strangler himself. Lou wasn't sure which was worse. "That's why we came to you right away," he said. "It's, uh . . . it adds a new twist to the investigation."

"Sure the hell does." Burnell stood again and walked to the window, his back to the detectives. Finally he turned. "If our guy was so intent on copying the Bayside Strangler, why didn't he use collars for the first two murders?" This time the captain sounded as if he did expect an answer.

"Maybe he didn't know about them then," Lou said. Which would mean they were dealing with a copycat and not the Bayside Strangler himself. But it also meant the killer was somehow getting inside information, either because he was part of the investigation or had access to it. Lou didn't want to think about that.

"Or maybe it's just part of the game for him," Keating suggested. "That seems to be a big part of what excites him."

"I thought this type of killer liked to have an authentic signature. Isn't that what you've been telling me?"

"That was Dr. Dunworthy," Keating explained. "We were only passing along what he told us."

"But the dog collar was part of the Strangler's signature." The captain seemed as eager as Lou to discount the possibility that their killer was the actual Strangler.

"Only in three out of five of the murders," Keating pointed out. "Could be, too, he dropped the collar with Bailey and Parkhurst simply to throw us off."

Burnell glared at Keating. "I thought you told me earlier these recent crimes were different." Burnell tapped his fingers on his desktop. "That we were looking at a copycat."

"We still think that, but you were asking for an explanation—"

Burnell cut him short. "Let's just hope the Bayside Strangler is in his grave."

Lou couldn't resist. "Actually, he'd be at the bottom of the sea. As bits of ash."

Burnell ignored the comment. "I want this kept quiet, understand? I'll keep support personnel in place for you, but you're to keep the details close to the vest."

"Malkin knows," Lou pointed out. "And so do the first cops to the scene."

"And we can't shut the DA's office out," Keating added.

"Do the best you can. Just remember that strategy sessions and case updates are between you two and that woman from the DA's office, period. And me, of course. Anybody else, it's on a need-to-know basis only."

As if they'd been broadcasting case findings over the airwaves. Burnell could be a pain in the ass sometimes. "Anything else?" Lou asked. "We'd like to get back on the case."

"Just that there's going to be a lot of media interest in this. We have to balance the public's desire for information against our need to run a meticulous investigation."

"Right."

"Evidence compromised is no evidence at all. You can leave the door open on your way out."

Lou waited until they were around the corner. "How'd he make it to captain anyway? Couldn't have been charisma."

"Pass the test and kiss ass, Lou. That's the ticket."

"Leaves you out of the running, doesn't it?" Not that Keating had any aspirations in that direction anyway as far as Lou was aware.

"I could pass the test. All it takes is some work."

Lou grinned. "It's the second part, Bryce. You'd never make the kiss-ass threshold."

Keating didn't rise to the bait. Didn't respond at all in fact. He pushed ahead at a brisk clip in silence.

"Something bothering you, Bryce?

"Beyond the fact that we've got a third body?"

"Hey, no need to bite my head off," Lou grumbled. He decided that Keating must have gotten out of bed on the wrong side that morning. "Where are you off to?"

"Macy's. On the off chance that one of the salespeople remembers seeing a lone man lurking around on Saturday afternoon. Want to come along?"

Lou shook his head. "I've done my bit with the clothing stores, thank you. I'll see if I can't squeeze some information out of Malkin."

\*   \*   \*

Lou found Malkin pouring coffee into a mug shaped like a skull. "You want some?" the coroner asked.

The coffee in the coroner's office was notoriously bad. Lou half suspected they made it with formaldehyde instead of water. "No, thanks." He eyed the mug. "It doesn't bother you drinking from that?"

"Never really thought about it before, but no. And it's a sure-fire way to keep people from using my cup." He set the Pyrex coffee pot back on the burner. "You're here about the body we just picked up, right? I won't have the preliminary report for at least another day."

"Give me your impressions, top of your head."

"That's not science, Lou."

"I understand that. But this is an important case. I won't hold you to it."

Malkin took a sip of coffee. "What is it you want to know?"

"How long she's been dead, for one thing."

"You know that's not easy—"

"Approximately, Earl. That's all I'm asking."

"Thirty-six to forty-eight hours, give or take."

So the chances were she'd been killed right away. "Strangled like the others?" Lou asked.

"Appears that way. Now let me get to work or I'll never get the report to you."

"I need to take a look at the bathing suit," Lou said.

"It's still on the corpse."

Lou nodded.

Malkin raised a thin eyebrow. "You aren't going kinky on me, are you?"

"She apparently tried on a pink bikini last week at Macy's. I want to know if it's the same suit he dressed her in."

"I was wondering about the clothing. The others have been dressed to the nines. Come on." Malkin lead Lou to the tile and stainless-steel room down the corridor where the newly arrived bodies were catalogued. "She's on the far table."

Lou wasn't excited about lifting the sheet to look at a dead woman in a bikini. Maybe he should have invited Maureen Oliver to do it; after all, she seemed to know clothes. Or Kali, since the DA's office was so interested in this crime.

He peeled back the sheet, noting what he could of the fabric and cut of the bathing suit. Pink, many shades, like the tie-and-dye projects Nikki had done in high school. Tie-and-die. How appropriate. He wondered if the killer had had the same thought.

Back in the car, he called Carla O'Neill and asked her to describe the pink bikini Ruby Wings had tried on at Macy's.

"V-neck, thin straps," she said. "It was a mottled material. Tie-dye, as I recall."

The same goddamn suit. And their killer was probably gleeful as hell at the joke.

# CHAPTER 35

Lou didn't watch much in the way of talk shows. But when he'd read in the paper that Al Gomez was going to be on the Bill McDonald show that afternoon, he'd made note of it. Not only was Gomez on the short list of people who knew the details of the Bayside Strangler murders, he had a personal interest in seeing Owen Nelson fall flat on his face. Maybe it *was* a stretch to think Gomez would resort to murder. Keating thought so. But Lou wasn't ready to toss the idea aside just yet.

Now, at a quarter till four, Lou had fifteen minutes to find a television. He finally decided on The Watering Hole, owned by an ex-cop and frequented by many of Lou's co-workers. It was nearby, and as Lou recalled from the couple of times he'd been there, it had a television. At four o'clock in the afternoon, he didn't imagine he'd have a lot of competition for the remote.

He was right about the television but wrong about the competition. There were only three other patrons in the place, but they were glued to a show featuring scantily clad teenage girls. Lou slid onto a bar stool and ordered a beer.

"Hey, Lou, haven't seen you around much. Not like your partner, who practically makes this place his second home." Pat had been on the force when Lou first started. Took a bullet to his shoulder in a domestic dispute and decided there were better ways to earn a living. Lou wasn't sure he'd found one of them, however.

"Yeah, well, Bryce has his own style." Lou paid for the beer. "I was hoping to catch an Al Gomez interview at four. What are the chances of convincing those three that television sex will rot their brains?"

"Not a problem. They're not even regulars, just some dentists in town for a convention."

The three men weren't happy about the switch. They finished their drinks and left. Lou moved down the bar to a seat with a clearer view of the television.

McDonald introduced Gomez and started off the segment with a rehash of the Bayside Strangler murders and the Davis trial. Gomez looked every bit the role of slimeball lawyer in his fancy, double-breasted suit and bow tie. He was in his element, yammering nonsense about minority convictions, death penalty abuses and police transgressions. If there was one thing worse than a lawyer, it was a manipulative, self-serving lawyer. And Gomez fit the description to a T.

He talked rapidly, seeming never to pause for a breath, and managed to get in a couple of digs at Owen Nelson as well as broad praise for Tony Molina. The discussion then turned to the recent spate of murders. Gomez had plenty to say about that, too, some of it inaccurate and highly speculative, most of it inflammatory.

Fifteen minutes into the program, Lou had about had his fill of Gomez. Only the fact that he hadn't finished his beer kept Lou from heading for the door. He'd half tuned out, wondering if he should stop for take-out or brave an attempt at pork chops in the kitchen, when Gomez said something that brought Lou back to the present with a jolt.

"Did you catch that?" Lou asked.

"Catch what?" Pat was drying glasses at the other end of the bar.

"What that jerk Gomez just said."

"Wasn't listening. What did he say?"

"He said, 'in light of the third murder'."

"What third murder?"

"Precisely."

They'd been very careful over the airwaves not to mention the victim or any of the details about the most recent murder. And given the location of the crime scene, interest from the press had been minimal. Bodies turned up in that part of the city with alarming frequency.

So how had Gomez known this latest murder was connected to the other two?

Lou put his beer aside. "Where's this program filmed, any idea?"

"San Francisco. One Embarcadero Plaza. I know cuz my wife's niece works in the same building."

"Thanks." Lou paid for his beer.

"Hey, don't be such a stranger from now on, okay?"

"Sure thing, Pat. See you around."

Lou headed across the Bay Bridge against the afternoon commute. Traffic was still bad, but the distance was short. He walked into the station's outer office at five minutes before the hour.

A young man sat behind the desk. "Can I help you?"

Lou showed his badge. "I'd like to talk to Al Gomez."

"There's no one here—"

"He's today's guest on the Bill McDonald program."

"They're in the middle of—"

"I'll wait."

"This isn't how we usually—"

"Let me know as soon as they're finished in the studio."

The young man seemed flustered. He made a call, covered the mouthpiece and whispered into the phone. All Lou was able to make out was, "yeah, the police." But whoever he'd checked with must have given the go-ahead, because ten minutes later Lou was ushered down a hallway and into a tiny, bright room where Gomez sat removing pancake makeup from his face.

"You need it on television," Gomez explained defensively. "Otherwise you fade into nothing." He was a big man. Not tall, but solidly built and carrying probably forty pounds over his optimal weight. His suit looked expensive and fit him as though it had been cut just for him. Defending slime apparently paid well.

Lou introduced himself. "I'd like to talk to you a minute."

"Official business?"

What did Gomez think? That Lou was a fan? "I've got a couple of questions, is all."

Gomez smoothed his oily hair, then nodded toward the door. "Mind stepping outside? I'm dying for a cigarette."

"This real killer you keep alluding to," Lou asked when they were standing on the open-air landing, "the one who you claim is responsible for the Bayside Strangler murders—do you have any proof he exists?"

Gomez pulled a cigarette from a silver case and lit it. "It's not my job to offer proof."

"It's not your job to make unsubstantiated accusations either."

"Certainly you didn't make a special trip here to discuss the scope of my job?"

"I came because I'm trying to find a killer and I thought you might be able to help."

"You thought wrong."

Lou hadn't imagined it possible, but he disliked Gomez more in person than at a distance. "It doesn't bother you that innocent women are being killed?"

"It apparently doesn't bother you that innocent men are being executed."

"You honestly believe Davis was innocent?"

Gomez flicked ash on the cement. "Tell me again why you're here, detective."

"We've got a copycat killer prowling around out there—"

"You've got a killer out there, all right, but he's no copycat."

"It's someone who knows the details of the Bayside Strangler murders," Lou said, ignoring the interruption. "That's a very short list, and your name is on it."

Gomez looked momentarily stunned, but he was too smooth a showman to let it trip him up. He offered a supercilious smile. "Are you implying that I killed those women?"

"You might have. Or had someone do it for you."

"Really, detective. Why would I do that?"

"You've gotten a lot of publicity out of these murders."

"So have other people, including Owen Nelson and his buddy Jack Jackson." Gomez laughed. "Of course the publicity Nelson's gotten isn't so good."

"It would be easy enough to check where you were when the murders took place," Lou said. "To check transfers in and out of your bank account, as well."

The lawyer's eyes narrowed and his nostrils flared. "You smear my name and I'll sue you for everything you've got."

"You wouldn't get much." Lou offered a blatantly false smile. "Is it true that you and Tony Molina are old friends?"

"We grew up in the same neighborhood in Los Angeles. . . ." Gomez stopped mid-sentence as the question hit home. "You think he's behind this? Jesus, you are sick."

"The real sicko is whoever is killing these women."

"Well, it's not me, and it's not Tony. I can't believe you even—"

"You made a comment on the air earlier," Lou said. "About a third victim."

"Did I?"

Lou nodded. "What makes you think there's been a third victim?"

"I must have heard it somewhere."

"Yeah? Where?"

Gomez ground out his cigarette. "Are you telling me the information is wrong?"

"I'm not telling you anything."

"That makes two of us." Gomez turned on his heel and went back inside.

Lou watched him leave, and wondered. Maybe it wasn't such a farfetched scenario, after all.

Almost five o'clock, and the sky outside Kali's office window revealed no hint of evening darkness. She was always happy when the shortest days of the year were behind them. Real spring might still be months away, but she felt relief that they were at least headed there.

Working a knot in her neck with her fingertips, she looked again at the city map spread out on her desk. Today's crime scene was in the southern part of the city, ten or so miles from either of the previous crime scenes, and even farther in terms of social climate and attitude. Inhabitants of the more advantaged parts of the city rarely made it to the tumbledown neighborhoods, and vice versa. Yet their killer was obviously familiar with both.

He was also familiar with an undisclosed detail of the Strangler murders—the dog collar. In theory, that narrowed the field of possibilities. But it was also a troubling development.

Kali reached into her purse for a breath mint and found the scrap of paper on which Nathan had written his number. Had she been too short with him this afternoon? Yes. No. Yes. How could she find him attractive and pleasant, and still feel there was something odd about him? Bad energy, she thought. How very California.

Out of curiosity, she looked up the main number for Global Investment, called and asked for the personnel department.

When the phone picked up, Kali asked to speak to someone about verifying employment. She was transferred to a woman whose voice was so flat, Kali thought at first she was talking to a machine.

"Hello," Kali said. "I'm with K&O Financial in Petaluma." She used her own initials because she wasn't quick enough to think of anything more clever. "I'm checking references on a former employee of yours who has applied for a job with us. A Mr. Nathan Sloane, who worked for your company until just last week."

"We no longer give recommendations or evaluations," the woman told her.

"Can you tell me if he left on good terms?"

"Sorry, just dates of employment. Would you like me to check those?"

"Please."

She put Kali on hold, which was actually a commercial for the company's financial services. Kali listened to the loop three times before the woman came back on to ask, "What was that name again?"

"Nathan Sloane."

"I'm sorry, ma'am, we have no record of anyone by that name."

"He transferred from Boston. I imagine he wasn't with your office long. Would there be any way to check with the Boston office?"

"We don't have a Boston office. Only Los Angeles and the Bay Area."

"I see. Maybe I have the wrong information," Kali said.

"Or maybe this applicant hasn't been truthful. I don't know how it is in your experience, but we're seeing that more and more all the time."

"So true," Kali said obliquely. She disconnected, tapped her fingers on her desk, then called one of the office investigators. "I'd like you to check the registration on a cell phone," she said and gave him the number.

"Can you give us a day or two?"

"Sure." Returning the receiver to the cradle, she looked up to see Bryce Keating standing in her doorway. She hoped he wouldn't ask about the call, hoped he hadn't overheard the conversation at all, in fact.

He regarded her from the doorway. "Got a moment?"

"Of course. Anything more on Ruby Wings's murder?"

Bryce shook his head. "I talked to the salesclerks at Macy's in Walnut Creek, where she apparently tried on the bathing suit. No one remembers seeing anything or anyone unusual on Saturday. Then again, they don't remember seeing Ruby or her friend Carla either."

"I imagine it's a madhouse there on Saturdays."

Bryce took a seat, sliding his legs out in front of him. "Lou talked to the friend. Sounds like the swimsuit Ruby was wearing when we found her matches the one she tried on when they were shopping. I had the store check sales records. There were no sales of that particular suit on Saturday or anytime this week."

"That's not the only Macy's in the area," Kali reminded him.

"I know. I put Maureen Oliver on it. I also looked into the dog collar. It's a common brand and style. I doubt we'll trace him through that." Bryce pulled at an earlobe. "Lou and I talked to the captain. He wants this kept quiet. Even within the department."

"Warding off hysteria about the return of the Bayside Strangler?"

"Partially that, and partially . . ." Bryce paused. "The killer has to be someone close to the Strangler case. Someone who knows details that weren't made public."

"I had the same thought." There was a sour taste in her mouth merely acknowledging the possibility. "It should help you narrow the field, though. There can't be that many people who are familiar with the case."

Bryce ran his palm over the rounded, plastic arm of the chair. "The list is probably longer than we might expect." He seemed lost in thought; then he stood abruptly. "You want to continue this over a drink?"

Despite previous hints of interest on Bryce's part, the suggestion caught her by surprise. "Socially, you mean?"

"Better than nonsocially." He gave her a quick grin. "But if you're busy or you'd rather not—"

"I'd love to."

He seemed pleased by her answer. Also, she realized in retrospect, a bit uncomfortable with the asking. So much for his reputation as a local Don Juan.

"I've got a few things to finish up," Bryce said. "How about we meet in the lobby in about twenty minutes. Does that give you enough time?"

"Perfect." She was doubly relieved that she hadn't agreed to meet Nathan Sloane after work.

Kali and Bryce left the building in a bustle of humanity that made conversation difficult. With his hand lightly on the small of her back, Bryce guided her to the edge of the sidewalk. It was a simple, casual gesture, but it quickened her heartbeat with its familiarity.

"Anyplace in particular you'd like to go?" he asked her.

"Your call, but no loud sports bar."

He laughed. "You must think I've got no class."

Class actually wasn't one of the qualities she associated with Bryce, but she didn't necessarily see that as a negative either.

She was looking at his eyes, which she noted were a warm brown and not at all unreadable as she'd previously thought, trying to formulate a witty comeback, when a young man on Rollerblades zipped by. He clipped her and sent her sprawling to the ground. Her shoulder and hip took the brunt of it, but her palms scraped the pavement, as did her chin and one knee. In the first instant, she felt nothing but the shock of suddenly finding herself on the ground. Then the pain came rolling in, so sharp that it took her breath away.

She saw Bryce start after the boy on Rollerblades, weaving between pedestrians, hollering, but he turned back almost immediately. He was kneeling beside her now, amidst a small gathering of passersby. "Are you hurt badly?" he asked.

"I don't think so." She was breathing hard against the pain of freshly scraped skin. She flexed her arm and her wrist. "Shaken and sore, but I seem to be in one piece."

Circling her with his arm, Bryce helped her to her feet.

"What's with kids today?" said a man in the crowd. "That punk shouldn't have been on the sidewalk and he shouldn't have been going as fast as he was."

"Almost looked like he went straight for her," said a gray-haired woman.

Kali looked at her palms and saw the blood beginning to seep to the surface. "I think I'll take a raincheck on the drink," she told Bryce.

"Looks to me like you could use a double."

Her hands stung so badly, she could feel tears. Something cold and alcoholic wasn't such a bad idea really.

"Come on," Bryce said. "My place isn't far from here. We can get you cleaned up there. You can't drive in the shape you're in anyway."

He slid an arm around her and helped her to the car. Her left ankle hurt if she put too much weight on it and she would have had trouble walking without his help. But more than that, his arm around her was comforting.

He drove more slowly than the last time she'd been in the car with him. Cautiously even, as though she might break if he took the corner with any speed at all.

"I should have gone after him," Bryce said.

"He was on Rollerblades. You'd never have caught him. Besides, I'm glad you stayed to help me."

"Fat lot of help I was."

"You were." She smiled. "Are."

"You sure nothing's broken?"

"Yeah. Nothing more serious than minor scrapes."

He parked in a garage under a row of town houses along the estuary and ushered her to what appeared to be a penthouse suite on the third floor.

She'd expected a bachelor pad, either sleek and hi-tech or rumpled and terribly messy. But what she encountered was a tasteful and eclectic mix of furnishings in a room with polished hardwood floors and high ceilings. The far wall was all bookshelves, crammed with books, she noticed, not trophies or memorabilia. The television was small and far from new.

Bryce led her to the limestone-tiled bathroom, where he washed her hands with a soft cloth and then applied an antiseptic cream. "It's going to smart for a while," he said.

It did. She yelped. "Hurt like hell is more like it."

"We should do something about the rest of you, too."

Kali looked at herself in the mirror. She was a mess. Wet and dirty. Her nylons and blouse were torn, and the side of her face looked as if she'd been in a barroom brawl.

"I can do it myself," she said. As nice as it was to have Bryce hovering over her, she wasn't about to play helpless patient.

"Why don't you get out of those wet and muddy clothes first. I've got a robe you can use."

He disappeared and returned a moment later carrying a velour robe embroidered with his initials. Kali suppressed a smile. Never in a hundred years would she have predicted that Bryce Keating was the monogram type.

"Holler if you need help." He started to close the door behind him. "You like margaritas?"

"Love them."

"There'll be one waiting for you when you finish there."

Kali dabbed at the remaining scrapes, which weren't as bad as they appeared once the surface grime and blood was off. She slipped out of her stockings and blouse, and into Bryce's robe. It was a blue and green striped velour, very dapper and way too big for her. She cinched it tight, then turned her nose to sniff for the scent of aftershave or soap. Nothing.

The margarita was ice cold, the way she liked it. And smooth as silk. None of this bottled mix that was so popular in some circles. After the first sip she could feel the pain of her scrapes and bruises recede. Kali sat at the dining table, intentionally avoiding the bulky and very inviting sofa beyond. She wasn't sure whether it was herself or Bryce she didn't trust.

He took a chair to her left.

"Nice robe," she said.

"A gift."

From a woman, no doubt. Kali experienced an unexpected stab of jealousy.

"It's clean," Bryce said. He ran his tongue over his lower lip. "I've never worn it."

"How come?" She caught him glance at the deep V where the robe flapped open at the neckline. She pulled it closed and held it there.

"I get up, I get dressed. I've never had much use for a robe."

Not a gift from anyone who knew him well, it seemed. Kali took odd comfort in the knowledge. She took another sip of her drink, angling it for a fresh taste of salt.

He smiled. His eyes crinkled.

"We were talking about the case," Kali said after a moment.

"We were?"

"Back in my office." A hundred years ago. "We were going to continue the conversation over drinks."

The smile broadened. "There must be better things to talk about."

Or do, she thought, taking another sip. The margarita was strong. She must be half-soused already to be thinking the things she was. "Such as?"

He touched her cheek above the abrasion. "How's it feeling?"

"Better."

His fingers grazed the skin at the nape of her neck. The pleasure was so intense she gasped involuntarily. And when he kissed her, she knew that she'd been a fool to think that avoiding the couch would be enough.

# CHAPTER 36

Gloria was on the phone when Kali limped into work the next morning. She looked up as Kali approached, adjusted her glasses, then held a hand over the receiver. "What happened to you?" she asked.

"I got hit by a kid on Rollerblades."

"Ouch."

"It's not as bad as it looks."

Gloria's expression registered doubt. She reached for the message slips tucked under the edge of her blotter and handed them to Kali. "There was another call, too, only he didn't leave his name."

Kali glanced at the call slips on her way to her desk. One was from the department investigator she'd asked for information about Nathan's cell phone; the other was from Lou Fortune. She tossed the slips onto her desk and hung up her coat. Then she uncapped the latte she'd picked up at Peet's on the way in and tried to clear her mind of the tangled thoughts she'd been tripping over since Bryce had delivered her back to her car in the wee hours of the morning.

She was a little angry at herself for succumbing (how could she have allowed herself to be so easily charmed?) and at the same time giddy with the memory. As a lover, Bryce was both gentle and passionate (a beguiling combination no doubt borne of ample experience), but what caused her heart to flutter still this morning was the shadow of vulnerability she'd detected behind the tough facade. Or maybe that was part of his persona, too. The man did have a reputation, after all.

At least she'd had the good sense not to stay the night. That was something. But she wasn't sure she wanted to face him just yet, either. Or talk to him. And if she returned Lou's call, the chances were good that Bryce might answer.

Well, so what? It wasn't like they were sixteen years old.

She picked up the phone and punched in the number before she had a chance to reconsider. But she felt a wave of relief when it was Lou who answered.

"You got some time to talk?" he asked.

"Sure."

"Probably best if you come over here. Bryce isn't in yet, but I just called him and he's on way."

"Has something come up?"

"I'll explain when you get here."

Kali eyed her latte. "Ten minutes okay?"

"Should be perfect."

She walked into the homicide room just as Bryce was hanging his black leather jacket over the back of his chair. The sight of him made her heart race, but she avoided his eyes.

Lou caught sight of her and did a double take. "Whad'ya do, take a header?"

"With some major help from a fast-moving Rollerblader."

"Kids today got no manners. No respect at all."

"This one sure didn't." Kali was bruised and sore, but she felt better than she evidently looked, given what was becoming the standard reaction to her appearance.

She took a seat across the desk from Lou. Out of the corner of her eye, she saw Bryce angle his chair so that he was facing them. But he avoided looking straight at her.

"Did you call a meeting, Lou?" Bryce asked. "Or did we all just happen to end up here at the same time?"

"The captain's all fired up this morning. Since you two dragged in here late, I've been the one catching the heat. Kali can at least claim injuries. What's your excuse, Bryce?"

Kali caught Bryce giving her a long sideways look. His mouth tweaked with the hint of a smile. Just enough to affirm silent communication. She felt better for it.

"I didn't get to sleep until late," Bryce said.

Lou raised one bushy eyebrow. "That little black book of yours keeps you busy, doesn't it?"

Bryce frowned. "What little black book?" The tone was pure innocence, but Kali saw him give Lou a pointed look, which apparently missed its mark.

"You mean you've got more than one?" Lou guffawed, seemingly pleased with his attempt at humor. "Anyway, in light of yesterday's discovery, I thought we needed to talk." He turned to Kali. "You've heard the captain wants us to keep the lid on this?"

She nodded. "Bryce told me. The trouble is, everyone at the scene yesterday already knows about the dog collar."

"They may know about it in *this* case," Bryce said. "But chances are they don't know the significance. Not unless any of them worked the Strangler case."

"They may even think it's some fashion statement," Lou added. "Way people dress these days, who can tell?"

"So what we've got," Kali said, making sure she hadn't missed something, "is a killer who has access to information about the Bayside Strangler case that wasn't made public."

"That's it in a nutshell."

Lou licked his finger and rubbed at an ink spot on his hand. "That's a good place to start. Who has inside knowledge about the Strangler investigation?"

"The two lead detectives," Bryce said. "Both are now retired, right? And the cops who worked the original crime scenes where the victims had collars." He turned to Kali, all business this time. "How many was that?"

"Three. The first victim didn't have a dog collar, and neither did Wendy Gilchrist."

"There's got to have been a handful of others in the department, too," Bryce continued. "Records clerks, evidence techs, support people of all sorts."

"A similar handful of people in the DA's office," Lou said. "Anyone there you think maybe we should look at?" He addressed the question to Kali.

"There were three of us working directly with Owen. Me, Anne Bailey and Corey Redmond. Since the dog collars weren't part of the prosecution's case, I don't think anyone else in the office would have known about them."

Keating frowned. "What about Corey Redmond?"

"He married a woman with money and connections. Works for his father-in-law. He has twin daughters. I got a Christmas card from him. Not a likely candidate for serial killer." Of course, Dwayne Davis hadn't seemed the type either, she reminded herself.

They lapsed into a momentary silence; then Bryce said, "What about Jack Jackson?"

Kali frowned. "What about him?"

"Did he know about the dog collars?"

"I'm not . . . wait, yes, he did. I remember Owen saying part of the deal with the book was that Jackson had to omit the confidential stuff. Owen specifically mentioned the dog collars when he was telling me. But why would Jack—"

"With crimes like this, looking for the *why* won't get you very far," Lou said. "Though in Jackson's case, publicity might be a factor."

"Or maybe writing about the Strangler murders triggered some fantasy of his own," Bryce said. "Didn't Dr. Dunworthy say that the copycat phenomenon was often based on a killer's fascination with the original murders?"

Kali nodded. "A fascination that the copycat killer then tweaked to make his own. Just the way our killer has done."

"Jackson had to have been pretty steeped in it. He covered the trial, interviewed the victims' families, as well as Davis himself, as I recall."

That much was true, but Kali couldn't picture Jack as a killer. He might not be above elbowing his way into a story, but as a person, he was a gentle teddy bear.

"You know who else is neck deep in murder?" she offered. "Dunworthy. He also knows the details of the Strangler murders."

Bryce whistled low under his breath. "Wouldn't that be something—the expert on serial killers, a killer himself. And the guy is strange."

"Strange how?" Lou asked.

"Imagine one of the Seven Dwarfs with a European tailor," Bryce said. "And he practically breaks into a pant when he starts discussing the mind of a serial killer."

Kali laughed at the description. It was a bit of a caricature, but not far off.

Keating scooted his chair closer to the desk and addressed Kali. "Lou had a thought the murders might be political."

"Political?"

"To embarrass Owen Nelson."

She made a face. "I'm no fan of Molina's, but I wouldn't go so far as to suspect him of murder."

"Not Molina himself," Lou said, "but someone in his camp. What's more, Al Gomez is a childhood friend of his. He's been pissed at Owen Nelson since the day Davis was convicted."

"You're saying Gomez is a potential suspect?" Her first reaction was that respected members of the legal profession didn't commit murder. But on further reflection, she had to admit there was a certain logic to the idea. Gomez certainly knew the details of the Strangler case; he'd defended Davis, after all. And he'd made a name for himself protesting what he claimed was Davis's wrongful conviction. The recent murders had been fuel for his fury.

"I talked to him last night," Lou said. "He knew there'd been a third murder."

"It's hard to keep a crime quiet," Kali pointed out. "Even when we withhold official comment."

Lou nodded. "But it hadn't made the news yet. And there's been nothing from our department connecting Ruby Wings's death to the other two."

Kali tried to remember what she'd read in the paper this morning. Her mind had been on more pleasant thoughts than murder, but as she recalled, there'd been nothing but a very short piece about the murder of an Oakland woman whose body had been found by a drainage canal. Nothing tying it to the other murders.

"You're saying Gomez knew things he couldn't have known unless he was personally connected to the crime?"

Lou crossed his arms on his belly. "I wouldn't go that far, although I wouldn't rule it out, either. But he *did* know the cases were related."

They lapsed into silence. Lou's broad face scrunched in concentration, while Bryce's expression was impenetrable. Kali's mind bounced from denial to thinking anything was possible.

"We should also think about members of your department," she said at last.

Bryce gestured to himself and Lou. "Meaning the two of us." He seemed more amused than put out.

"And whoever else was privy to information about the dog collars in the Strangler case," Kali explained. "I imagine there's been a lot of internal discussion."

"It might surprise you to know," Lou grumbled, "that most of us are too busy to gossip."

She could have debated the point, but all this speculation was getting them nowhere. "What I think might be more useful," Kali offered, "is looking at how our killer chooses his victims. Anne worked on the Strangler case, but the others don't have any obvious connection. Nothing obvious to me anyway."

"To me either," Lou conceded.

Bryce rubbed his cheek. "Maybe he started with Anne because of her connection to the Strangler case, which he was copying, and then as he's made the killings more his own, he's moved on to a wider choice of victims."

"But still, why these particular women?" Kali pressed the point because she thought it was important. "We know the murders weren't opportunistic. The killer took a photo of Jane, and he broke into Ruby's house. He had to have crossed paths with them at some point earlier on."

"Like with Lancaster and the windows," Lou said. "I still think we were on the right track there."

"You're forgetting, Lancaster was in jail when the third murder took place."

"I don't mean he did it, Bryce. Just that there's some similar connection to the victims."

"There's still Larry Silva's gas station," Kali reminded them. "Anne's husband was going to look through the credit card statements, but I'm thinking we should get a court order for receipts from all three victims. If it's not the gas station, it might be something else."

The phone rang. Lou picked it up, then reached for a pen and jotted something on a nearby slip of paper. "That was Maureen Oliver," he explained, when he'd disconnected. "Someone bought a size twelve bathing suit, same style as Ruby Wings was wearing when we found her body, at the Hilltop Macy's last Sunday. Eleven-fifteen in the morning, to be precise."

"The day after she'd tried on a similar suit in Walnut Creek," Kali noted. "Cash sale?"

"Of course. Our guy isn't stupid."

"Does the clerk remember who bought it?" Bryce asked.

"Maureen was leaving that to one of us. The saleswoman is working today so it should be easy to check."

Lou looked at Bryce. "This one has your name in it."

Bryce laughed. Pushing back his chair, he explained to Kali, "Lou feels like a bull in a china shop when it comes to women's clothing."

"You heading out now?" Lou asked. "I'll walk to the car with you."

Kali felt Bryce's gaze linger in her direction; then he turned to his partner. "Fine, let's go."

Okay, so she wasn't going to get a chance to talk to Bryce alone. Maybe it was just as well. Still, she was over the hard part. Granted, the first few minutes had been awkward, but once she'd gotten past that, she'd been able to deal with Bryce as though last night had never happened. And he'd apparently had no trouble doing the same. Maybe he'd already forgotten, in fact. Or didn't consider anything about the evening worth remembering.

She'd been back at her own desk only about ten minutes when her phone rang. Bryce Keating's voice caught her by surprise. She could tell from the background noise that he was calling on a cell phone.

"I'd hoped we'd have a chance to talk this morning," he said.

"We just did."

"In private." He paused. "I don't know how to do this, really, but I want to . . ." Another pause. He started over. "I know I've got a reputation, but it's not totally accurate."

Not totally inaccurate either, she was willing to bet. "No?"

"I mean some of it's deserved, but not . . ." He sounded almost embarrassed. "Anyway, what I wanted to say is, last night was different."

"Different, how?" But she thought she knew. It had been a foolish move for both of them. A crime of passion, so to speak. And now he wanted to make sure they could still work together, no hard feelings.

"I don't want to blow it, Kali." His voice was suddenly earnest, like a kid's. "The playboy reputation is . . . well, it's not who I really am. But I'm not sure I know how to do it right anymore, either. And that's what I want. I don't want it to be a game this time."

She took a moment to digest his words. They weren't what she'd expected. Touching, but discomfiting in their own way. "I don't think you're in any danger of blowing it." She laughed to lighten the mood. "Not yet, anyway."

"If I head that direction, conk me in the head, would you?"

"You bet." Good thing no one was there to see her beaming like an idiot.

She'd just managed to tuck away the smile when the phone rang again. She picked up thinking it might be Bryce again.

Instead, it was Nathan. Kali felt the warmth drain from her.

"Hey, how about lunch today?" he asked.

"I'm . . . I wasn't planning on taking a lunch break. I got in late this morning."

"Just a short one. I have to be in your neck of woods for a job interview this afternoon."

"That was fast. You just left Global Investment a week ago, didn't you?"

"Like I said, I didn't get along with my boss. I'd sort of started putting out feelers before I quit."

So Global Investment *was* the company name he'd give her. She hadn't been mistaken. He heart was pounding in her chest, but she wasn't going to let the matter drop. "You never worked there, Nathan. I called, looking for you. They'd never heard of you. And they don't have a Boston office."

Silence hung heavy in the air. "I can explain," Nathan said at last.

"You think explaining a lie makes it better? I don't think so."

"Wait. Kali, please. It was stupid of me to make up a story like that. I did it to impress you."

"Impress me, why?"

"That night we met, I fell for you the minute I laid eyes on you. It was like, wow, an arrow straight to the heart. I've heard about that happening, but I never thought it would happen to me. I'm usually pretty reserved."

Could have fooled her. "That doesn't explain the lie."

"It was more of a story than a lie."

Kali wasn't sure she understood the difference, but she let him go on.

"You're a classy lady. I mean, that's apparent to anyone who sets eyes on you. And I figured you probably wouldn't want anything to do with someone who wasn't what you might call an 'even match'."

"So what *do* you do for a living?"

"At the moment, I drive a taxi. But I didn't always," he added hastily. "I was in sales before this. Regional manager for all of northern California. Then I got sick and lost my job. It's an American story in a way. Happens to a lot of people."

"I wonder how many of them pretend to be something they're not?"

"Everyone pretends to some degree." His voice dropped a few decibels. "Even you."

"How do I pretend?"

His voice took on a teasing tone. "I don't know, but I'd like to find out." Then he was serious again. "It was wrong telling you I worked someplace I didn't. I'm sorry I misled you, but it was only because I wanted you to like me." He paused, maybe waiting for some assurance on her part that she did. "So how about another chance. Have lunch with me today, okay?"

"I can't, remember? I'm working through lunch today."

There was a moment's silence on the other end. "If you'd gotten home at a decent hour last night, you'd have been in the office on time this morning." His delivery was almost playful, but there was ice at the core.

"What do you mean?"

"Remember how we were talking about pretense? Look in the mirror, Kali. Take a long, hard look at yourself before you jump on others."

"Nathan, I—"

"Why don't you just say it? You think I'm a no-account loser. You think you're too good for me, don't you? You think—"

Kali lowered the phone quietly into the cradle. He wasn't just a liar; he was loony, and a bit scary.

# CHAPTER 37

The end of a workday. The office was quiet. Owen sat at his desk and closed his eyes. He was tired. Not simply end-of-the-day wound-down and spent, but weary to his core. It weighted his bones and clouded his mind. He couldn't even remember what bounce and enthusiasm felt like anymore.

His interview that afternoon for the Channel Four news roundup had not gone well. It had gone very badly, in fact. Owen had stumbled over questions he could easily have turned to his advantage, and had failed to press key points he'd outlined in his mind. What's more, the latest election poll showed that while his name recognition had gone up a couple of points, his popularity among voters had actually dropped.

Now they had a third murder, and a killer who was clearly privy to undisclosed details about the Strangler case.

With a stab of nostalgia for simpler times, Owen recalled a book he used to read to Alex years ago—*Alexander's Terrible, Horrible, No Good, Very Bad Day.* Alex had been particularly attached to the story because he shared the lead character's name. In the book, at the end of a day where everything went wrong for him, the young Alexander announced he wanted to leave his troubles behind and run away to Australia. His mother, in explaining that trouble wasn't something you could run from, told her son, "Some days are like that, even in Australia." It had become something of the family mantra for bad days, but right now Owen had reached the point where he thought taking a flyer to Australia might not be such a bad idea.

Finally pulling himself from his internal slouch, Owen turned to the stack of files on his desk. Through the window, he could see that the sky had darkened with twilight. A crescent moon was barely visible above the horizon. Owen switched on the antique desk lamp that had been a Christmas gift from Selby. It gave the office a soft, homelike atmosphere, which helped a little.

He was reviewing the lead attorney's notes on an upcoming rape case when Owen heard a shuffling at his door. He looked up to see Jack Jackson standing there, brown paper bag in his hand.

"I was hoping if I waited until late enough in the day," Jackson said, "I wouldn't be disturbing anything."

"There's no end to the work that needs doing around here. But come in anyway. My heart's not in the work right now."

"Tough day?"

"Tough month, and showing no signs of letting up."

Jackson held the bag up in one hand. "I brought you something. Sounds like you can use it." He pulled a bottle of eighteen-year-old Balevenie single-malt scotch from the sack. Seventy-five dollars a bottle when Owen last looked.

"I can't take a bribe," Owen said, only half in jest.

"It's a gift, Owen. Or how about a peace offering for interrupting your evening the other night?"

"I still can't take it." Some prosecutors bent the rules, but Owen had been careful his whole career to avoid anything that might smack of impropriety.

"Okay, I'll keep it for myself." Jackson grinned. "How about a drink?"

Why not? He wasn't getting anything done anyway. "Sure. Thanks." Owen pulled two glasses from the credenza. Jackson poured a couple of fingers of the dark liquid into each glass.

Jackson sank into an upholstered chair in the corner of Owen's office. "Good ad you're running on television. I saw it for the first time the other night."

"That's Les Amstead's doing. He's got his fingers on the pulse, but it's costly."

"I bet. But you've got big backers from what I hear. Silicon Valley money, as well as Hollywood. There are a lot of people who share your centrist view, Owen."

"Fewer now than last week." Owen brought the glass to his face and sniffed. Rich and mellow. Then he took a sip and swallowed slowly, savoring the taste. "Good scotch," Owen said with a smile. "I'm glad you bought yourself a bottle."

"Better than the rotgut we used to drink in college, that's for sure."

Owen thought he could probably sacrifice good scotch for a chance to be young again. "How are things with you these days, Jack?"

"Good. I've started another book."

So that's what this was about. "As a follow-up to the one we wrote on the Bayside Strangler?"

Jackson shook his head. "This one's a novel."

"A novel, huh?" Owen was relieved that it wasn't another true crime book, though he was sure Jackson had his eye on a series of articles about the recent murders. "What's it about?"

"Politics and murder. And sex, of course. I'm drawing loosely on some of my experiences covering the crime beat."

"Should be a winner." Half the people Owen had met lately were writing novels. It was a crapshoot as far as he could tell, which ones actually got published, much less demanded attention. Jackson had a leg up, though. Not only was he a journalist and someone who knew the crime field firsthand, he had a best-selling nonfiction book to his credit.

"So what brings you here bearing gifts?" Owen asked.

Jackson feigned insult. "Do I have to have an ulterior motive?"

"No, but I'm sure you do." He smiled.

"Actually, I *was* curious about this most recent murder. A young woman, Ruby Wings."

So Owen's instincts had been right all along. Jackson wasn't about to let go of a story. "What is it about the murder that makes you curious?"

"I understand she was found near a drainage canal. Strangled."

"Right."

"Hers was the house that was crawling with police a couple of days ago. Including Fortune and Keating."

"You telling me or asking?"

Jackson ignored the question. "Is this connected with the Strangler copycat case?"

Owen said nothing. Jackson wasn't really looking for an answer anyway. What he wanted was details.

"I won't say anything until the word's official," he promised.

"Sorry, Jack. You've got to get it from the cops in charge."

"Come on, we're a team. We help each other out."

It was an arrangement beneficial to both of them. But Owen had always been careful not to interfere with an ongoing investigation.

"I hear the victim had a dog collar around her neck," Jackson said.

"Where'd you hear that?"

Jackson focused on the amber liquid in his glass. "I've got my sources."

"I'm not going to confirm or deny anything."

"Neither of the other victims was wearing a collar, were they?"

"Jack, when this thing goes to trial, if you want to follow it like you did before, that's fine by me. You know I'll share anything I can. But I can't—"

"You're jumping the gun talking about a trial, aren't you? Last I knew, you weren't any closer to getting this guy than you were the morning of the first murder."

"Catching him is not my job," Owen pointed out.

"Funny how your name keeps popping up, though. Must be that pesky Bayside Strangler connection."

"Which the press continually shoves in people's faces."

Jackson raised a hand in surrender. "I understand why you might be upset, but our job is to report the news, not rewrite it in order to make people feel better." He poured himself another shot of scotch. "You want some more?"

"I'd better not."

"I've interviewed friends and family of Jane Parkhurst. What strikes me is that she's different from the other two."

The reference to "other two" wasn't lost on Owen, but he let it pass. The more he protested the notion that the murders were linked, the more certain Jackson would be.

"She's older, for one. And as far as I've been able to determine, she had no involvement with or interest in the Bayside Strangler murders."

Owen frowned. "You've lost me."

"Anne Bailey was a lawyer with the prosecution, right? And Ruby Wings's mother was on the jury that convicted Davis."

"What?" Owen rocked forward, spilling what little was left of his drink. "Who told you that?"

Jackson grinned. "I'm an investigative reporter; my sources are confidential. But I'll tell you one thing—you talk to enough people, you'll eventually get answers."

"Do you know more than you're telling me, Jack?"

He looked suddenly drained, as tired as Owen felt. "No. I probably know less. All I've got are pieces of information with no logical connection." He finished his drink and rose to leave. "But maybe next time you'll remember this is a two-way street."

Owen noticed he'd left the bottle.

Kali was sitting in her car with the engine off, a floppy-brimmed hat pulled down low on her head. She'd been there for fifteen minutes, watching the green stucco house across the street. The windows were still dark; there was no sign anyone was home.

She'd finally connected with the DA's investigator and gotten the registration name and address for the cell phone number Nathan had given her. The phone was registered to a Helen Branson at the address in Albany across from where Kali was now parked. The house was small and well maintained, like the other houses on the street. The kind of quiet, residential neighborhood populated by older couples and young families just starting out. There was a child's bike, still with training wheels, on the front porch.

Kali checked her watch. What was the purpose in staying longer? She'd already seen enough. Nathan had lied about more than where he worked. She felt anger bubbling in her chest. Anger at Nathan. Anger at herself for being part of it, however marginally.

Just then a car pulled into the driveway. A dented, older-model Toyota. A woman and a little girl got out and headed into the house. The woman appeared harried, walking several steps ahead and pulling the girl by her arm. No sign of Nathan. Was he out driving his cab? Did he, in fact, drive a cab? Kali wasn't sure what to believe. Nor did she care, except for the fact that she found his behavior disgusting. And she intended to tell him so.

Home again, she fed Loretta, sorted through the mail and contemplated her own dinner. She wished she'd thought to pick up something ready-made on her way. She wasn't in the mood to cook, and a dinner of cereal was a little too much like a dinner of kibble.

"Okay, already," she said to the prancing dog, who'd finished her meal before Kali had finished the mail. "Let me change into my walking shoes." Her own dinner would have to wait.

The street was winding and without sidewalks, which made nighttime walking difficult. Kali carried a flashlight, both to warn cars and to keep from tripping in the evening blackness. She didn't intend to go far in any case.

Passing Margot's house on her way home, she veered up the steep driveway. If Margot hadn't eaten yet, maybe she'd join Kali for pasta and salad. Cooking wasn't so bad when you were doing it for someone besides yourself.

Kali rang the bell. When there was no response, she knocked. "Margot? Are you home?"

Nothing but the scuffing and barking of the dogs inside. Margot's car was there, so maybe she was in the shower, or simply not interested in company.

As Kali turned to leave, she heard a moan coming from the far side of the carport. She rounded the side of the car, sweeping the area with her flashlight. The beam connected with something out of place and Kali froze.

Margot's crumpled form was slumped on the pavement. Her clothing was torn, her face bloodied.

"Margot?" Kali knelt down and put a hand on Margot's neck. Her pulse was weak, her skin clammy. "Hang on," Kali said. "I'm going to call for an ambulance."

Yanking Loretta by the leash, she raced next door and told a neighbor to call 911, then hurried back to Margot's side. Margot groaned again and mumbled a few words Kali couldn't make out.

Kali held her hand. "You're going to be okay. Just hang in there." It seemed an eternity before she finally heard the sirens in the distance.

The paramedics arrived first, followed not long after by two uniformed patrol officers. They were strapping Margot onto the gurney when Bryce showed up.

"What are you doing here?" Kali asked, surprise overshadowing all other emotion.

"Victim's alive, Bryce," said the taller of the cops. "No need for homicide detail."

"Glad to hear it." He turned to Kali. "I heard the call on the police band and recognized the street as yours. I thought you might have been hurt."

The paramedics began moving Margot toward the ambulance. Her eyes were closed, and an oxygen mask covered her nose and mouth.

"Is she going to be okay?" Kali asked.

"We're not the ones who can answer that."

"Which hospital? I'll follow."

"What happened?" Keating asked.

Kali had given a brief account to the responding cops, but she told the story again. There was little she could add to what was patently obvious.

The taller patrolman listened in, interrupting once to clarify a point. "What can you tell me about the victim?" he asked when she'd finished.

That was always a wide-open question, and especially so with Margot. "What do you want to know?"

"She keep a lot of valuables in the house?"

"Not that I'm aware. She has a pair of diamond earrings, but she was still wearing them just now."

"Married or single?"

"Divorced."

"Bad feelings?"

"Not at all."

"Do you happen to know her ex-husband's name and address?" The cop had his pen poised to take the information down.

"Ex-wife, actually."

Both the cop and Keating stared at her.

"Margot used to be a man," Kali explained. "Still is, sort of."

"You and . . . she are, uh . . ." The cop finished the question with a vague sweep of his hand.

"Neighbors and friends."

"What do you mean 'sort of'?" Keating asked.

"I need to get to the hospital," Kali said. "You figure it out."

It was close to midnight before Kali was allowed to see Margot. She was in a room near the nurse's station, lying flat on her back in the large hospital bed. Her head was heavily bandaged, one eye was swollen shut and she was hooked up to an IV, but she was conscious and able to talk, though hoarsely.

"The police said you were the one who found me." She even managed a smile. "Thanks."

"How are you feeling?"

"Right now, just dandy. They gave me a shot of something that worked magic. When it wears off, I'll probably hurt like hell."

"But you're going to be okay?"

"Nothing's broken, if that's what you mean. They're keeping me overnight because of the head injury. A concussion, the doctor says. And they want me to stay flat, which is no fun. But am I okay?" Margot bit her lower lip. "I don't know. I guess this was an introduction to the dark side of being female. I'm not used to looking over my shoulder."

Kali touched her hand. "Men get attacked, too." But she knew what Margot was talking about. Women's experiences were different from men's. "What happened anyway?"

"I'm not sure. I remember getting out of the car, reaching for my purse . . . and then suddenly there was someone there. He'd been hiding in the shadows, I guess. He came from behind me. Next thing I knew, his hands were on my neck. . . ." Margot touched her neck, which Kali could see was chafed and bruised. Her eyes filled with tears. "It was so awful, Kali. That pressure on my throat, the panic, the disbelief. All at once. I couldn't breathe. I was sure I was going to die."

"You were lucky."

"Very lucky. It probably helped that I'm stronger than most women. I struggled with him. I don't remember anything after that, but I do remember fighting back. I think I got one pretty solid punch in."

"Did you get a look at him?"

"The police asked me the same thing. All I remember is that he was Caucasian, and his hands were soft. It all happened so fast."

"How tall?"

"Taller than me, maybe six feet. I keep trying to call up other details. I almost get there, then poof, they're gone." Margot paused. "The funny thing is that after all that, he didn't even take my purse."

Not funny at all, Kali thought, if the purse wasn't what he was after.

# CHAPTER 38

"You mean the woman who was mugged is actually a *man*?" Lou choked on his doughnut. He looked at Keating, trying to decide if his partner was pulling his leg.

"Apparently so. Or maybe a little of both."

At least Nikki hadn't tried to change herself into a man. Lou supposed there was something to be grateful for in that. Just thinking about it gave him the jeebies. "The guy who attacked her—uh, him must have gotten a real surprise."

"Certainly not what he bargained for." Keating polished off what was left of his banana and tossed the peel into the trash.

"Who's handling it?"

"Montera. Crimes against persons. I doubt there will be much in the way of follow-up, though. The victim is apparently going to be okay, and there were no witnesses."

Your garden-variety mugging didn't rate much investigative attention. Especially when there were no witnesses and no evidence. "How'd you end up there anyway?" Lou asked, reaching for a second doughnut. Someone from the night shift had left practically a whole box.

"I was listening when the call went out from dispatch."

"Dispatch handles lots of calls, Bryce. How often do you go out of your way to offer backup?" Lou didn't get a response, which didn't surprise him. He'd more or less figured it out as soon as he'd learned the victim was a neighbor of Kali's. On some levels, Keating wasn't all that hard to read.

Just then Maureen Oliver approached them from across the room. As usual, there was the enviable spring of youth to her step. "I've got something here that might interest you two."

"What's that?" Lou took a bite of chocolate glaze. How could Keating be satisfied with a banana when there were doughnuts to be had?

"I've been going over the phone records for the three victims, like you asked. No overlap that I've seen. I also compiled a list of commonly called numbers for each of them. There was one number Ruby Wings called at least daily." She paused to make sure she had their attention. "It's Jack Jackson," she said. "His cell phone, not his work or home number."

"Jackson?" Lou looked at his partner. "What's that about, you think?"

"He's been hounding us for information on this. And never once did he let on that he'd known her."

Maureen Oliver cocked her head. "I can't think of anyone I call every day, even among my friends."

Lou couldn't either. And then to keep quiet about it. Something didn't set right. "Guess we'd better ask him."

They went to the newspaper office first. The woman behind the front desk told them Jackson was working from home.

"You got an address?" Lou asked. It would save them the trouble of looking it up.

"Just a minute." She checked a directory and wrote the information out on a slip of paper.

The woman was middle-aged and appeared bored, something that was increasingly common, in Lou's experience. Were perky young receptionists a thing of the past? They were probably working in dot-com land now, making twice what he was.

The address was in Montclair. Older homes, nice neighborhood. Somehow Lou had expected something a bit flashier from Jackson.

A woman answered when they rang the doorbell. Dark hair, a round face, a few pounds too heavy for the blue velour pants and shirt she was wearing.

"We're looking for Jack Jackson," Lou explained.

"He's working and doesn't want to be disturbed."

Lou held out his badge. "Oakland Police."

Her face brightened. Not the usual reaction. "I'm sure he'll make an exception for *you*," she said. "He's been complaining about what trouble he's had reaching anyone there." She stepped back from the door. "Come in. I'll go get him."

Several moments later, Jackson came down the stairway. Lou could hear his wife running water upstairs.

"Hey, this is what I call service," Jackson said. "You've been stonewalling me for days and now I get a personal visit. Why the change of heart?"

"We're here about Ruby Wings," Keating told him.

"Good, that's the case I've been calling about."

The guy still didn't get it. "How come in all these calls to us," Lou asked, "you never mentioned you knew her?"

Jackson's face collapsed. It wasn't often you saw a journalist at a loss for words, but Jackson seemed unable to find the ones he wanted. Finally, he shrugged. "I'd met her. Didn't seem worth mentioning."

The guy must think they were stupid. "When did you meet her?" Lou asked.

"She called me about a year ago. It was when there was a lot of stuff in the news about Davis and the Bayside Strangler because the conviction had just been upheld on appeal."

"Why'd she call you?"

"She was trying to line up a speaker for a Rotary luncheon. She'd read my book, as well as some of my newspaper pieces, and thought the subject would be of interest to the members."

That didn't explain the pattern of phone calls. "When did you last talk to her?"

"I can't say for sure. Why?"

"Last couple of months?"

"Maybe. I don't really remember."

Keating rocked forward. "You're lying, Jackson. Her phone records show she called you nearly every day until about a week before her death."

A muscle in his jaw flexed. Jackson glanced up the stairway toward the second floor, then spoke in a lowered voice. "Let's step outside. I don't want my wife to overhear this conversation."

Once he'd closed the door behind them, he said, "We were seeing each other." His tone was still hushed.

Lou's wasn't. "An affair, you mean."

"Shh. Please. It isn't something I'm proud of." He wrung his hands. "It was over before she died."

"Who called it off, you or her?"

"It was mutual."

Keating made a face. "Are her friends going to agree with that assessment?"

"Maybe it was more me than her." Jackson rubbed his cheek with his knuckle. "I finally realized I'd made a big mistake getting involved with her."

"How'd she react when you broke it off?" Lou asked.

"She was upset." Jackson took a breath. He sounded nervous.

"When was this?"

"End of December."

Just in time for the holidays, Lou thought. What a gift. "The phone calls continued, though."

"I know. She wouldn't leave me alone. Kept begging me to reconsider. She even called the house a couple of times."

Keating brushed a spider off the porch railing and stepped on it. "You must be relieved that she's dead."

Jackson shook his head emphatically. "No, you're wrong about that. I cared for Ruby. She was a lot of fun. Her murder has been tearing me up inside, and there was no one I could even talk to about it."

"Certainly not your wife." Keating's tone was nasty.

Jackson ignored the remark. "It was the same killer as the other two, wasn't it?"

"Same as what other two?"

"The Bayside copycat. Don't play dumb with me."

"What makes you think it was the same?" Lou asked.

"You two are on the case, for one thing."

Keating stuck a hand in the pocket of his black leather jacket. "Have you been clothes shopping lately, Jack?"

He laughed. "What's that got to do with anything?"

"Have you?"

"I don't know. I may have bought some shirts."

"Macy's?"

"Nordstrom's isn't my style."

"Do you remember when that was?" Lou asked.

"Jesus, what's with you two?" He looked from Keating to Lou, and the expression on his face turned dark. "Wait a minute, this is all somehow related to Ruby's murder and you think I might be involved? That's crazy. You're wasting your time, believe me."

"Why should we believe you?"

"I'll tell you what you should be looking at—the connection

between the victims and the Bayside Strangler case, that's what. Anne Bailey was an attorney on the case; Ruby's mother was a member of the jury. I don't know what Jane Parkhurst's connection was, but maybe you ought to find out."

"Whoa." Lou wasn't sure he'd heard right. "Ruby Wings's mother sat on the jury in the Strangler case?"

"Yeah. That's why Ruby was so interested in it, which is how she hooked up with me. But the point is, your killer's not only copying the Strangler, he's selecting victims who are somehow connected. Your killer knows the Strangler case well."

Keating smiled. "Sounds like you, Jack."

Lou scratched his cheek as they headed back to the car. "You think it might be him?"

"He's on the short list of people who knew about the dog collars in the Bayside Strangler case. If you think about it, Jackson is the perfect guy to be our killer."

"How's that?"

"He covered the Bayside Strangler in depth. He knows more about the murders than just about anybody else. And he probably relived Davis's fantasies in his own mind when he wrote the book. If they happened to mesh with his own . . ."

"Davis was a trigger, you mean?"

Bryce nodded. "Or he could have done it simply for the attention. Hell, maybe he even set the whole thing up just to get the Wings woman. The first killing took place not long after they broke up."

"You're drifting pretty far out there, Bryce."

"Could be. Still, we should keep an eye on him."

Lou nodded. "I wonder if the captain will authorize a tail."

"If not, you and I are going to be pulling double duty for the next couple of weeks."

Kali had not had a restful night. With Margot's attack and Nathan's lies vying for space in her mind, she'd alternated between fretful sleep and troubled wakefulness. First thing this morning, she'd called the hospital and reassured herself about Margot's condition. Dismissing Nathan from her mind was harder.

Twice during the day, she'd been tempted to call him and give him a piece of her mind. But both times she'd hesitated. She was hardly one to appoint herself a member of the morality police, and all she really wanted was to be rid of Nathan Sloane.

Still, it rankled her to sit by and say nothing. She was looking at the phone, again thinking about calling, when it rang.

She experienced a prickle of pleasure when she recognized the voice on the other end as Bryce's.

"How is your neighbor doing?" he asked.

"Better. I talked to her this morning. She still has a horrible headache, but the tests came back normal. Unless she takes a turn for the worse, they'll probably release her tomorrow."

"That's good." He paused, and Kali expected some disparaging comment about Margot's gender. Or at the very least, some reaction of curiosity. Instead, he asked, "Was there anything about the attack you think might relate to our murders?"

It took Kali a moment to process the question, and when she did, her knees grew weak. "You think it was the killer who attacked her?"

"I think it's worth exploring. She said he tried to strangle her."

"Attacks on women aren't uncommon."

Bryce hesitated a moment. "Does your friend have any connection to the Strangler case?"

"Margot? Not likely." Kali wasn't sure where Bryce was going with this. "Why?"

"Anne Bailey worked on the original Bayside Strangler case. Turns out Ruby Wings was having an affair with Jackson. No only that, her mother sat on the jury that convicted Dwayne Davis. It could be the killer is targeting women who have some affiliation, however tenuous, to the original case."

"Whoa." There was a lot for Kali to absorb, and her mind was still half floating along on the sound of Bryce's voice. She, too, had an affiliation to the original case. "How did you learn all this?"

"Maureen Oliver discovered that Ruby Wings made repeated calls to Jackson's cell phone. When we talked with him, he admitted the affair, though reluctantly. He was the one who pointed out that two of the victims had connections to the Strangler case."

"What about Jane Parkhurst?"

"No link that we've discovered, but that doesn't mean there isn't one."

"Have you talked with Ruby Wings's mother?" Kali asked.

"She died a couple of years ago. Cancer. But it could be the killer is somehow seeking revenge for Davis's conviction."

"Or it could all be coincidence." Kali didn't want to think about the other possibility. She couldn't imagine how Margot was connected to the Strangler case, but Kali most definitely was. As strongly as Anne Bailey, in fact.

"I think you ought to be careful," Bryce said. "And I'd like to talk to your friend." There was a beat of silence; then his voice grew softer. "Can we change the subject for a minute?"

"Sure."

"You want to have dinner with me tomorrow night?"

"Love to."

"I was hoping you'd say that."

Had he really had any doubt? She sat for a moment after hanging up, savoring the anticipation of an evening with Bryce Keating. Hell, an evening and night. She began mentally going through her closet, trying to decide what to wear.

Finally she pulled herself from the reverie, called the office where Jane Parkhurst had worked, and spoke with several of her co-workers. Not only was there no apparent connection with the Strangler case, Jane hadn't even been living in the Bay Area at the time. She'd been married then and living in Portland, Oregon.

Kali reached for Jackson's book—dedicated, she noted with irony, to his wife—and turned to the section that talked about the jurors. Sure enough, there'd been a juror named Celia Wings. But she wasn't, Kali noted, a particularly vocal juror, nor had she been convinced initially of Davis's guilt. Besides, why target a juror's *daughter* when there were actual jurors the killer could have gone after?

The more she thought about it, the more she decided it had to be a coincidence that Anne and Ruby both had ties to the Strangler case. And Margot's only connection was Kali herself, which was pretty darned tenuous. Not that Kali really thought the attack on Margot had anything to do with the murders.

But what if it *was* the killer? Kali made herself hold on to the thought a moment, to climb inside and think about what it might mean. Her stomach churned, but her mind remained blank.

Heading home for the evening, Kali stopped by the hospital to visit Margot, and then the grocery store. She would have made do with what was in the house if she'd had only herself to think about, but she knew she was almost out of dog food.

And since she was there anyway, Kali picked up chicken breasts and string beans for herself. She was rounding the produce aisle when she saw a familiar-looking male turn the corner at the other end.

Nathan?

She sped up and rounded the corner to the next aisle. When she didn't see him, she decided she'd been hallucinating. She finished her shopping and headed to the express checkout. She'd no sooner slid into what she gauged to be the shortest line than he stepped in behind her.

"Hey, this is a surprise." Nathan put energy into making it sound authentic, but Kali was sure it wasn't.

"What are you doing here?" The line moved ahead and Kali placed her items on the conveyor belt.

"Shopping. How about you?"

"I meant, in this store."

His eyes narrowed. "Why, is something wrong with this store?"

"It's kind of far from where you live."

There was a subtle shift in his expression. He shrugged. "I was in the neighborhood."

"Drop off a fare close to here?"

"As a matter of fact, yes."

Kali paid for her purchases and dropped her wallet back into her purse. "Who is Helen?" she asked.

The question clearly caught him off guard. He seemed momentarily stunned, then quickly recovered. "My sister. Why?"

His sister. Couldn't he do better than that? It was an excuse so old and tried, you'd think he'd have trouble delivering it with a straight face. "You live with your sister?"

"It's temporary. Until I get a regular job and some money in the bank. How'd you know about Helen?"

"Your cell phone is registered to her."

He gave Kali a calculated smile. "So that's what this is all about. You thought she was someone I was involved with?"

"Just curious." She wished he weren't such a good liar. It was hard to tell what the truth was.

"I'm flattered you're so interested."

"I said *curious,* not *interested.*"

The smile grew smug. "If you say so."

She paid for the groceries and left Nathan in line. In the parking lot, Kali spotted a green cab parked near the entrance. It was dented in a few places and belonged to an independent company she'd not seen before. She jotted down the license number and the name of the company. Then she went to her own car and sat there, watching the cab. She didn't even turn on the engine until she'd seen Nathan get into the cab and drive off.

# CHAPTER 39

The day had blossomed with the hint of spring, and Lou was feeling good. It happened this way every February—a short teaser of sunny, warm days fragrant with the scent of daphne and jasmine. The spell wouldn't last. Winter was sure to slam back onto the scene with a vengeance, just as it did every year. For the time being, though, he was enjoying the respite from rain and cold.

Keating, on the other hand, seemed not to have noticed. Between sips of straight black coffee that made up his entire lunch, Keating was poring over Jack Jackson's book on the Bayside Strangler. They were sitting at an outside table in the City Center plaza where the flowering cherries were in bloom and pots of tulips danced in the sun, but Keating had hardly looked up from his reading.

Lou bit into his hamburger. It was stacked high with lettuce, tomato and pickle. "What are you looking for?" he asked.

"I'm not sure."

In the twenty-four hours since they'd discovered that Jackson was involved with Ruby Wings, Keating had talked about little else but the guy's potential as a suspect. Lou wasn't so sure he bought into it, but he wasn't sure he didn't, either. He knew cops who'd gone bad. Why should a crime reporter be any different? Or maybe it was the fascination with things criminal that drew them to their professions in the first place.

"We know Jackson smokes," Keating said. "And we found cigarette butts at two of the crime scenes."

"Pretty slim evidence." Lou picked up a french fry.

Keating marked his place in the book with a napkin. "I know

we don't have much to go on, but think about it, Lou. Jackson knows the Strangler crime inside and out. He's studied it from virtually every perspective—the victims' families, the cops, attorneys and jurors. Even Davis himself."

"Except Davis claimed he was innocent."

"Maybe he was," Keating said with growing excitement. "Maybe it was Jackson all along."

Lou took another bite of hamburger and chewed slowly. He wasn't even sure Keating was serious. "I guess anything is possible," Lou said. That was a cardinal rule of homicide investigation. You didn't categorically rule out anything. But you didn't jump to conclusions either.

"The captain okayed the tail," Keating said. "So we're freed from that drudgery."

"He must be getting soft. I was sure he'd tell us to take a hike."

"There are a limited number of people who know the details of the Bayside Strangler murders, and Jackson is one of them."

That's what they came back to every time. Their killer was someone who was familiar with the Strangler case. They'd put together a list of people who fit that category. Jackson and Gomez were the two with something obvious to gain from the publicity surrounding the murders. Owen Nelson was at the other end of the spectrum, with the most to lose. But there were more than a dozen other names on the list, from Dunworthy to low-ranking police personnel. And Lou was sure there were others who should have been on their list and weren't.

"You know," Lou said, "the dog collar might be something our killer came up with it completely on his own."

Keating wasn't buying it. "If it was only the collar and none of the other similarities, I might agree with you. But combined with everything else, I'm sure he knew."

"So where do we go from here?"

"I want to look back over the file on the Gilchrist murder since Kali is convinced there's a tie-in between that murder and our current ones. You want to follow up with that friend of Ruby Wings and see what she can tell us?"

"Assuming she even knew Ruby was involved with Jackson."

"Women talk," Keating said. "I bet you five dollars she knew."

From his tone, Lou figured Keating was speaking from experience.

Keating picked up his lunch tab, pulled out his wallet and slid a couple of ones onto the table. "I'm outta here. Catch you later this afternoon."

Lou took his time finishing his burger, then drove to Carla O'Neill's house in Crocker Highlands and punched the bell. He was admiring the pots of Iceland poppies on the porch when she opened the door.

"What can I do for you, detective? Something more about Ruby's death?"

"Just a few questions. Can I come in?"

She hesitated. "Actually, I'd rather talk out here if you don't mind. I've got a house full of kids. My turn with the babysitting co-op." She turned back and said something to a young boy inside, then stepped onto the porch, partially closing the door behind her. "What is it you want to know?"

"Why didn't you tell us that Ruby was having an affair?"

A string of expressions passed over Carla's face. Surprise, guilt, and then horror. "Is that who killed her?" She closed her eyes and took a deep breath.

"We don't know who killed her," Lou said. "But withholding information only makes our job that much harder."

"I'm sorry. I didn't say anything because I didn't want to cause trouble. He was married."

"You know him?"

Carla shook her head. "Ruby called him Jack. I'm not even sure that's his real name. Ruby was very quiet about the whole thing. She knew I didn't approve."

"So you never met him?"

"No. I saw them together once, though. By accident. He's not all that much to look at. A little on the heavy side."

"What was their relationship like?"

"Hot, at least in the beginning. Ruby was the instigator, I think. She met him and went after him. But I don't imagine he put up much of a fight." Carla paused, her forehead creased in thought. "I don't know much about his marriage except that he couldn't have spent a lot of time with his wife because he was with Ruby a couple of times a week. Then right before Christmas, he started acting more distant. And a couple of weeks ago he told her it was over."

"How'd she take it?"

"Hard. She'd convinced herself he was going to leave his wife for her." Carla's tone made it clear she'd seen through that line even if her friend hadn't.

Lou was uncomfortable asking the next question. He cleared his throat. "Did Ruby, uh . . . did she say anything about unusual sexual practices?"

Carla's eyes narrowed. "What, precisely, are you asking?"

He hadn't asked it well, Lou realized. "Did you get the impression this Jack had odd tastes or was into anything kinky?"

"Kinky?"

"Bondage, clothing fetishes, that sort of thing."

"Ruby didn't talk much about him at all. Like I said, I didn't approve and she knew it. And when she did mention him, it was more about love and how nice he treated her. . . ." Carla paused. "Now that I think of it, though, she did show me a dress he bought her. Narrow and slinky. He made her model it for him." Carla lowered her eyes. "Without underwear."

To Lou's way of thinking that was hardly kinky, but it *was* interesting that Jackson wanted to see her dressed in a certain way. Much like their killer.

Kali was meeting Bryce at the restaurant at six-thirty. At a quarter to six, she went into the office rest room to touch up her makeup. Blusher, mascara and lipstick. She brushed her teeth and unclipped the hair that was pinned back from her face. She'd worn a knee-length black skirt with the burgundy cashmere sweater that always brought compliments.

There was something laughable about having a first date with a man she'd already slept with, but in some ways that made it even harder. She liked Bryce Keating. Liked him better the more she got to know him. And she wanted him to like her.

Back at her desk, Kali checked her watch. Still time to kill. She called Margot, whom she'd driven home from the hospital earlier in the day.

"You doing okay?" Kali asked.

"Just fine. I'm glad to be home again. Though I have to admit I'm looking over my shoulder more than before."

"I hate the idea of your being alone on your first night back." Kali felt she ought to have at least offered to cancel her date with Bryce to stay with Margot, but she hadn't.

"I've got friends besides you, Kali. If I didn't want to be alone, I'd call one of them. So have a good time tonight and don't worry about me."

The e-mail icon popped up on her computer as Kali was saying good-bye. She clicked on it. Two new messages. One was a many-times forwarded collection of lawyer foot-in-the-mouth remarks sent to her by Nina.

The other consisted of a single word—SLUT.

The return address was a string of numbers from one of the free services. The kind of account anyone could set up. She had no way of knowing whom it had come from.

She felt ill. What upset her wasn't just the message; it was the sense of being watched and judged from behind the cloak of anonymity. In fact, the longer she looked at the screen, the more violated she felt. Kali closed out the computer and sat silently in her chair, hugging herself. The pleasure she'd felt in anticipation of the evening was gone.

She did, finally, manage to get herself to the restaurant. It had opened about a year ago and enjoyed nothing but favorable reviews. Light continental cuisine in an atmosphere that was upscale without being glitzy. True Berkeley chic.

Although she was late, Bryce was even later. He arrived with a flurry of apology.

"I'm not usually late, scout's honor." He held up three fingers. "Especially when it's something I'm looking forward to as much as I am to having dinner with you. I'm glad you waited for me."

It hadn't crossed her mind not to.

Bryce gave the hostess his name and she ushered them to a table near the window. He hung his black leather jacket over the back of the chair and leaned forward with his arms on the table.

"I got a last-minute call." Bryce was still explaining his late arrival. "A worker at the car wash on Broadway found Jane Parkhurst's eyeglasses in the trash."

"How did you know they are hers?"

"Her name was on the case. The guy called because he recognized the name from the papers. But here's the really interesting part. They were folded inside a week-old *Chronicle* along with some candy wrappers like one we found in front of Ruby Wings's house."

"You think it was the killer who dumped them there?"

"Almost has to be. The trash gets emptied twice a week, which means our guy has been at the car wash in the last three days. We're hoping to get prints, but that's a long shot."

It was an eerie image, the killer at the car wash. So close, yet so far. He was walking around, getting his car washed, buying groceries, just like everyone else. "Does the car wash keep a record of who's been through?"

"Only people who pay by credit card."

The waiter came to take their drink order. Kali ordered a glass of merlot and Bryce followed suit. "And why don't you bring us a plate of the bruschetta," he said.

"I wonder why he waited so long to get rid of them," Kali said when they were again alone.

"My guess is that they fell out of her purse or pocket into his car, and he didn't discover them until recently." Bryce took a sip of water. "I'll say one thing for him, he's got good taste in candy."

"What do you mean?"

"Dove dark chocolates. That's the type of candy wrapper."

Kali felt a prickle at the back of her neck. "Dove dark? The little candies in red foil?"

"Yeah. You like them too?"

She swallowed, but her mouth was suddenly dry. "I found a couple of them in a paper sack on my deck last week. I assumed it was garbage from a neighbor blown in by the wind. And then I found another one a few days later, loose."

Kali could tell from the look in Bryce's eyes that he was thinking the same thing she was. "It's probably just coincidence," she said, though she didn't believe it for a minute.

Bryce shook his head. "I don't think so."

She was grateful that he took her fears seriously, and at the same time alarmed that he didn't try to reassure her. "You said the killer might be targeting women connected with the Strangler case."

Bryce touched her arm, a simple gesture that was surprisingly comforting. Like a promise to protect her. "You've got something that none of the victims had," he said. "Forewarning. Nonetheless, I think you ought to take precautions."

She nodded mutely. How did one take precautions against a deranged killer?

"Is there someone you could stay with for a while?"

"I don't know. I'll have to think about it." Of the names that came immediately to mind, none was easily workable. And it was hardly fair to put a friend in danger.

The waiter brought their wine and appetizer. "Are you ready to order?"

"Give us another couple of minutes," Bryce said. Then he turned back to Kali. She could see the tension around his eyes. "Do you know how to use a gun?"

"Not well enough to trust my life to it."

Bryce was silent. Finally he said, "I'll take you to the shooting range, but it usually takes more than one afternoon to get comfortable enough to do any good."

"I'm not sure I'd ever get there." Kali had grown up with guns, and at one time she'd been pretty good at hitting beer cans. But shooting at a person was something different. She wasn't convinced she'd have the nerve, no matter what the situation.

"We don't know for certain that the killer is going after women associated with the Strangler case," Bryce said. "It's just a theory. And nothing's come up that connects Jane Parkhurst to that case."

Maybe that was because they hadn't looked in the right place. Kali sipped her wine. Her hand shook. The day had not been kind to her nerves. "Can you find out about somebody for me?"

"Related to the investigation?"

She considered lying, but knew she'd regret it. "I don't think so. His name is Nathan Sloane."

"An old boyfriend?"

"No, although I went out with him once. He keeps popping up in places where I don't expect to see him. And he's . . . well, odd somehow." She didn't mention the e-mail but she suspected it was the sort of thing Nathan might do.

Bryce studied her a moment. "I'll see what I can find out."

"Thanks."

The waiter reappeared and took their order. Caesar salad and grilled salmon for both of them. And Kali ordered a second glass of wine. She'd have to slow down, but for now it helped stave off the panic that was just under her skin.

"Let's talk about something besides the murders," she said.

Bryce caught her gaze and held it. He smiled. "Like what?"

"Anything." She liked his smile. The way it lit his eyes. "Tell me why you're a cop."

"I couldn't stand the idea of being stuck behind a desk all day."

"You could have been a mailman."

"The uniform sucks."

"Seriously, why are you?"

He ran a thumb down the stem of his glass. "It was either that or wind up in prison myself. I had a few brushes with the law as a kid. But I was lucky. The officer on juvenile detail became my mentor instead of my enemy."

"So you followed in his footsteps."

"Yeah. I'd like to say it was all about doing good and giving back, but in truth, I think a lot of the attraction for me was in the power and respect. . . ." He laughed. "Or what I thought at the time was power and respect. The reality is a bit different. But I also discovered I liked the idea of holding people accountable. Truth, justice and all that other rot. How about you, why did you go to law school?"

"Something about those same quaint notions of truth and justice."

Over dinner she learned that Bryce's idea of fun included mountain biking, backpacking, and white-water kayaking. That he was a decent tennis player and a lousy golfer. His taste in movies ran, not surprisingly, to heavy action films, but he appreciated good drama as well. And books. He was something of a history buff, couldn't carry a tune worth a darn, and had never traveled outside the U.S. except for short excursions to Mexico when he was younger. The conversation rarely strayed to more deeply personal matters, and when it did, he managed to deflect the focus back to her. But it was comfortable conversation. Bryce was knowledgeable and articulate, and laughed easily. He was just the tonic she needed for the evening.

When they'd finished dessert, he ran a finger along the inside of her arm. "Do you like to dance?"

"Love it, do you?" She would never have predicted that Bryce was the dancing type.

He took her to a club in Emeryville that featured a local band. The lead guitarist greeted Bryce by name.

"Are you a musician as well?" Kali asked.

"Far from it."

But he was a good dancer. And when the music turned slow, he held her close, one hand at the small of her back, the other bent under her chin. He kissed her cheek, her eye, her ear. His breath was warm and sweet.

"You want to come to my place for the night?" she whispered.

"Yes. But I'm not going to."

"Why not?"

"I told you before, I want to do this right."

"Right?" Kali stopped moving to the music.

"I don't want to rush it."

She laughed. "We already did."

"I know. But I have a reputation to live down. I want this to be different."

She wasn't going to beg him, for God's sake. She tried not to let her disappointment show. "I guess I should be flattered."

He kissed her forehead. "It's not rejection, Kali. Quite the opposite."

Bryce did follow her home, however. He checked the house for prowlers and made sure she locked the door when he left.

By the time she crawled into bed, part of her was glad that he hadn't agreed to stay. The other part ached for him.

Saturday morning Kali was up early. She drove into Berkeley, where she picked up an assortment of pastries at The Bread Garden and two lattes at Peet's, then delivered them to Margot, pulling up the long, steep driveway to park near the house, as Margot had on the night she was attacked. Even in broad daylight, Kali was cautious.

"You read my mind," Margot said, eyeing the bakery bag eagerly.

"In this case, not hard to do."

Margot led the way to the kitchen. She was wearing teal silk lounging pajamas that seemed more elegant than practical, but the glamour effect was offset by the bruises and scrapes on her face.

"How are you feeling?" Kali asked.

"As long as I don't move, I'm okay."

"How about emotionally?"

"Can't we stick with the easy questions?" Margot reached for a croissant.

Kali waited for an answer. Friends didn't let friends fall through the cracks.

"Okay, so I'm not a hundred percent. Being attacked is a humbling experience, let me tell you that. It's something I relive several times every hour. If I were a real woman, without the extra strength . . . I don't like to think what might have happened."

"And you didn't get a look at him at all?"

"It was dark."

"But you must have an impression."

Margot shivered. "He was taller than me. Soft hands. That's all I can remember. I'd really prefer to talk about something else."

"One more question. Have you found any Dove candy wrappers around your yard?"

"Not that I recall. But between the dogs and the kids next door who keep tossing balls in my yard, I'm so used to finding stuff that doesn't belong, I don't pay much attention. Why, is it related in some way to my attack?"

Kali shook her head. "I don't know. Probably not."

Half an hour later Kali got back into her car and drove across the street to her own home. She entered the house through the garage, making sure the garage door was shut before unlocking her car. It wasn't until the afternoon, when she went out the front door to check the mail, that she noticed the box on her porch. A white box, the sort a department store might used for gift items.

She took it into the kitchen and lifted the lid. Inside was a glossy eight-by-ten photo of herself standing on her back deck. And a yellow rose. The attached card read, "In anticipation."

# CHAPTER 40

What Kali noticed first wasn't her pounding heart or the legs so weak she could barely stand. What struck her right away was the taste in her mouth. A tinny, sour taste she recognized as fear.

She peered at the photograph, trying to figure out when it might have been taken, and came up blank. Not surprising, considering the screaming in her head, so loud and shrill that it made thought impossible.

She remained rooted to the sunny spot at the far end of the kitchen where she'd opened the box. Frozen in time. Unable to think, unable to move. As if by holding the moment she could prevent what came next.

Loretta's whining by the side door finally propelled her to move. Kali peeked through the window and, seeing nothing to cause alarm, let the dog out. She set the deadbolt, then went to the phone and called Bryce.

When she couldn't reach him, she left a message, then tried his cell phone and got a "customer not available" announcement. Panic rose in her throat. She called the detective bureau. Come on, Bryce, be there. But he wasn't, and neither was Lou. She left another message, let Loretta back into the house, then pulled out a chair and sat. She shifted and twisted, unable to get comfortable, and soon found herself pacing instead. Check your messages, she urged Bryce silently, then aloud. "Check them, damn it."

The phone remained silent.

Finally, Kali collapsed onto the sofa and hugged her knees to her chest. Now that the initial shock had worn off, she felt oddly disconnected. It was like being on an airplane miles above the earth. Nothing existed but the moment.

Then, in a sudden sweep of memory, she was flooded with images from the crime scenes. As if stung, she leapt from the sofa. She was *not* going to be a victim.

Kali pulled the phone book from the drawer in the kitchen. Corner flower stands were abundant around town, but most did not carry long-stemmed roses. Those generally came from true florist shops. Still, there were a lot of florists, Kali realized, as she ran a finger down the listings, and most, if not all, had been contacted by the police previously in the course of the investigation.

But she had to do something.

Using her cell phone in order to keep the ground line free, she began working her way down the list alphabetically. By the time she got to the Gs she was ready to give up. It was an exercise in futility. Then the woman who answered at Giabaldi's Flowers and Gifts surprised her. Yes, she had sold a single long-stemmed yellow rose the previous day. To a man.

Kali's heart was beating so fast and furiously she found it difficult to speak. "I don't suppose he paid for it with a credit card, did he?"

"It was just that one rose. Why?"

The words that tumbled from Kali's mouth weren't those she'd planned. Rather than get into an explanation that involved the DA's office, which was just as likely to elicit wariness as cooperation, she found herself playing the role of hapless female.

"He left it at my house but the card apparently blew away. I think I know who it's from, but before I make a fool of myself, I want to make sure."

The woman chuckled. "I can see that might be a problem."

"Can you describe him for me?" Kali asked.

"You're in luck, dear. I can do better than that. When the young man paid for his purchase, a business card fell from his billfold. I noticed his name because it's the same as my maiden name. We talked about being related but couldn't find a common ancestor anywhere."

Kali's heart skipped a beat. "What was the name?"

"Keating."

A single word packing the weight of a wrecking ball. It hit Kali square in the chest.

"Keating," she asked to make sure she'd heard right. But she knew she had.

"Yes." The woman hesitated. "It sounds like you were hoping it was someone else. That's too bad because he seemed like a nice young man to me."

It had to be someone else with the same last name. A coincidence. A fluke. Not Bryce.

"Jeans and a black leather jacket," the woman added. "A good-looking guy, if you ask me."

Kali had no idea what she said to get herself off the phone. She hoped she hadn't simply hung up on the woman.

Bryce? Impossible.

Or was it? He clearly had inside knowledge about the Strangler case. And there was nothing to say he *hadn't* been behind the murders. When Margot was attacked, he'd been right there in the neighborhood, after all. She tried to think what his motivation might be. Attention as detective on the case? Fulfillment of his own fantasies, as Dunworthy predicted? She wondered what he'd been doing at the time of the Strangler murders.

Her head argued with her gut. It wasn't possible; it was. She felt sick to her stomach.

She went into the bathroom, splashed water on her face and brushed her teeth. The apprehension she'd felt on discovering the rose was now layered with anguish. It clawed at her insides.

The phone rang. Kali jumped. Don't let it be Bryce, she prayed. She waited for the machine to pick up.

"Kali, this is Lou Fortune returning your call. I'm at 510-63—"

She grabbed the phone in mid-sentence.

At first Lou thought she might be high. Her sentences rambled, and her voice had an unnatural tenor, almost as though she were talking without breathing. Once he understood the gist of what she saying, he wondered if she might be psychotic as well. Now that he was off the phone, though, no longer dealing with a woman on the brink, he tried to be objective.

Was there any chance in hell she might be right?

His immediate response was a resounding *no*. Even Kali herself had seemed unsure. There had to be another explanation. A different Keating. Or a flower for a different purpose.

As much as Lou tried to keep the doubts at bay, they drifted, like smoke, through the cracks and crevices of his mind, and settled square in the center of his thoughts.

Okay, so the idea wasn't totally impossible. But his own partner?

Keating was a cipher. A maverick cop who lived by his own code. Lou didn't always agree with his methods or approach, but in the short time they'd been working together he'd seen nothing that made him think Keating wasn't also a good cop.

On the other hand, Lou was a good cop too. He knew better than to let personal feelings interfere with the job. That was one of the basic tenets of police work.

Before he'd found Kali's message, he'd been working in the garden. Now he changed into clean clothes and headed out to speak to the florist who'd sold the yellow rose. He took along a photo of Keating.

Giabaldi's Flowers and Gifts was a small store wedged between a check-cashing service and a pawnshop. Lou didn't see much in the way of gifts—just some balloons and greeting cards—but the glass-paneled refrigeration unit was brimming with floral arrangements. Lou suspected the bulk of their business came from wired deliveries instead of off-the-street purchases.

A young man was behind the counter. Lou asked to speak to the woman who'd been working earlier that day.

"She's gone. Can I help you?"

Lou showed his identification. "Can you tell me where I might find her? It's important."

The man looked worried. "She was going off to see her cousin or something. She's not in trouble, is she?"

"No, I just wanted to ask her about a sale."

"She should be back in a few days."

*Days.* By then it might be too late. "Do you have a number where I can reach her?"

The man shook his head. "Sorry. I got the impression it was up north somewhere. Susanville, maybe. I can give her a message when she gets back."

"Don't bother. I'll catch her later."

Lou sat in his car, drumming his fingers on the steering wheel. He was resisting this whole line of inquiry. But having opened the door in his own mind, he wanted to see it through. Finally, he started the engine and drove to Keating's place. Better just to confront him and get it out in the open.

Lou rang the bell, waited, then knocked on the door. No answer. When he determined Keating wasn't at home, he turned a few moral somersaults before searching out the spare key out from under the step where he knew Keating hid it and letting himself in. He didn't like what he was doing, but what if he did nothing and Kali got killed? He'd like that less. He hoped she'd taken his advice to go away for a bit.

Lou started in Keating's bedroom. Night stands, dresser, closet, and then into the second bedroom, which was used as an office. Lou wasn't sure what he was looking for. It could be clothing, pictures, anything that might implicate Keating in the murders.

He didn't find it.

Lou settled in on the living room couch to wait for his partner.

After talking with Lou Fortune, Kali went back to pacing from room to room. At first, Loretta followed her, prancing eagerly across the hardwood floor in search of excitement. When none was forthcoming, the dog curled in a sunny spot near the window.

Kali wasn't sure Lou had even believed her. He'd sounded skeptical. As well he might, she scolded herself. Bryce was his partner, after all.

Kali wasn't sure what she believed herself. But she felt better for having shared her suspicions with Lou.

Suddenly she had a thought that stopped her cold in her tracks. What if they were in it together? No, she was losing her grip. She felt suddenly light-headed. She went into the kitchen to find something to eat, and realized she couldn't stomach the thought of food.

The niggling doubt wouldn't let up. Had she mistaken the fox for the farmer? Surely, there must be someone she could trust.

She tried calling Owen and got a busy signal.

"Keep your eyes open," she told Loretta, who opened hers only long enough to give Kali a plaintive where's-the-fun-in-this sort of look. "I'm going out for a bit." *And then we're leaving,* Kali added silently. Lou had been right in suggesting Kali not stay at the house.

* * *

Kali parked directly in front of Owen's, then went to the door and rang the bell. It was Selby who answered. She was wearing jeans and a T-shirt, and was drying her hands on a dishtowel.

"Sorry to disturb you," Kali told her. "I was hoping to speak with Owen."

"He's out golfing with some bigwigs from southern California and won't be back until much later."

"Oh." That was a blow she wasn't prepared for. The emotional turmoil of the day caught up with her. She felt tears threatening.

"Is something wrong, Kali? You seem upset."

"I need to talk to him."

"I don't have any way to reach him." Selby took her arm. "Come inside and have some tea, why don't you. I just put the kettle on. Or maybe you'd like something stronger?"

"Tea sounds wonderful. Thank you."

They moved into the kitchen. Kali took a seat at the center is-land while Selby prepared the tea. The room was large, with a hand-crafted copper hood over the stove and granite slab counter-tops. The cabinets were cherry, and above the sink a large bay window looked out onto an expansive garden as attractive as any Kali had seen on the pages of a magazine. More than lovely, it was a safe haven. Kali felt herself growing calmer.

"How do you take your tea?" Selby asked. "Sugar? Lemon?"

"Just plain. This is a great kitchen."

Selby smiled. "It is, isn't it? We thought of moving after we de-cided to get married, or rather I did. I wasn't keen on the idea of living with ghosts."

"Ghosts?"

"Marilyn. Everyone says when you marry a widower you should start over in a house that's *yours*, not *theirs*."

"Makes sense."

"Yes, it does." Selby climbed onto the high bar stool next to Kali. "I was ready to sell it and move on. Several real estate agents pointed out that the house was in bad shape and we'd do better to fix it up first. Marilyn had let things go to pot, and she didn't have much decorating taste to start with. Not that I'm faulting her; she had her own problems. But by the time we'd fixed things up, it no longer felt like Marilyn's house. It was mine and Owen's, and I loved it."

"That's the problem with well-meaning advice," Kali said, finding the small talk comforting. "It doesn't always fit your particular situation."

Selby nodded. "We were also worried what Alex's reaction would be if we sold the house. Not that he spends much time here." A pained look crossed Selby's face.

"How do you two get along?"

A bitter laugh. "We don't."

"You came into a situation that was already pretty volatile from what I understand."

"Our marriage seemed to make things worse, though."

"It can't be easy."

"Mostly Alex ignores me. It's Owen who gets the brunt of his hostility, though I thought things were getting better. Then they had another fight last night. Alex wanted the two of them to go to the auto show, but Owen had already scheduled his golf game. . . ." Her voice trailed off and she took a sip of tea. "It's not all black and white either. Owen can be demanding. He has a tendency to think he knows best, which is not what kids want to hear. And he has a way of throwing his success in Alex's face."

"Not a formula for peace."

"Sorry," Selby said, with a smile. "You didn't come here to listen to me whine." And then her face darkened. "It's about the investigation, isn't it? Has there been another murder?"

The calm she'd felt only moments before shattered. Kali felt the tea rise up in her throat. The next murder would be hers. "Not yet," she stammered. "But I . . . well, I need to talk to him as soon as possible." She was already on her feet, ready to take her leave.

"What is it? Are you okay?"

"I need to be going. Thanks for the tea, Selby. Tell Owen to call me as soon as he can."

Hearing Keating's key in the door, Lou placed the *Newsweek* he was reading back on the sofa table. His palms were suddenly damp. He wiped them on his pants leg. He'd been on the verge of leaving a dozen or so times during the two hours he waited, but he knew confronting Keating head-on was the only way.

Keating came through the door whistling, a bag of groceries in one hand. He stopped dead in his tracks when he saw Lou.

"What the fuck?"

"Set the groceries down, Bryce."

"What's going on?" But he put the bag on the floor.

Lou unholstered his gun and set it on the coffee table. "Put yours there, too," he said.

"Are you nuts?"

"Do it, Bryce. We need to talk."

Keating reached under his jacket and removed his gun. His expression registered confusion, not fear. That was a good sign, Lou thought.

"What about the Ruger?" Lou said.

"I haven't got it on me."

"Let's see."

Keating raised first one leg and then the other, pulling the hem of his jeans above his sock line. "Now, you want to tell me what this is all about?"

"Did you buy flowers yesterday?"

"Why would I buy flowers?" Again, the confusion sounded genuine.

"You weren't at Giabaldi's Florist on San Pablo?"

"Never heard of it."

"Woman who works there claims you were."

"Well, she's wrong. What in the hell's going on, Lou?"

Keating wasn't acting like a man with something to hide. Lou was aware it could be a trick. Keating was clever. But his responses seemed so genuine, Lou was inclined to trust him.

"We've got a problem, Bryce. The woman at the florist says you bought a single yellow rose there."

Keating's jaw dropped. "Whoa, hold on. You think *I'm* the killer? This is some kind of joke, right?"

"It's not a joke. The woman says you dropped your business card."

"Jesus. You think if I were actually the killer, I'd be stupid enough to drop my business card?" Keating waved his arms wildly. "Anybody could have picked up that card."

Lou nodded. "But she described the man as well built and wearing a black leather jacket. What's more, the man *told* her his name was Keating."

"Holy shit." Keating tossed back his head, then paced to the far side of the room. "It's a game for him, remember? This is just the sort of stunt he gets off on. Let's go to the florist's now. Ask the woman to her face if it was me."

"No need. I believe you. But I had to ask."

"How did this come up, anyway? Did she call the department?"

Lou shook his head. "Kali got a rose. And a note."

If there'd been any doubt in Lou's mind, Keating's reaction put it to rest. Keating jerked as though he'd touched a live wire. His face went white.

"When?"

"This morning. You obviously haven't checked your messages."

Keating grabbed his gun from the table. "Call her. Tell her I'm on my way over."

"Bryce, wait. She's not going to—"

But Keating was already out the door.

# CHAPTER 41

Kali pulled into the garage and closed the door behind her. She entered the house, checked the front and side doors, and then the windows. Everything looked to be secure. She went into the kitchen to check her phone messages. None.

Loretta was sleeping contentedly in the corner.

"You're a lazybones today," Kali said. "I didn't even get my usual greeting."

The dog raised an eyelid, looked at her, and shuffled her rear paws against the floor. Kali scratched behind her ears, and Loretta's eye closed again. A dog's life, Kali thought. She wished hers were as carefree.

She'd decided to take Loretta and leave town. Stay in a motel until she figured out whom she could trust and whom she couldn't. She'd pack a suitcase, take a couple of hundred dollars from the ATM, and they'd be off before nightfall.

The afternoon was already beginning to turn to twilight. She needed to hurry.

The doorbell startled her. She jumped.

"Kali, are you there? Open up. It's Bryce." He knocked loudly.

Kali froze. She heard him rattle the door, then heard his footsteps as he made his way around to the back of the house. The windows were curtainless. She'd be visible, like a bug under glass.

Silently, she retreated down the hallway to her bedroom. The windows there were high enough that the room was secluded from anyone standing at ground level.

Her whole body was shaking. She sat on the bed and reached for the phone to dial 911.

The phone was dead.

A wave of panic hit her, and then she remembered her cell phone. It was in her purse.

In the kitchen.

Kali didn't want to leave the sanctuary of her bedroom, but she had to reach the cell phone. She was ready to make a quick dash for it when she heard a rustle of movement from the bathroom.

An involuntary moan escaped from her lips. Her chest felt tight, as though it were being squeezed in an iron vice.

She turned to see Alex. His broad frame filled the open doorway.

In her confusion, all she could manage to say was his name. He smiled at her. "Hello, Kali."

"What are you doing here?" Her first thought was that Owen had sent him, but she realized at once that made no sense.

"Don't play dumb. You know why I'm here." He held a rope taut between his hands.

She shook her head, then took a step backward.

"I've been thinking about this moment for weeks now."

Her heart raced. She could hear the rush of her own blood in her ears. Alex, not Bryce.

"It was you," she stammered. "You left the flower and photo on my doorstep."

"Yep." He smiled. "You thought it was the cop, didn't you? I found his card in my dad's stuff. It was a nice touch, if I do say so myself."

"Why, Alex? Why any of this?"

"Because I wanted to." He moved closer, backing Kali toward the wall.

"Wanted to," she echoed. "What did any of us ever do to you?"

"That's not the point."

"I don't understand."

"You wouldn't. No one does." Alex's eyes flashed with anger. "My father the know-it-all district attorney, the smart-ass who thinks he should be governor—he had plenty of time for the Bayside Strangler, but he was too busy for me or my mom."

"This is about him?" Kali's throat was so dry, it hurt to talk.

"No, it's about me!" Alex squared his shoulders. "I'm just as strong and clever and important as that stupid Dwayne Davis. He didn't even kill all those women."

"What do you mean?"

"It was *me* who did Wendy Gilchrist."

The murder that had been different all along. The murder that most closely resembled the three current ones. Her head was spinning. "Why?"

"The bitch laughed at me."

"So you killed her." Keep him talking, wasn't that the advice she always heard?

"I didn't mean to. I only meant to show her she couldn't get away with it."

"Get away with what, Alex?"

"She used me. Led me on like she'd give me anything I wanted, you know? Like she was hot for me. Oh, man, was she hot. Then suddenly she tells me to get lost, that she was only trying to make this other guy jealous."

"So her death was an accident," Kali said, striving for the voice of reason. "And then you made it seem like the Bayside Strangler did it."

"Wasn't hard. He was all over the news. All I had to do was send her a yellow rose. I didn't know there was supposed to be a stupid note with it." Alex laughed. "And then my dad winds up prosecuting the guy. What a joke."

"Yeah." Kali was trying to show she understood, though she didn't. "But that was a long time ago, Alex. Why kill more people now?"

"It was just going to be one. Make people think the Bayside Strangler was still around, that my dad screwed up big time. Poof, there goes the election."

She didn't even try explaining how fuzzy his logic was.

"Turned out to be fun, though." Alex's expression was slightly crazed. "And *I* was the one pulling the strings for a change." He snapped the rope. "So to speak."

Kali had been listening for sounds from outside, hoping that Bryce hadn't left, but she'd heard nothing. Of course he was gone. He would have assumed she wasn't home.

She wondered if Lou had talked to him yet. She hoped not. But the damage was done. He would eventually learn she'd mistrusted him. Her heart ached at what she'd done. But she couldn't think about that now.

Kali inched to her left, away from the bed. The door to the hallway, her only means of escape, was behind Alex. She'd never get past him.

The master bath opened onto the bedroom diagonally across from them. If she made a sudden dash, could she reach it before he reached her?

She didn't see that she had any other options.

"Alex, listen to me. I'm your friend, aren't I? You don't have to do this."

He shook his head. "It's part of the plan."

"What plan?"

"My plan. I'll try not to hurt you, though." He moved forward.

Kali lunged to the side, but he grabbed her by the arm, twisting it until she thought it would break. She screamed and he loosened his grip. She turned, flailing at him with her arms. He grabbed her again and she kicked his shin, then aimed her knee at his groin. She missed, but it landed somewhere close enough to cause him pain. He cursed and released his grip.

Kali sprinted for the bathroom and locked the door behind her.

Her heart pounded frantically and her head felt light. Alex hammered on the door with his fist. The door was thin and the lock simple. It wouldn't protect her for long.

And then what?

With dismay, she looked around the windowless room. What had she gained? Nothing but a few minutes' reprieve. Worse, she'd backed herself into a corner.

In a frenzy Kali opened the cabinet drawers, tossing the contents. A disposable razor, with a blade that couldn't be removed. Useless. Nail clippers and cuticle stick, not much better. Hair brush, bobbypins, makeup, hand cream. Drawers full of junk, and not a decent weapon anywhere. Not even a glass bottle she could break for its jagged edge. The damn things were all plastic.

Alex was jiggling with the lock now, poking at the spring mechanism. Even without the universal key, all it would take was a little pressure in the right spot.

Panic gripped Kali, sucking the air from her lungs. She didn't want to die like a cornered animal.

She didn't want to die, period.

She flung open the cabinet doors beneath the sink. More junk. And an aerosol can of ant spray.

Kali grabbed it just as she heard the lock spring click. Alex charged through the door. Aiming straight for his eyes, Kali held her breath, turned her head, and sprayed the poison, never letting up on the button.

Alex cursed, lashed about, and Kali ducked out the door. She ran out front, smack into Lou and Bryce.

# CHAPTER 42

When she thought about it afterward, what Kali remembered most vividly was the surge of relief she felt at finding Bryce on her doorstep—a momentary joy that was instantly overshadowed by a realization of all she'd lost by ever doubting him.

At the time, though, all Kali could do was point to the house and stammer disjointedly. "Alex . . . it's Alex. . . ."

"Who's Alex?" This was Lou asking. Bryce had his cell phone to his ear, calling for backup. Even without knowing the details, he'd read her panic correctly.

"Owen . . . Owen Nelson's . . . son." Kali was panting hard, gasping for words with what little breath she could manage. "He killed Anne and . . . the others. Wendy Gilchrist too. He was going . . . going to kill me next."

Lou put an arm out to steady her. "Are you hurt?"

Kali shook her head. "No, I . . ." She gulped for air, thinking how close she'd come. "I'm okay. I doused him with ant spray."

"I'm heading around back," Bryce said to Lou. "You take the front." He ignored Kali except to bark instructions that she stay out of the way.

Kali realized she was shaking and close to tears. She crossed to the other side of the street and collapsed onto her neighbor's low brick wall. Lou cased the front of the house, then positioned himself by the door. In the evening dusk, Kali had trouble seeing anything but shadowy forms.

Within minutes two patrol cars arrived and slammed to a stop. The officers sprang from inside, guns drawn. Lou beckoned to them and the three of them conferred briefly.

One of the officers returned to the patrol car for a megaphone. He called out to Alex to surrender.

The house remained quiet.

Several neighbors came out onto the street to see what the commotion was. Margot, her head still bandaged, sat down next to Kali on the wall.

"Someone's in your house?"

Kali nodded. She didn't want to explain it all just yet.

Still nothing from inside. Kali dug her fingernails into her palms. He hadn't gotten away, had he?

Then one of the uniformed officers shot what Kali later realized was tear gas into the interior. A few seconds later Loretta staggered out the front door. Kali was afraid the officer with the rifle might shoot the dog by mistake, but he merely pushed her aside with his leg, keeping the gun aimed inside.

Loretta circled, looking confused. When Kali started to go for her, Margot put a restraining hand on her arm.

"You don't want to get in the middle of it, Kali. Loretta will be okay."

"I think Alex drugged her. She hardly lifted her head when I came home, and look at her now."

"She may not be frisky, but she's alert and mobile. She'll be okay, trust me."

Just then Bryce circled from behind the house with a uniformed cop. Between them was Alex, handcuffed and coughing.

Kali felt the release of panic. They'd gotten him. She was safe.

Lou and Bryce conversed for a moment, then Bryce shoved Alex into the back of a patrol car. Bryce slid in beside him. As the car rounded the corner, she saw him look at her briefly, then turn away without acknowledgment.

How did you ask forgiveness for betrayal of trust? Was it even possible?

She gave a statement to an officer, then went back to Margot's to call her sister and ask if she could stay there for a few days. Even without the tear gas, it would take a while before Kali felt like sleeping in her own house again.

Lou took a long swallow of beer. Ice cold from the bottle, the way he liked it. What a weekend it had been. He was glad Keating had suggested they stop off for a drink. It had been almost midnight last night when they'd finished processing the paperwork, and today had been just about as full.

"Who'd have thought it was Owen Nelson's kid," he muttered. "We weren't even close."

"We actually weren't that far off, Lou. The murders *were* about Owen Nelson and the election, only not in the way we thought. And the killer was someone with ties to Gilchrist, like we figured. All that stuff Dunworthy gave us fits, too. The killer's sense of powerlessness, his personal interest in the Strangler case . . ."

"It's still a shock." Lou couldn't begin to imagine what it would feel like to have a kid who was a killer. Nikki's piercings and shacking up were hardly a blip on the screen in comparison. "A double whammy, too, cuz Owen Nelson inadvertently contributed to Alex's knowledge of the crimes. That's how he knew the details of the Strangler case and how he learned he'd overlooked the dog collars."

"Nelson told him?"

"I doubt it. But he probably talked to his wife and Alex eavesdropped. Nelson was also the link to how Alex chose his victims."

Keating reached for a fistful of salted nuts. "How so? Anne Bailey had the Davis connection."

"Right. And Alex knew her murder would get his dad's attention. Jane Parkhurst died because he associated her with selling the house. Owen's new wife remembers Parkhurst made some pretty derogatory comments about the former Mrs. Nelson's taste."

"And he targetted Ruby just because her mother was on the Davis jury?"

Lou shook his head. "I don't think that's it. He seemed surprised when I raised the point. Turns out he'd seen Jackson and Ruby together and figured killing her was a way to get Jackson's attention. The more attention he gets, the more publicity. I suspect it was Alex who fed information to Gomez, as well."

Keating smiled darkly. "I still love it that you all but accused Gomez of murder to his face."

"I'm not going to lose any sleep over it." Lou didn't like the guy and having him turn out not to be a murderer wasn't enough to raise him in Lou's esteem. "The kid's rationale for attacking Kali's friend is a bit less clear, though it seemed to make sense to him."

"Margot was lucky."

Lou nodded. He rolled the beer bottle between his palms. "I'll tell you the thing we really have to be thankful for. That you noticed the van parked in front of Kali's house and remembered it matched the description of the one that witness saw in the pharmacy parking lot the night Anne Bailey was killed."

"It was one of those moments that makes you believe in the power of the subconscious." The muscles around Keating's mouth pulled tight. His gaze went flat.

"You talked to her since this all went down?" Lou asked.

"Why would I do that?"

"You don't have to keep up a front with me, Bryce. I know there was something going between you two."

"Was."

"So you've dropped her already?"

"She thought I was a murderer, Lou."

"I hadn't ruled the possibility out myself."

"It's different."

"How?"

"You confronted me, for one thing. Instead of assuming the worst."

And theirs was a very different sort of relationship. "Okay, Bryce, it's your life. And God knows I'm the wrong guy to be giving advice. But if I was in your place, I wouldn't toss everything until I was sure that's what I wanted."

Owen read through the handwritten draft once more. It certainly wasn't his best speech, but it probably was his shortest. It said what he wanted to say, though, and that was the important thing. Owen was withdrawing from the primary, resigning as district attorney. He offered his most humble regrets and deepest sympathy to the families of the victims. There wasn't much else to be said.

He poured himself a glass of scotch and leaned back in the soft leather chair. He would miss this office. He would miss the job. The friends he'd made here and the satisfaction of thinking he could make a difference.

But while he'd been busy mending other people's wrongs, he'd neglected his own.

A wave of sorrow crashed down on him. For a moment it took

his breath away. Grief at all he'd lost overcame him. And at the core of that grief was the greatest loss of all. A son he'd loved like life itself. Whatever happened at the trial and after, the Alex who'd reached for his hand before crossing the street, who'd curled next to him at bedtime, who'd beamed at Owen when he caught his first fish—that Alex was gone forever. Had been gone for a long time, Owen realized.

And he would forever wonder how much his own failings as a father had contributed to the change.

Kali didn't return from her sister's until the end of the week. She'd stayed longer than she intended, in part because avoidance was easier. But also because she and her sister had gotten along better than ever before, and Loretta had loved the open yard and the attention of Sabrina's kids.

The first thing she did on returning home was open the windows and doors to air the house out. She checked her answering machine. The light was blinking furiously with messages from concerned friends. Nothing from Bryce.

Not that she was surprised, really. But she didn't realize how much she'd been hoping there might be until there wasn't.

She found a week's worth of mail and papers in a sack on the back deck, where Margot had left them for her. Kali tossed the papers, unread, into the recycle bin. She'd heard all the details she wanted at her sister's. She knew that the search of Alex's apartment had yielded enough evidence to support the arrest, and that his fingerprints matched those taken from Ruby Wings's bathroom and garage window. She knew that Owen had bowed out of the gubernatorial race and resigned as district attorney. Rumor had it that he and Selby were in seclusion at her family's ranch near Santa Barbara.

She'd have to write Owen at some point. When she figured out what to say. Bereavement notes she had down pat. But this was a first.

She made herself a cup of coffee and tackled the mail next. A plain white envelope with Bryce Keating's return address caught her attention, and she opened it with trembling fingers.

Two pages, typed. Nothing personal, not even a greeting. Just the information about Nathan Sloane she'd asked for.

The disappointment stung. She'd been hoping for something

that spoke to their relationship, even if he was angry with her. Not that she could really blame him for ignoring her after what she'd done.

She turned to the report.

Over a period of the last seven years, Nathan had had five restraining orders issued against him and two arrests for stalking, both of which involved jail time. He'd also spent close to a year in a psychiatric hospital. No record of violence, but he'd found plenty of other ways to harass his victims, all in the name of love. Kali was apparently not his only current target. A divorcee with a young child had filed charges last week when she learned he had access to her bank accounts. The woman was Helen Branson, and Nathan was back in jail.

Kali tossed the report aside. She sure knew how to pick them, didn't she? And when she finally found someone who was honorable and cared about her, what did she do but suspect him of murder.

Well, it was done and couldn't be undone. But she did owe Bryce an apology. She thought about writing a note, which would be far easier, but decided as part of her penitence to deliver the apology in person. She got into her car and headed downtown.

When she arrived in the homicide room, Bryce was at his desk going over some papers with Lou.

"Can I talk to you for a minute?" she said.

"Go ahead."

He wasn't making it easy. "I mean privately. Can we go outside?"

Bryce hesitated, then rose from his chair. "I won't be long," he told Lou.

They rode the elevator in silence. Outside the day was warm and sunny.

"I owe you a big apology," Kali said.

Bryce scuffed the sole of his shoe against the pavement. His face showed the strain of bound emotion. "How could you think I was a killer?"

"The woman at the florist said . . ."

"But you believed her!"

"I was scared, Bryce. We knew the killer was someone with inside information."

He looked at her straight on. "You knew me. You'd let me make love to you, for God's sake. And you were ready to believe a woman you never met?"

Kali thought about trying to explain. The yellow rose, the panic, the way the evidence seemed to fall into place. But she wasn't here to defend herself. In truth, she wasn't sure there was much to defend.

"You said to me that you wanted to do it right. You have, Bryce. I blew it. I regret that more than I can express. If it could be undone—"

"But it can't."

"I know. And I am sorry." There didn't seem to be anything more to say.

Bryce was silent.

"Thanks for the report on Nathan Sloane."

"I hope you weren't pinning your hopes on him."

"Far from it." If she'd had hopes set on anyone, it was Bryce.

"You know that Rollerblader who ran you down? Sloane paid him to do it. I think he expected to rush to your rescue himself."

"How'd you find that out?"

"The kid on wheels came clean."

The tumble she'd taken had led to the night she'd spent with Bryce. A memory she could hold on to.

"Well, I'm glad I got scraped. The cure was worth it." She smiled at him. "Take care, Bryce."

She started to leave and got no more than twenty feet before he called after her.

"Kali?"

"What?"

"Give me some time, okay? I'd still like to do this right."